BAD KITTY

Camp Daze

NICK BRUEL

SQUARE
FISH

A NEAL PORTER BOOK
ROARING BROOK PRESS
NEW YORK

For Jim, Catherine, Zoe, and Astrid

▛
SQUARE
FISH

An imprint of Macmillan Publishing Group, LLC
175 Fifth Avenue, New York, NY 10010
mackids.com

Our books may be purchased in bulk for promotional, educational, or business use. Please
contact your local bookseller or the Macmillan Corporate and Premium Sales Department at
(800) 221-7945 ext. 5442 or by e-mail at MacmillanSpecialMarkets@macmillan.com.

Library of Congress Control Number: 201794447

Originally published in the United States by Neal Porter Books/Roaring Brook Press
First Square Fish edition, 2019
Square Fish logo designed by Filomena Tuosto

ISBN 978-1-250-29409-8 (Square Fish paperback)
1 3 5 7 9 10 8 6 4 2

ISBN 978-1-250-23240-3 (special book fair edition)
1 3 5 7 9 10 8 6 4 2

AR: 2.8/LEXILE: 480L

• CONTENTS •

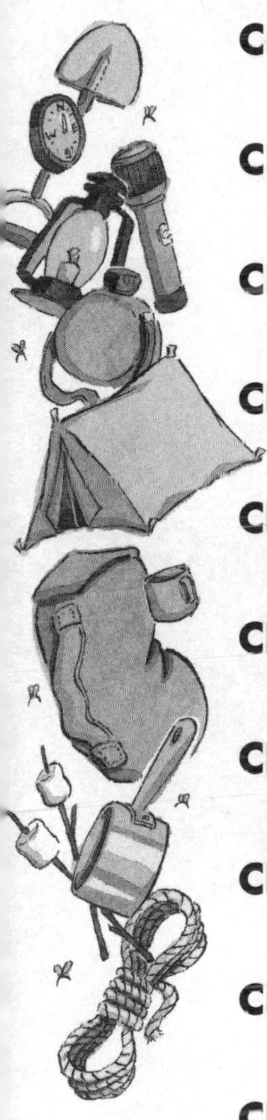

•CHAPTER ONE•
ONE FINE AFTERNOON

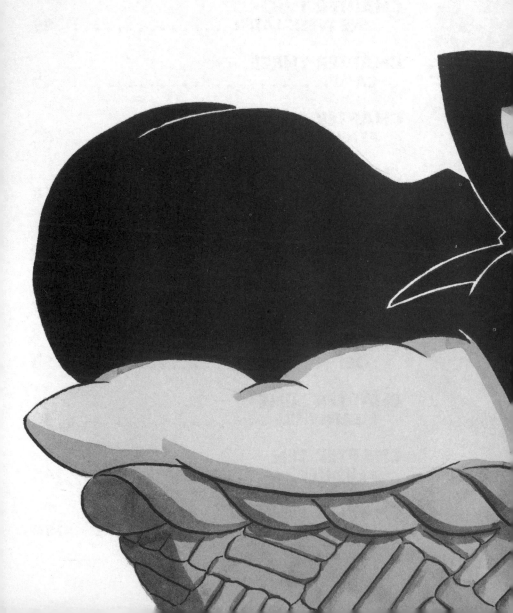

Good morning, Kitty!

Or perhaps I should say, "Good afternoon," seeing as it's 3:00 pm and morning ended hours ago.

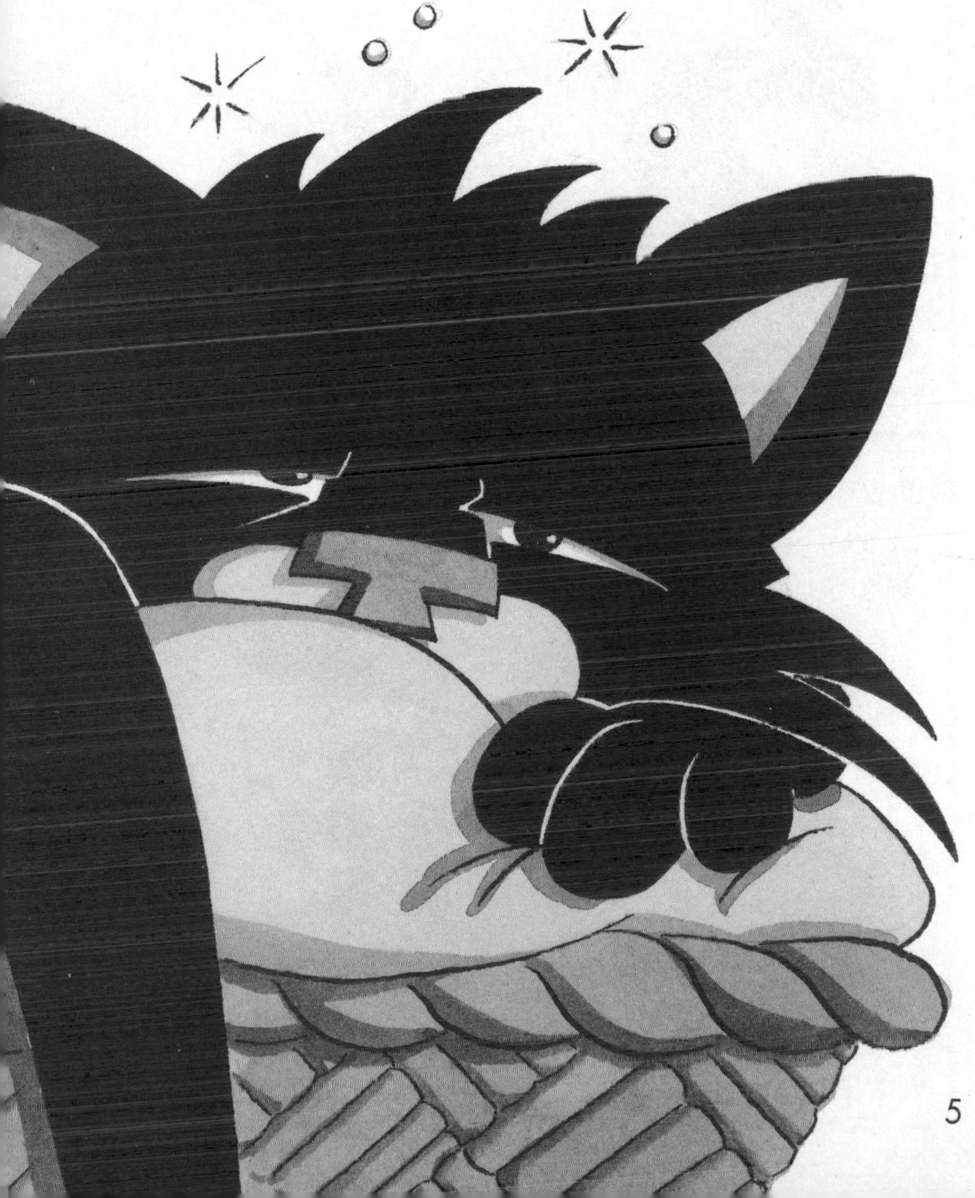

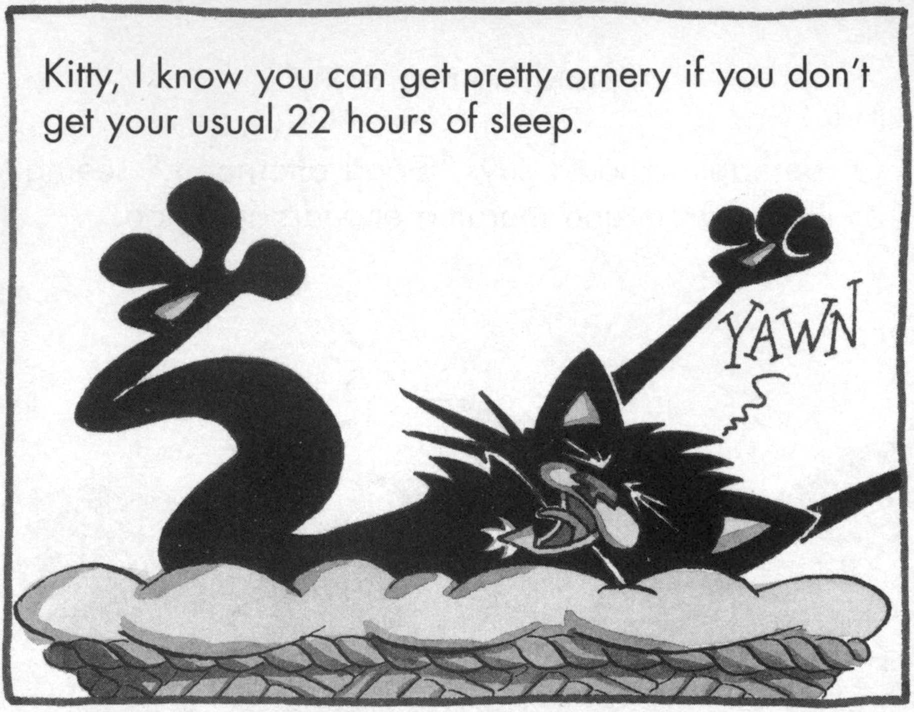
Kitty, I know you can get pretty ornery if you don't get your usual 22 hours of sleep.
YAWN

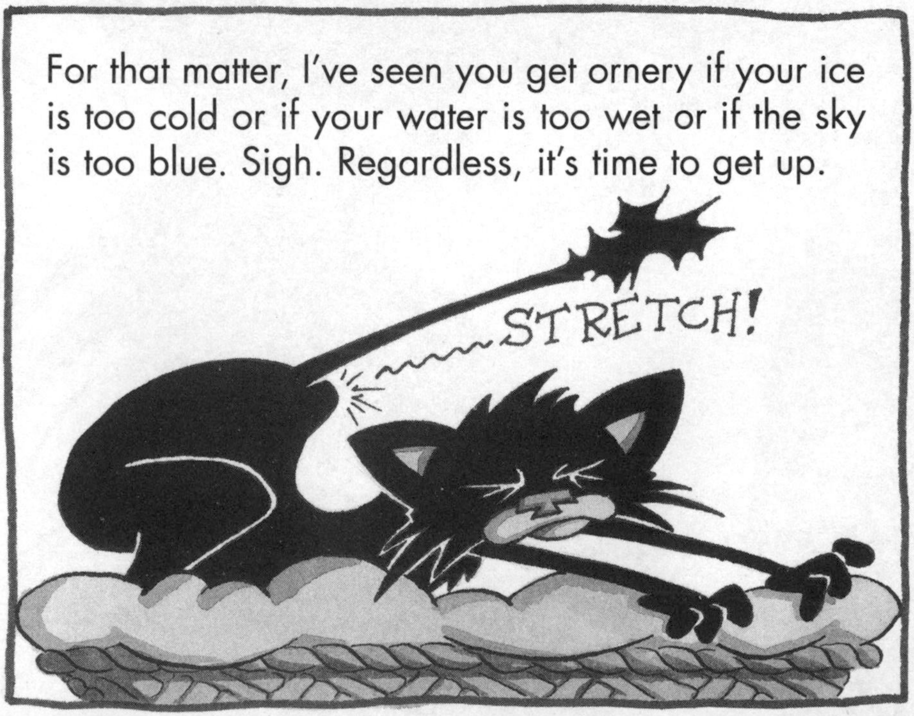
For that matter, I've seen you get ornery if your ice is too cold or if your water is too wet or if the sky is too blue. Sigh. Regardless, it's time to get up.
STRETCH!

Besides, your breakfast is ready, and I have a really, really, really BIG surprise for you today!

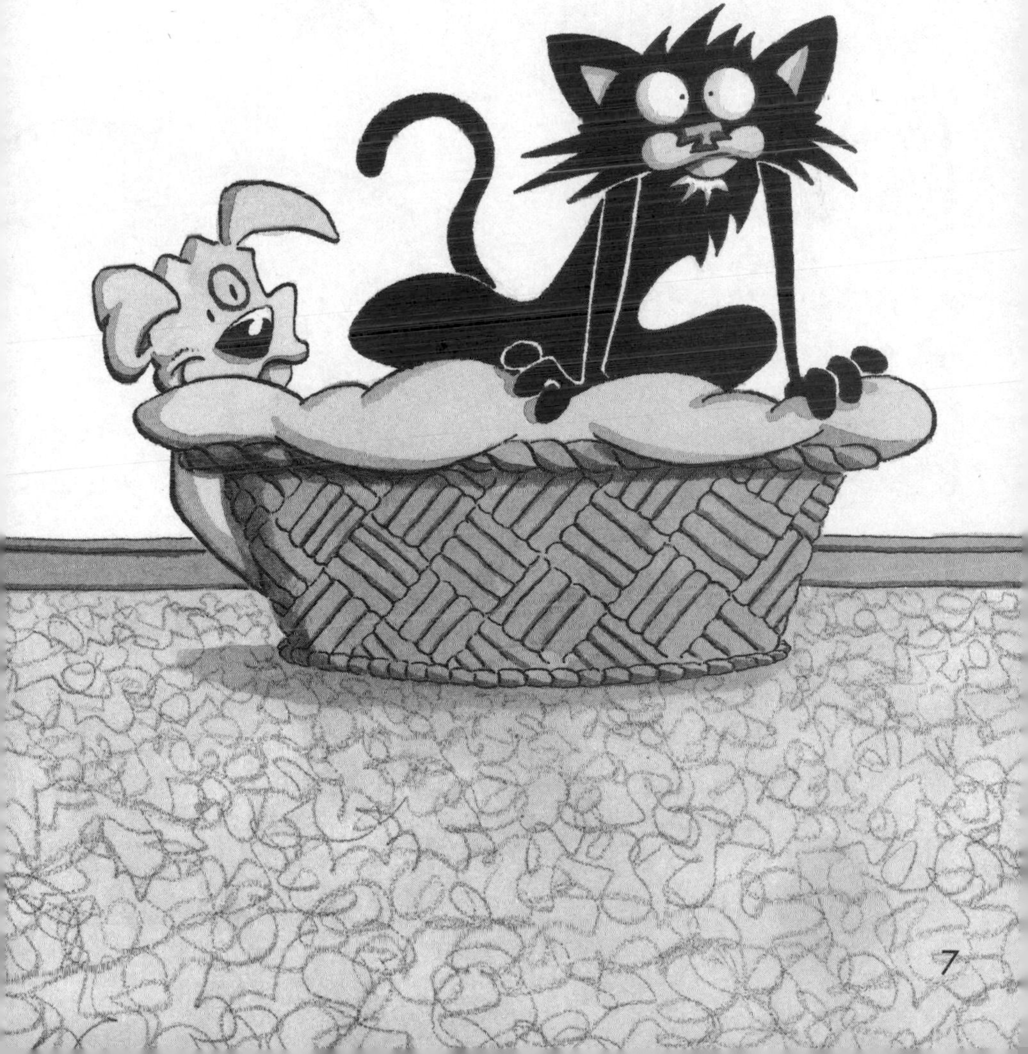

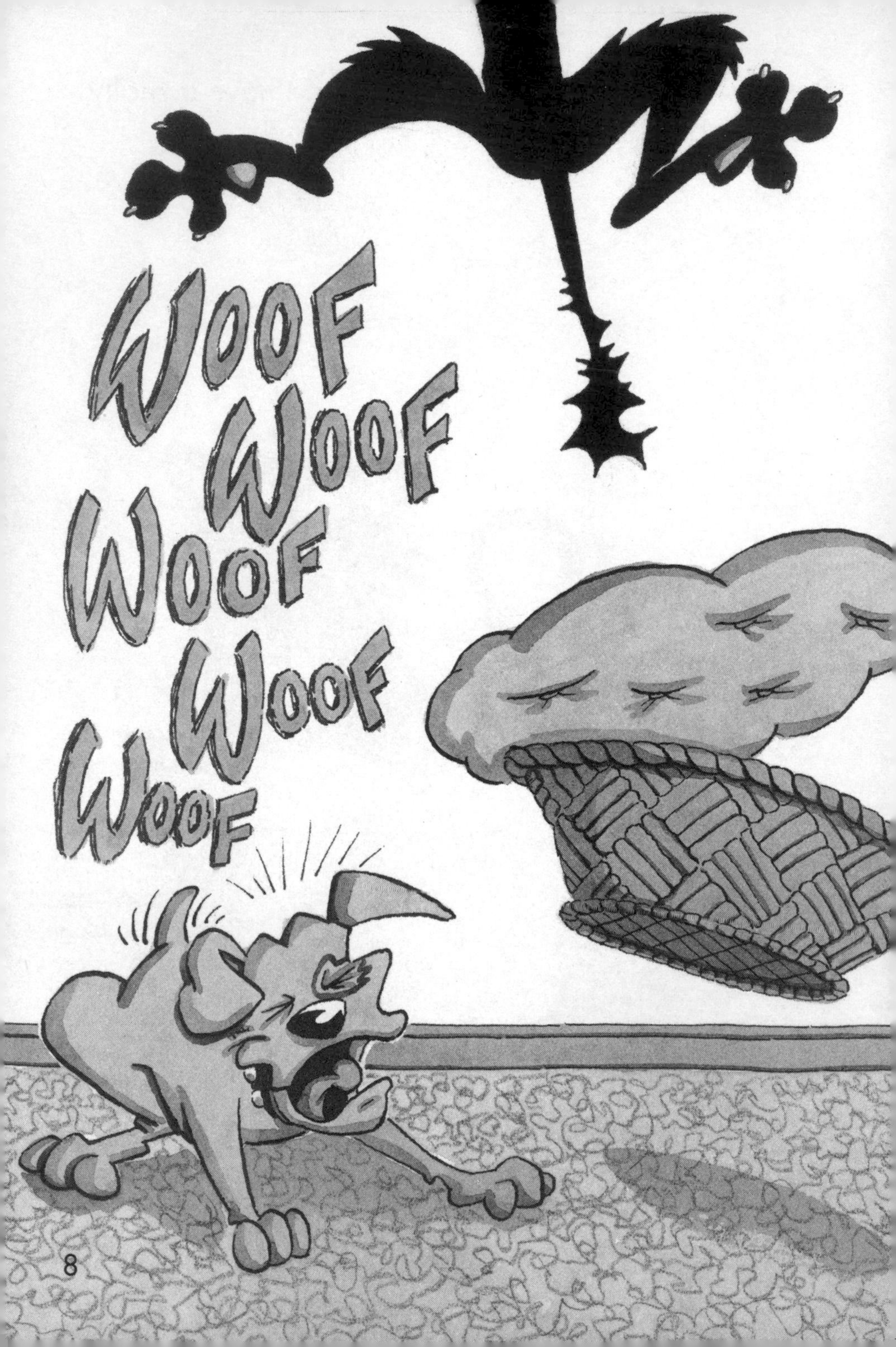
WOOF
WOOF
WOOF
WOOF
WOOF

Sorry, Kitty. That wasn't the surprise. Are you okay? Puppy has been waiting patiently all day to play with you, and I guess he got a little excited when he saw you were finally up. The really, really, really BIG surprise is . . .

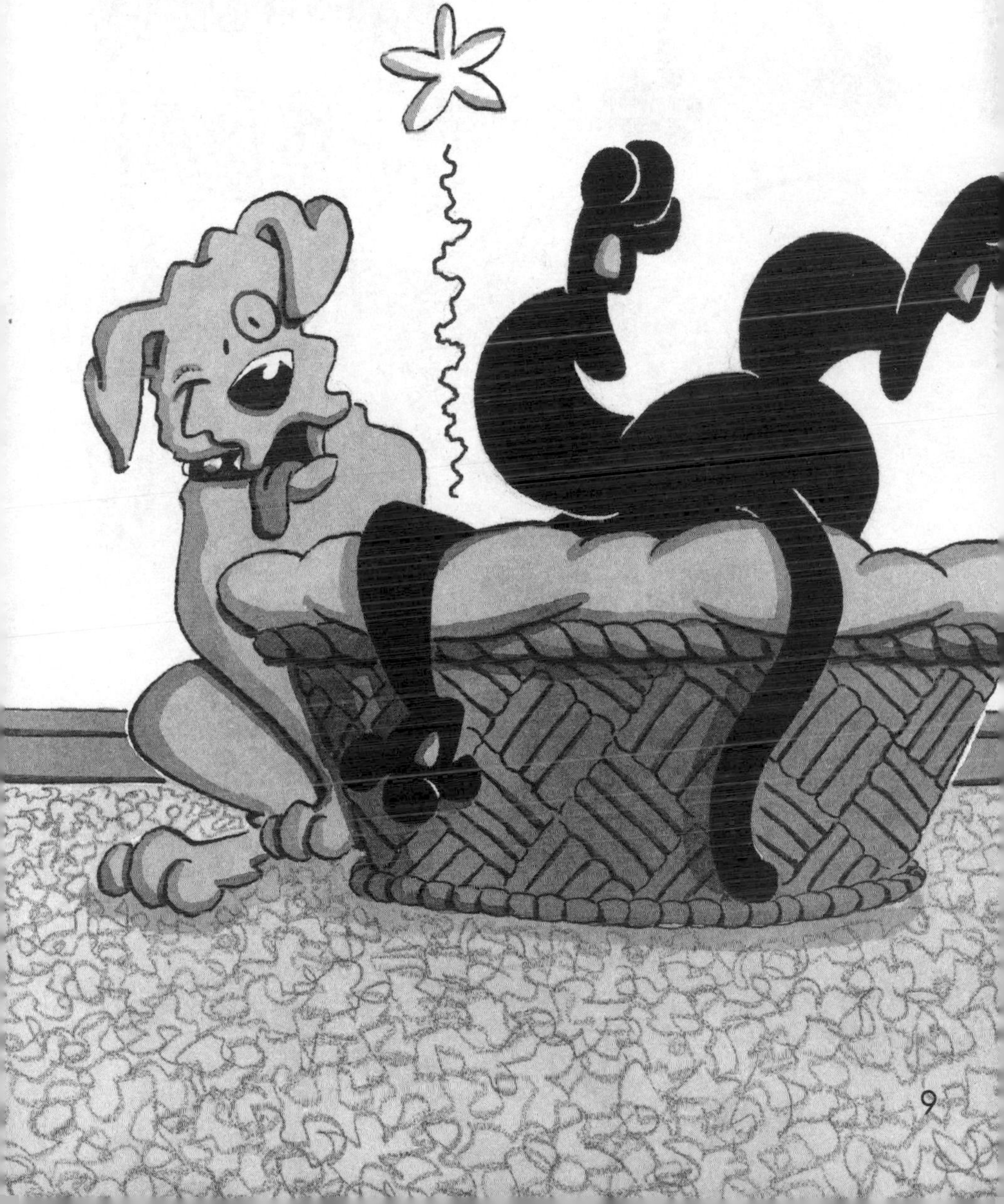

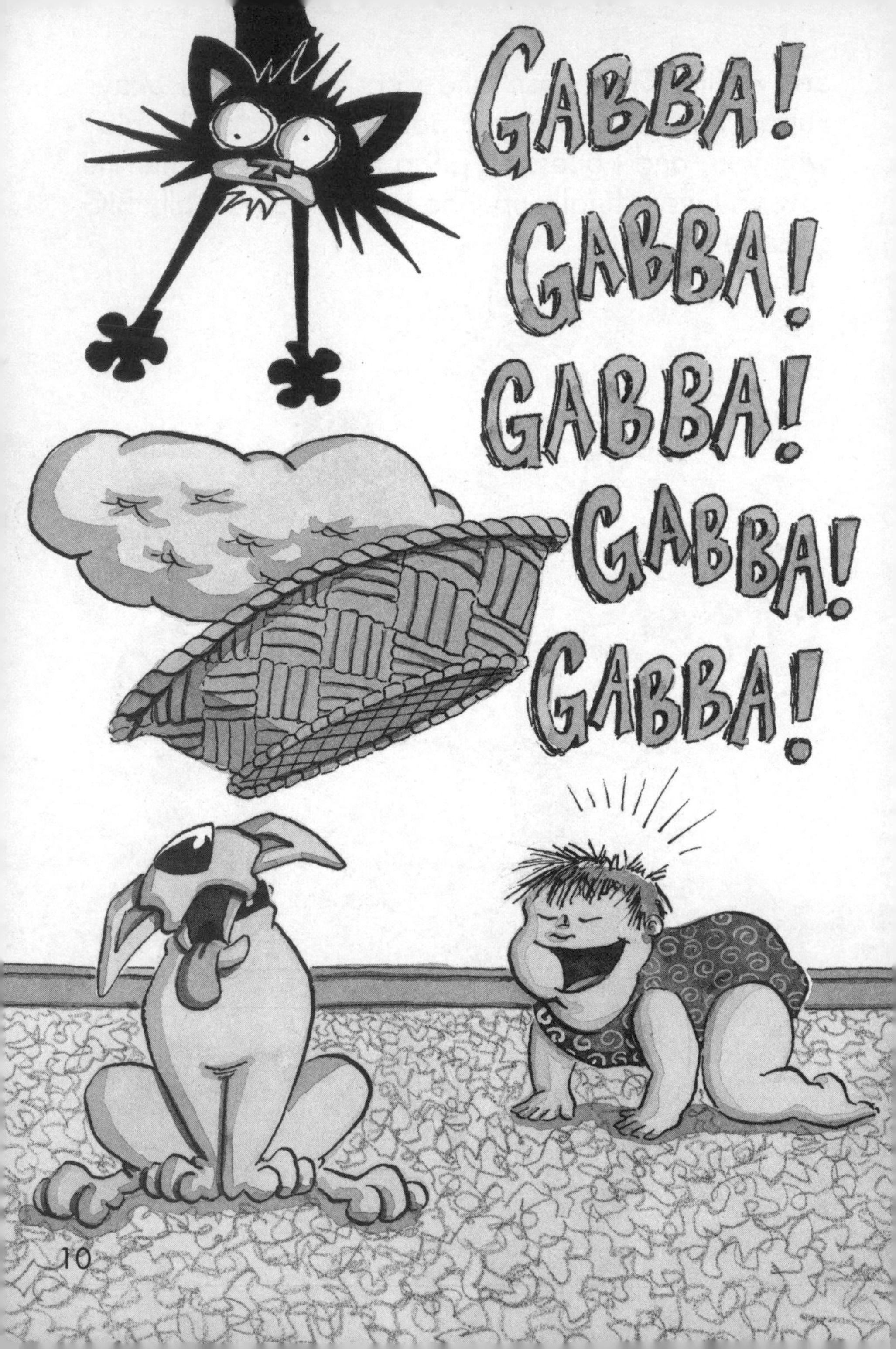
GABBA!
GABBA!
GABBA!
GABBA!
GABBA!

Sorry again, Kitty. That wasn't the surprise either. Baby has been waiting patiently all day to play with you, too.

Are you sure you're okay? That's twice now that you've landed on your head.

Anyway, the really, really, really BIG surprise is . . .

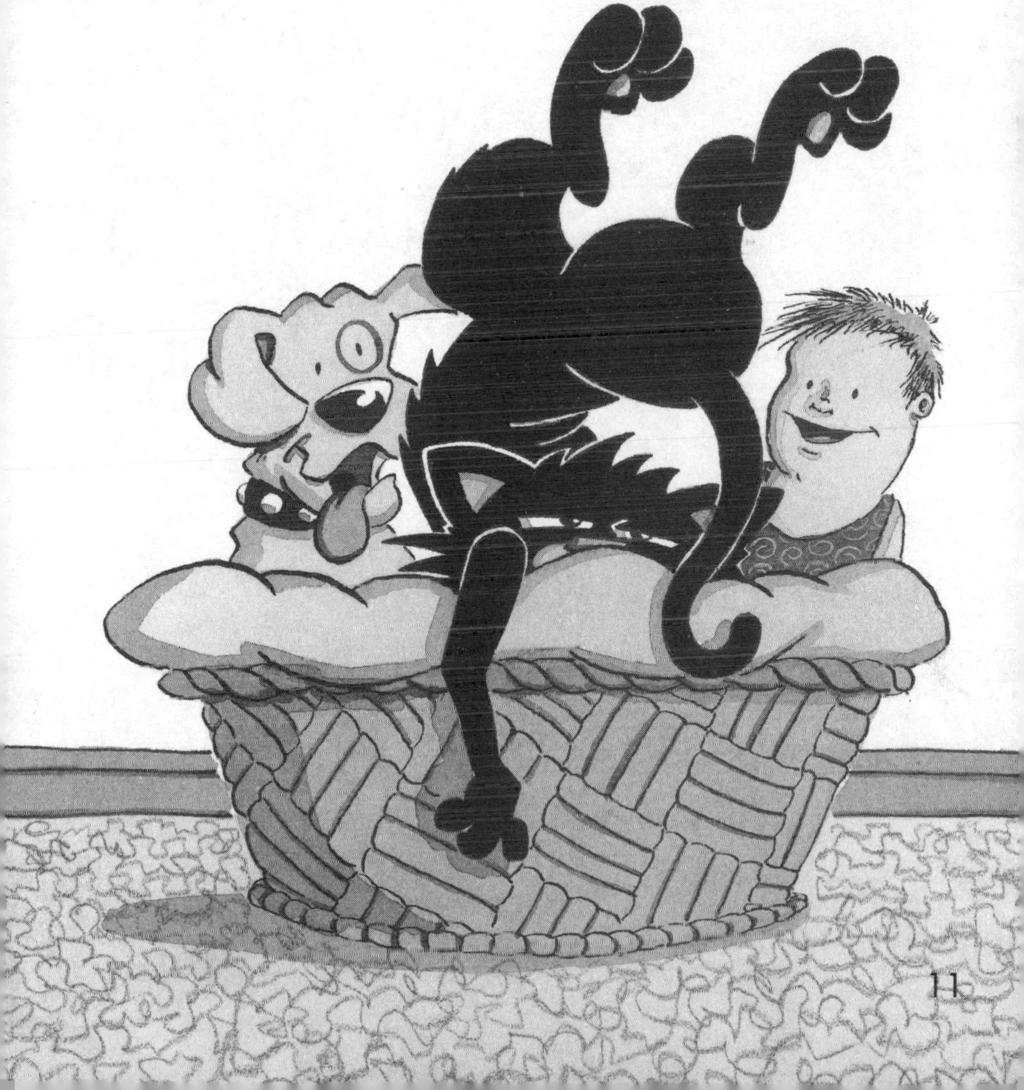

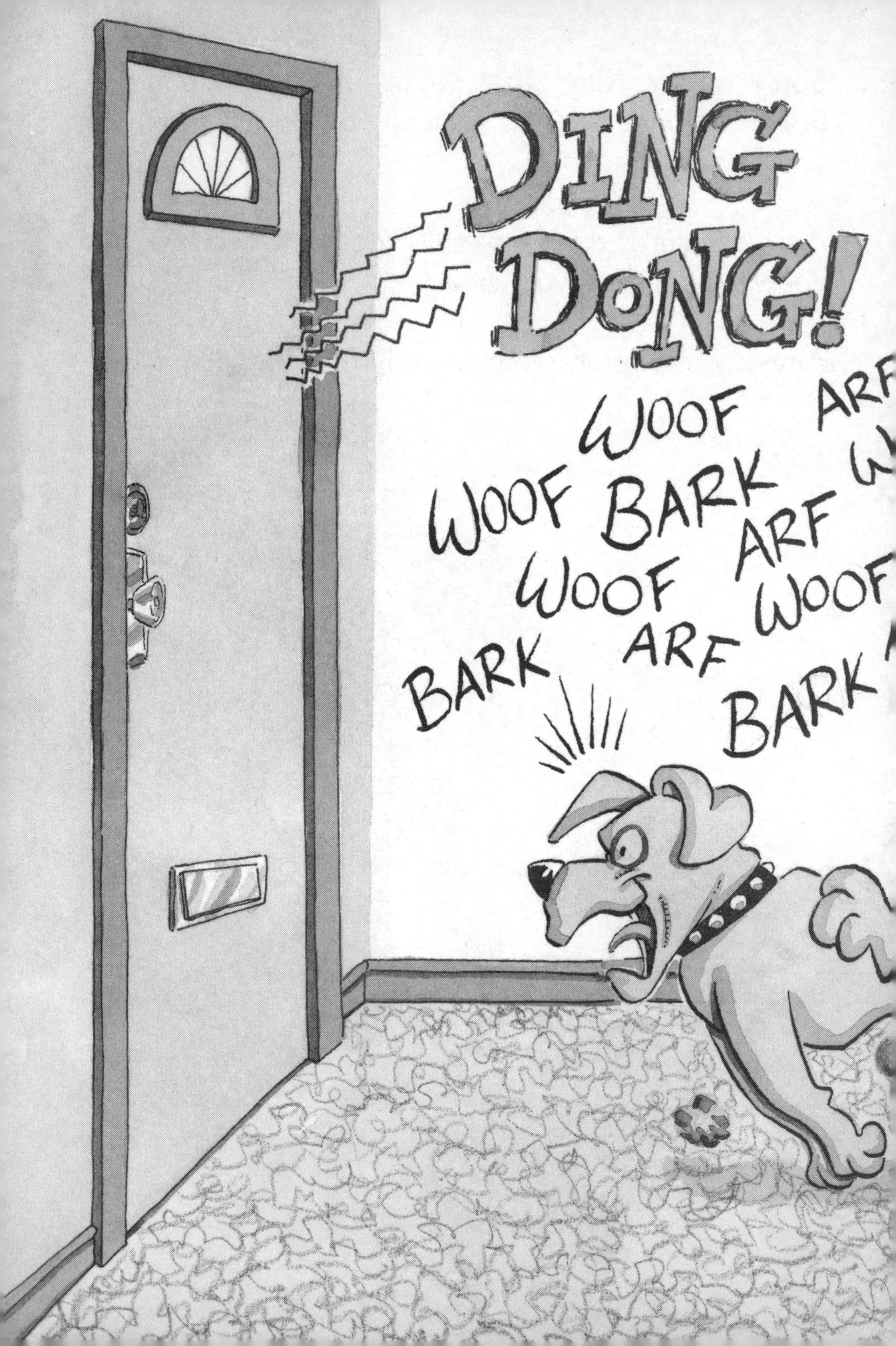
DING DONG!
WOOF ARF
WOOF BARK
WOOF ARF
BARK ARF WOOF
BARK

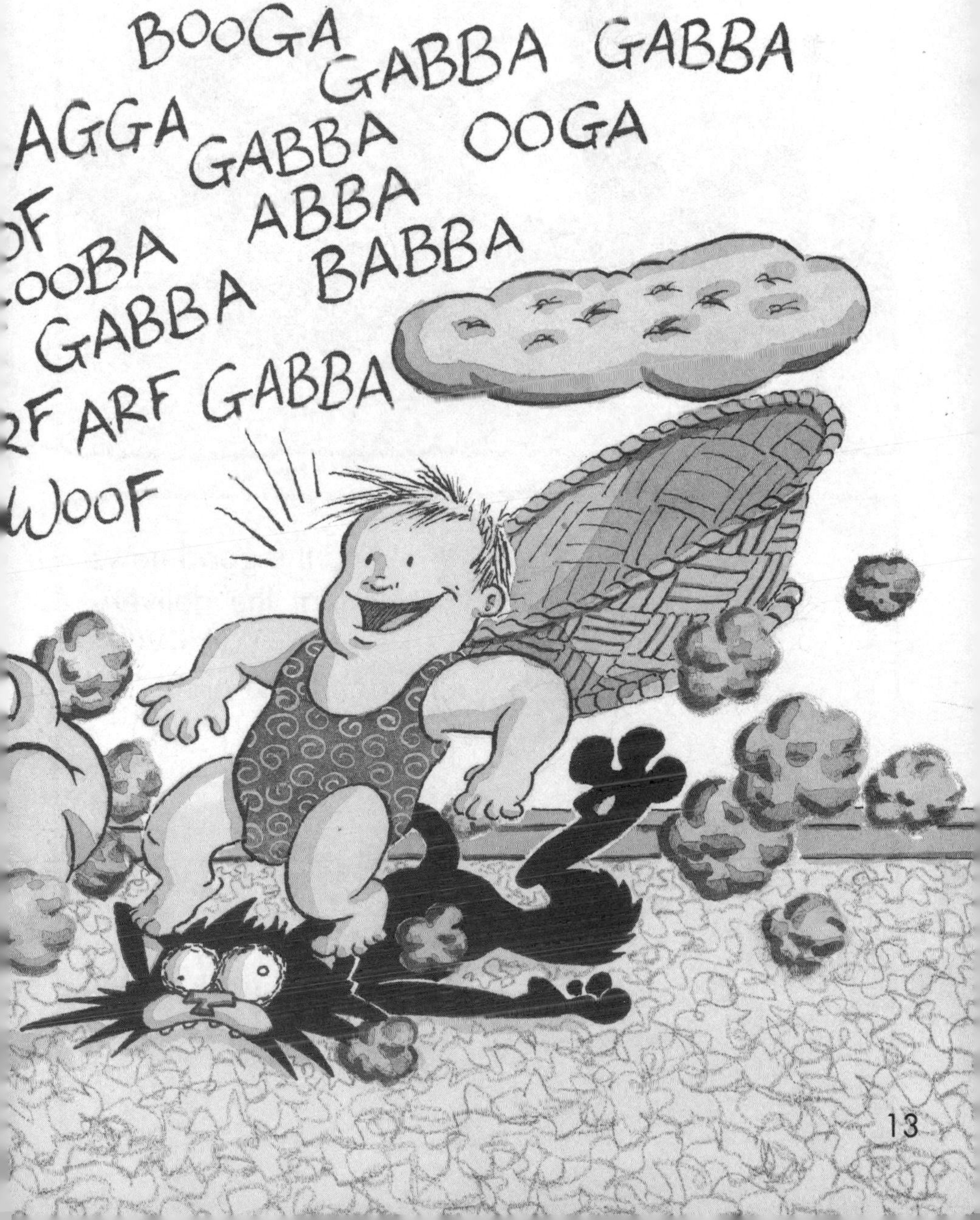
BOOGA
GABBA GABBA
AGGA
GABBA OOGA
OF
ABBA
OOBA
BABBA
GABBA
RF ARF GABBA
WOOF

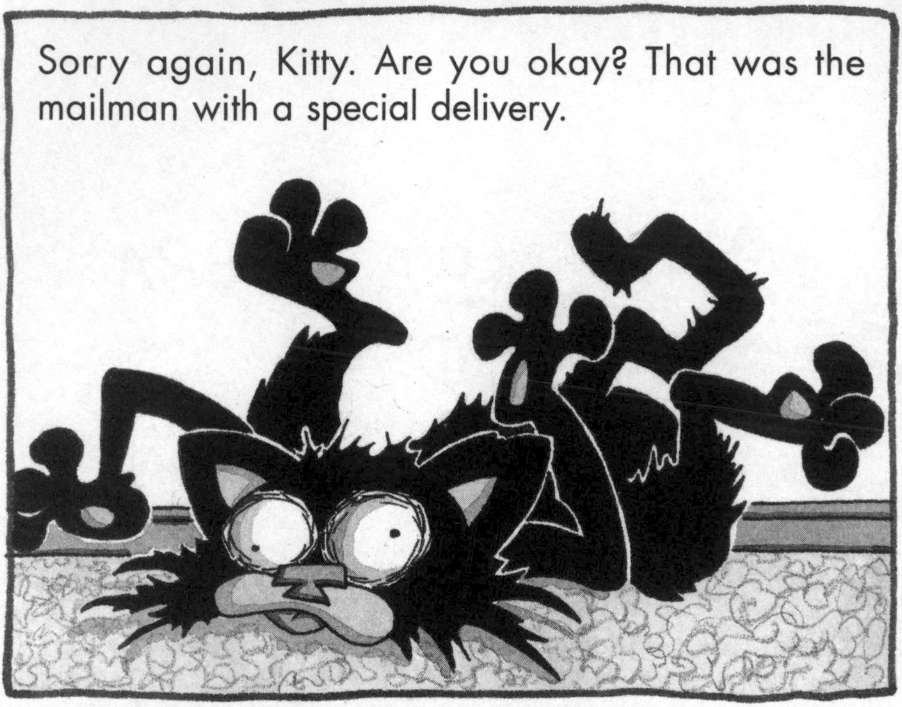
Sorry again, Kitty. Are you okay? That was the mailman with a special delivery.

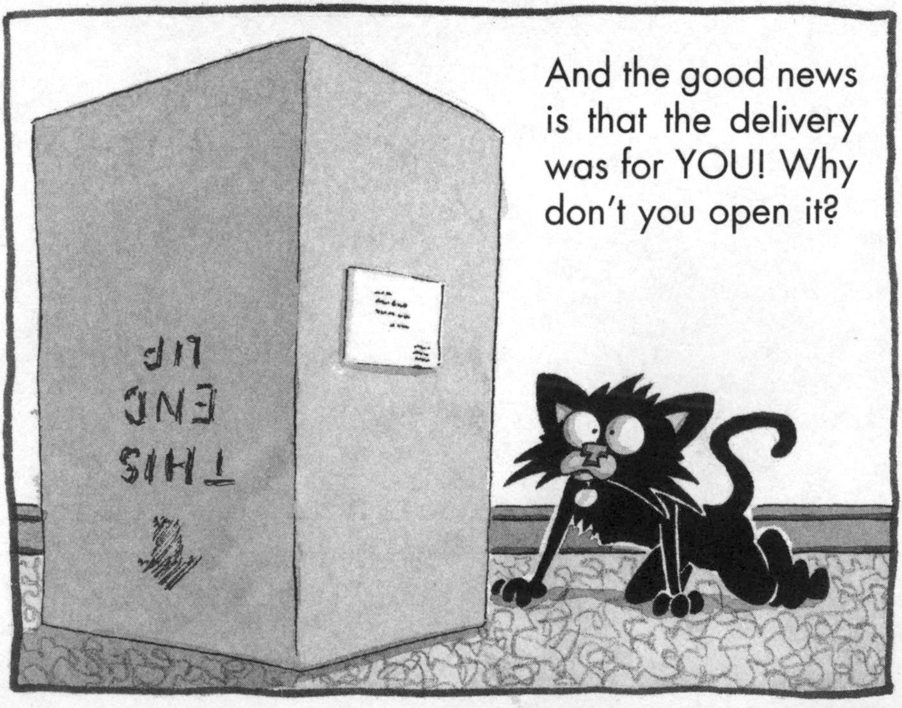
And the good news is that the delivery was for YOU! Why don't you open it?

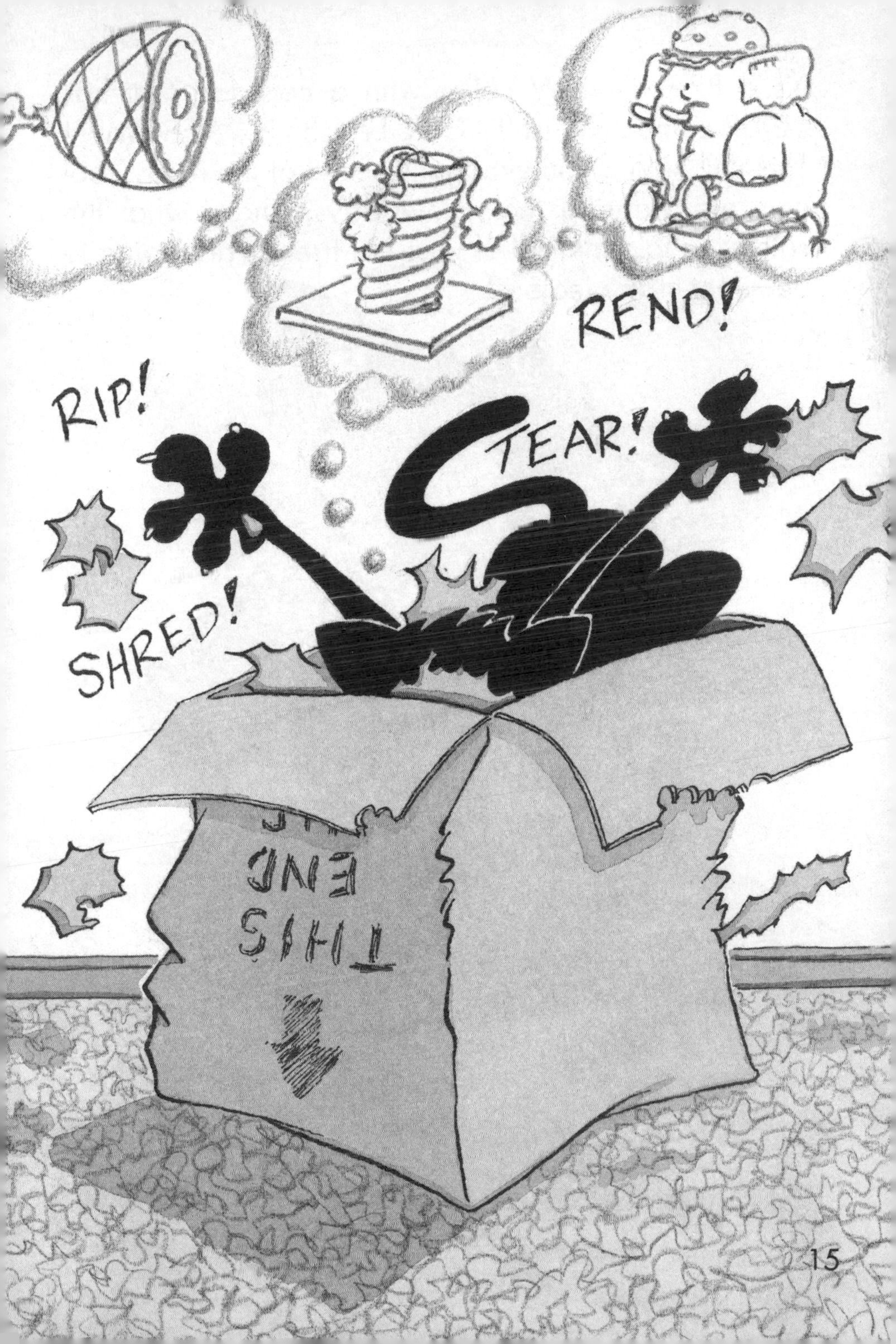
REND!
RIP!
TEAR!
SHRED!

It's a BRAND-NEW collar with a cool tag that has YOUR name on it! Isn't it COOL?! Isn't it AWESOME?! This will help if you ever get lost. All of the really cool cats are wearing them nowadays. That's what the salesman told me. All of your cat friends are going to be super-crazy jealous!

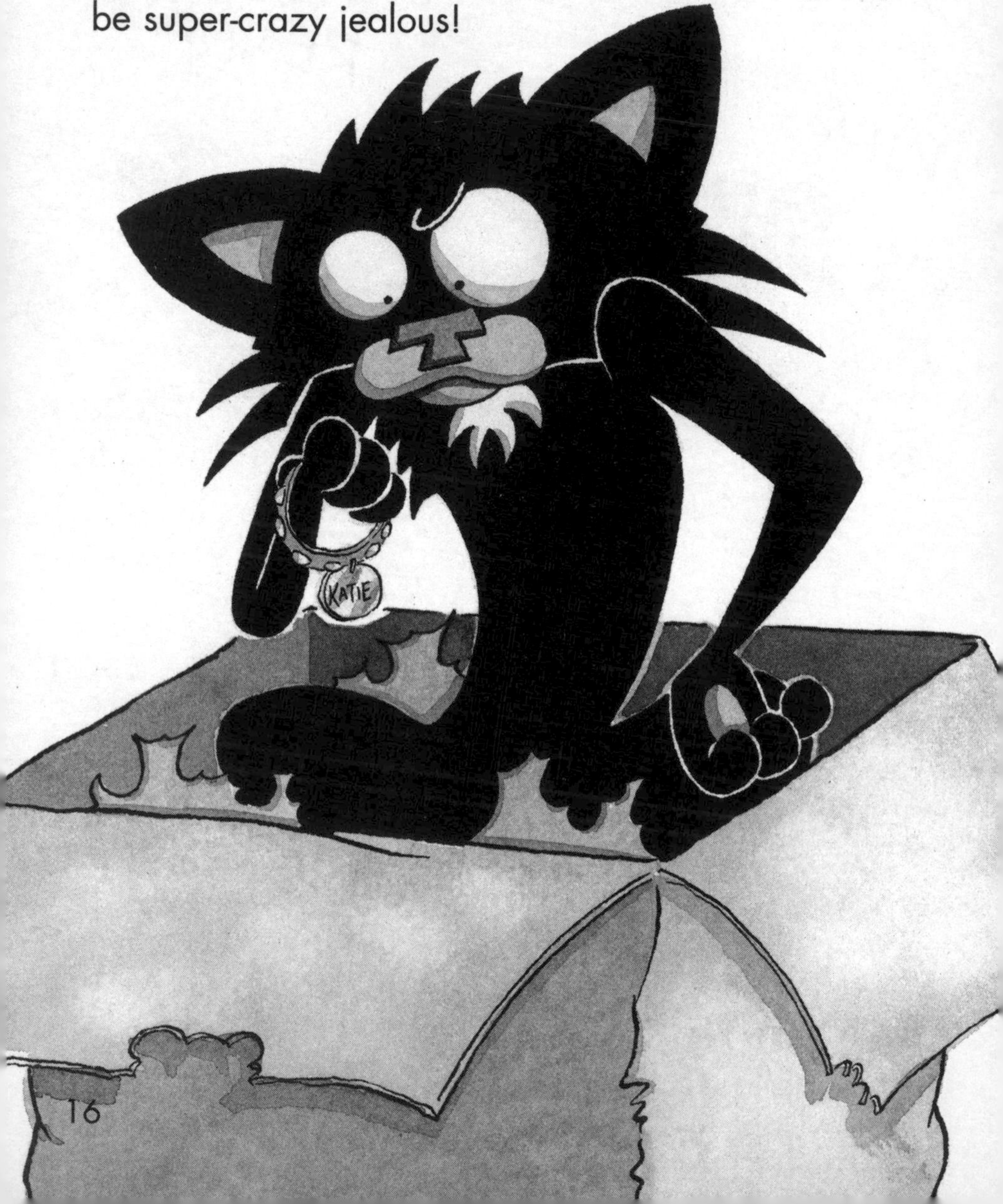
KATIE

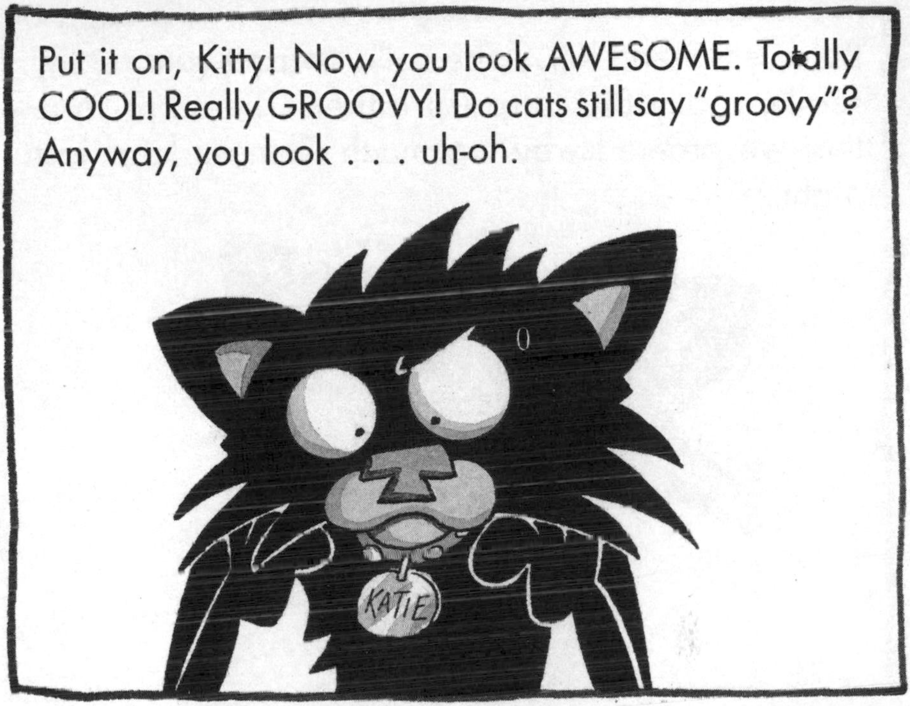
Put it on, Kitty! Now you look AWESOME. Totally COOL! Really GROOVY! Do cats still say "groovy"? Anyway, you look . . . uh-oh.
KATIE

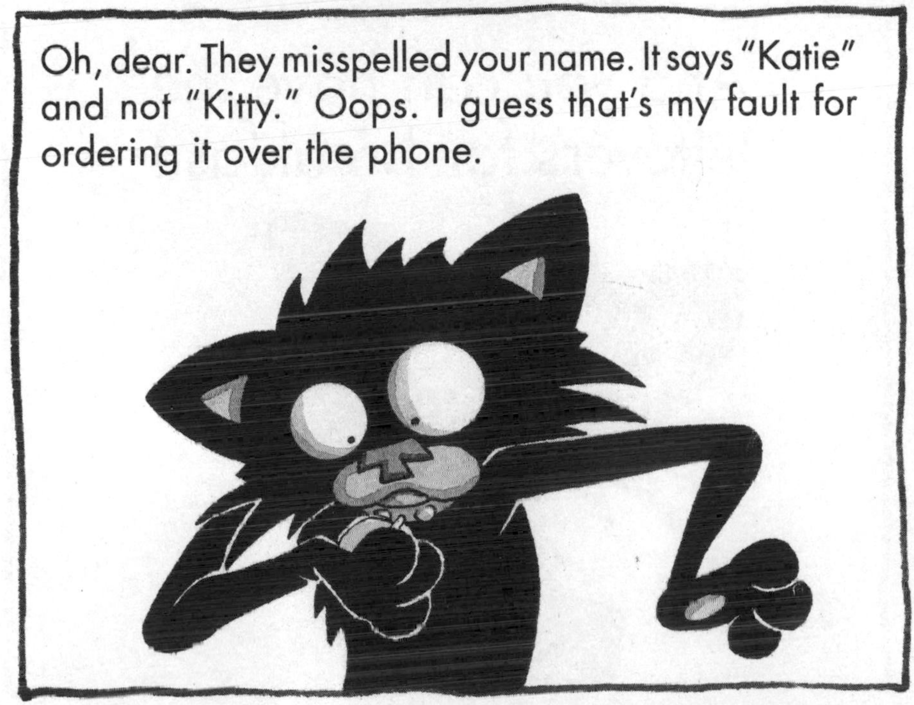
Oh, dear. They misspelled your name. It says "Katie" and not "Kitty." Oops. I guess that's my fault for ordering it over the phone.

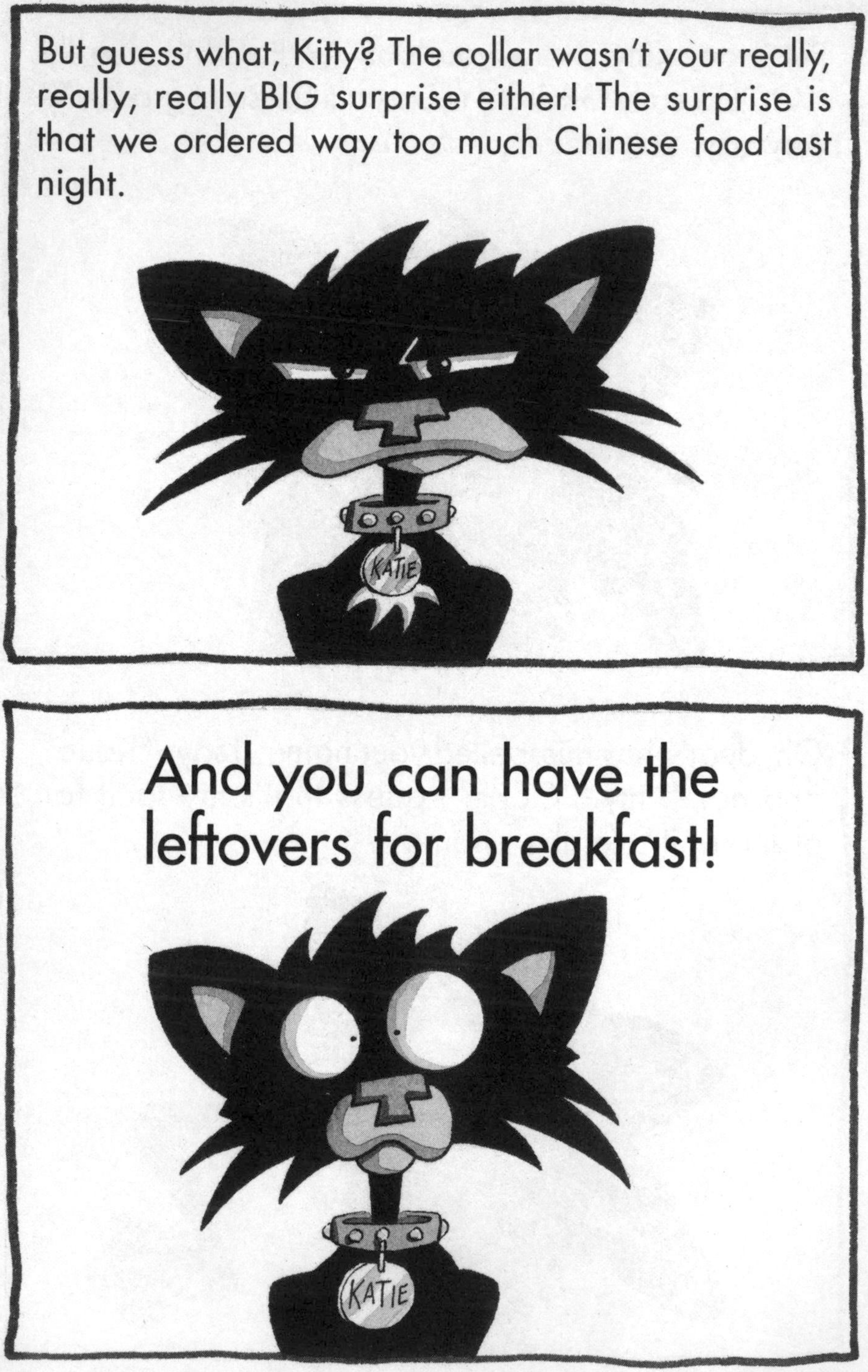
But guess what, Kitty? The collar wasn't your really, really, really BIG surprise either! The surprise is that we ordered way too much Chinese food last night.
KATIE
And you can have the leftovers for breakfast!
KATIE

There's chicken fried rice and beef lo mein and duck chow fun and shrimp with broccoli and scallops with mixed vegetables and fried dumplings and steamed dumplings and Shanghai dumplings and egg rolls and spring rolls and . . . and . . .

AND IT'S ALL YOURS, KITTY!

Bon appétit!

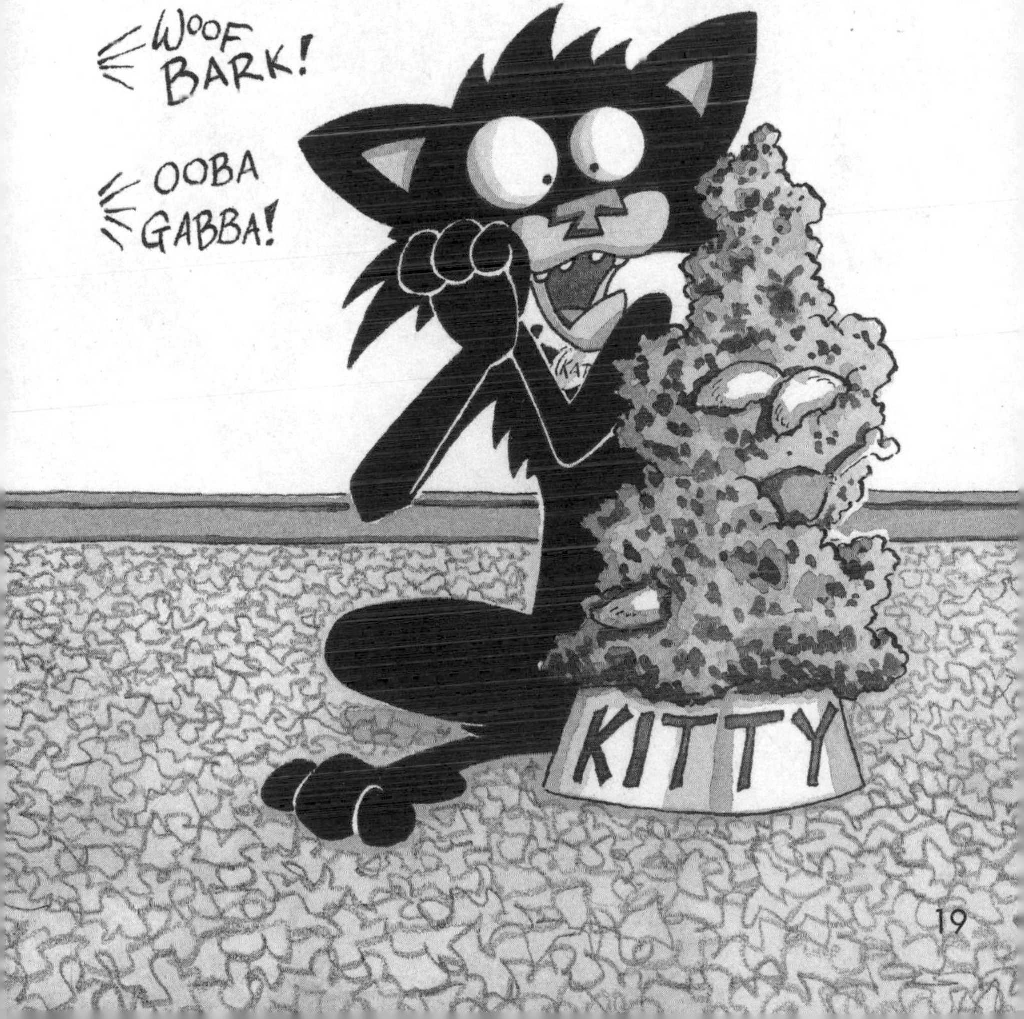
WOOF
BARK!
OOBA
GABBA!
KITTY

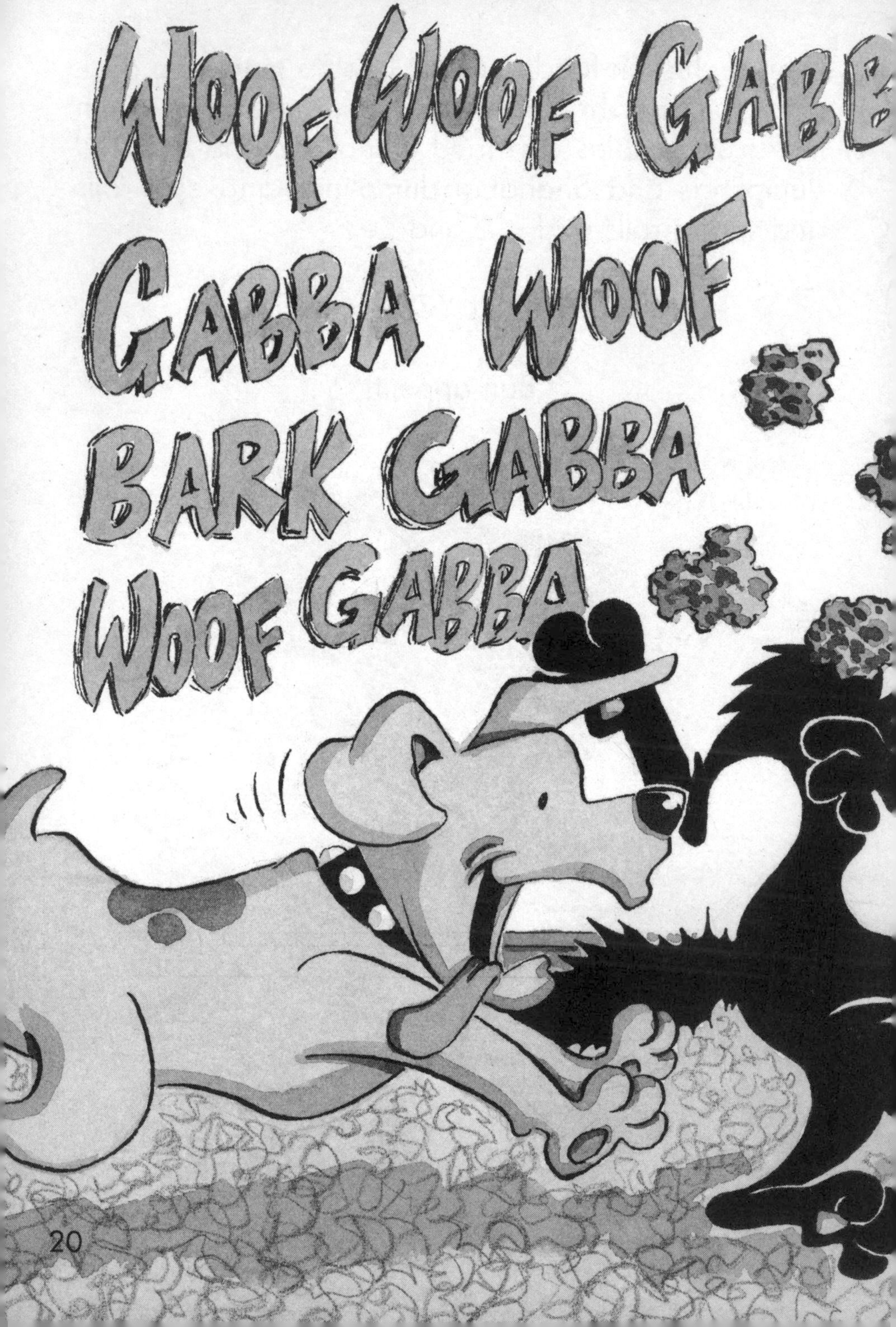
WOOF WOOF GABB
GABBA WOOF
BARK GABBA
WOOF GABBA

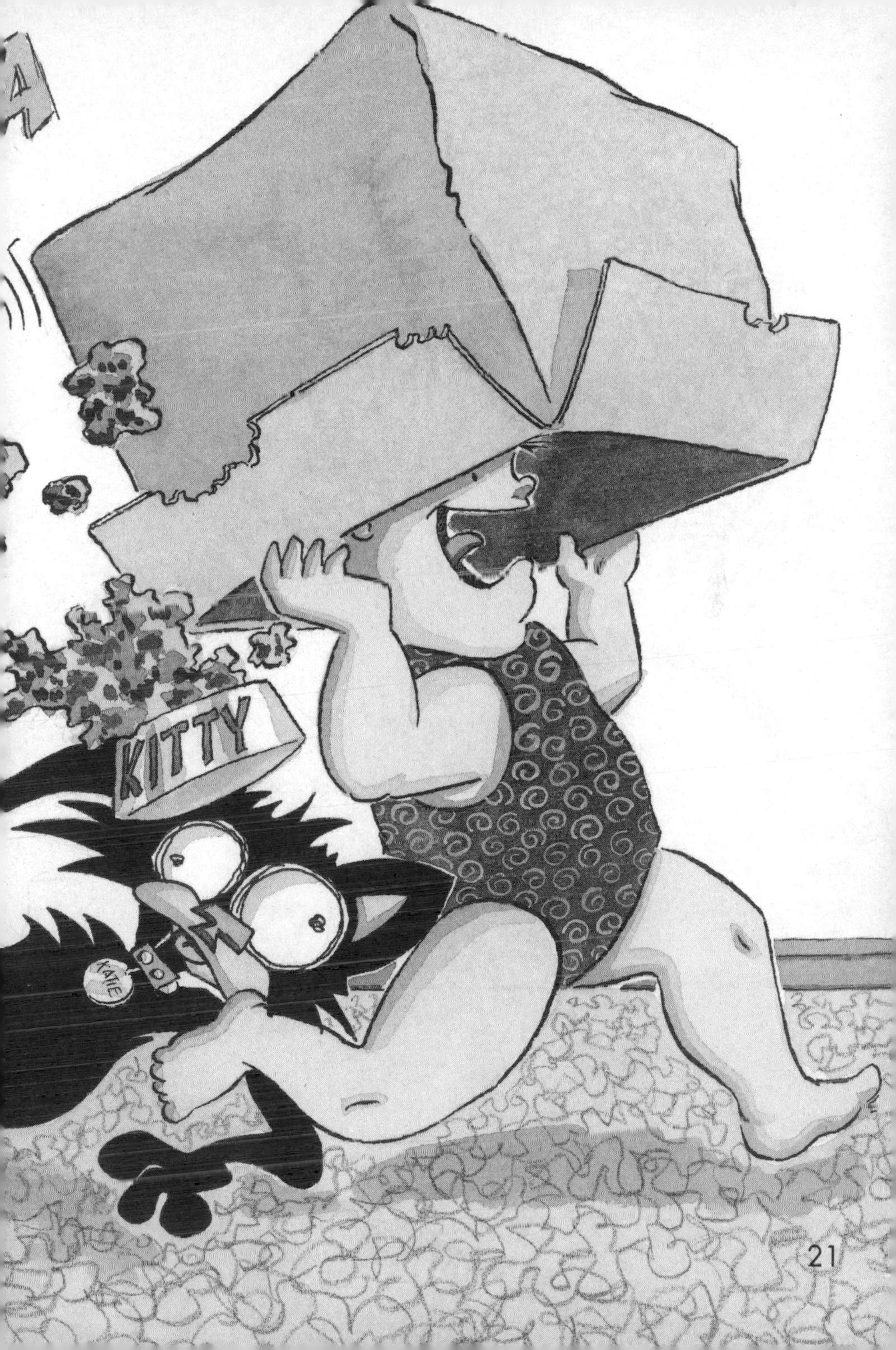
KITTY
KATIE

Oh dear.

What a mess.

Sorry about that, Kitty. I'll clean this up and get your usual breakfast: a can of gray chicken-flavored paste with green bits.

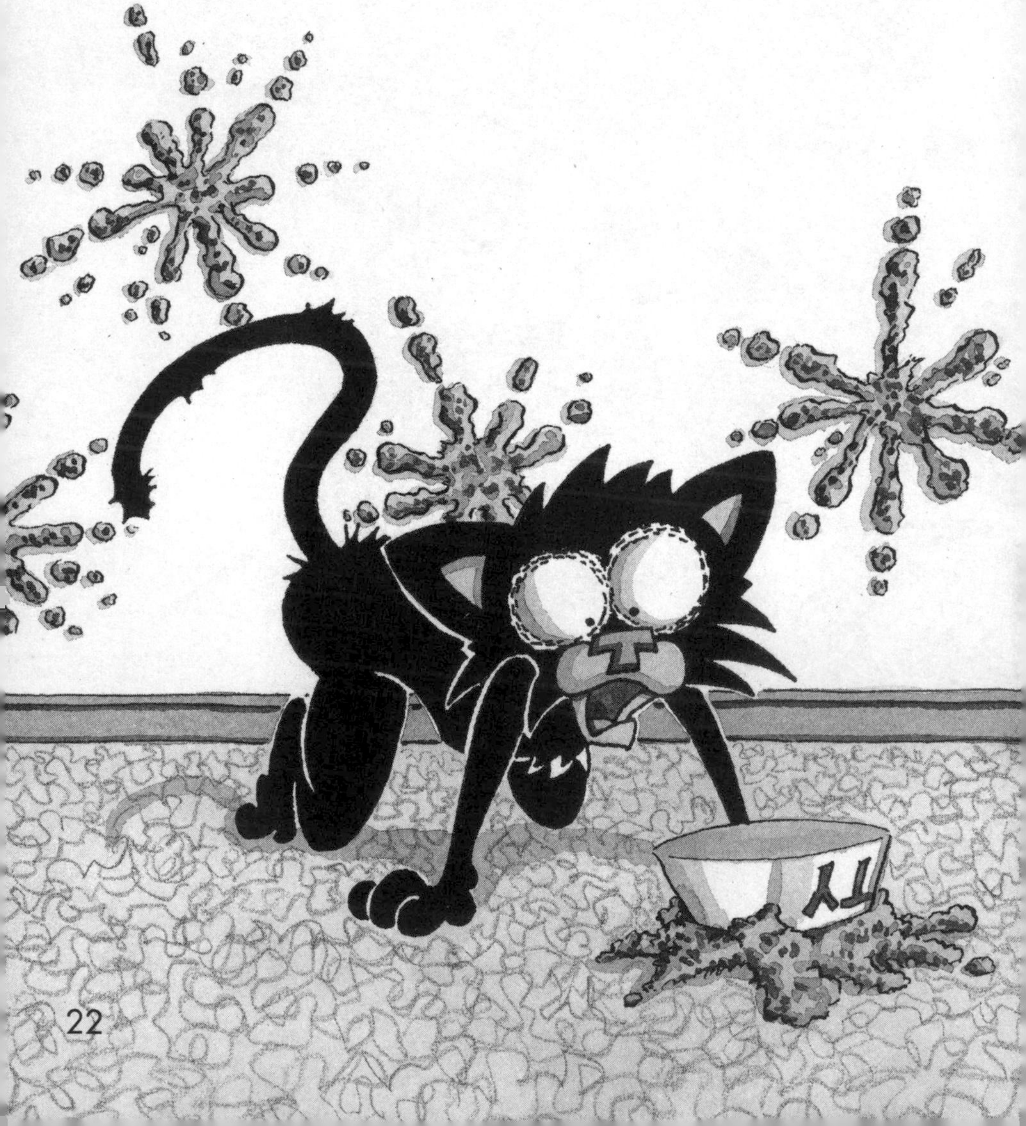

TY

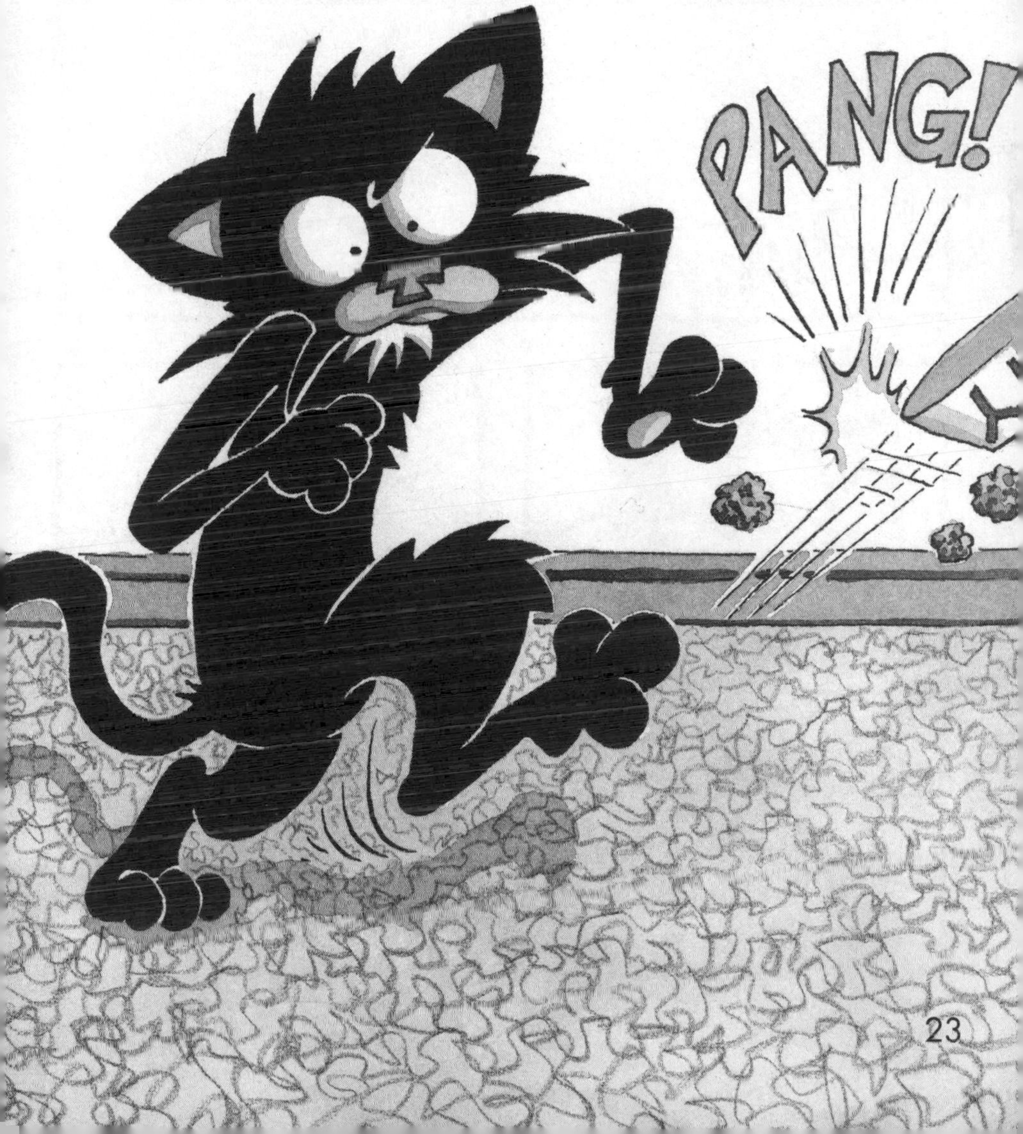
PANG!

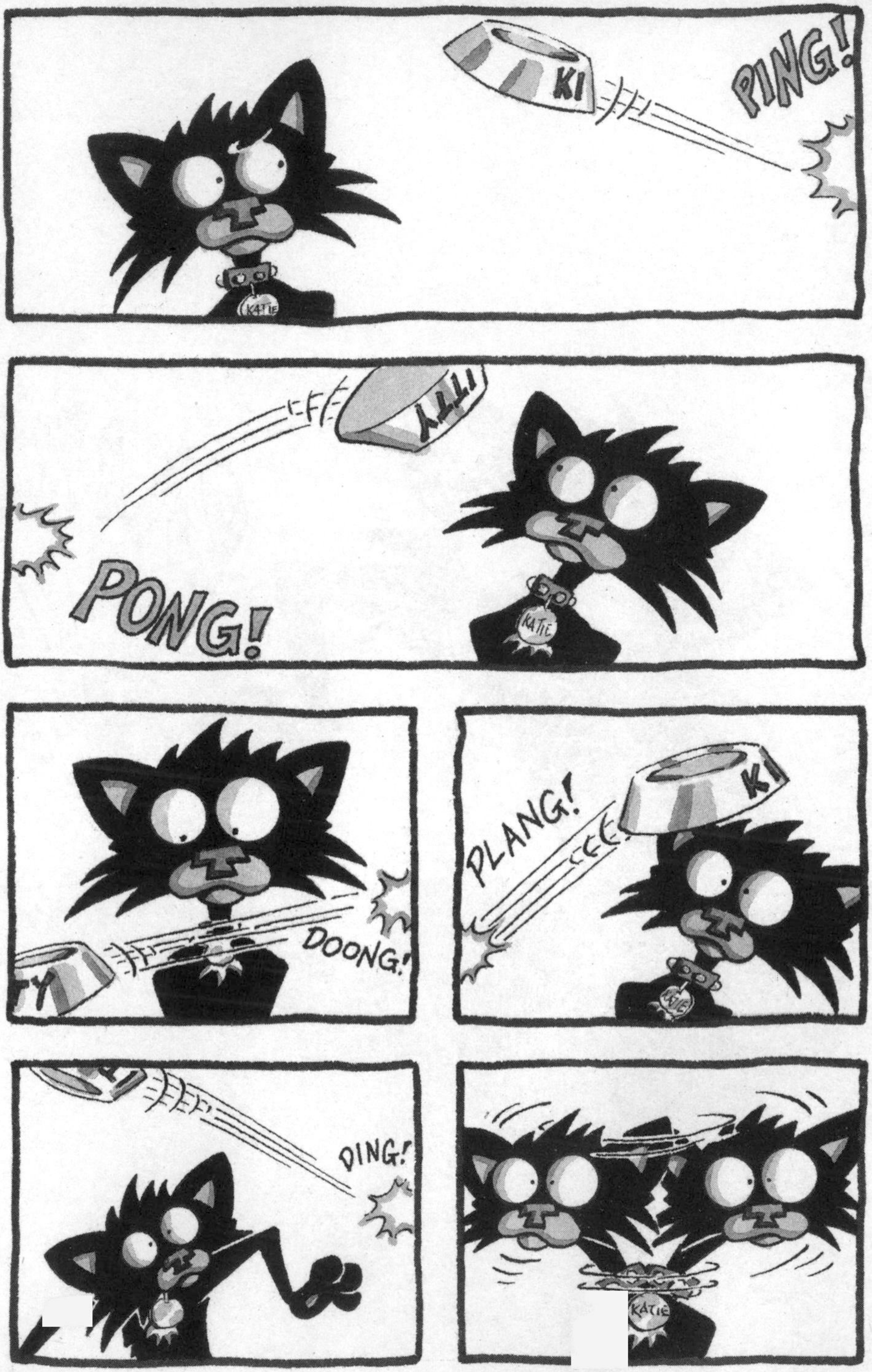
KI
PING!
KATIE
PONG!
KATIE
DOONG!
PLANG!
KI
DING!
KATIE

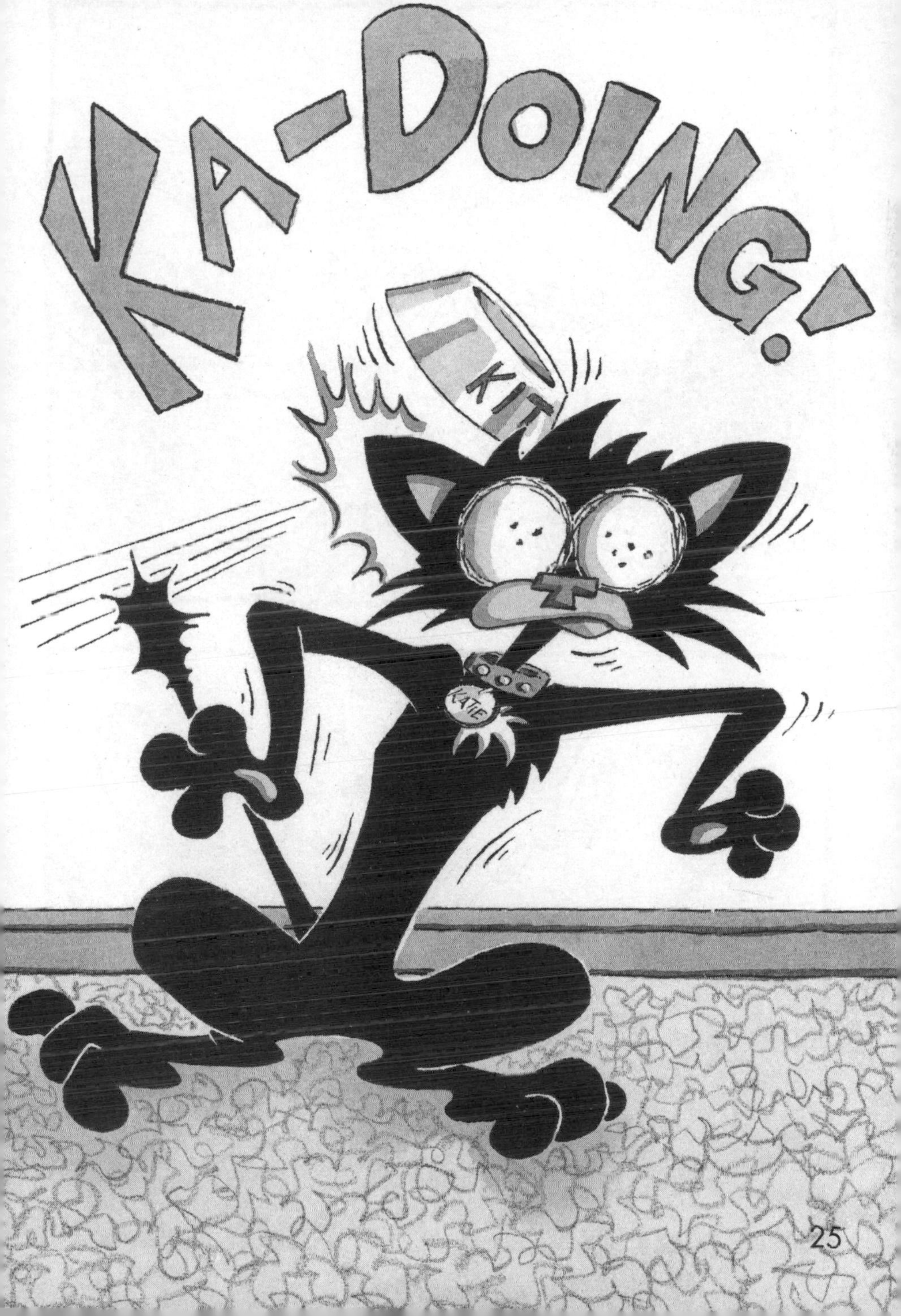
KA-DOING!
KIT
KATIE

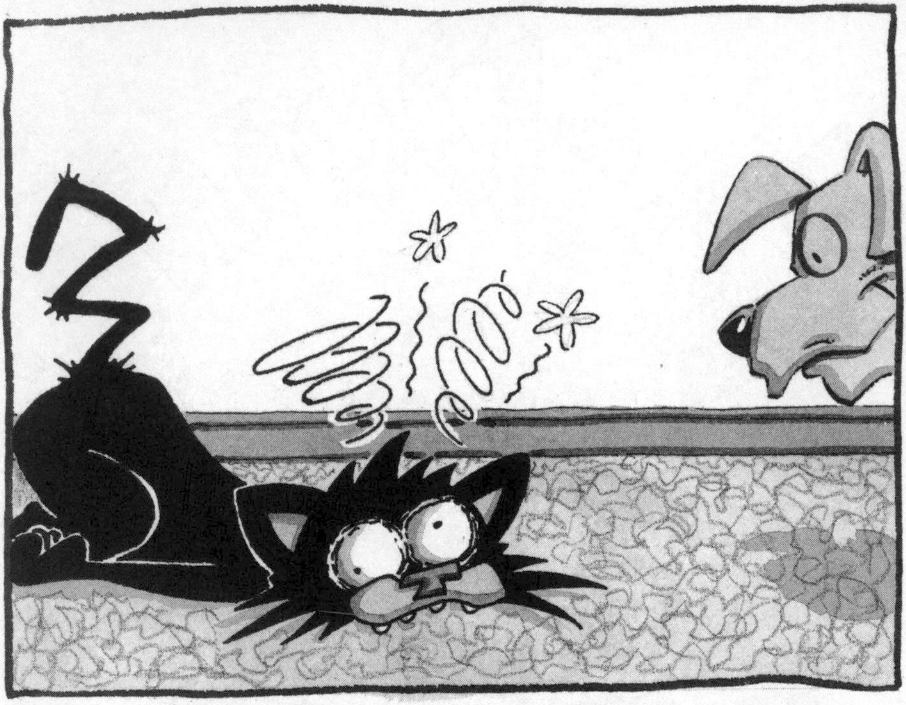

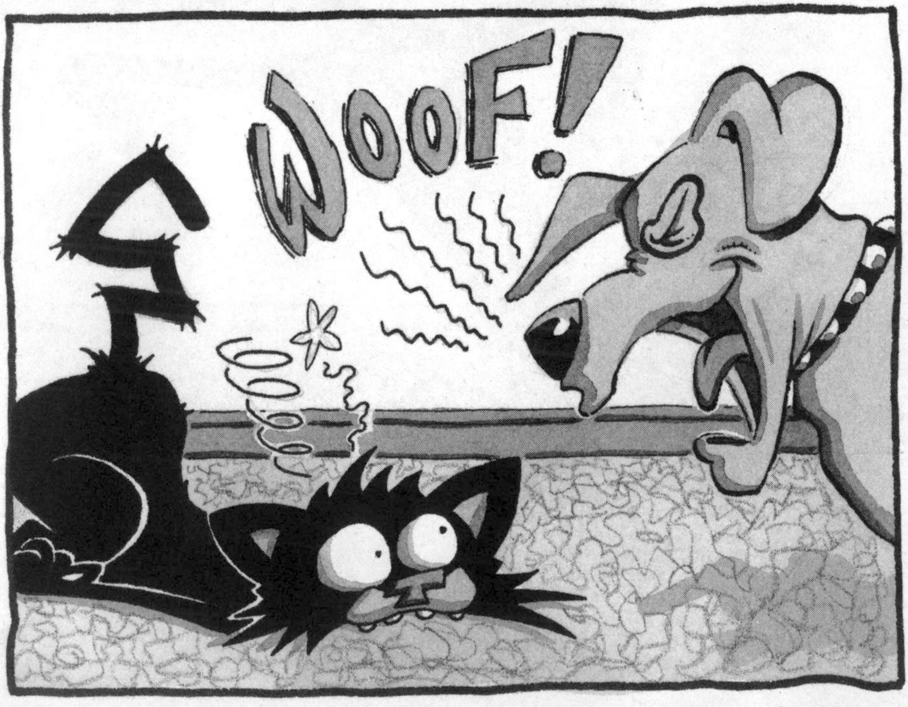
WOOF!

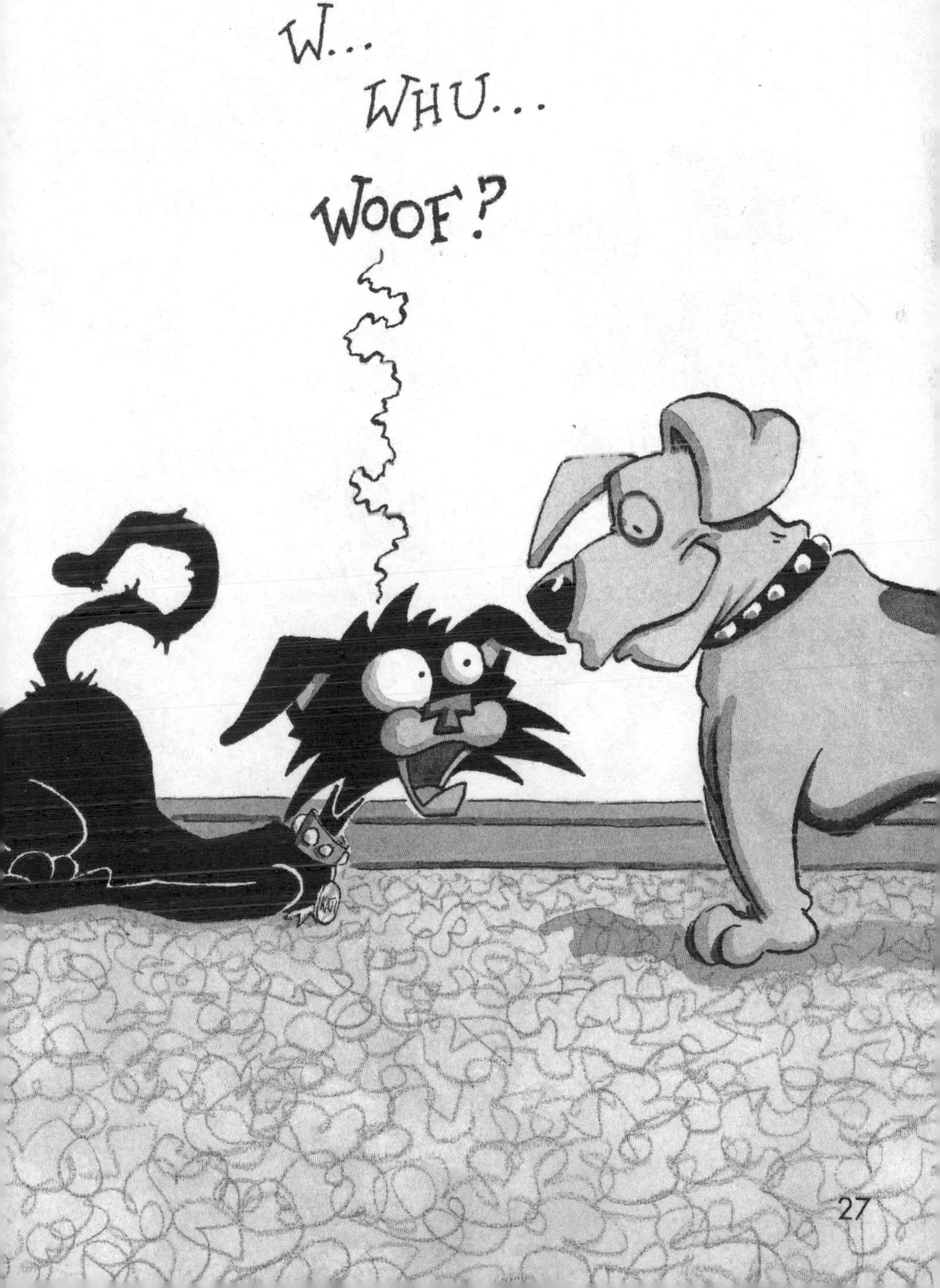
W...
WHU...
WOOF?

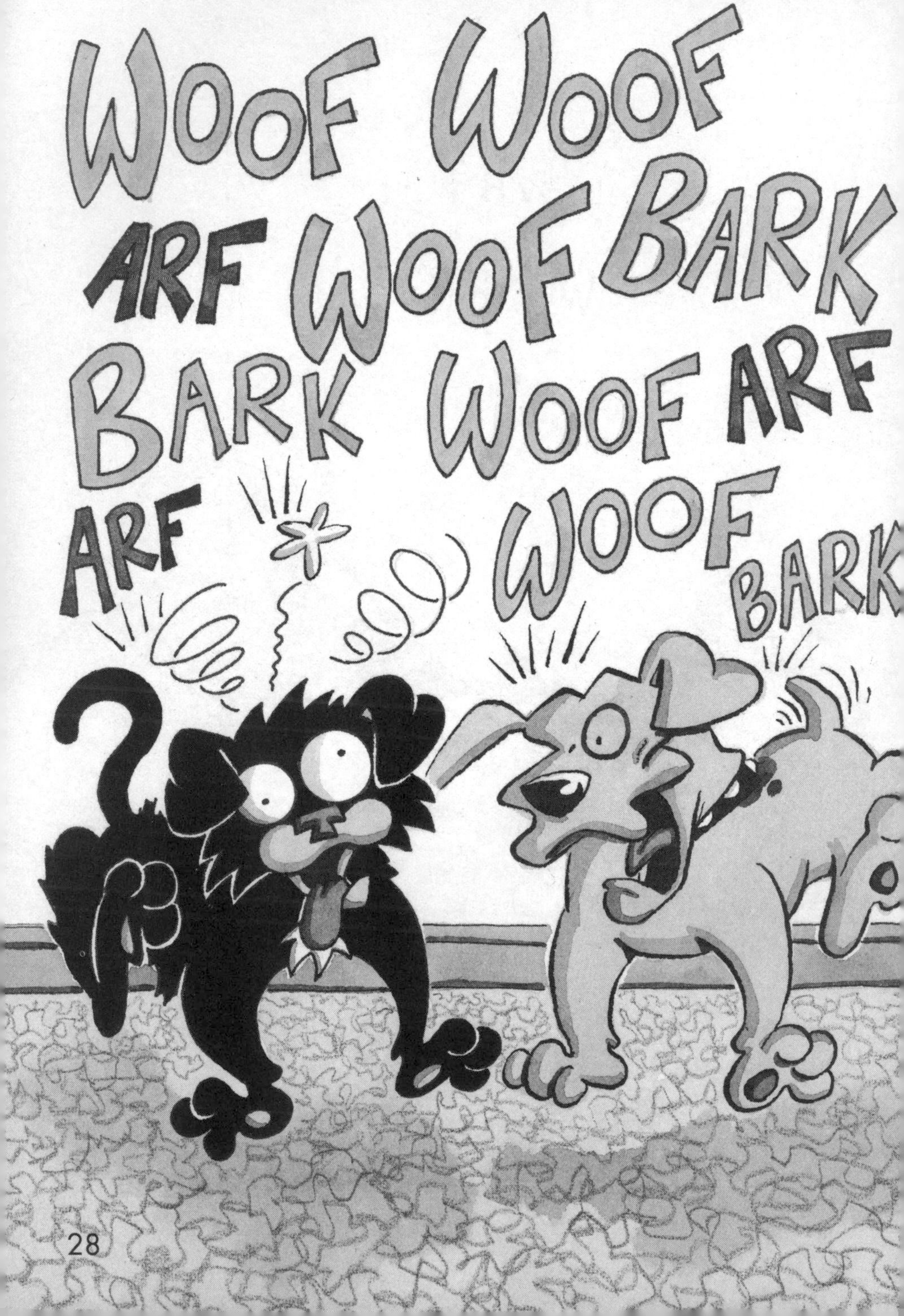
WOOF WOOF
ARF WOOF BARK
BARK WOOF ARF
ARF WOOF
BARK

•CHAPTER TWO•

ONE WEEK LATER

Hi, Puppy. You've been playing with Kitty a lot these past few days. But now you look exhausted. Why don't you lie down and take a nice, long nap?

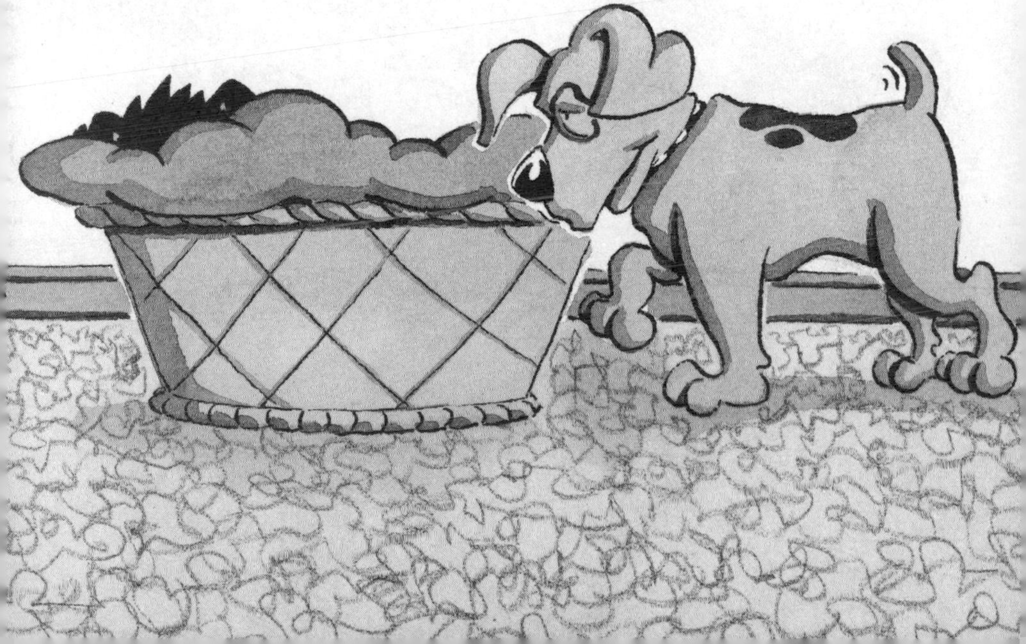

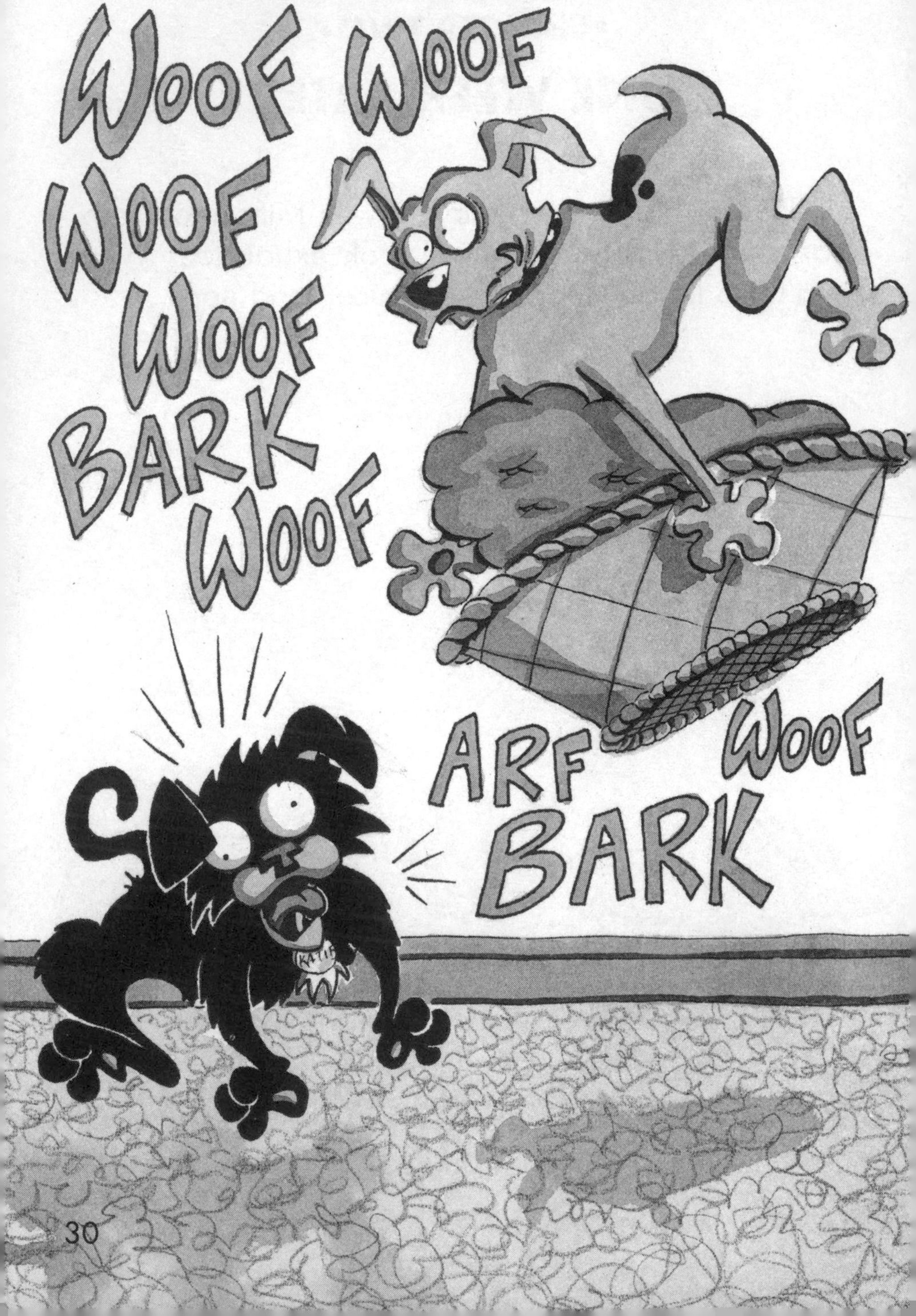
WOOF WOOF
WOOF
WOOF
BARK
WOOF
ARF
WOOF
BARK

KITTY! STOP THAT!

I'm thrilled that you and Puppy are suddenly getting along so well, but you've been playing with him nonstop for about a week now. He's turning into a nervous wreck. Just leave him alone for a little while and let him rest.

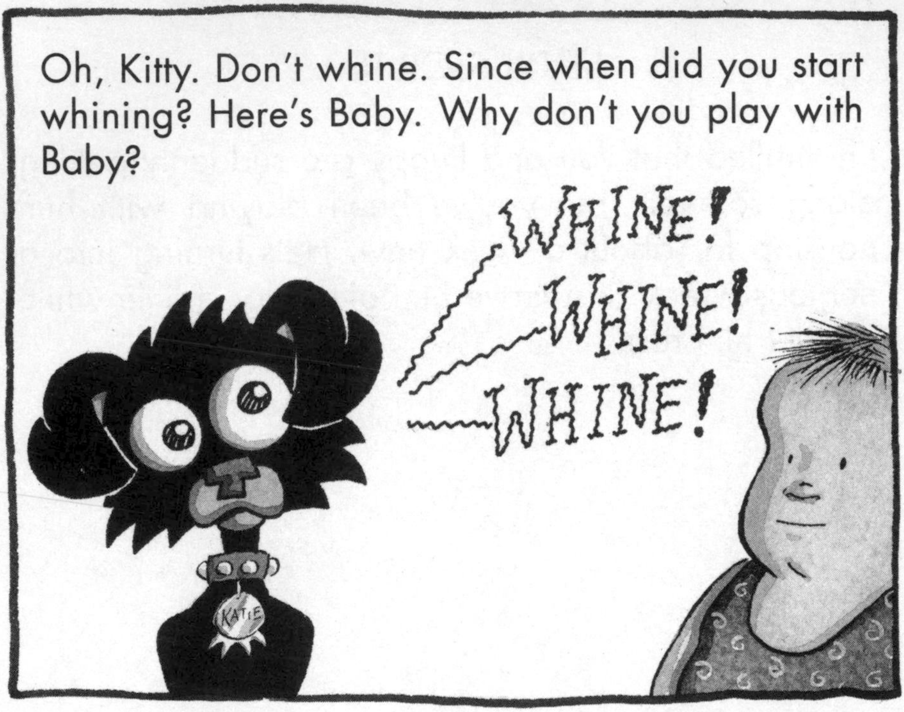
Oh, Kitty. Don't whine. Since when did you start whining? Here's Baby. Why don't you play with Baby?
WHINE!
WHINE!
WHINE!
KATIE

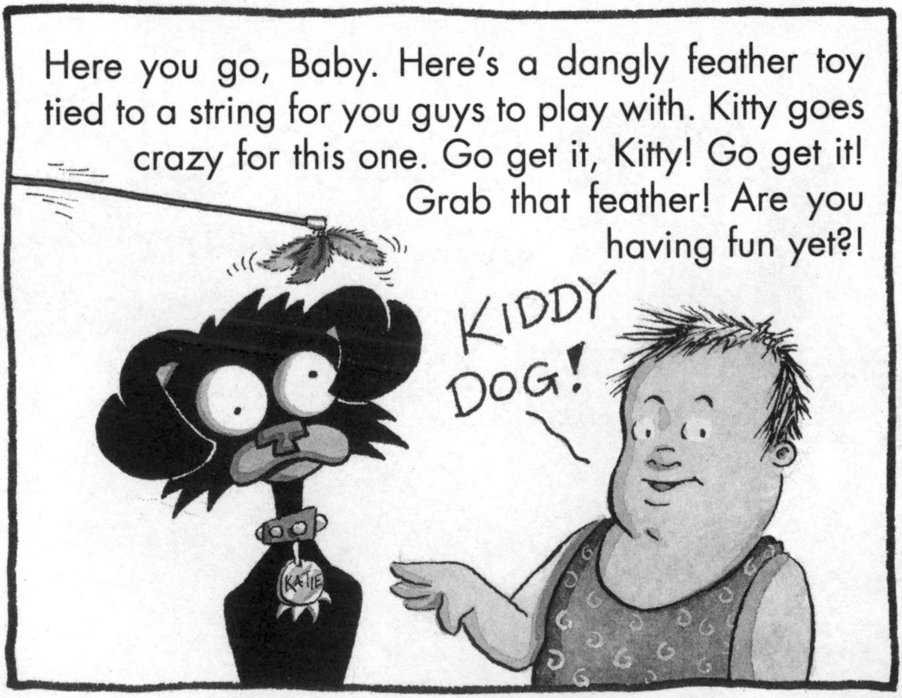
Here you go, Baby. Here's a dangly feather toy tied to a string for you guys to play with. Kitty goes crazy for this one. Go get it, Kitty! Go get it! Grab that feather! Are you having fun yet?!
KIDDY DOG!
KATIE

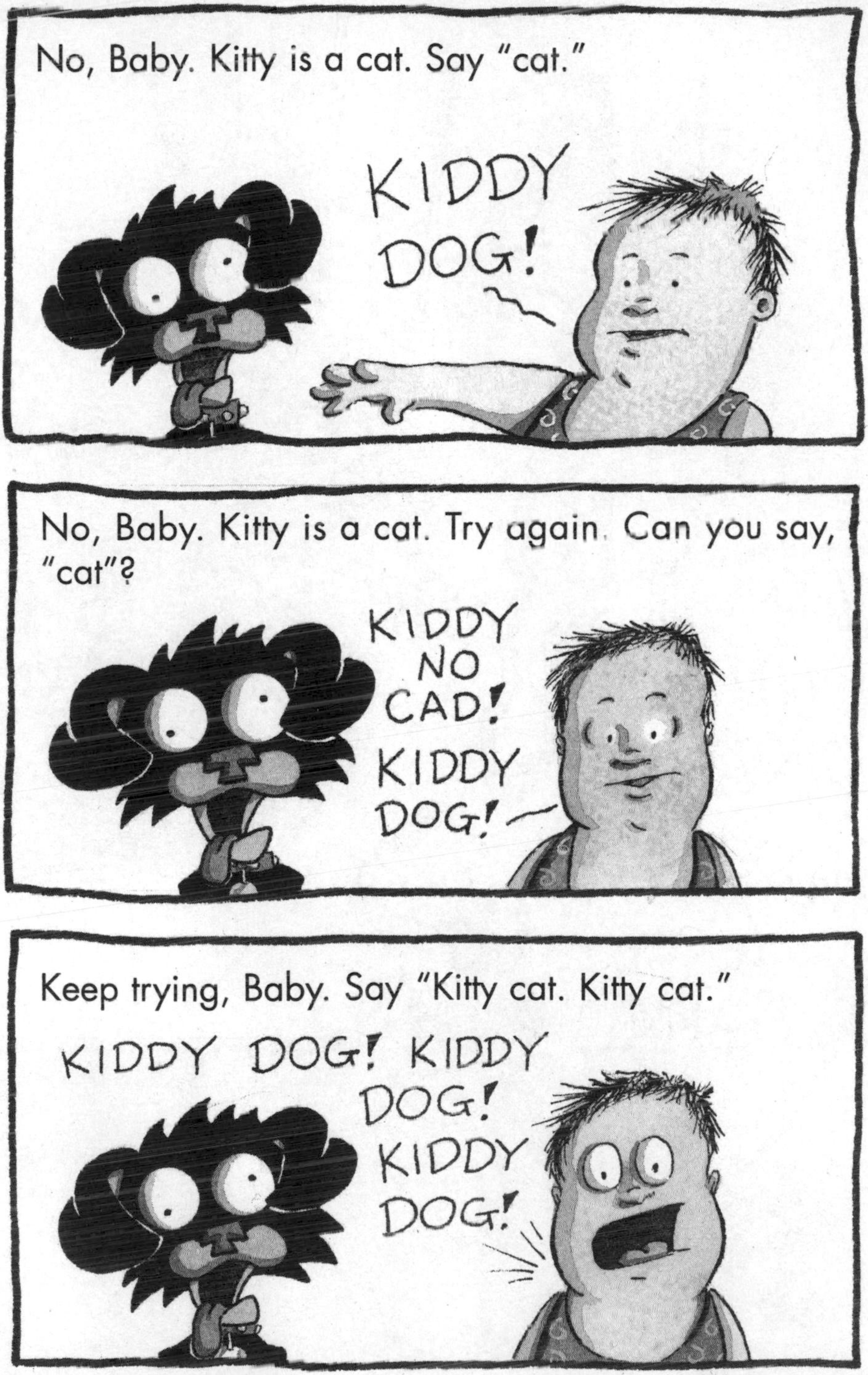
No, Baby. Kitty is a cat. Say "cat."
KIDDY DOG!
No, Baby. Kitty is a cat. Try again. Can you say, "cat"?
KIDDY NO CAD! KIDDY DOG!
Keep trying, Baby. Say "Kitty cat. Kitty cat."
KIDDY DOG! KIDDY DOG! KIDDY DOG!

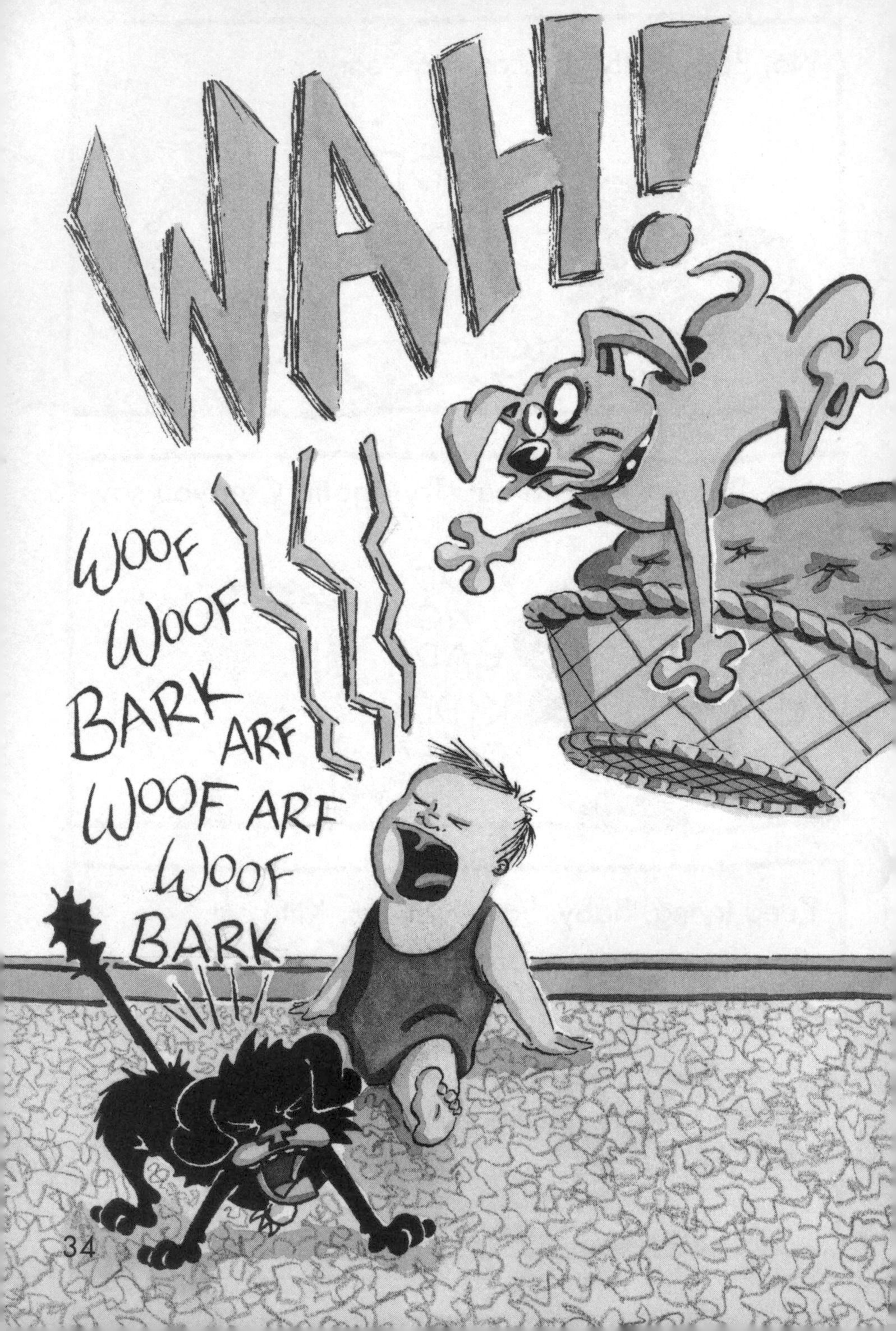
WAH!
WOOF
WOOF
BARK
ARF
WOOF ARF
WOOF
BARK

Wow, Puppy. You look pretty stressed out. Maybe you need a vacation. I think you need to go somewhere to relax and just be a dog.

But where? Hmmmmmmm . . .

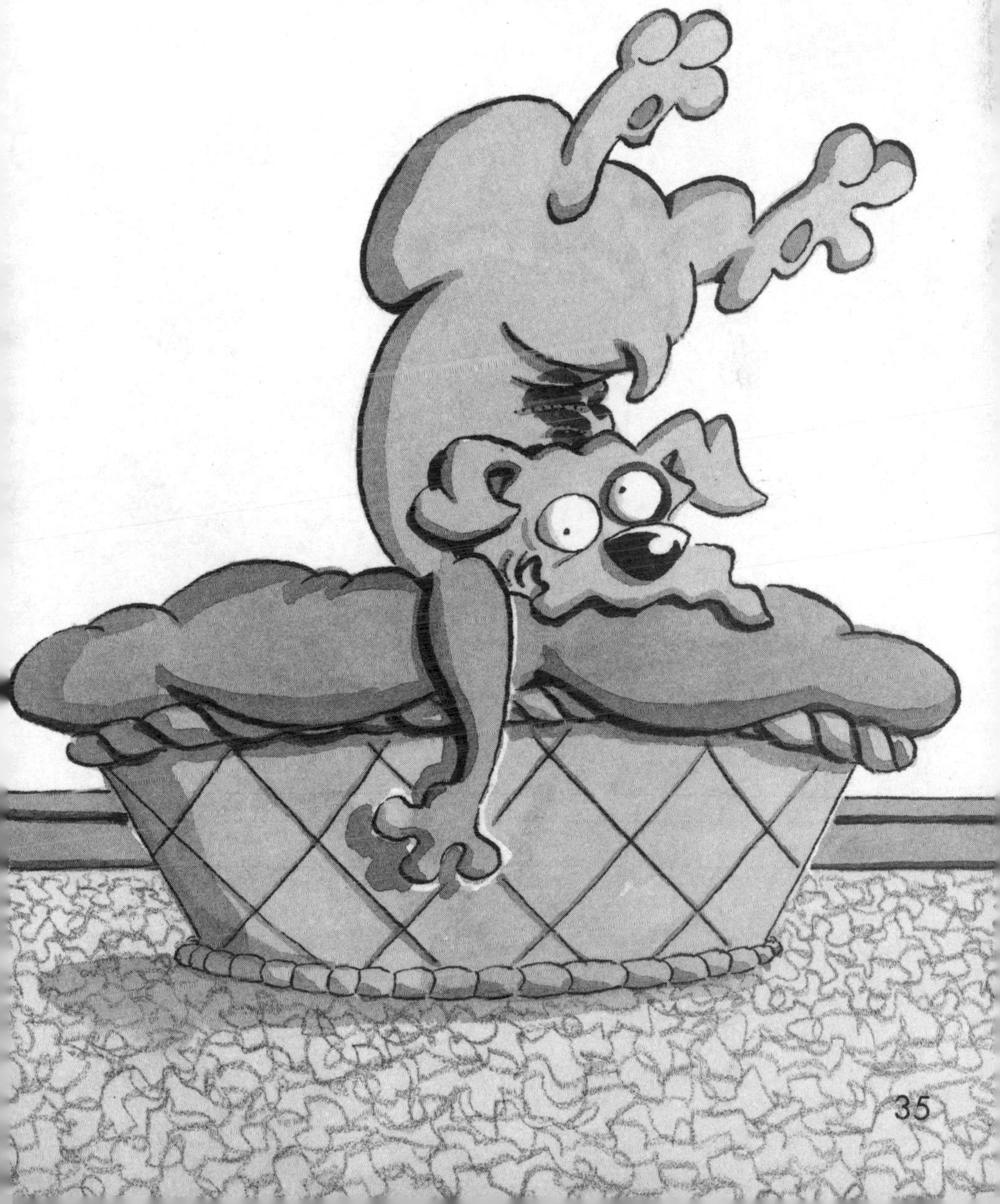

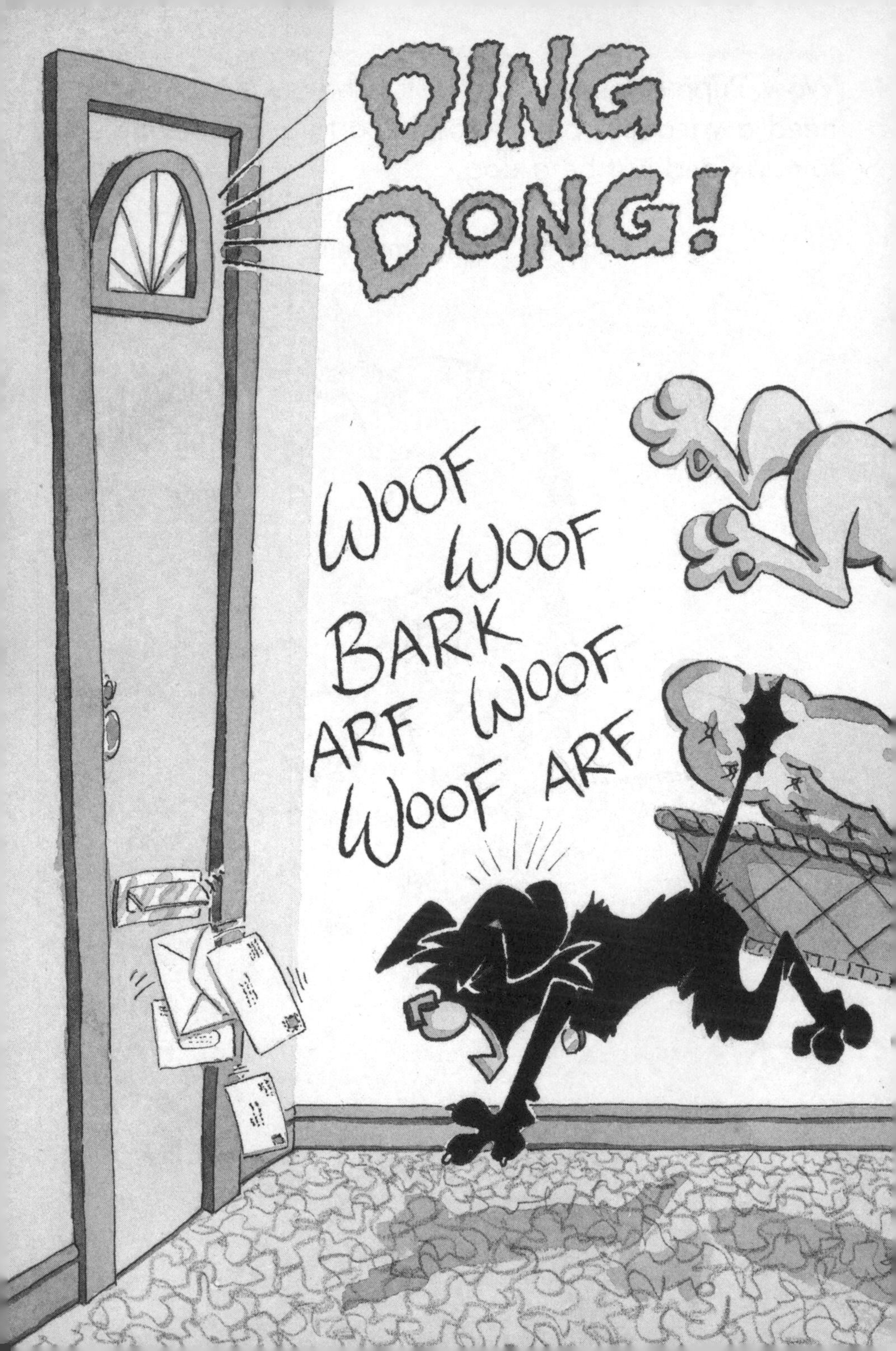
DING DONG!
WOOF WOOF
BARK
ARF WOOF
WOOF ARF

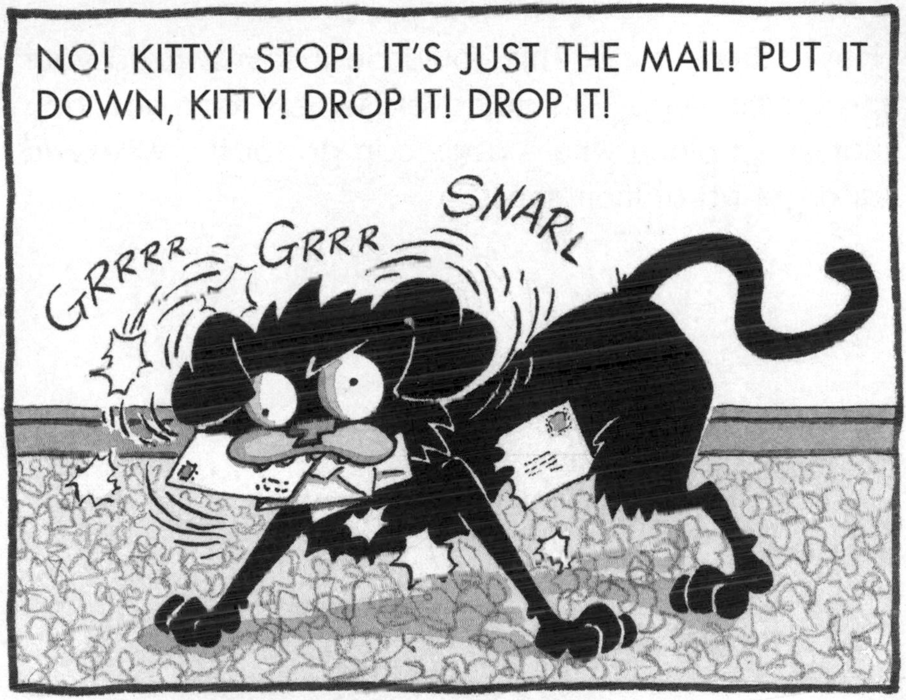
NO! KITTY! STOP! IT'S JUST THE MAIL! PUT IT DOWN, KITTY! DROP IT! DROP IT!
GRRRR
GRRR
SNARL

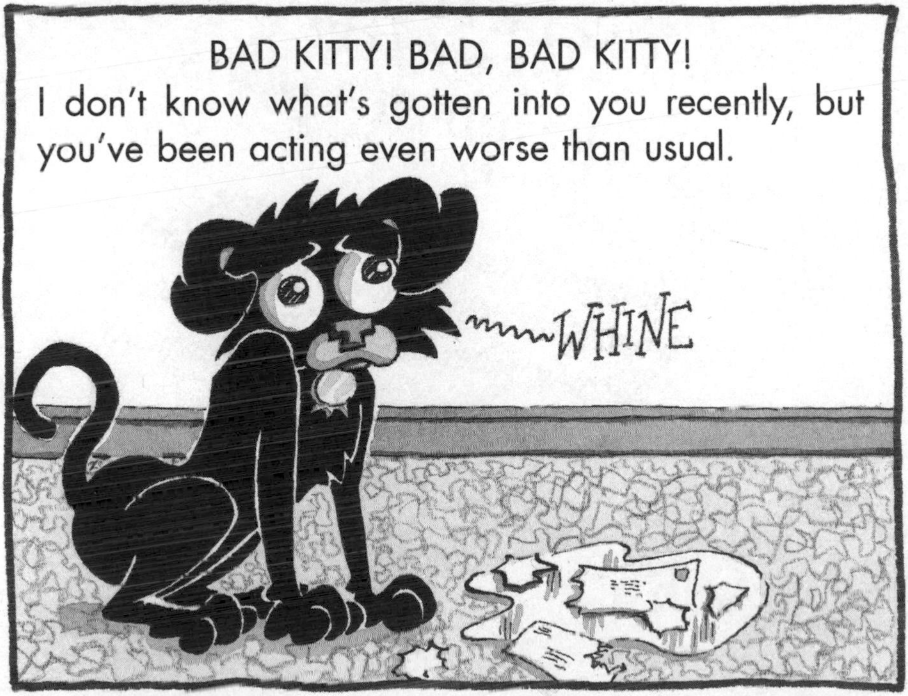
BAD KITTY! BAD, BAD KITTY!
I don't know what's gotten into you recently, but you've been acting even worse than usual.
WHINE

Hey! Check it out! This could be the answer to your problems, Puppy! It's an advertisement for a new dog camp—a place where dogs can go for the weekend and get rid of their stress.

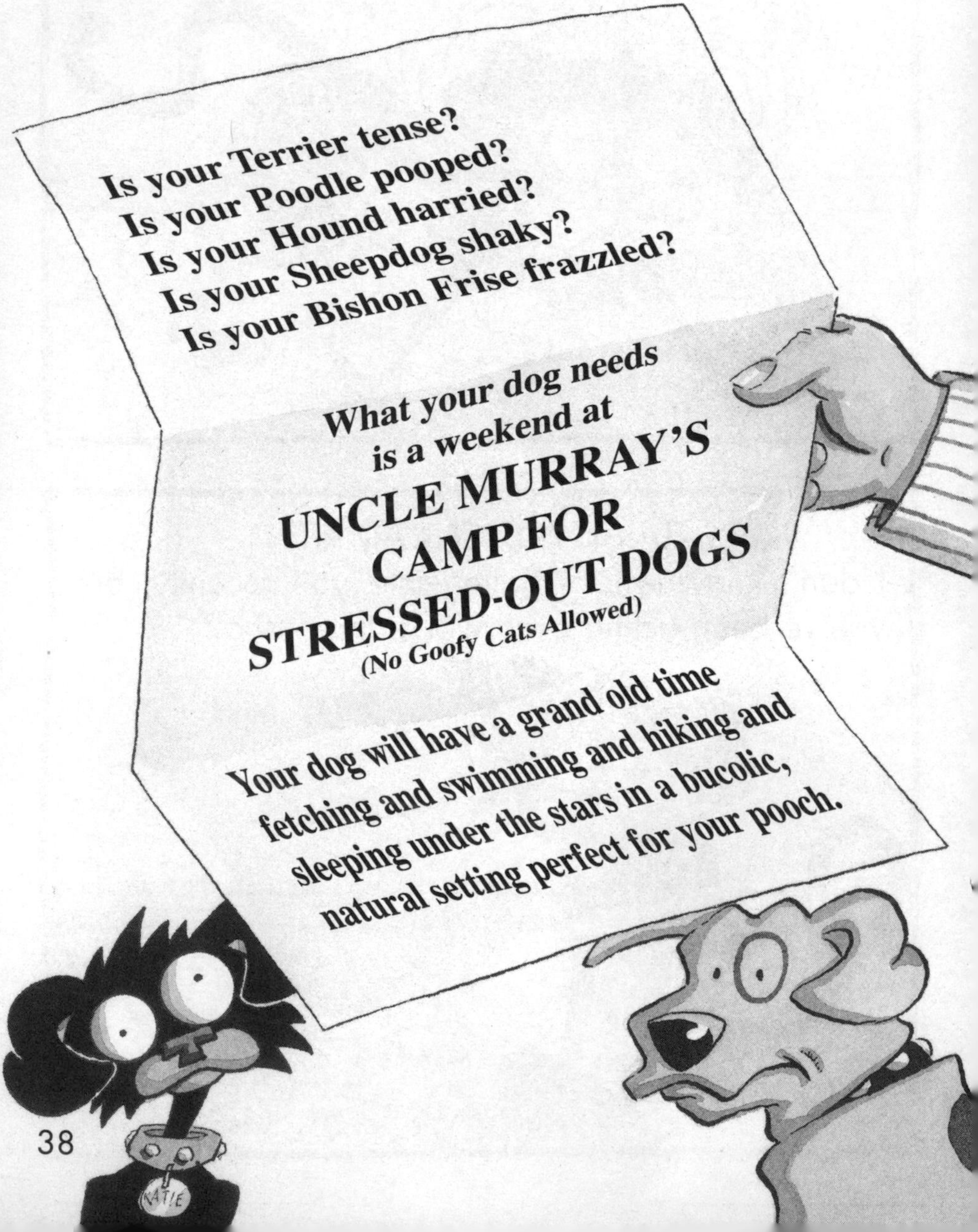
Is your Terrier tense?
Is your Poodle pooped?
Is your Hound harried?
Is your Sheepdog shaky?
Is your Bishon Frise frazzled?
What your dog needs
is a weekend at
UNCLE MURRAY'S
CAMP FOR
STRESSED-OUT DOGS
(No Goofy Cats Allowed)
Your dog will have a grand old time
fetching and swimming and hiking and
sleeping under the stars in a bucolic,
natural setting perfect for your pooch.
KATIE

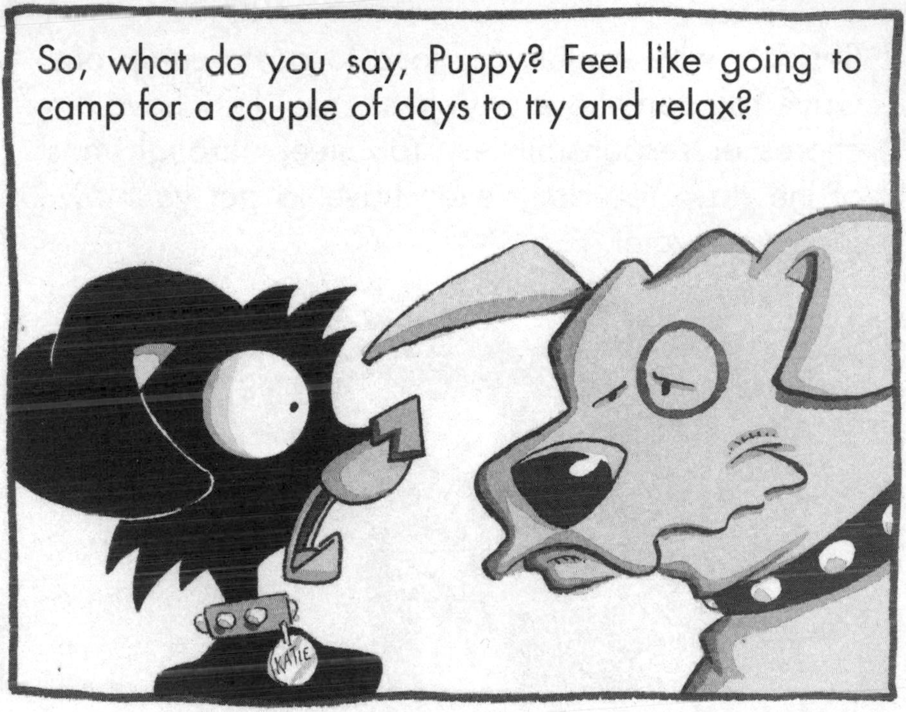
So, what do you say, Puppy? Feel like going to camp for a couple of days to try and relax?
KATIE

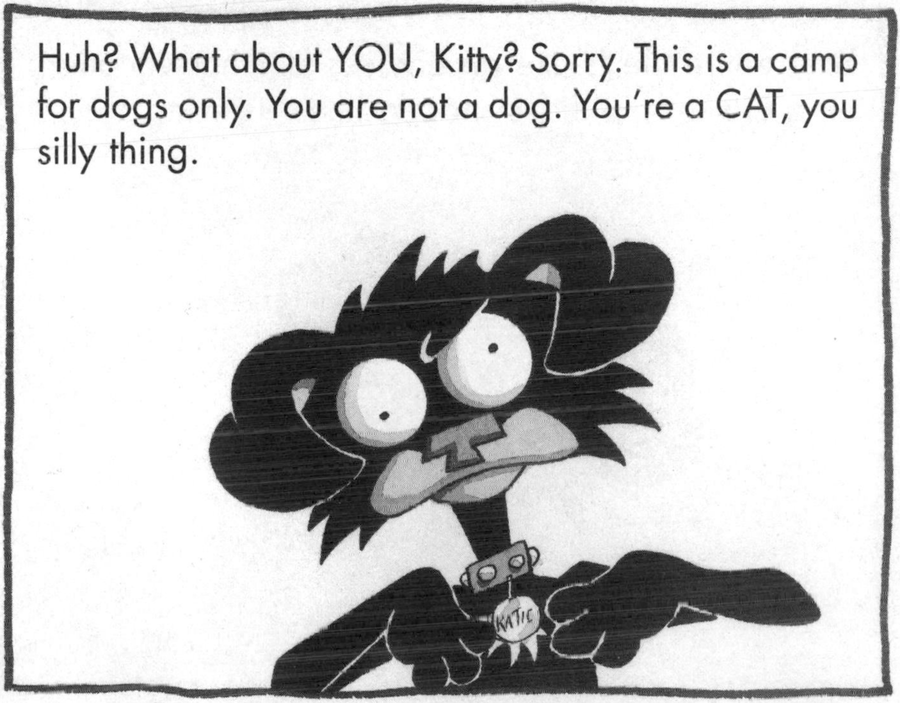
Huh? What about YOU, Kitty? Sorry. This is a camp for dogs only. You are not a dog. You're a CAT, you silly thing.
KATIE

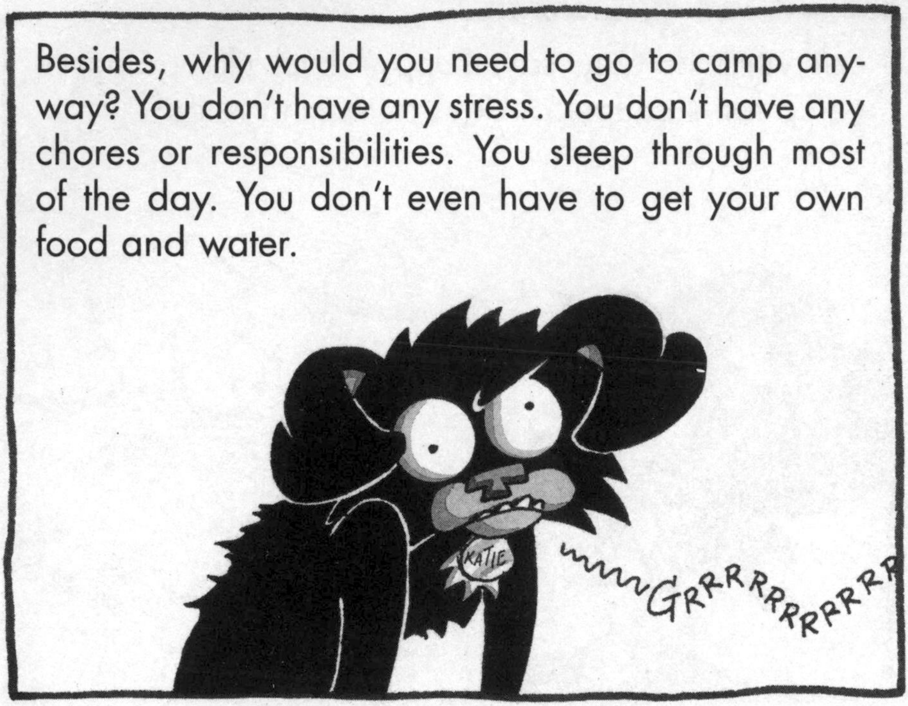
Besides, why would you need to go to camp anyway? You don't have any stress. You don't have any chores or responsibilities. You sleep through most of the day. You don't even have to get your own food and water.
KATIE
GRRRRRRRRRRR

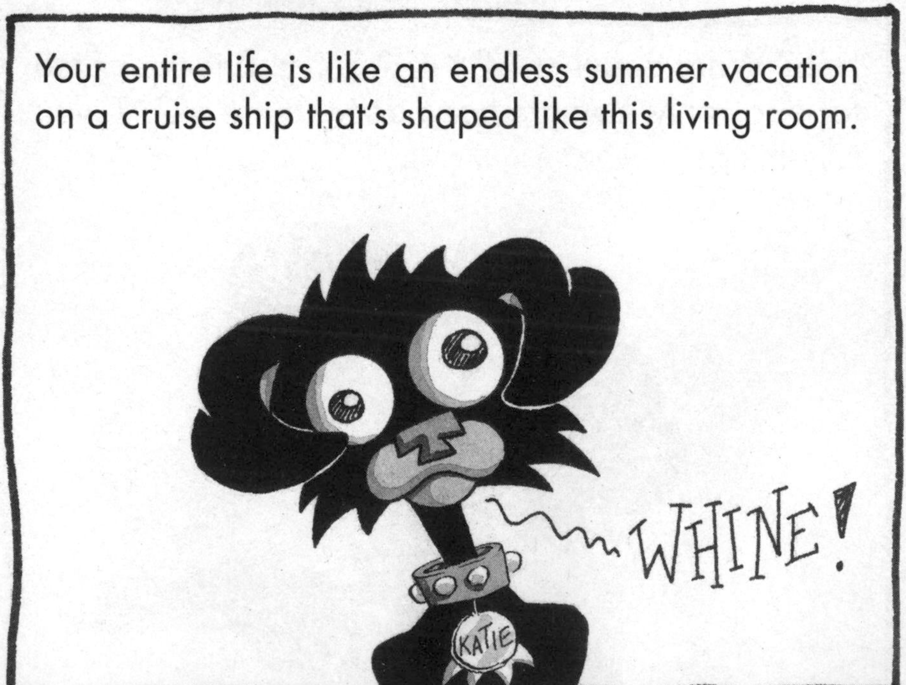
Your entire life is like an endless summer vacation on a cruise ship that's shaped like this living room.
WHINE!
KATIE

Let's go, Puppy. I'll help you pack.

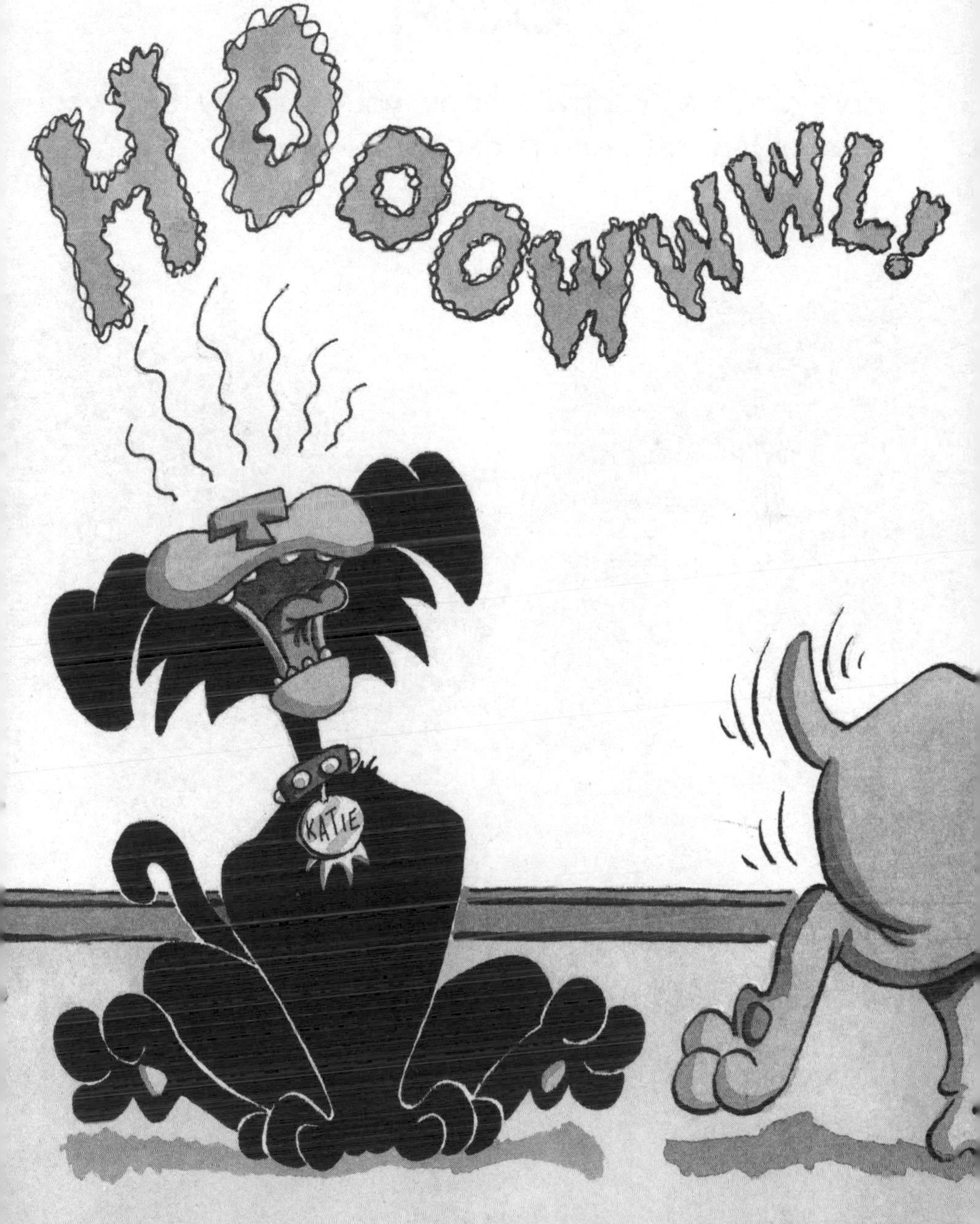
HOOOWWWL!
KATIE

•CHAPTER THREE•

CAMP!

Here we are, Puppy! I hope you're ready for two days of fun, rest, and relaxation.

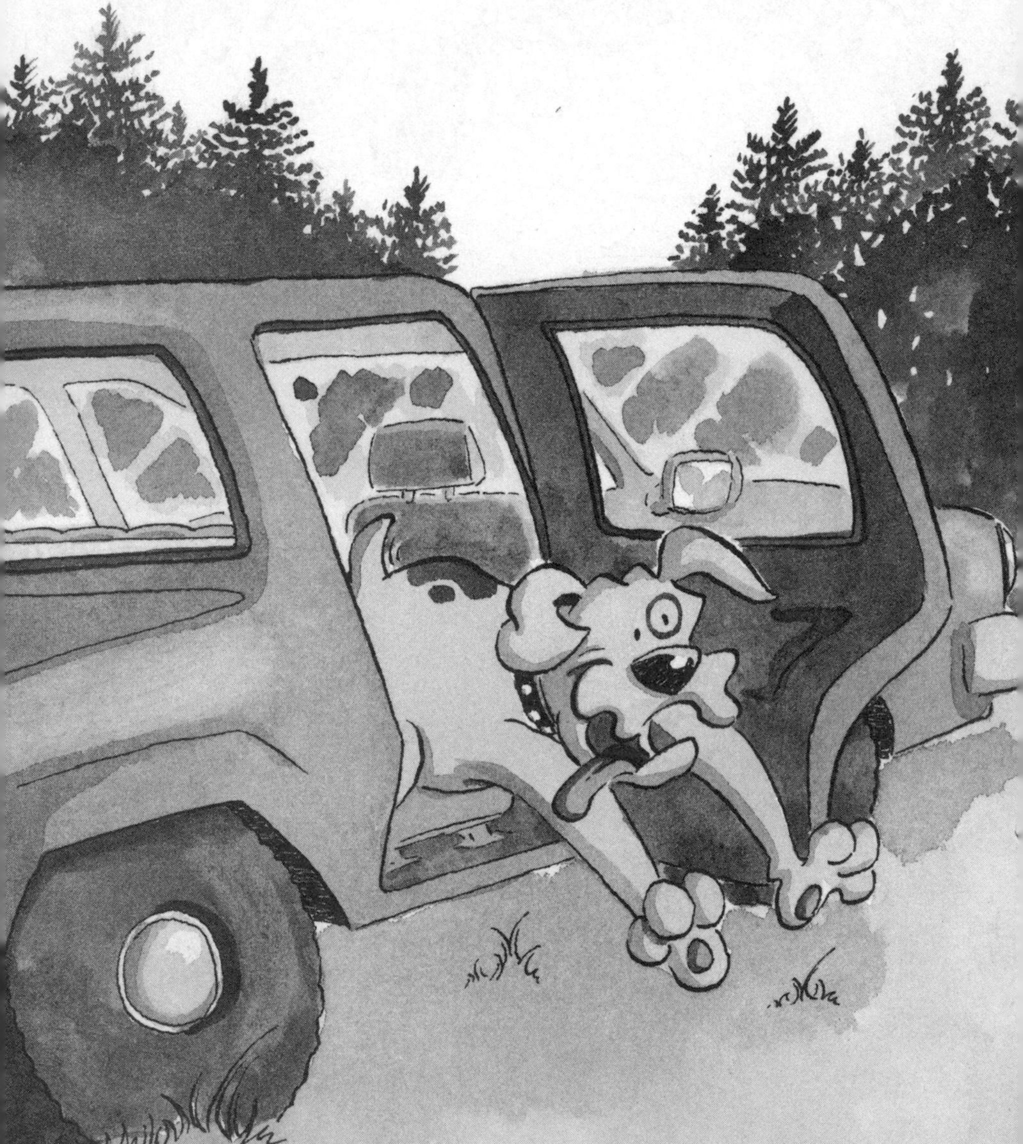

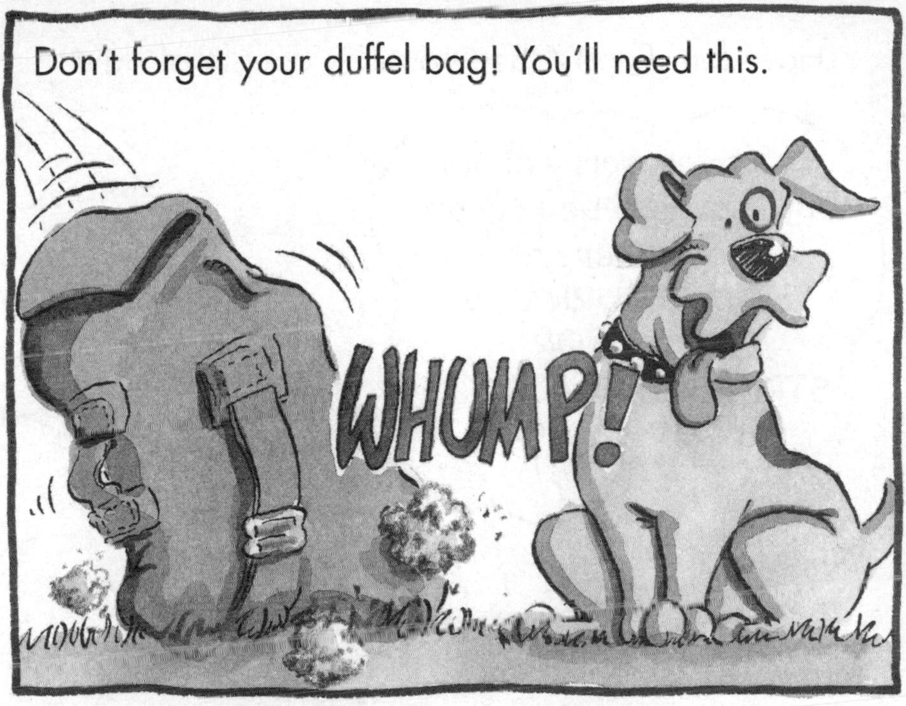
Don't forget your duffel bag! You'll need this.
WHUMP!

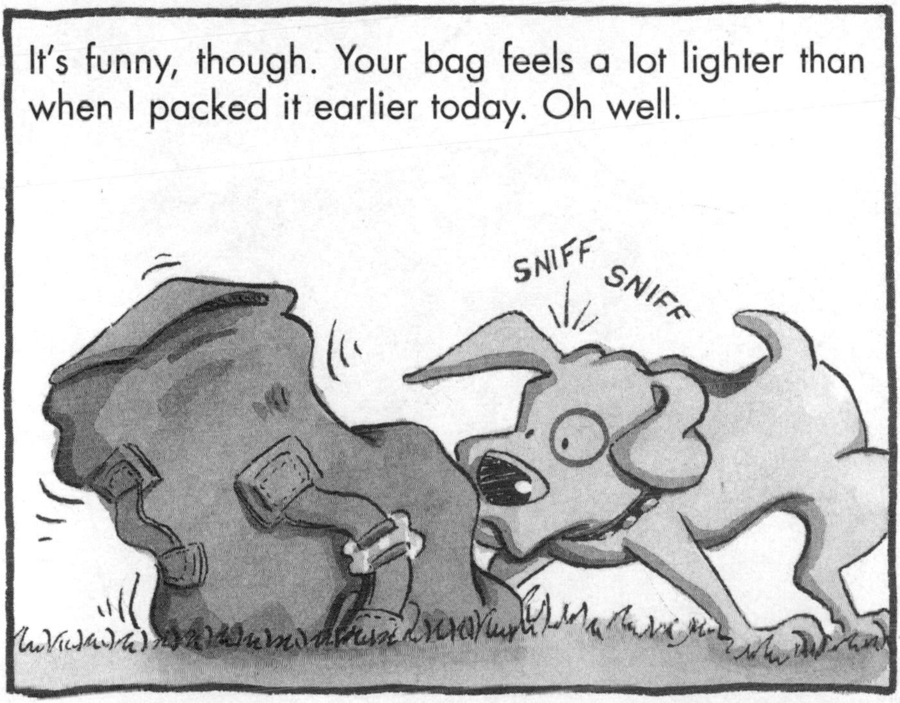
It's funny, though. Your bag feels a lot lighter than when I packed it earlier today. Oh well.
SNIFF
SNIFF

Have fun, Puppy! See you in a couple of days!

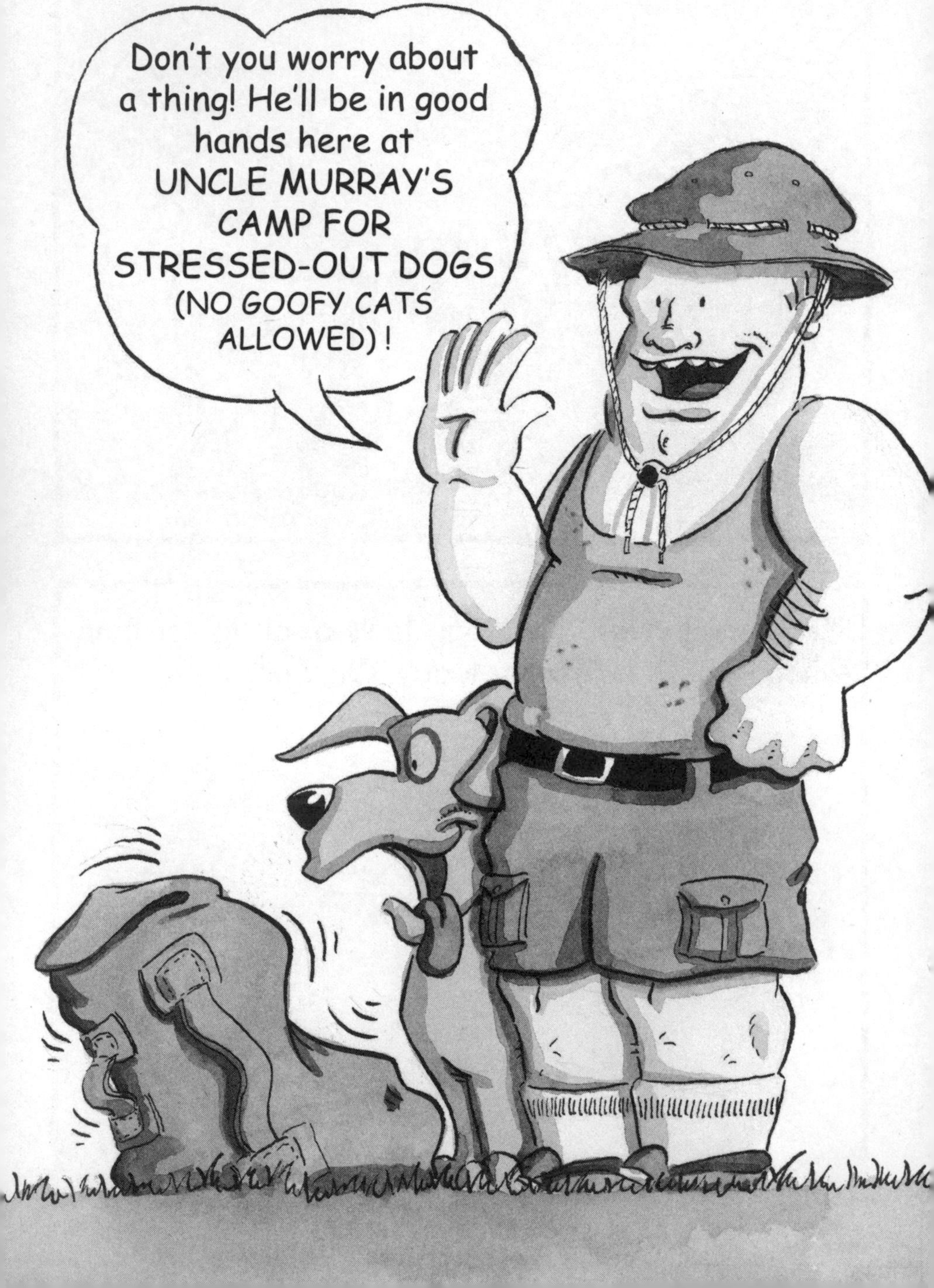
Don't you worry about a thing! He'll be in good hands here at UNCLE MURRAY'S CAMP FOR STRESSED-OUT DOGS (NO GOOFY CATS ALLOWED)!

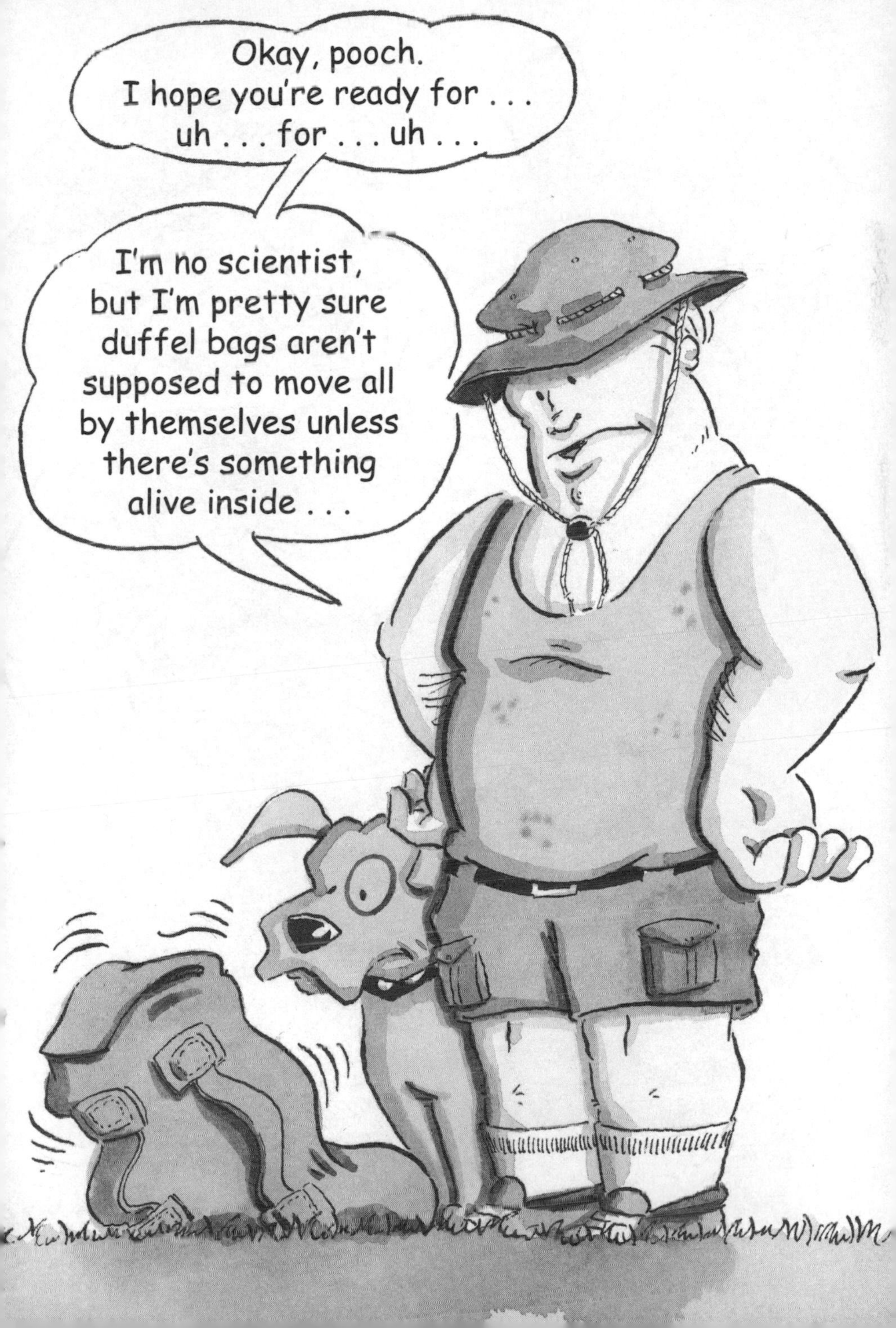
Okay, pooch.
I hope you're ready for . . .
uh . . . for . . . uh . . .
I'm no scientist,
but I'm pretty sure
duffel bags aren't
supposed to move all
by themselves unless
there's something
alive inside . . .

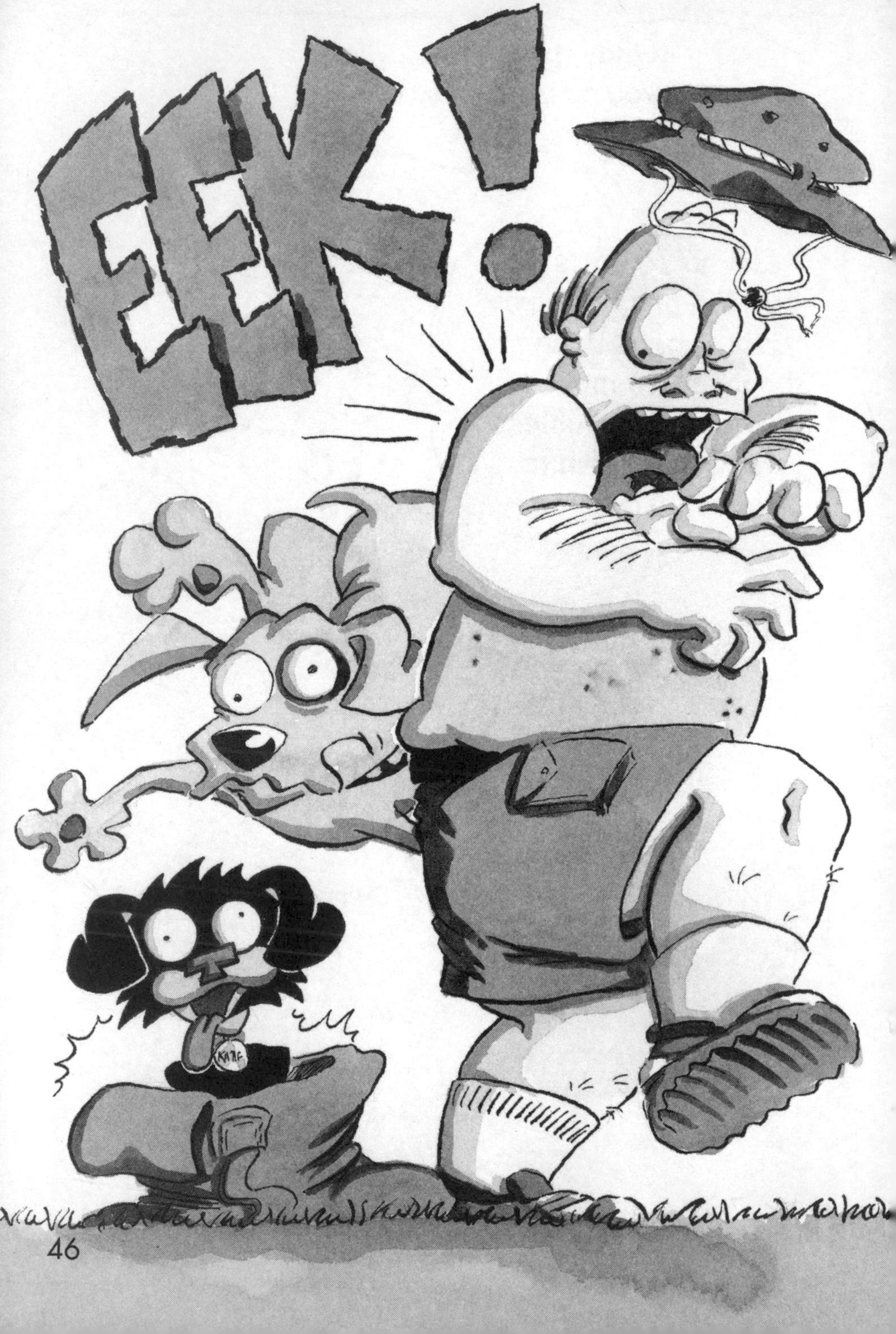
EEK!

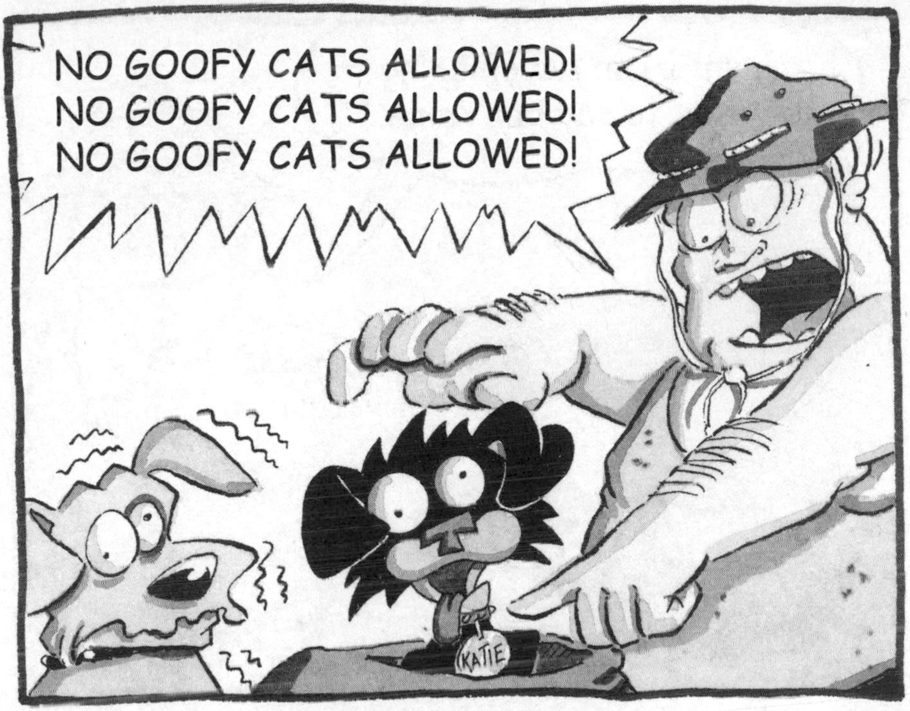
NO GOOFY CATS ALLOWED! NO GOOFY CATS ALLOWED! NO GOOFY CATS ALLOWED!
KATIE

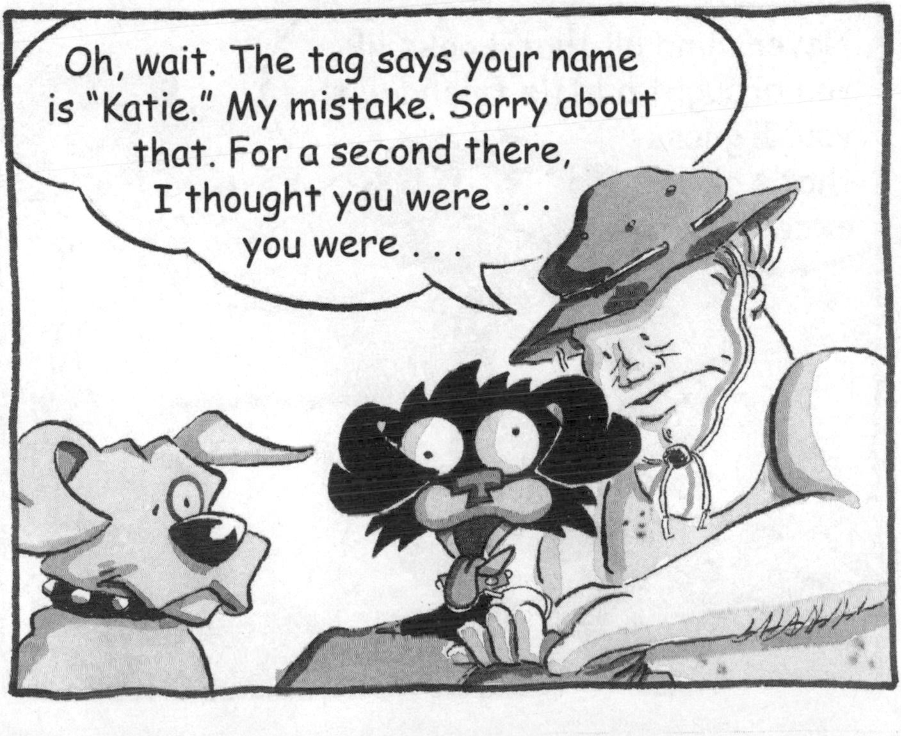
Oh, wait. The tag says your name is "Katie." My mistake. Sorry about that. For a second there, I thought you were . . . you were . . .

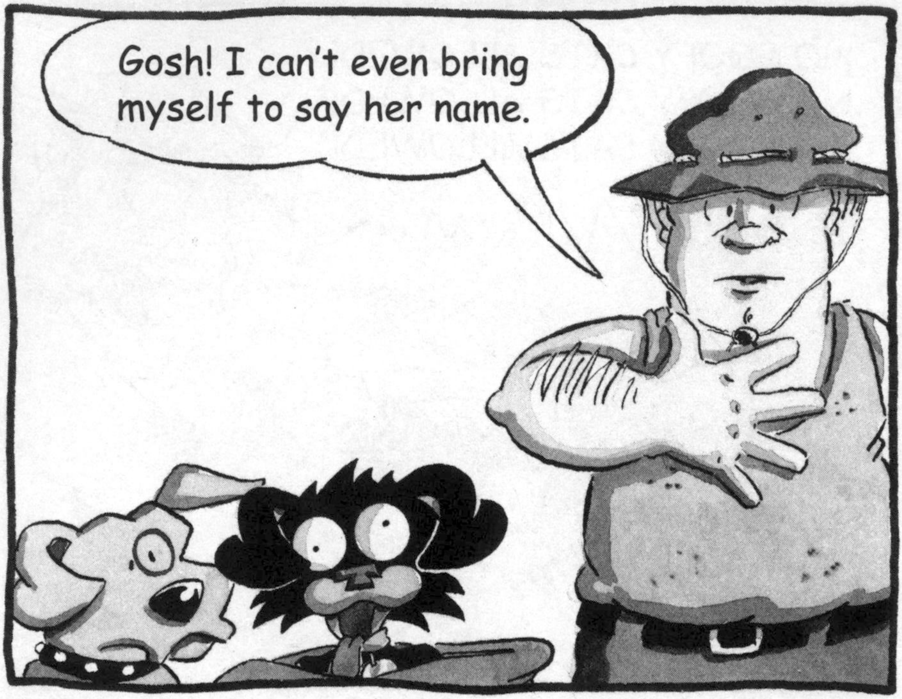
Gosh! I can't even bring myself to say her name.

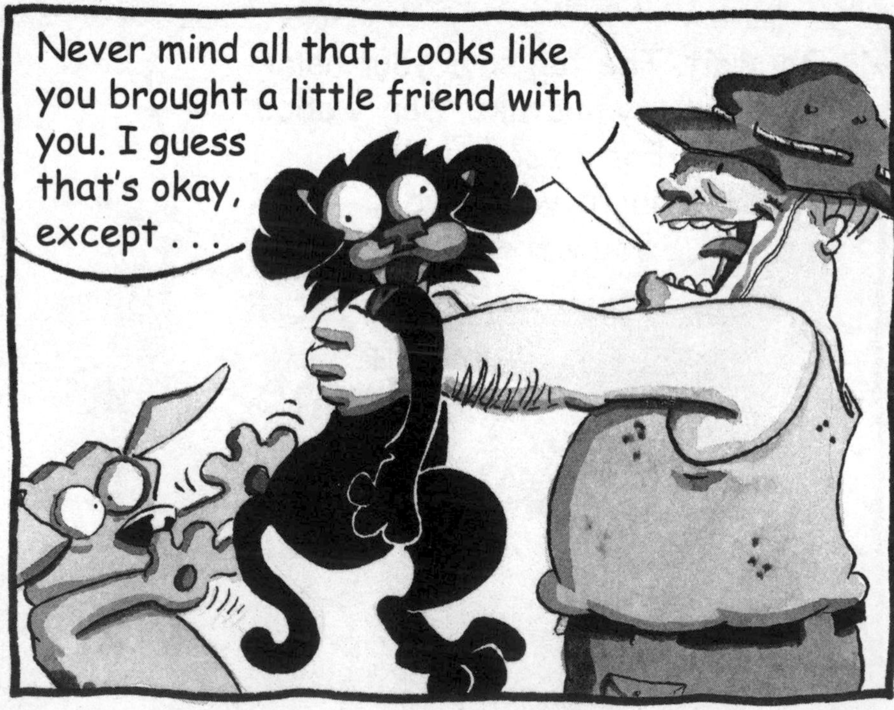
Never mind all that. Looks like you brought a little friend with you. I guess that's okay, except . . .

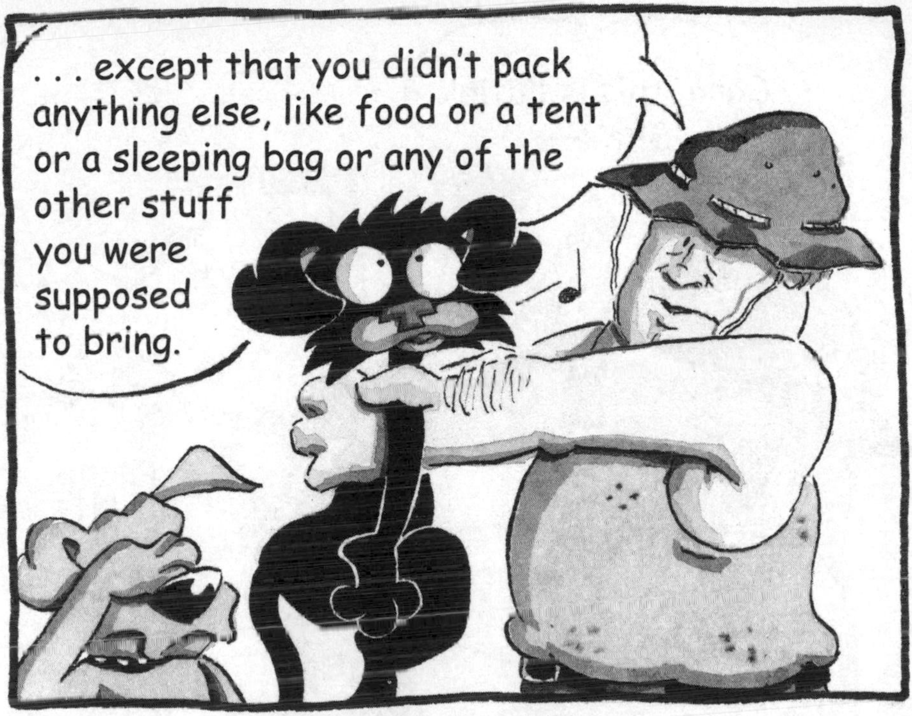
. . . except that you didn't pack anything else, like food or a tent or a sleeping bag or any of the other stuff you were supposed to bring.

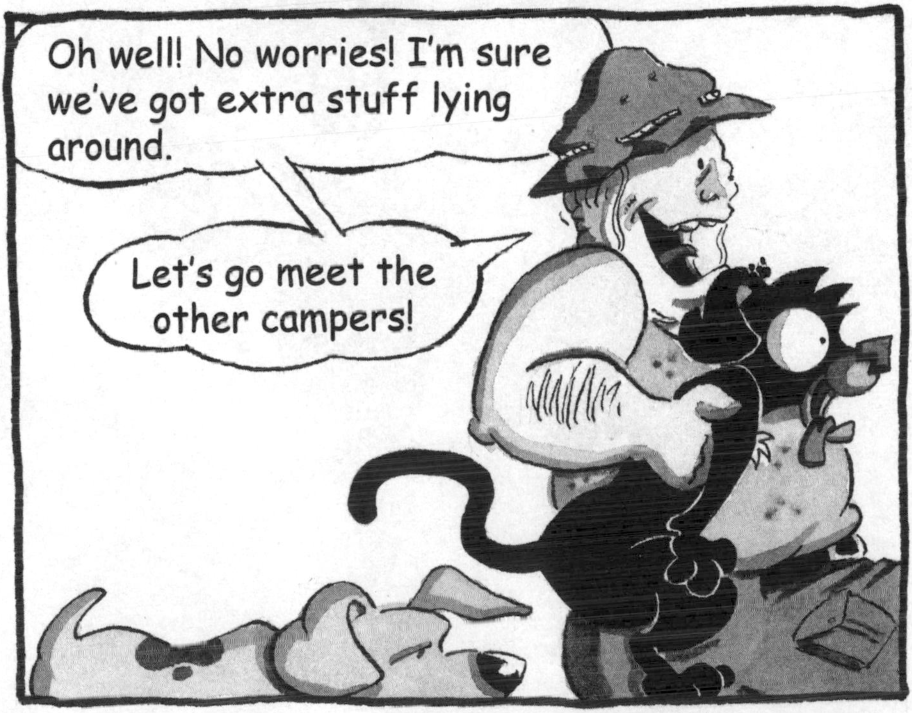
Oh well! No worries! I'm sure we've got extra stuff lying around.
Let's go meet the other campers!

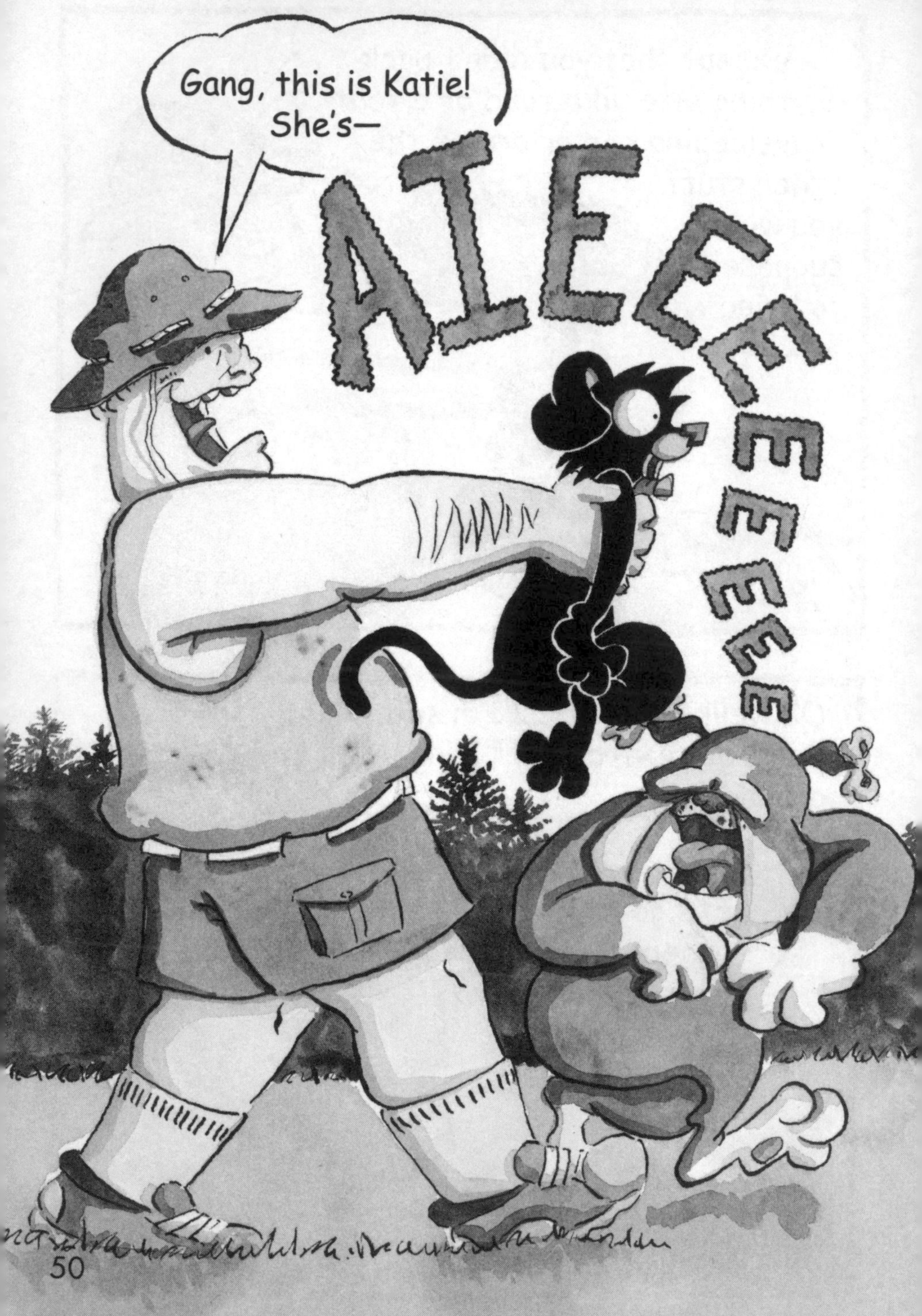
Gang, this is Katie! She's—
AIEEEEEEEE

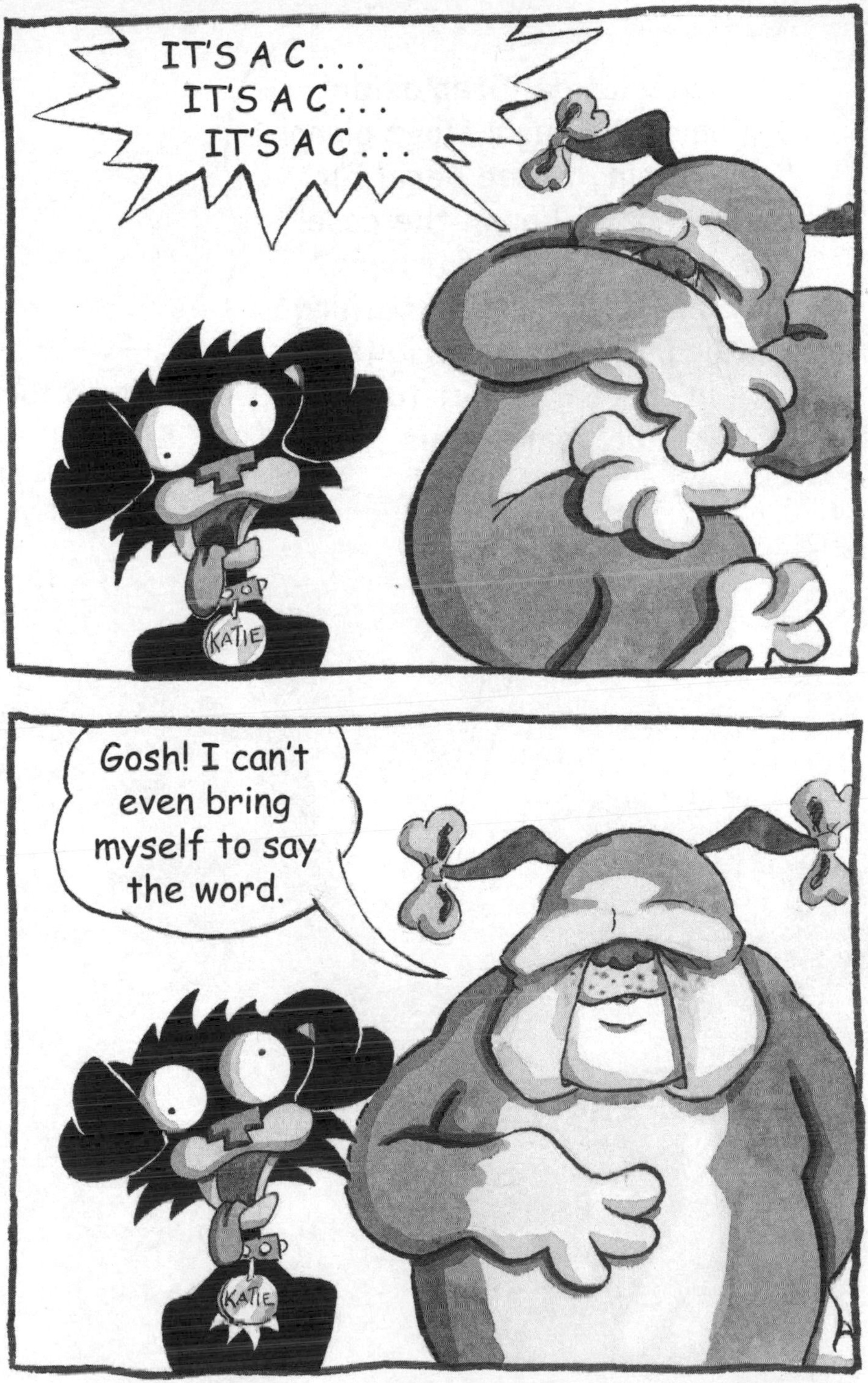
IT'S A C . . .
IT'S A C . . .
IT'S A C . . .
KATIE
Gosh! I can't even bring myself to say the word.
KATIE

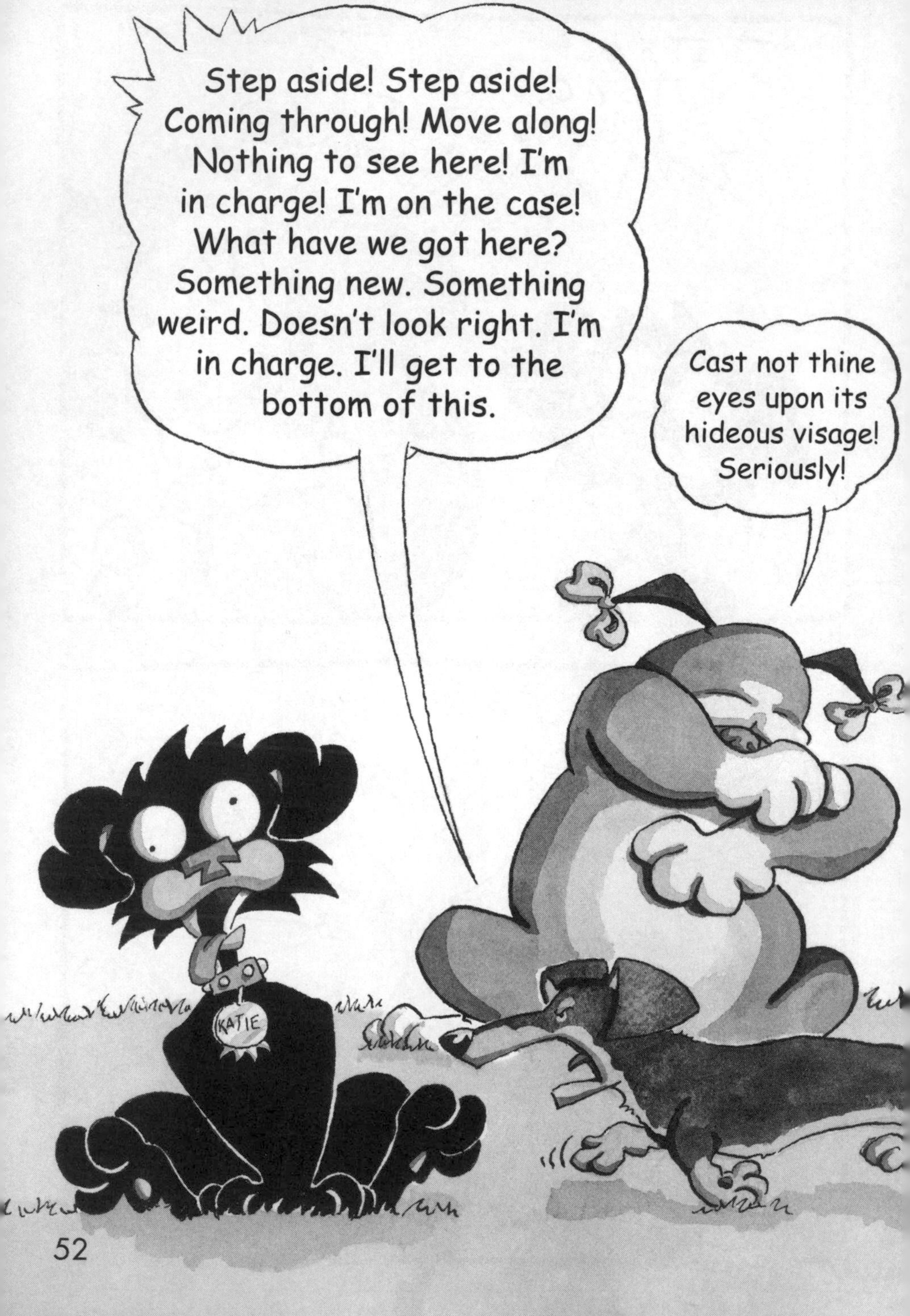
Step aside! Step aside! Coming through! Move along! Nothing to see here! I'm in charge! I'm on the case! What have we got here? Something new. Something weird. Doesn't look right. I'm in charge. I'll get to the bottom of this.
Cast not thine eyes upon its hideous visage! Seriously!
KATIE

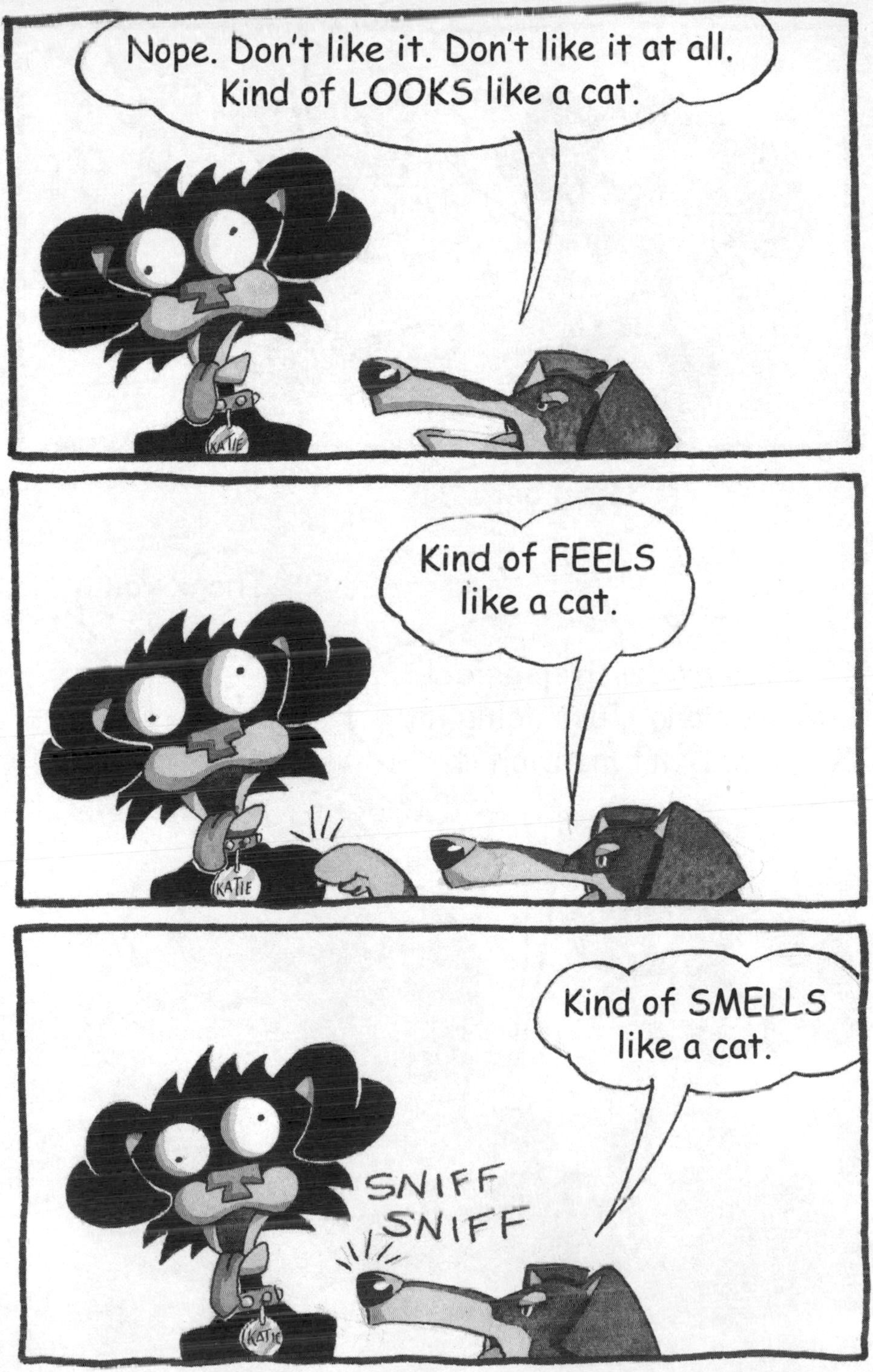
Nope. Don't like it. Don't like it at all. Kind of LOOKS like a cat.
KATIE
Kind of FEELS like a cat.
KATIE
Kind of SMELLS like a cat.
SNIFF SNIFF
KATIE

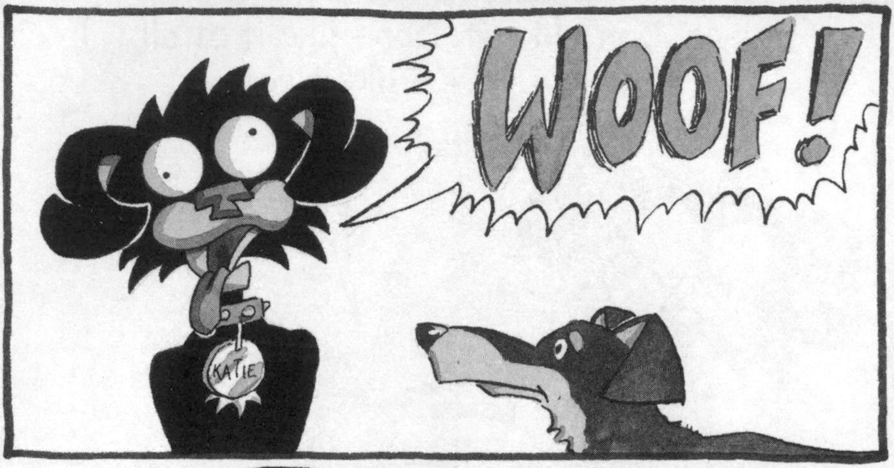
WOOF!
KATIE

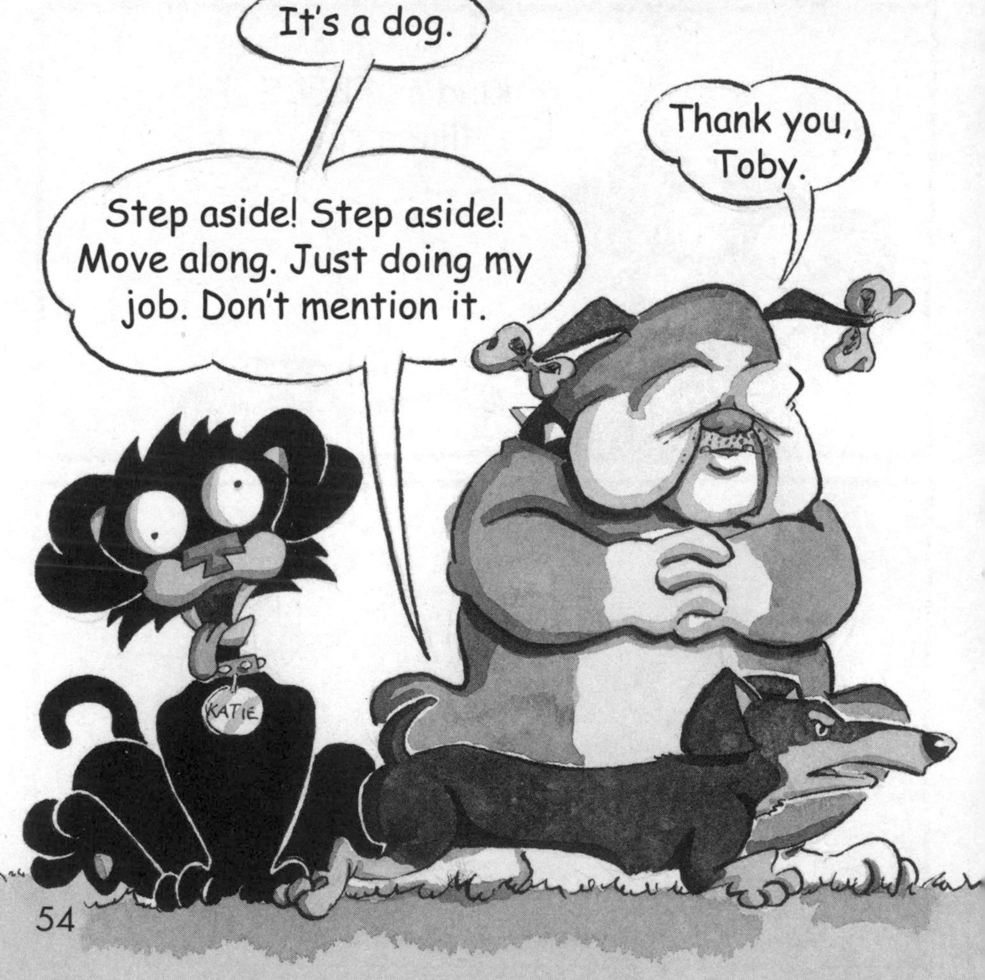
It's a dog.
Step aside! Step aside! Move along. Just doing my job. Don't mention it.
Thank you, Toby.
KATIE

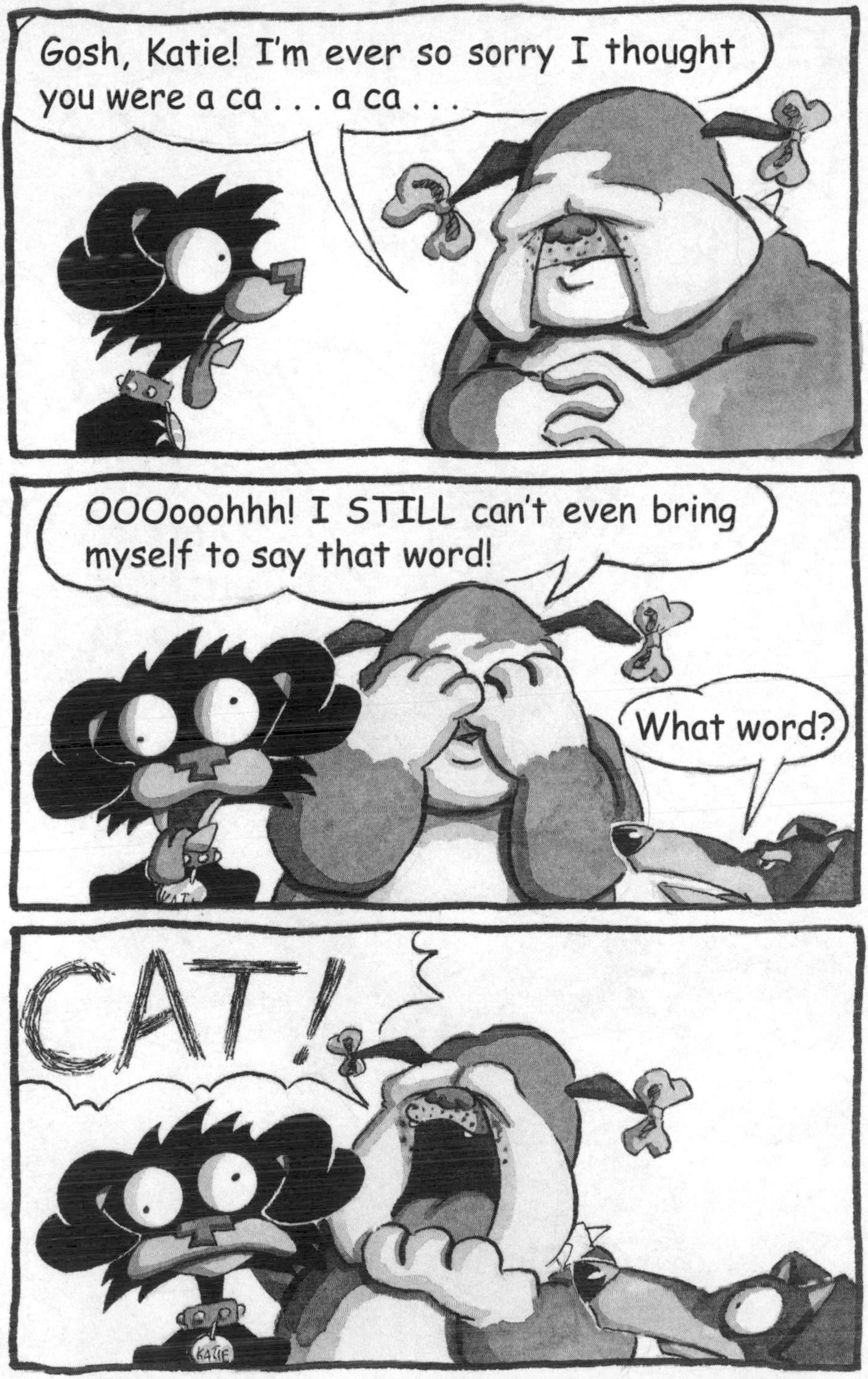
Gosh, Katie! I'm ever so sorry I thought you were a ca . . . a ca . . .
OOOooohhh! I STILL can't even bring myself to say that word!
What word?
CAT!
KATIE

CATS?! WHERE?! LET ME AT 'EM! LET ME AT 'EM!
GET THEM OFF ME! GET THEM OFF ME!
HOOOOWLL

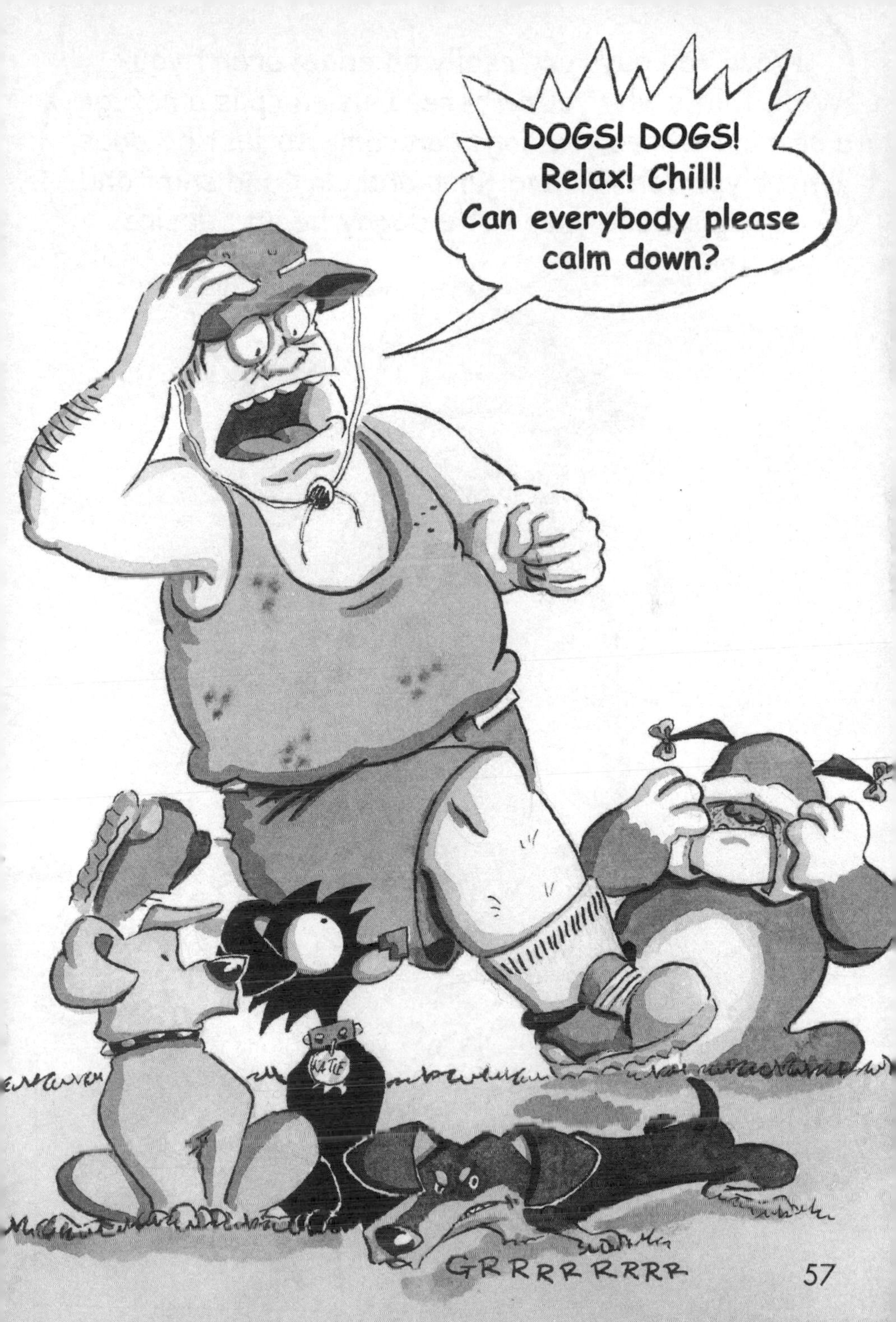
DOGS! DOGS!
Relax! Chill!
Can everybody please
calm down?
KATIE
GRRRRRRRR

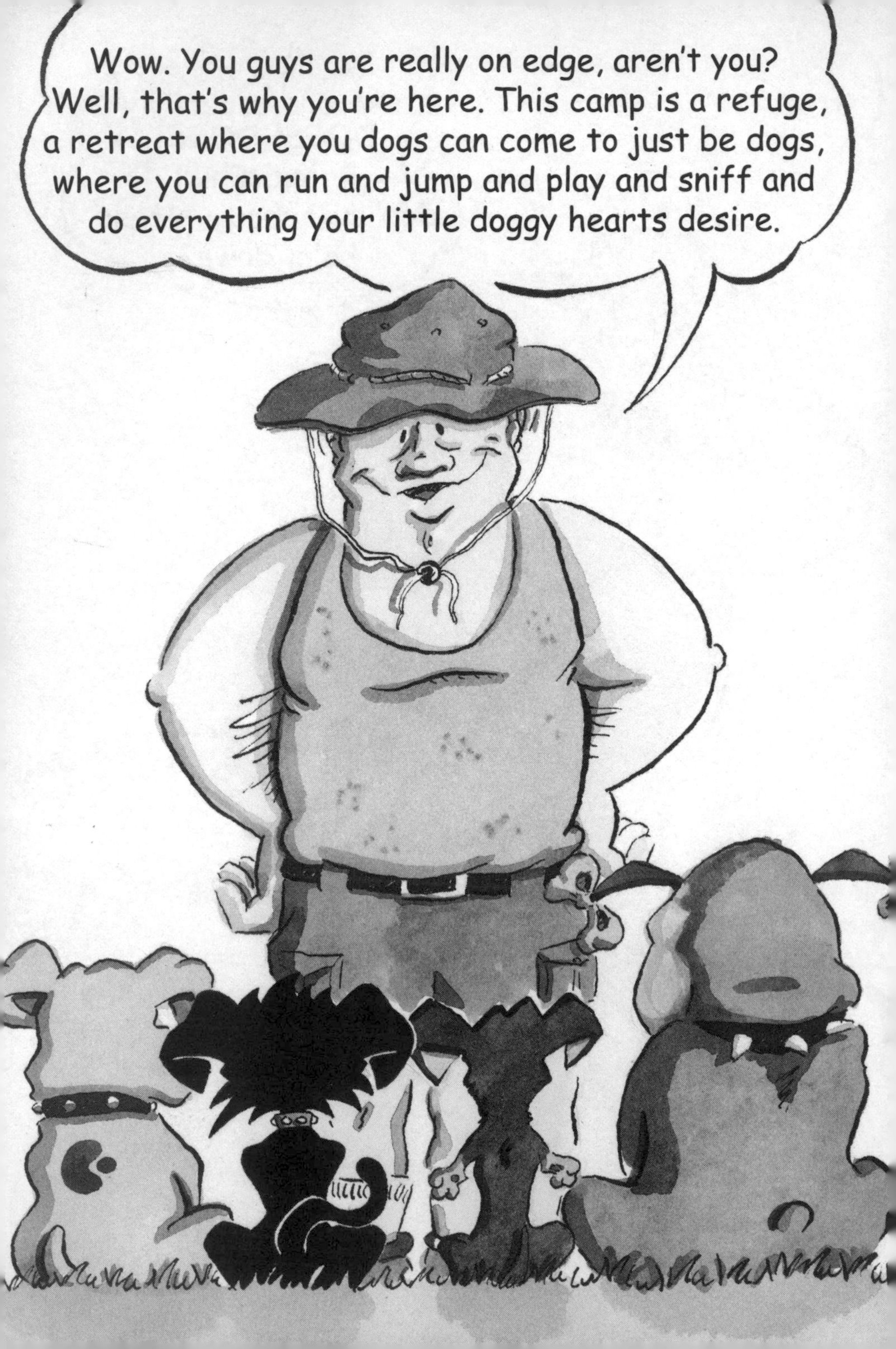
Wow. You guys are really on edge, aren't you? Well, that's why you're here. This camp is a refuge, a retreat where you dogs can come to just be dogs, where you can run and jump and play and sniff and do everything your little doggy hearts desire.

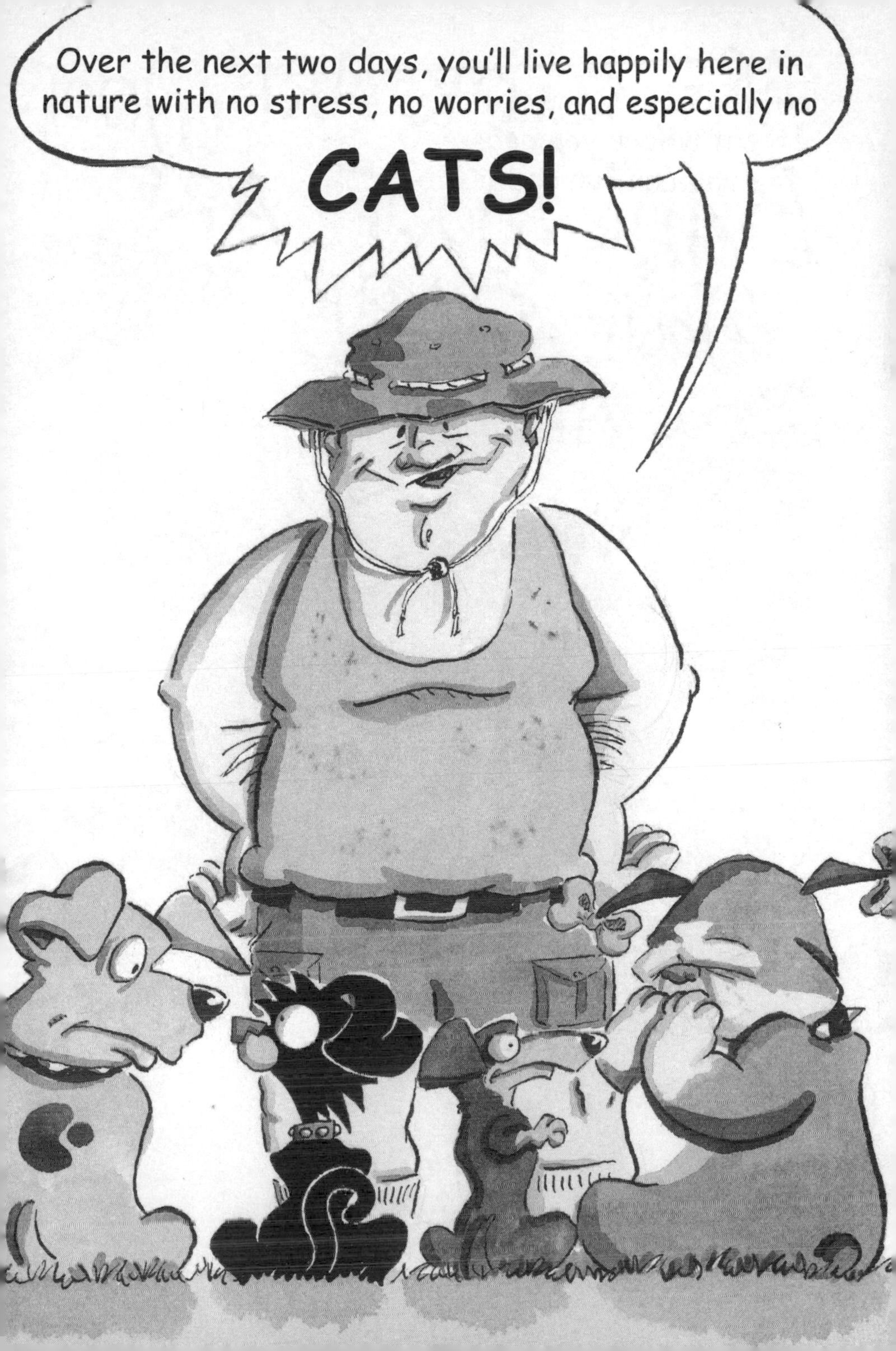
Over the next two days, you'll live happily here in nature with no stress, no worries, and especially no
CATS!

ARF BARK ARF WOOF
BARK WOOF ARF
WOOF BARK
ARF ARF
HOOOWLLLL
KATIE

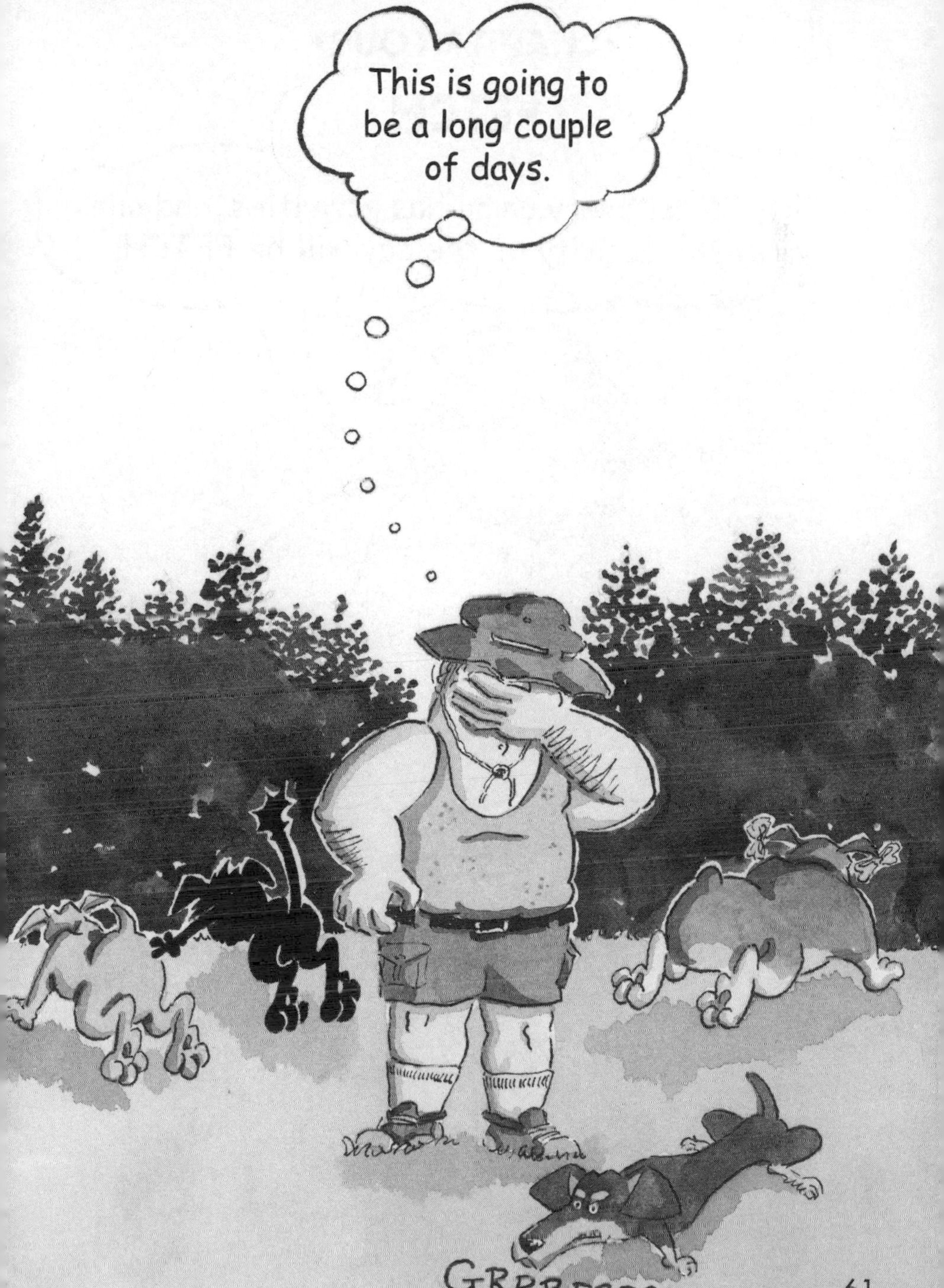
This is going to be a long couple of days.
GRRRRRRRR

•CHAPTER FOUR•

FETCH

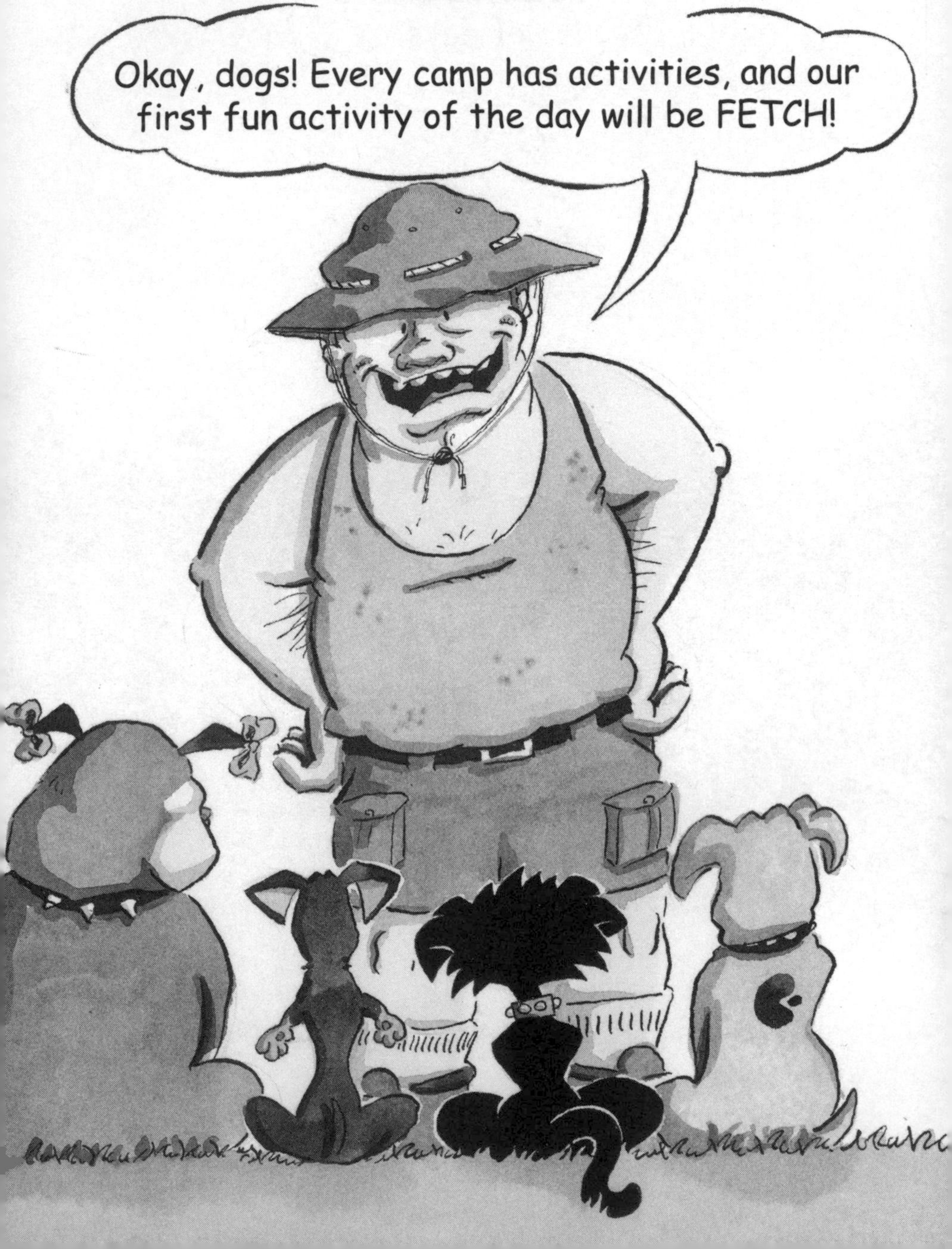
Okay, dogs! Every camp has activities, and our first fun activity of the day will be FETCH!

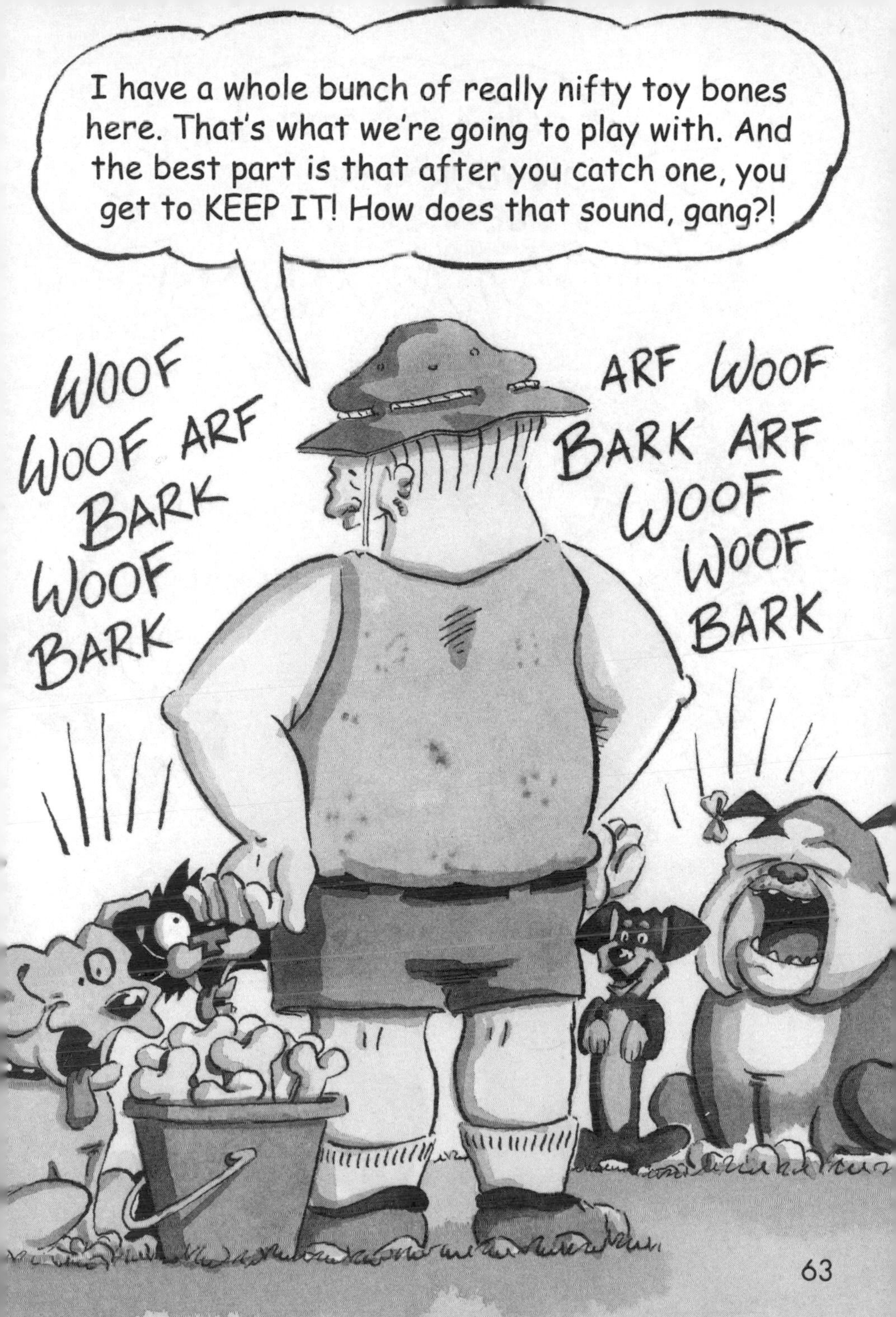
I have a whole bunch of really nifty toy bones here. That's what we're going to play with. And the best part is that after you catch one, you get to KEEP IT! How does that sound, gang?!
WOOF WOOF ARF BARK WOOF BARK
ARF WOOF BARK ARF WOOF WOOF BARK

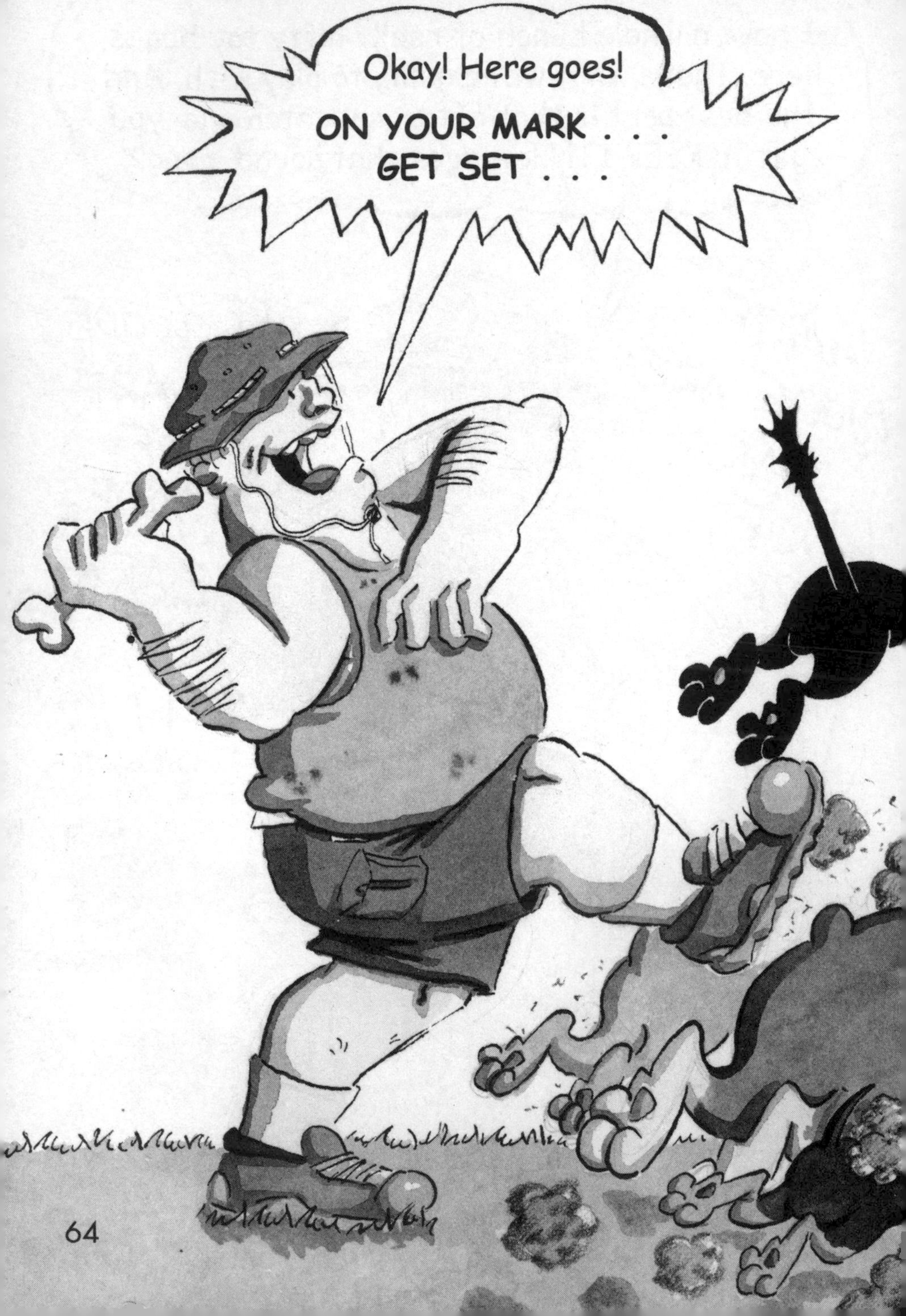
Okay! Here goes!
ON YOUR MARK . . .
GET SET . . .

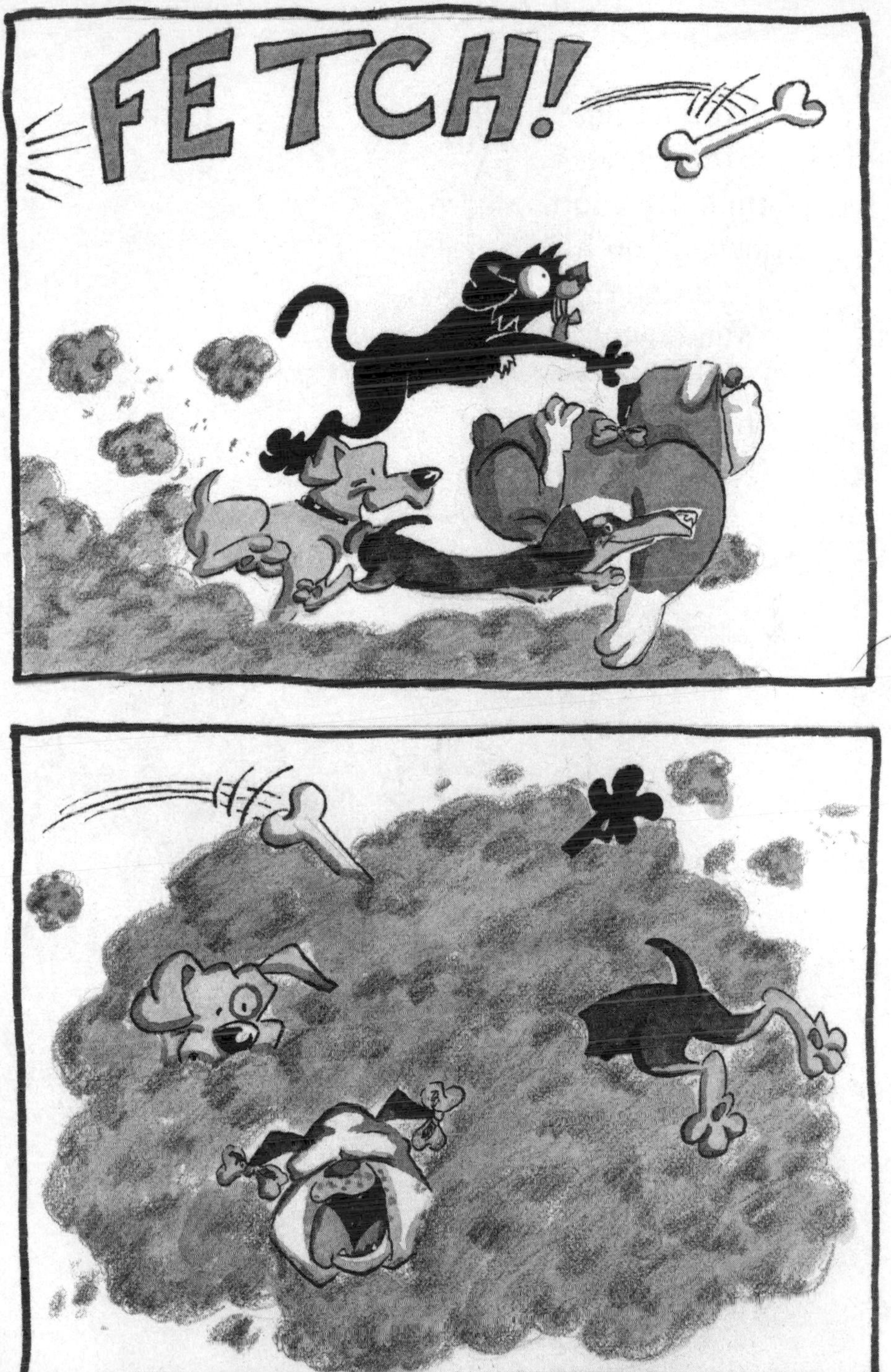
FETCH!

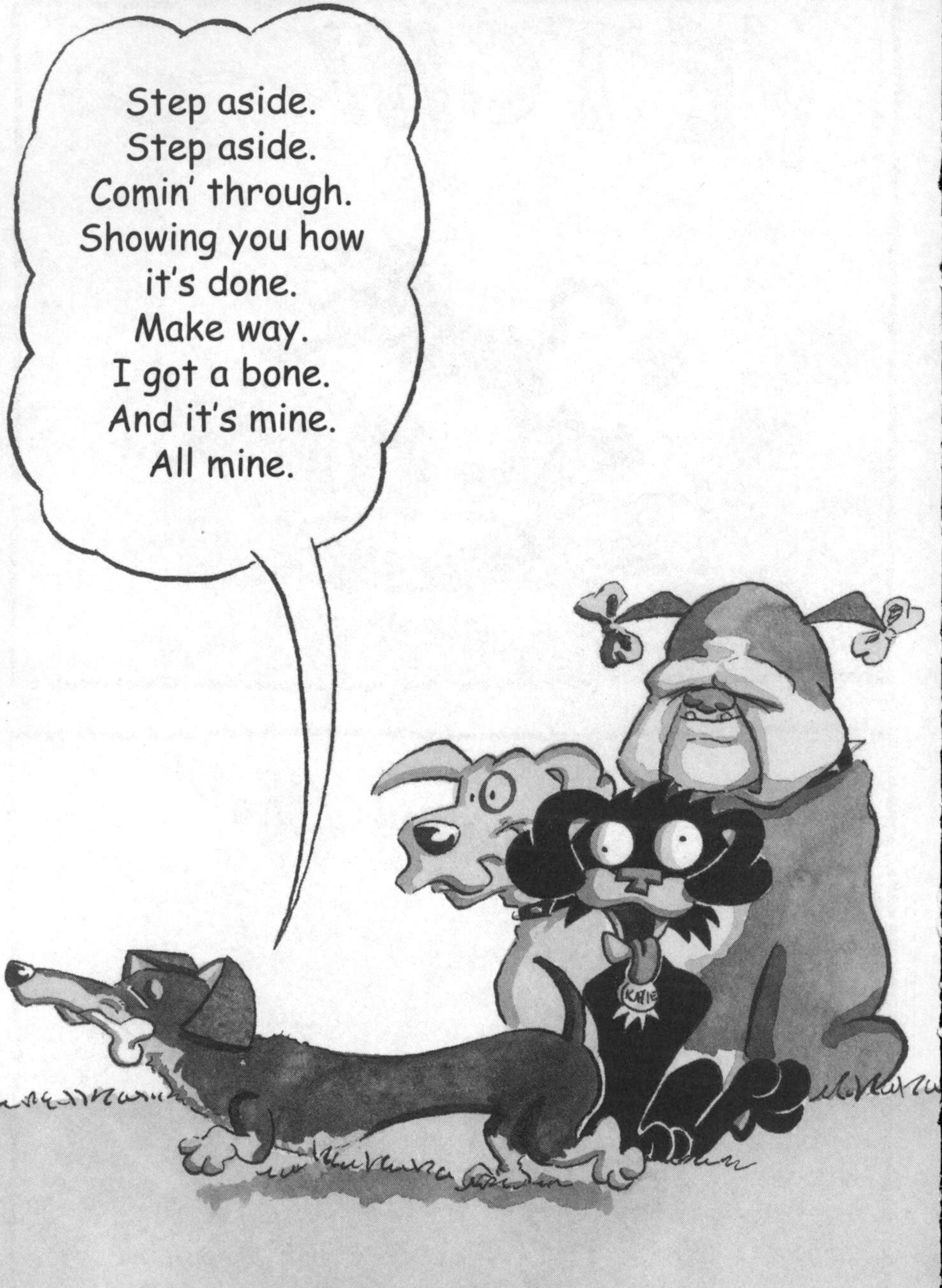
Step aside.
Step aside.
Comin' through.
Showing you how
it's done.
Make way.
I got a bone.
And it's mine.
All mine.

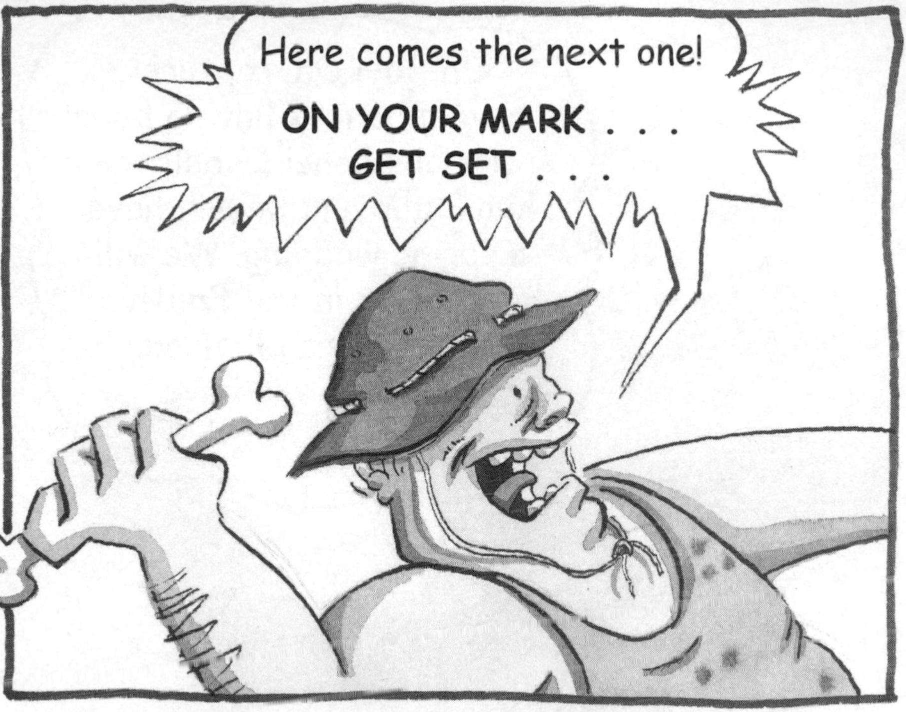
Here comes the next one!
ON YOUR MARK . . .
GET SET . . .

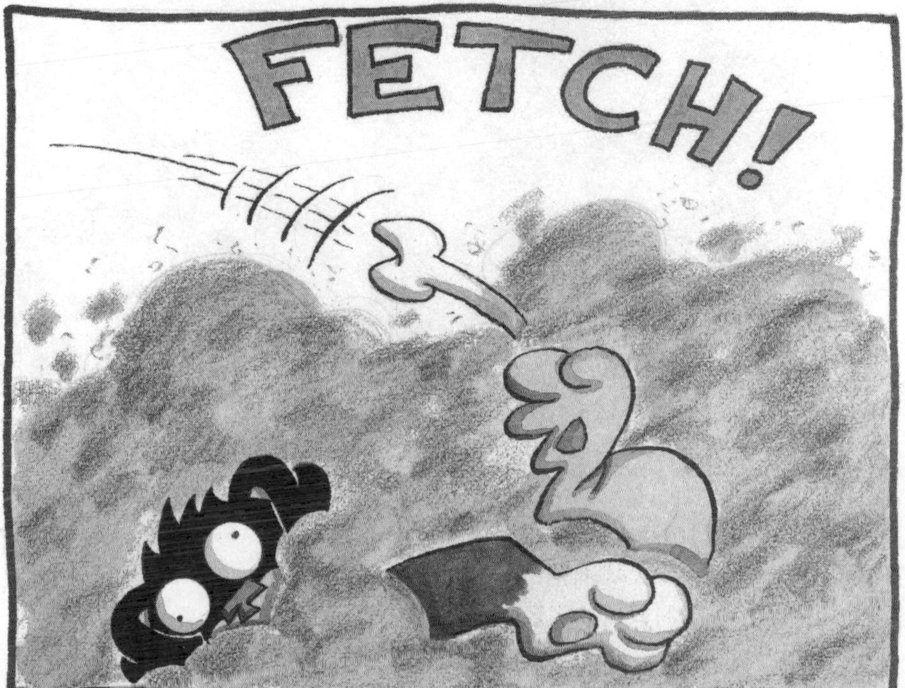
FETCH!

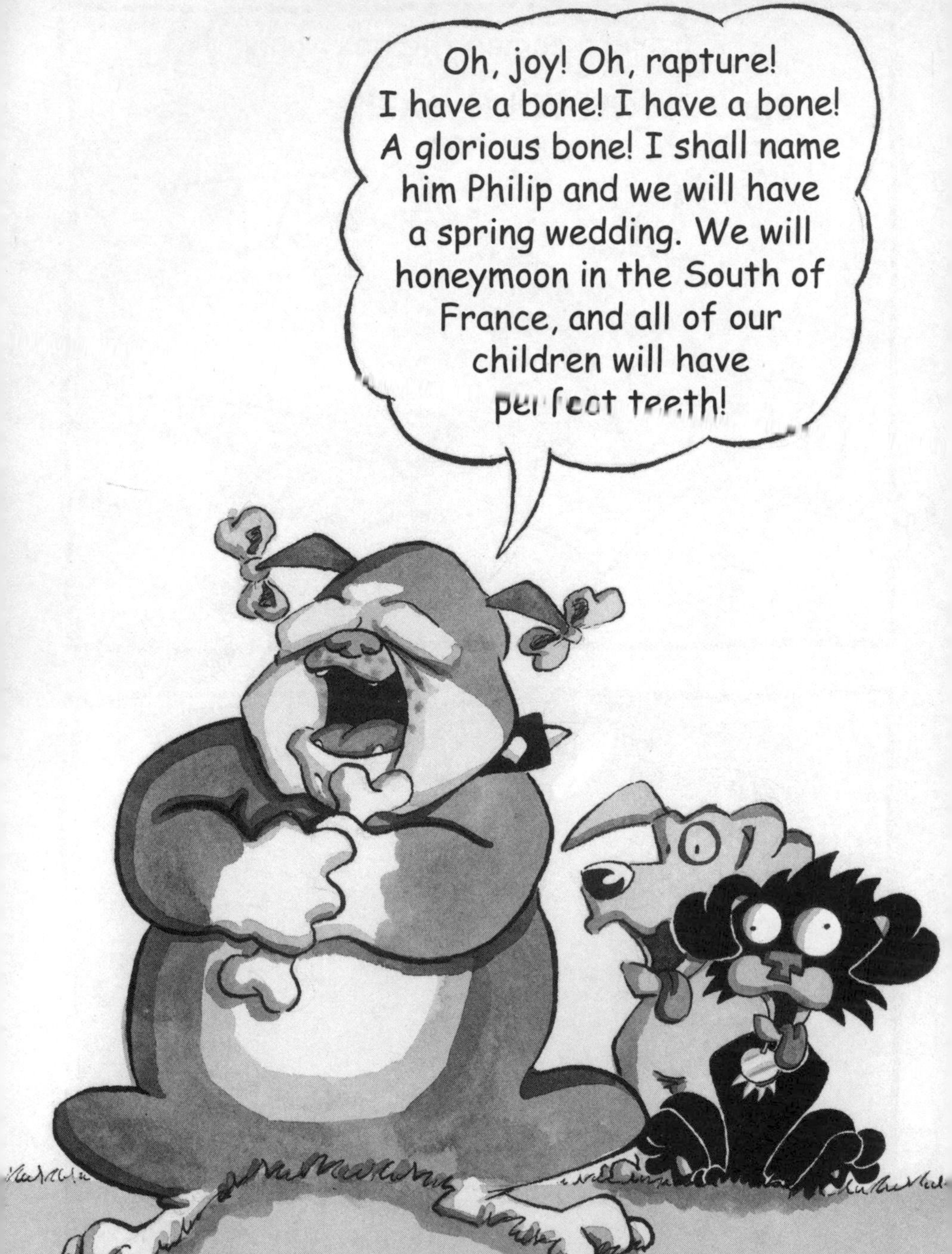
Oh, joy! Oh, rapture! I have a bone! I have a bone! A glorious bone! I shall name him Philip and we will have a spring wedding. We will honeymoon in the South of France, and all of our children will have perfect teeth!

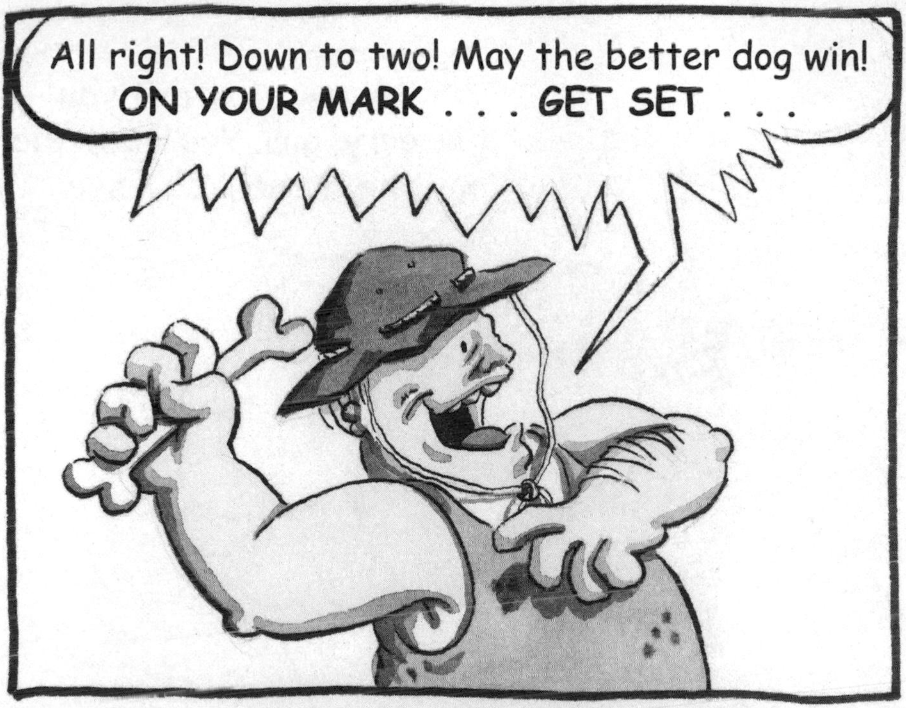
All right! Down to two! May the better dog win!
ON YOUR MARK . . . GET SET . . .

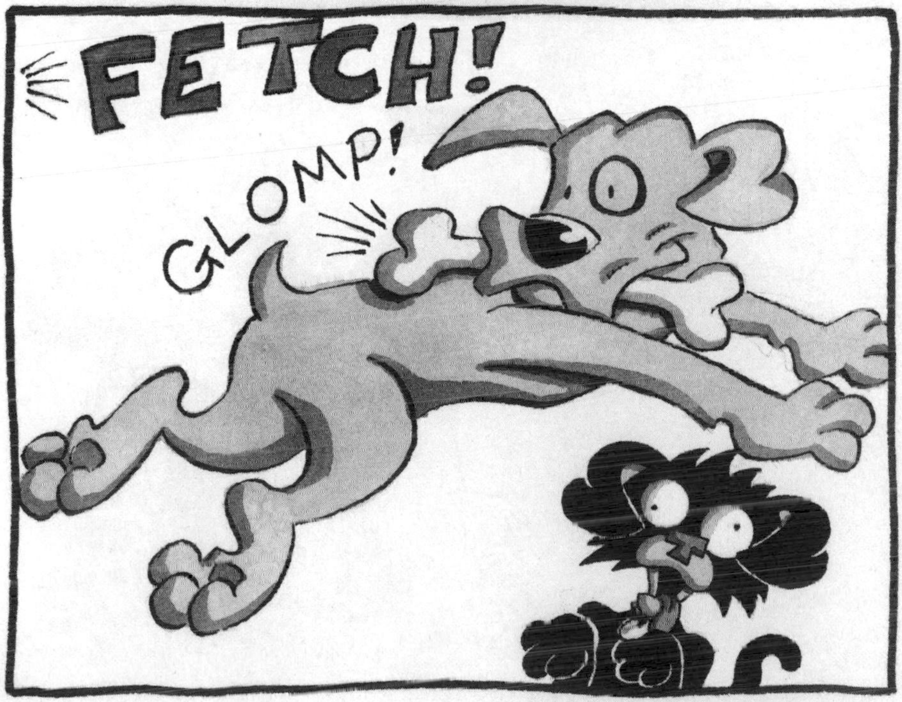
FETCH!
GLOMP!

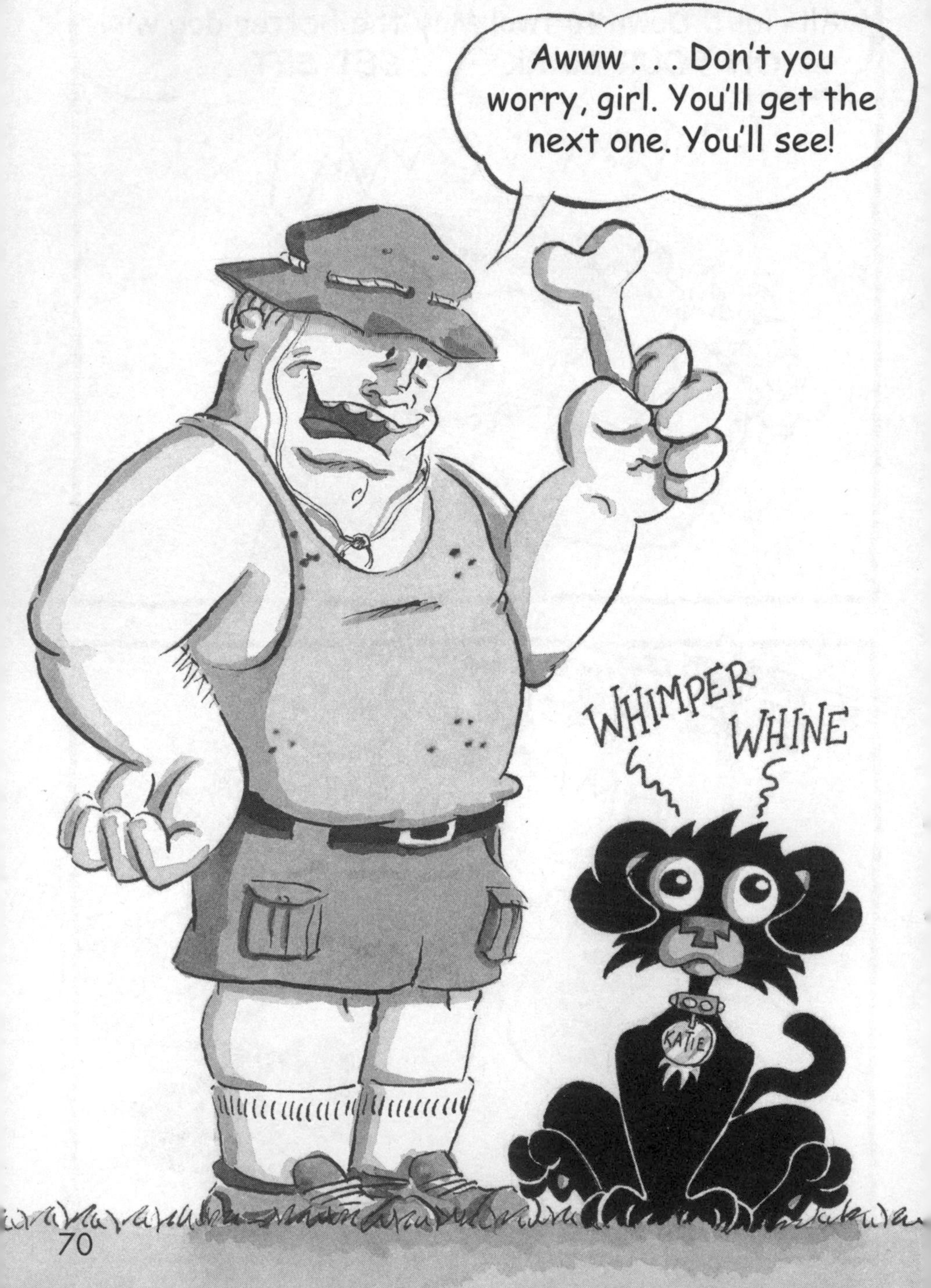
Awww . . . Don't you worry, girl. You'll get the next one. You'll see!
WHIMPER
WHINE
KATIE

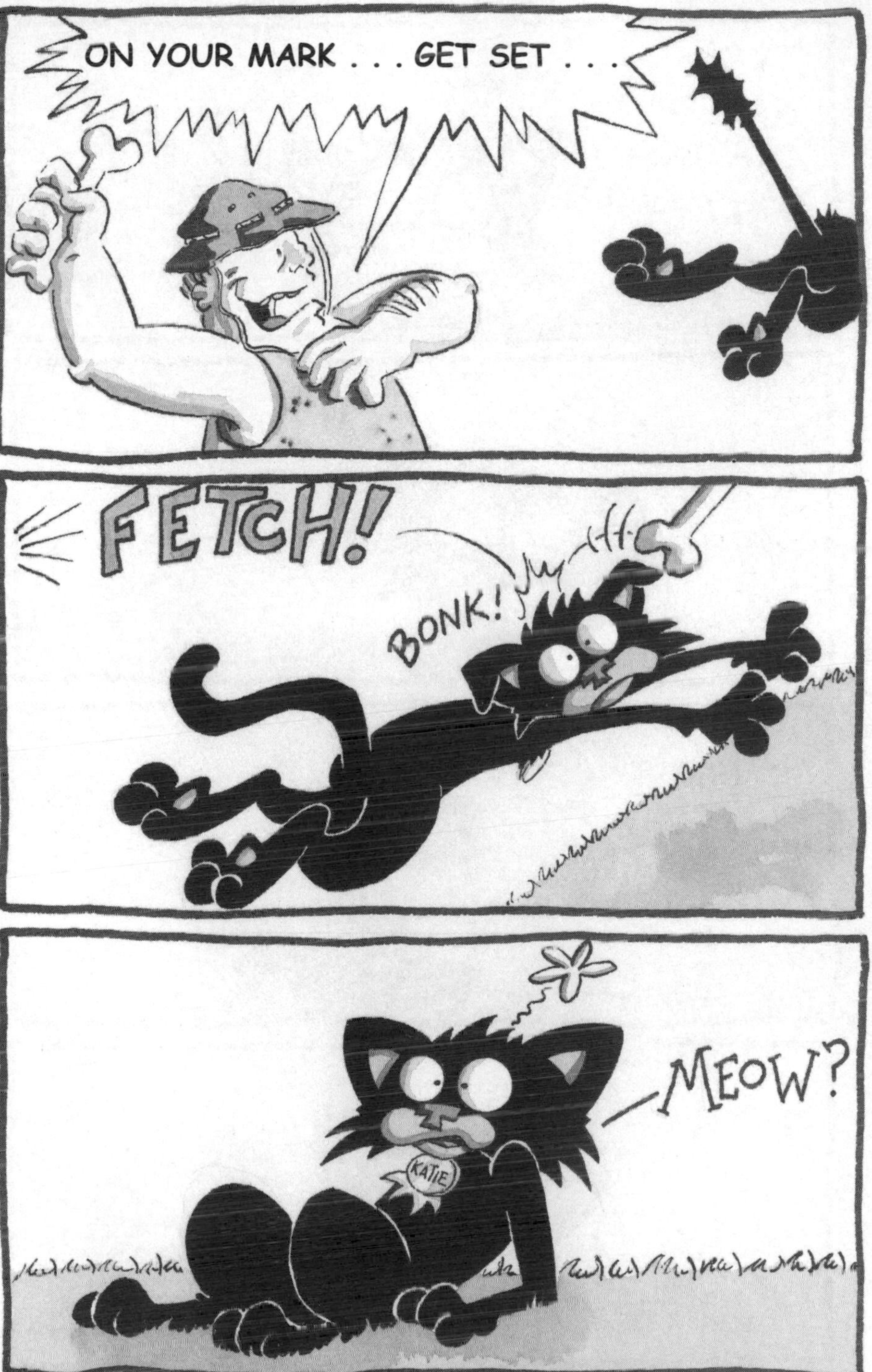
ON YOUR MARK . . . GET SET . . .
FETCH!
BONK!
KATIE
MEOW?

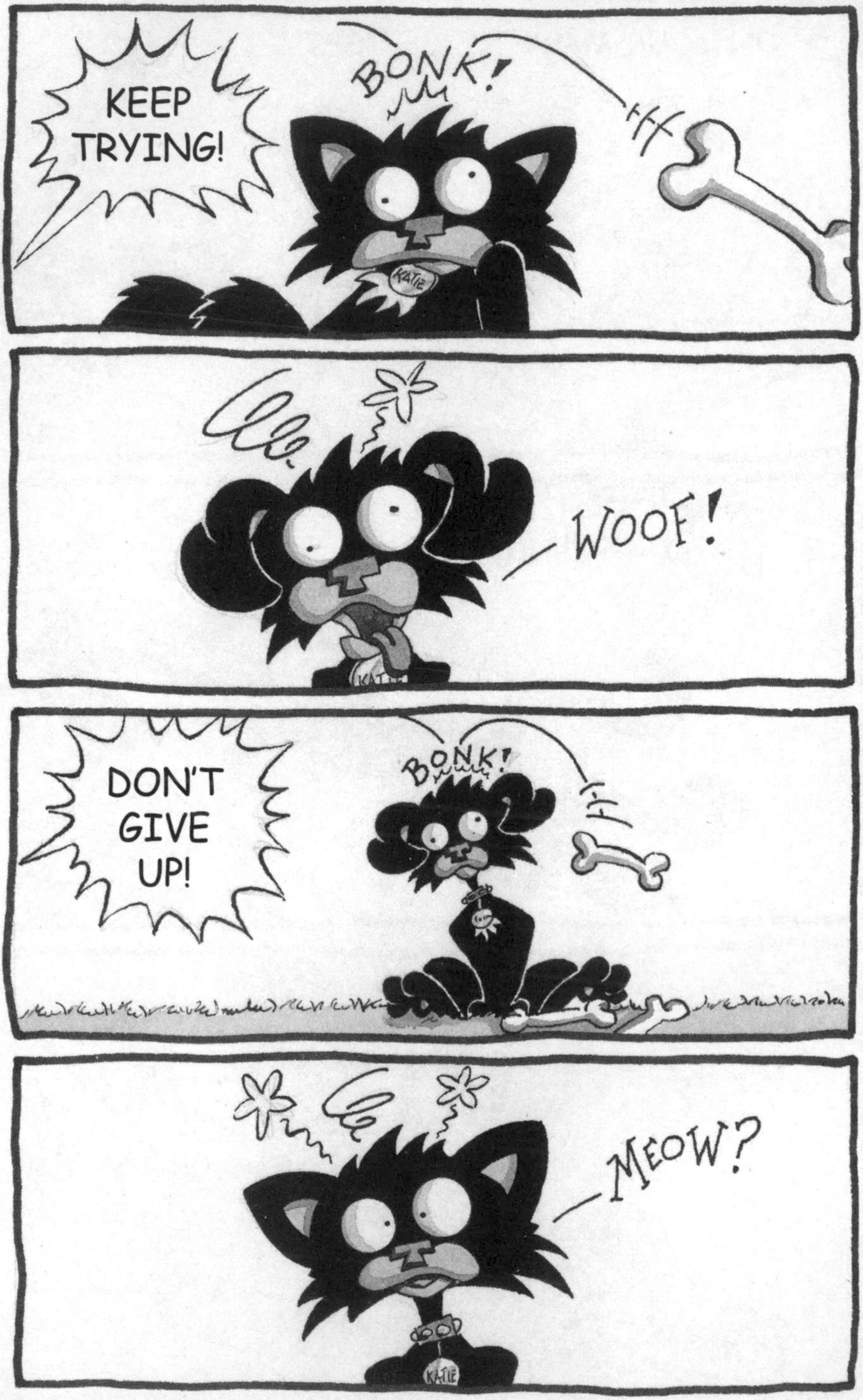
KEEP TRYING!
BONK!
KATIE
WOOF!
DON'T GIVE UP!
BONK!
MEOW?
KATIE

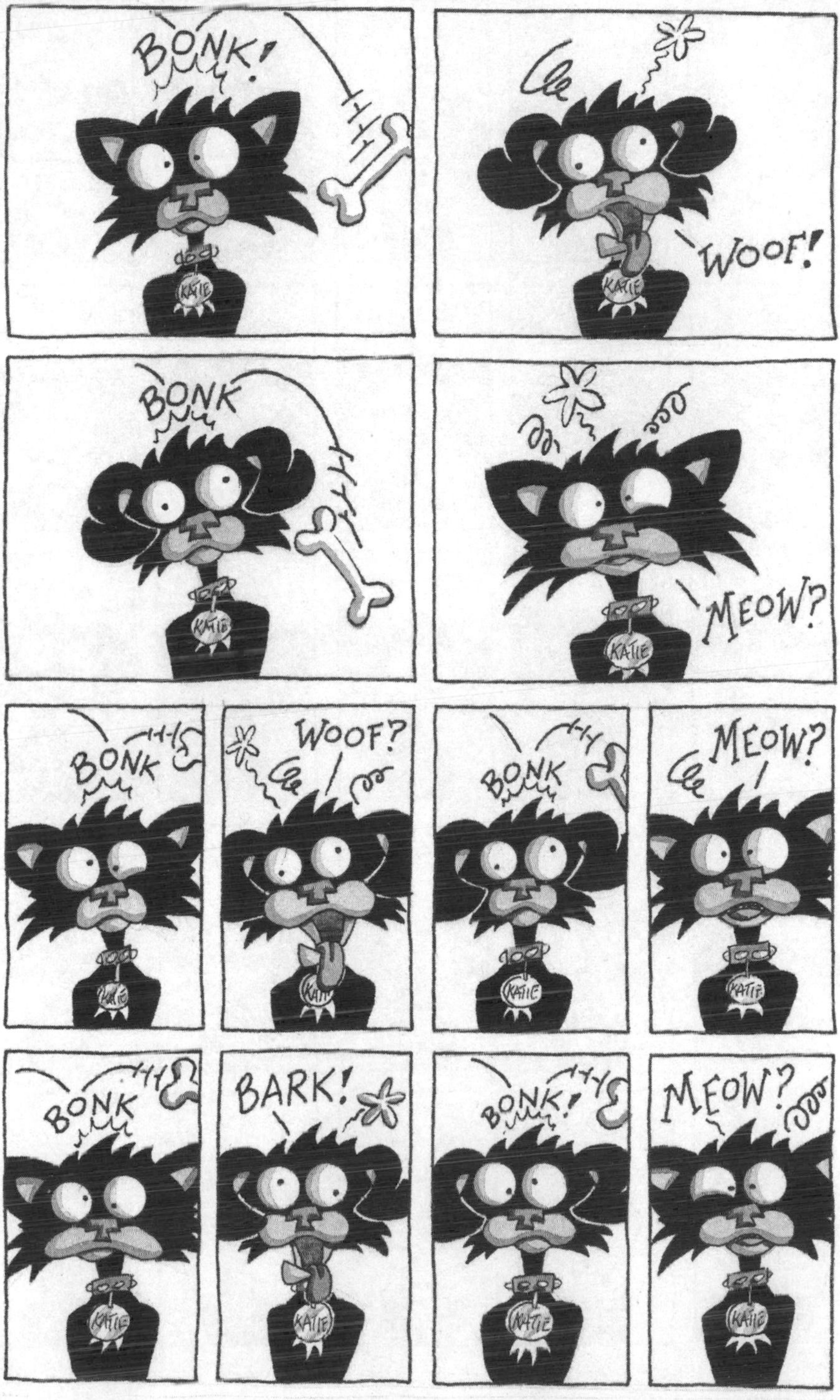
BONK!
WOOF!
BONK
MEOW?
BONK
WOOF?
BONK
MEOW?
BONK
BARK!
BONK!
MEOW?

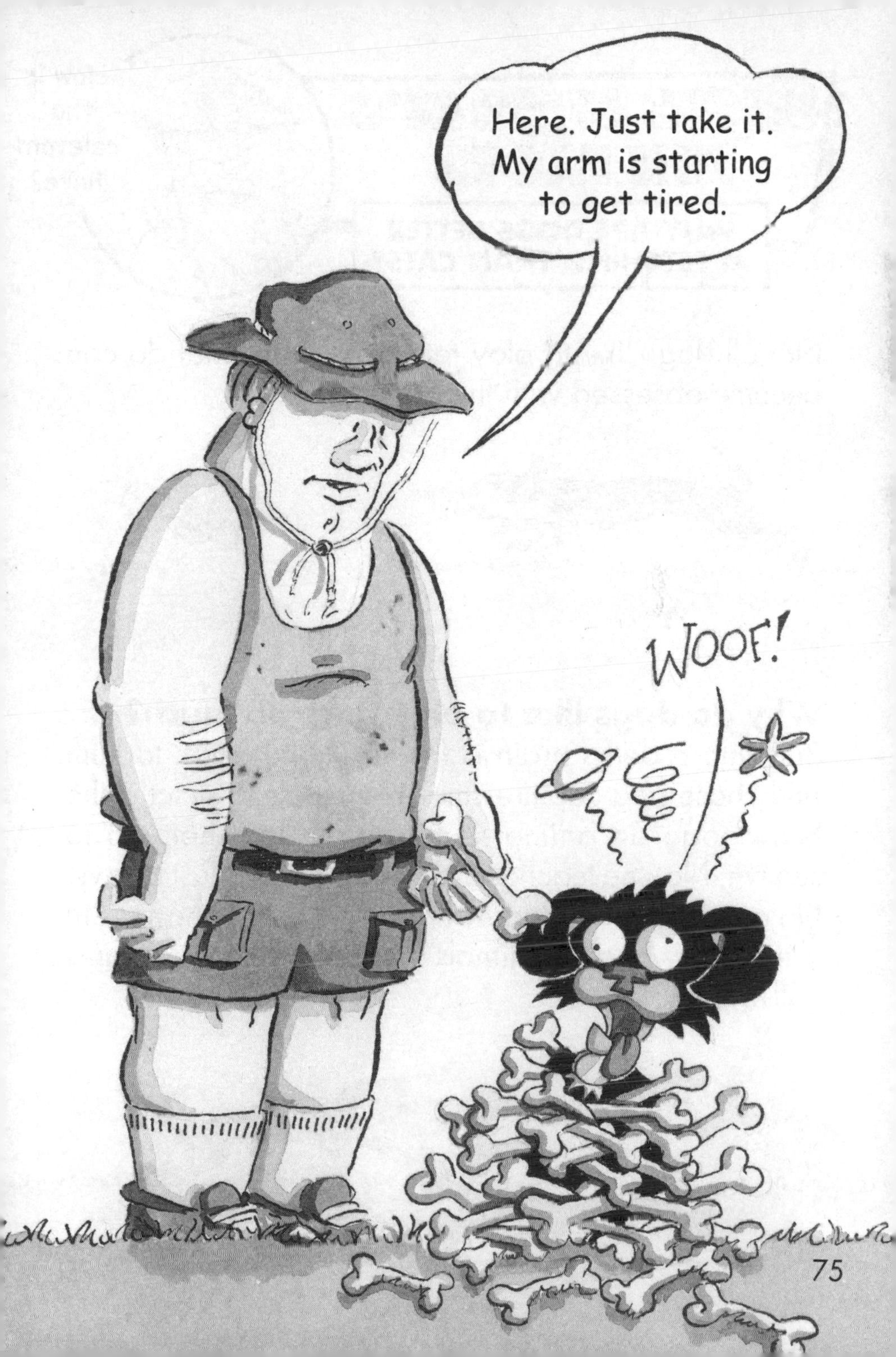
Here. Just take it. My arm is starting to get tired.
WOOF!

UNCLE MURRAY'S FUN FACTS

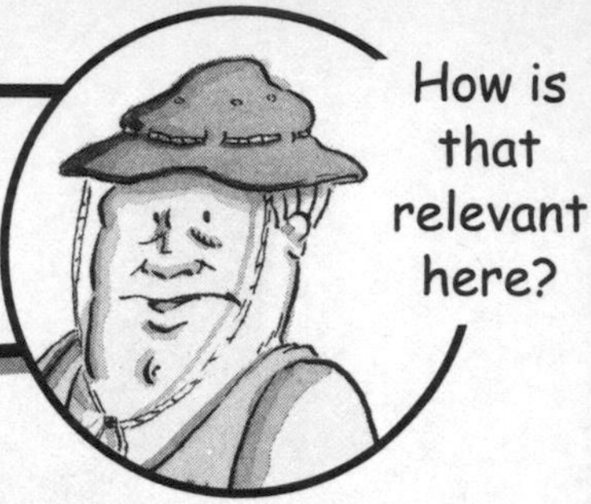
How is that relevant here?

WHY ARE DOGS BETTER AT FETCHING THAN CATS?

Not all dogs like to play fetch. But those that do can become obsessed with the game.

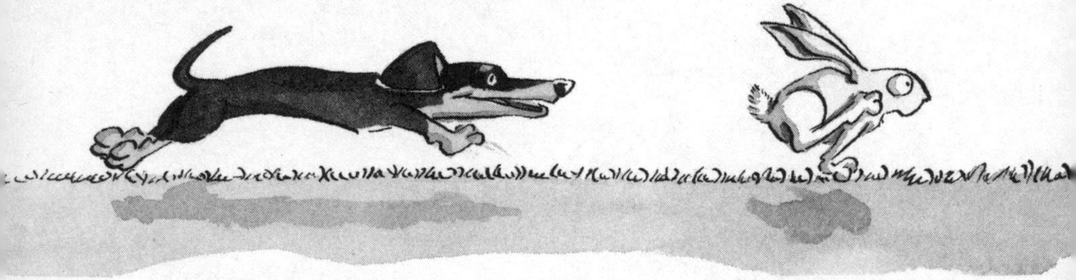

Why do dogs like to play fetch so much?
Built into a dog's brain is the instinct to fetch: to hunt and chase and capture smaller animals. Instinct is the knowledge an animal is born with that helps it to survive. No one teaches a bird how to fly. It just knows. No one teaches a dog how to fetch. It just knows. But without any smaller animals around, a stick or a tennis ball will do.

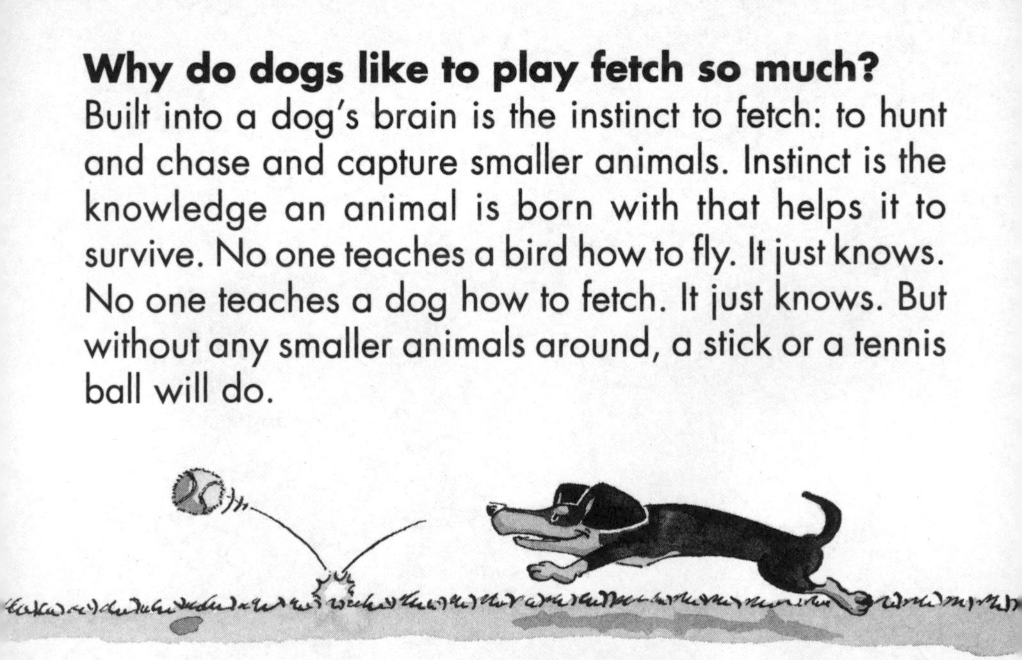

But cats are hunters, too. So why don't they play fetch?

A few of them do. Cats are natural born fetchers. Their mouths are perfectly designed to grab small items and animals and then carry them around. Think of a mother cat and how she will pick up and carry her kittens.

So why don't cats play fetch like dogs?

Cats just aren't generally as playful with people as dogs are. One reason is because cats like to conserve their energy. It's why they sleep so much. Their instinct tells them to rest as much as possible so they'll have the energy to hunt later.

Another reason is because they tend to be loners. Cats will be affectionate with their owners, but tend not to play with them the same way dogs do. This means that cats will often chase a toy you throw, but they'll rarely pick it up and bring it back.

More playful. More energetic. This all just goes to prove that dogs are better than cats. So, there.

•CHAPTER FIVE•

SWIMMING

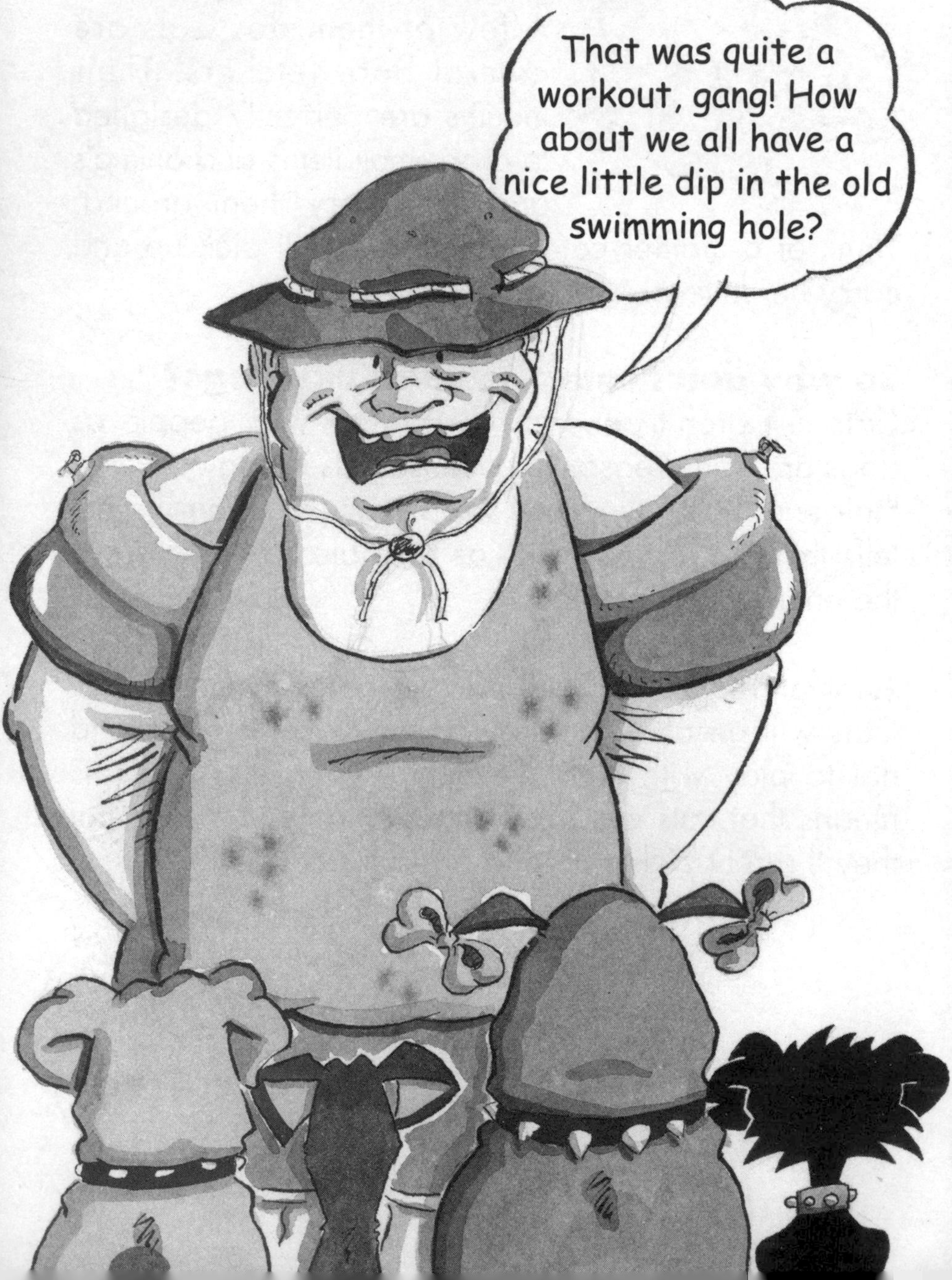
That was quite a workout, gang! How about we all have a nice little dip in the old swimming hole?

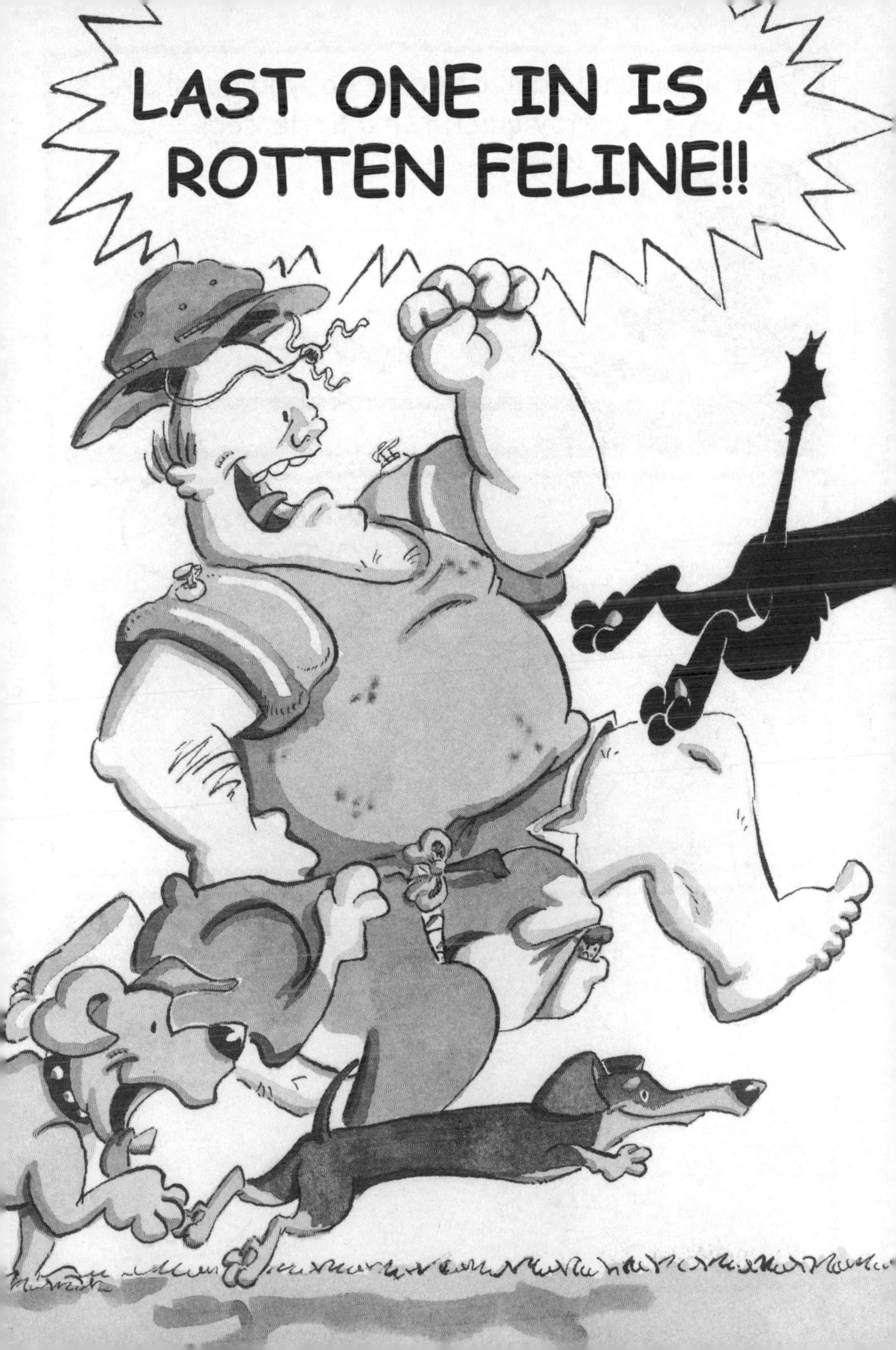
LAST ONE IN IS A ROTTEN FELINE!!

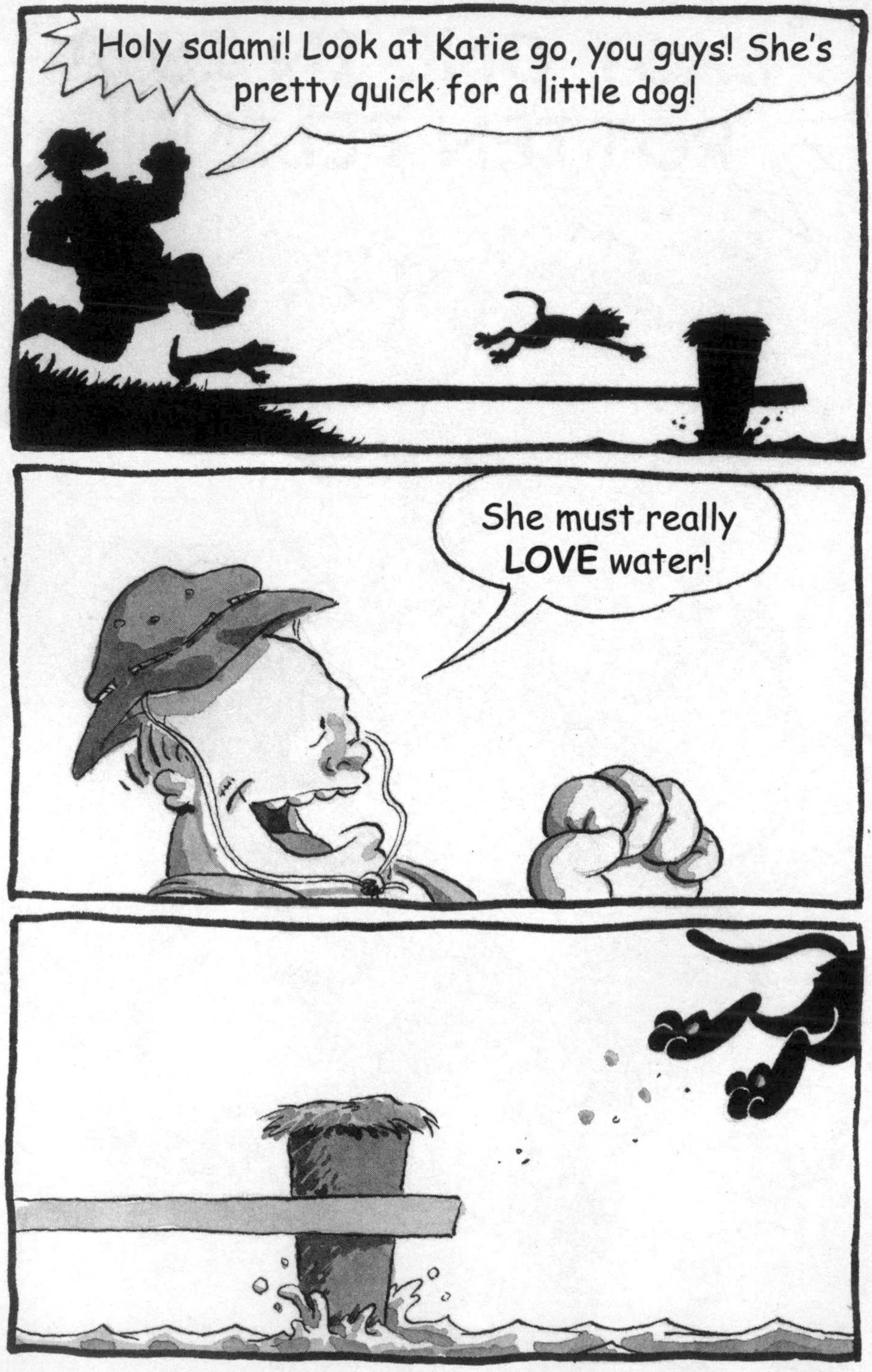
Holy salami! Look at Katie go, you guys! She's pretty quick for a little dog!
She must really LOVE water!

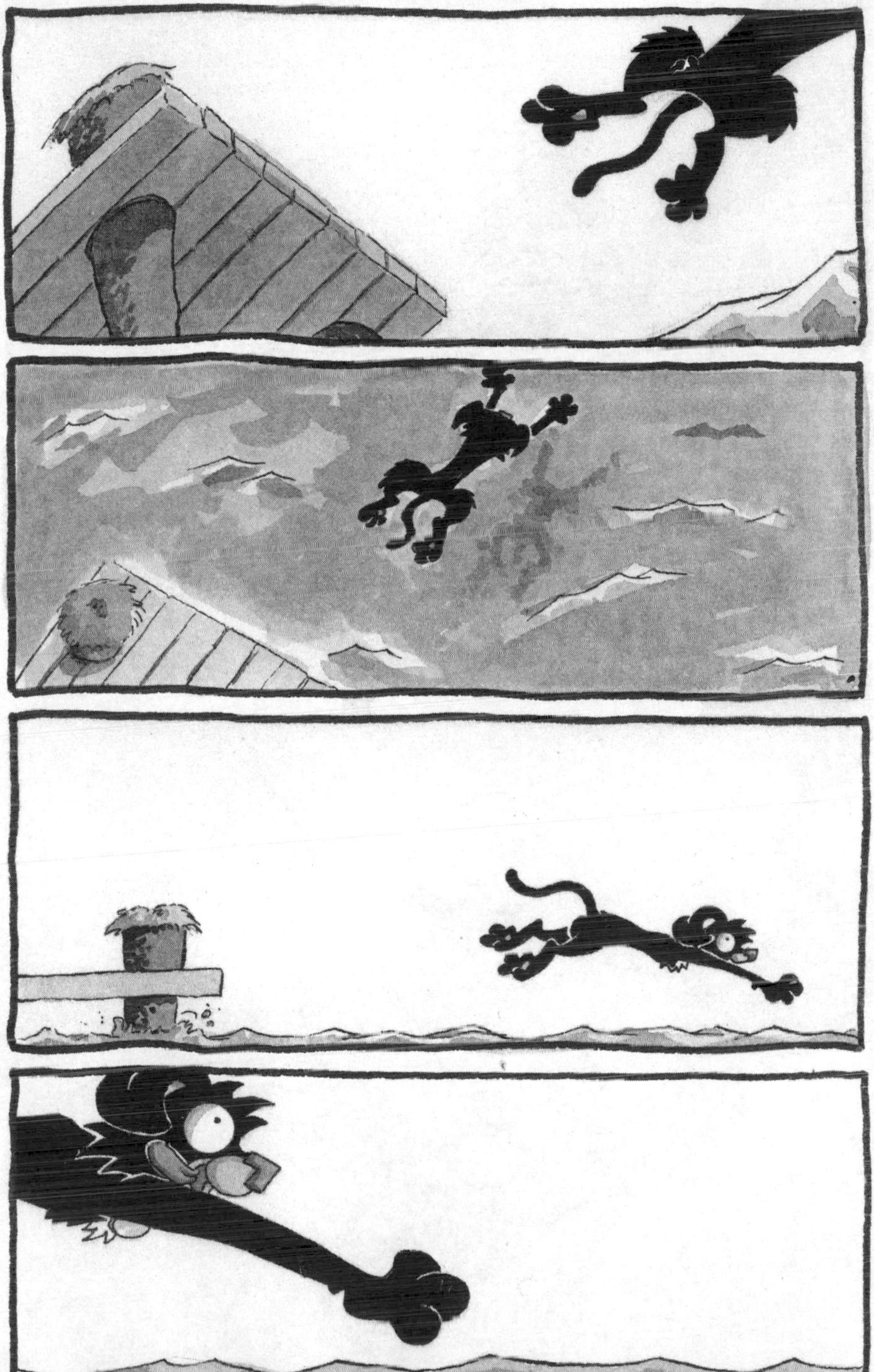

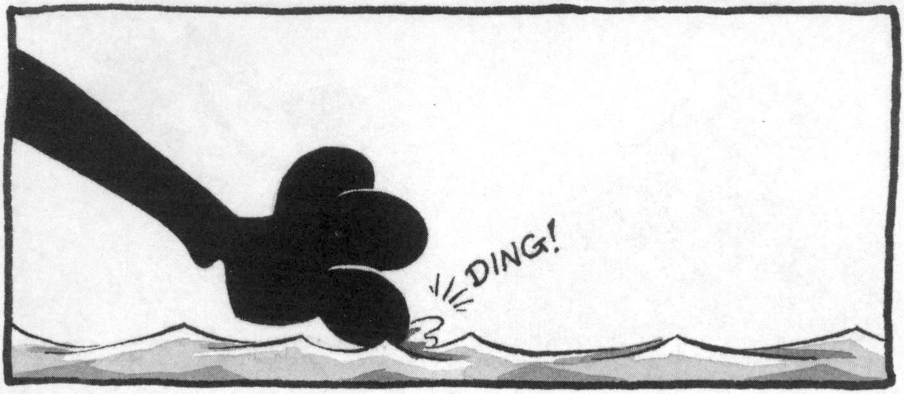
DING!

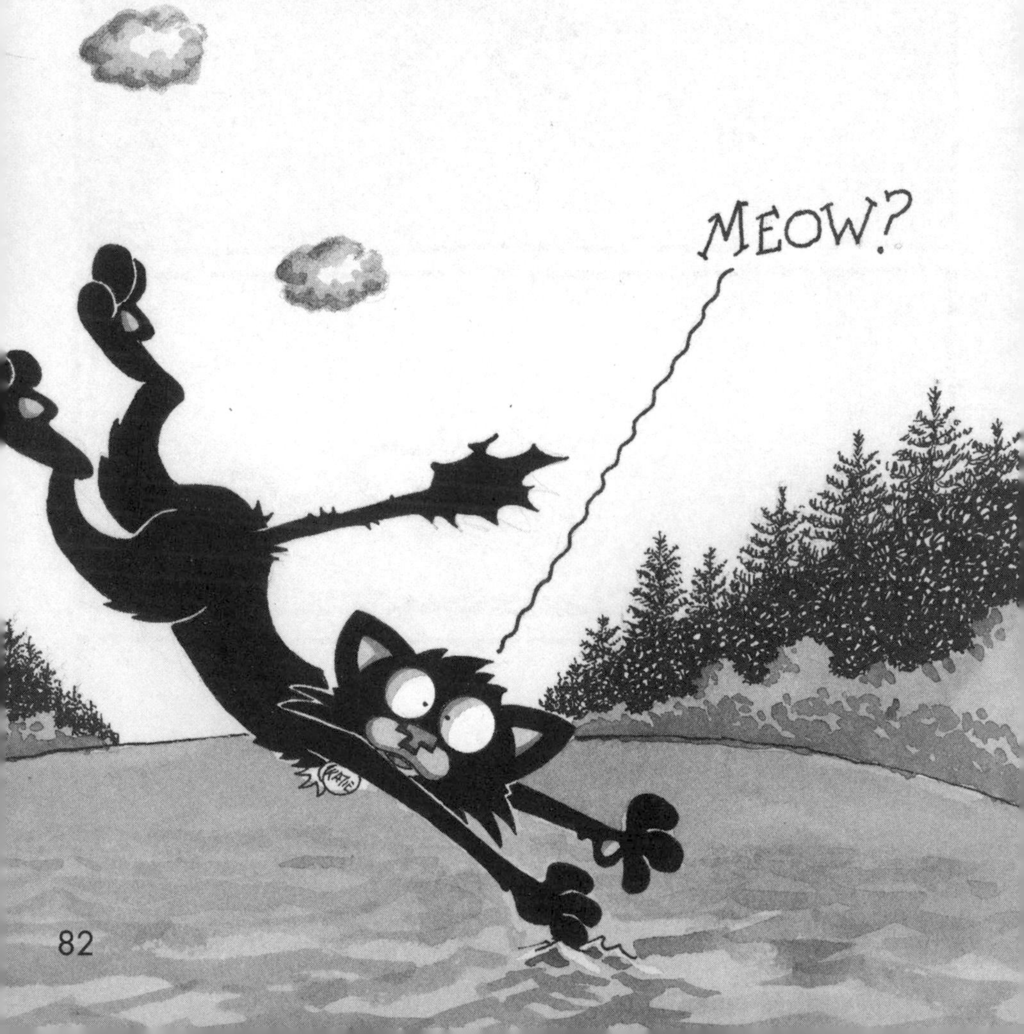
MEOW?

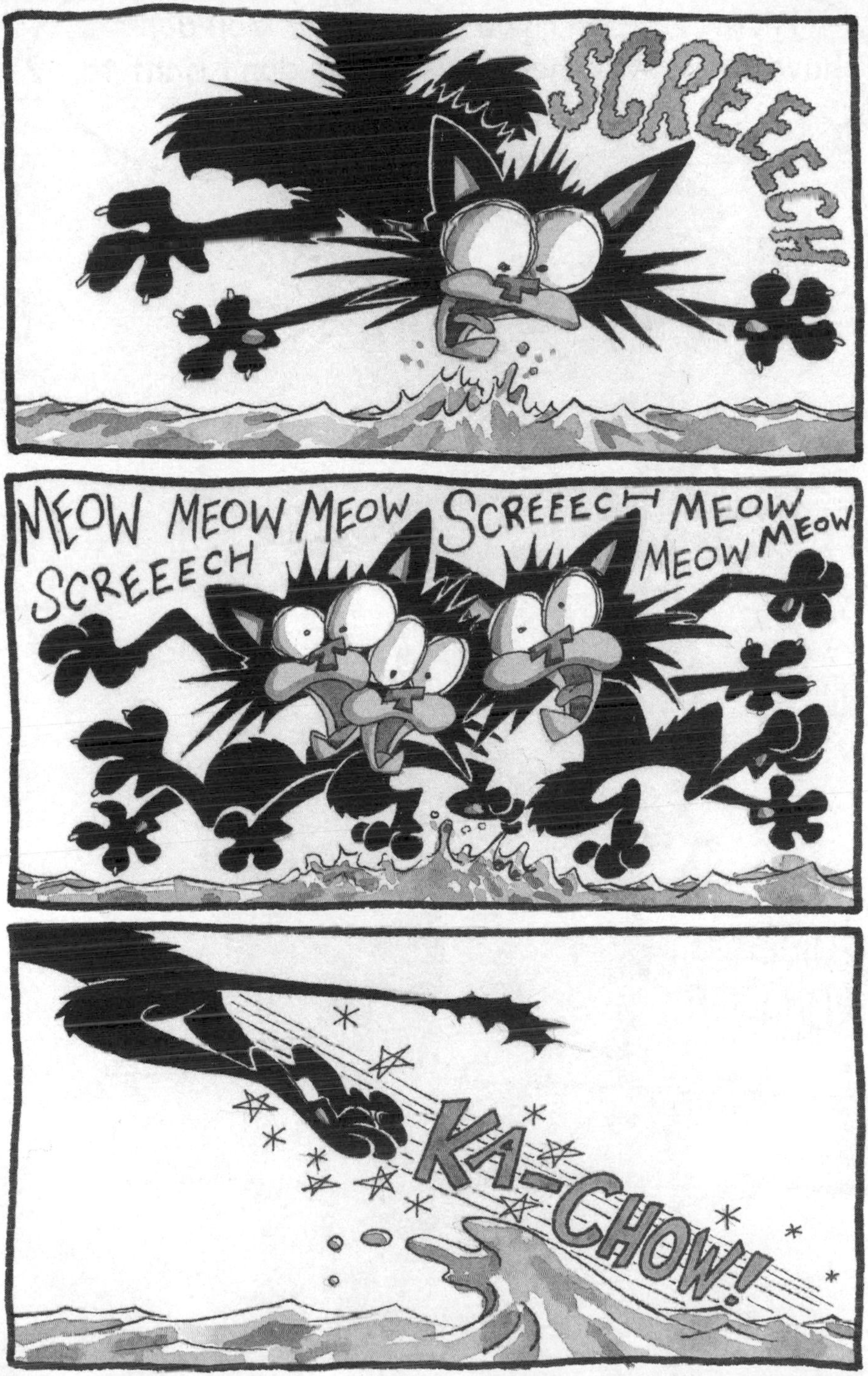
SCREEECH
MEOW MEOW MEOW
SCREEECH
SCREEECH MEOW
MEOW MEOW
KA-CHOW!

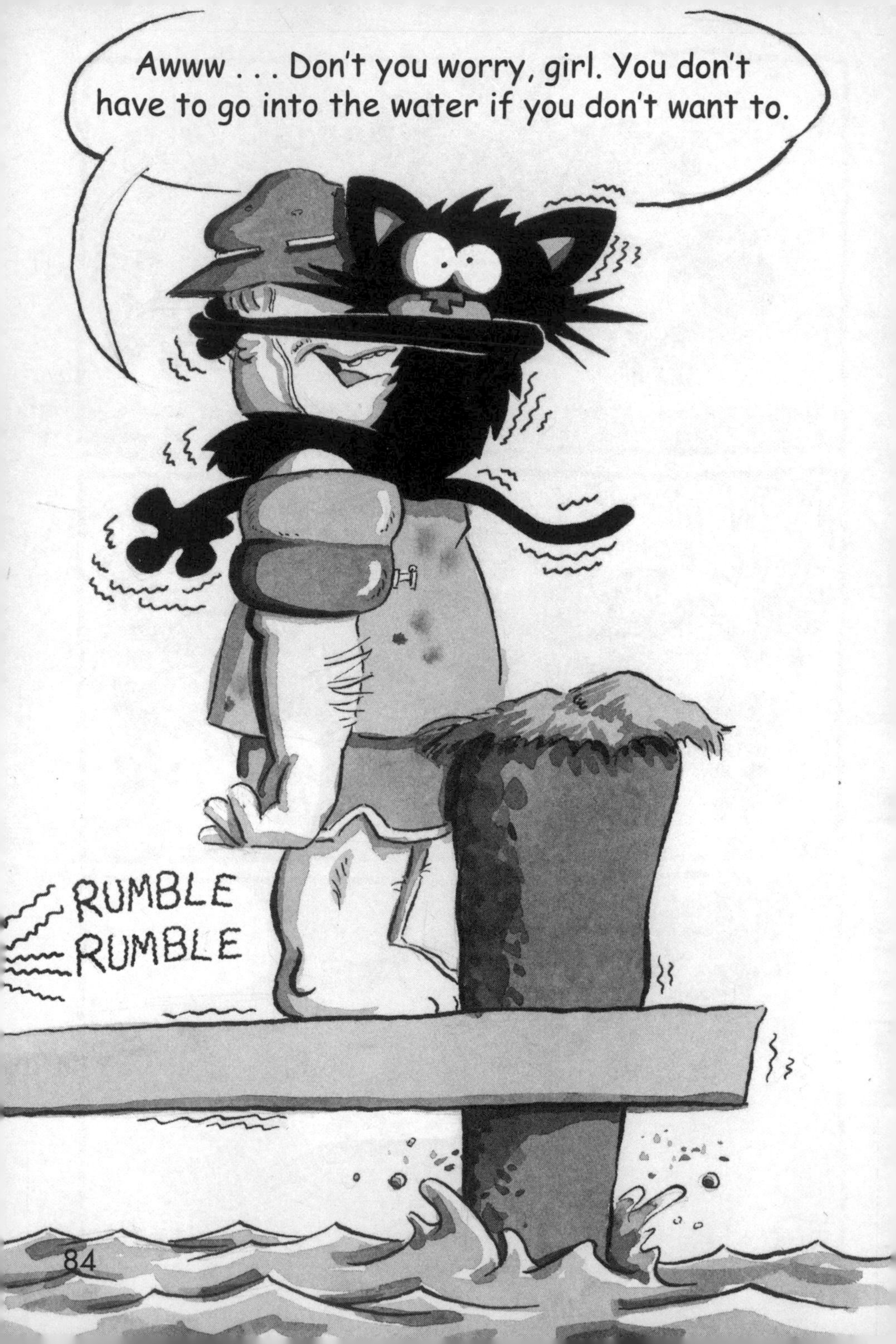
Awww . . . Don't you worry, girl. You don't have to go into the water if you don't want to.
RUMBLE
RUMBLE

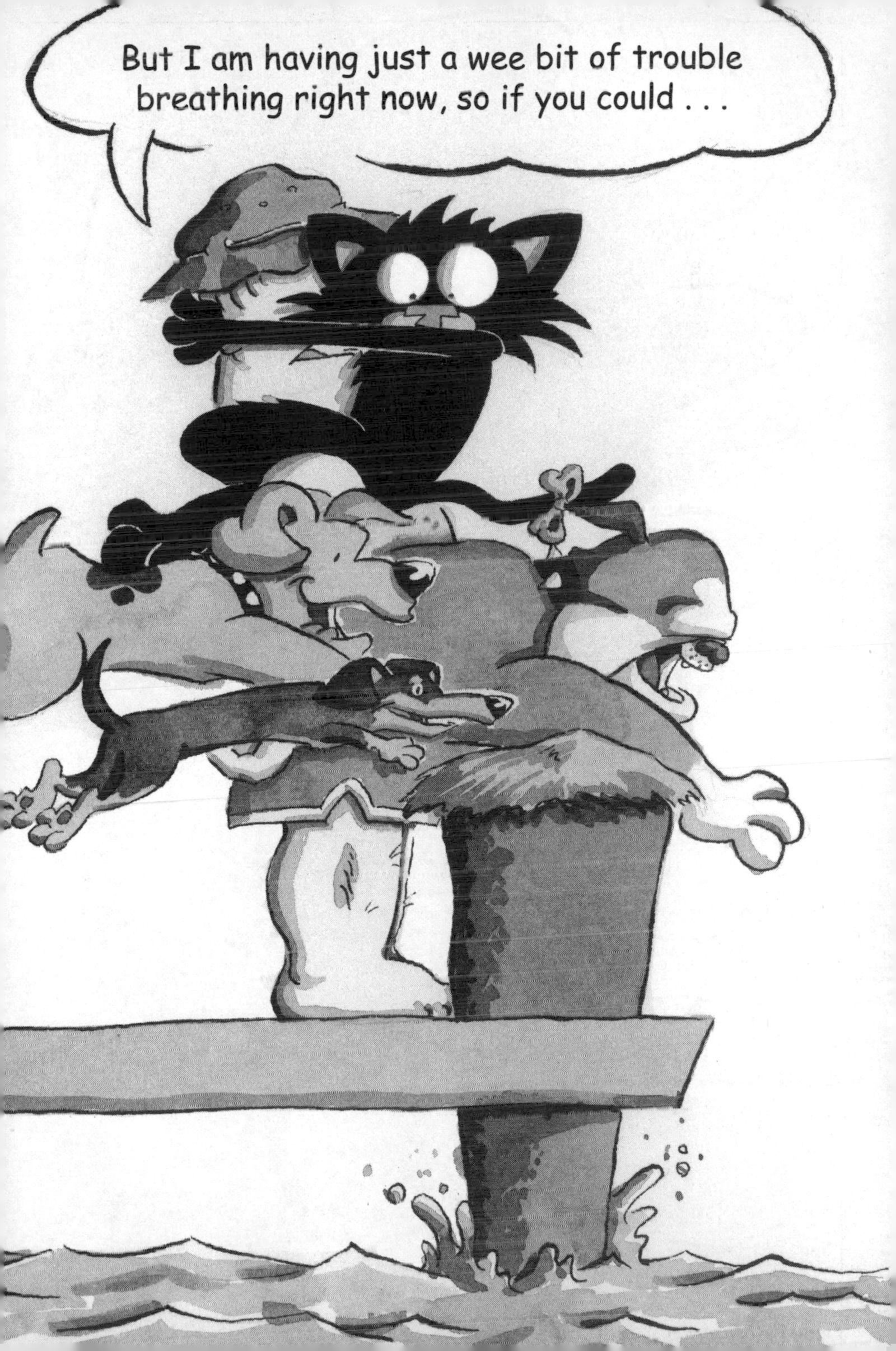
But I am having just a wee bit of trouble breathing right now, so if you could . . .

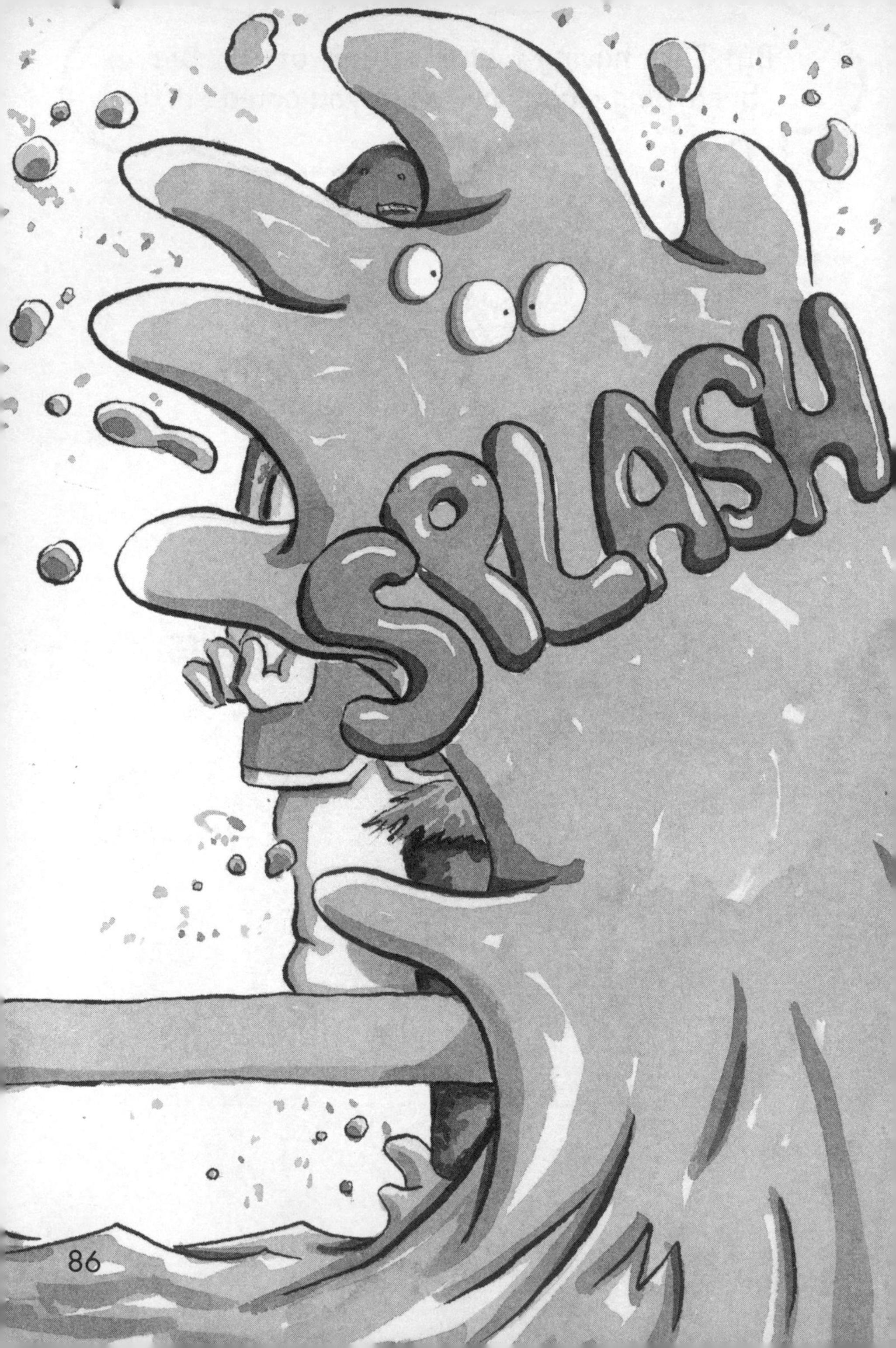
SPLASH

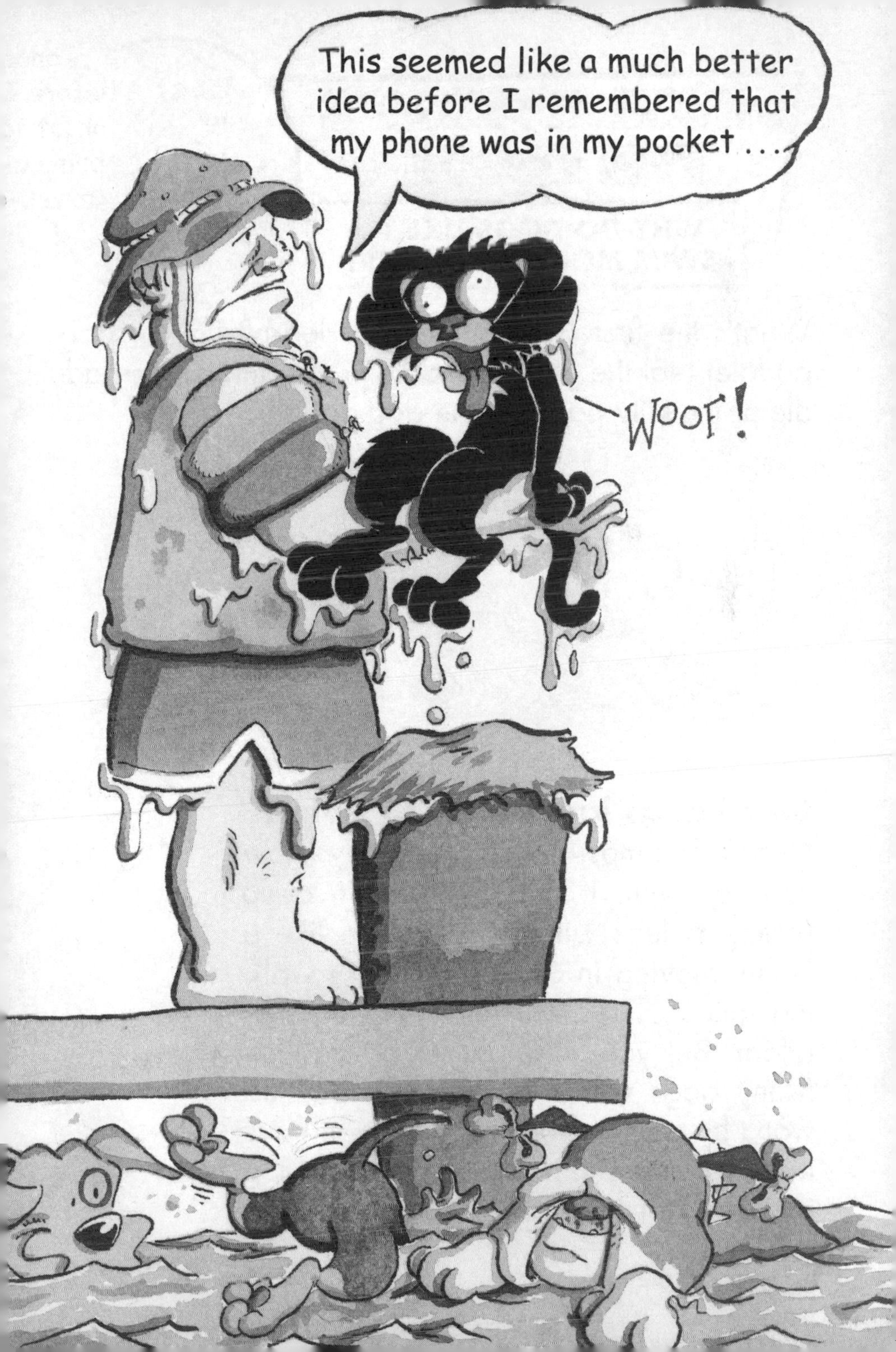
This seemed like a much better idea before I remembered that my phone was in my pocket . . .
WOOF!

UNCLE MURRAY'S FUN FACTS

WHY DO DOGS LIKE TO SWIM MORE THAN CATS?

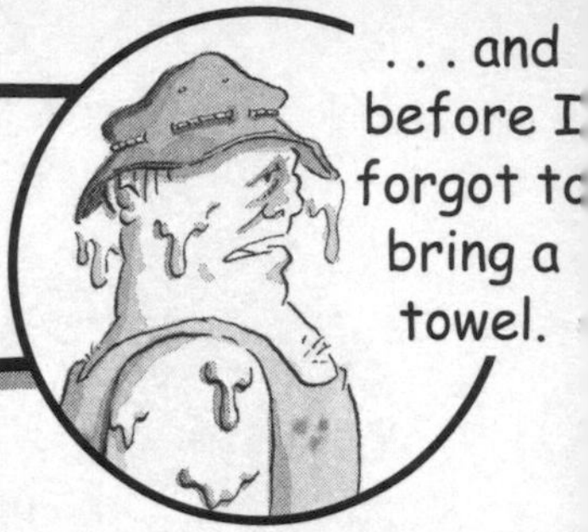
. . . and
before I
forgot t
bring a
towel.

What's the first swim stroke kids learn? It's the dog paddle! Not the giraffe paddle or the rhinoceros paddle or the kitty paddle. The dog paddle.

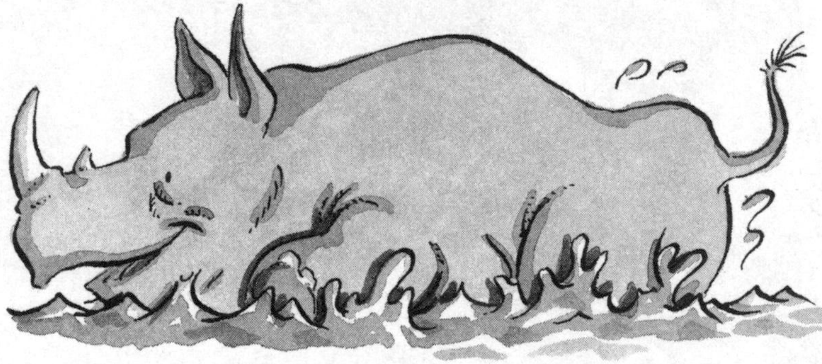

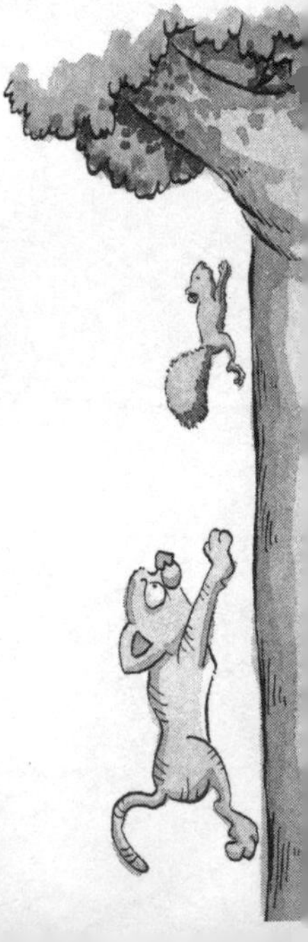

Do all dogs know how to swim?

Not all, but most dogs instinctively know how to swim. If a dog is put in deep water, its legs will begin trotting like a horse, moving in a motion like it's walking quickly. This will help the dog stay afloat. But you still have to be careful. Many dogs will try swimming, but just won't be able to float at all, so you have to be very careful before putting any dog in water that goes above its head.

Do cats also know how to swim?

They do, but they don't like it. A cat's instinct tells it to hunt for food on the ground and in the woods and in the trees, which is why they're better at climbing than dogs.

But the really big reason dogs generally like to swim more than cats is because cats HATE TO GET WET.

Like it or not, hairless cats, like yours truly, NEED a bath at least once a week.

A cat's fur is finer and softer than a dog's, so it doesn't dry as quickly. This means that if a cat gets soaking wet, it will stay wet for a long time and that can be very uncomfortable.

Dogs swim. Cats don't. Dogs win. So, there.

89

•CHAPTER SIX•

CAMPFIRE

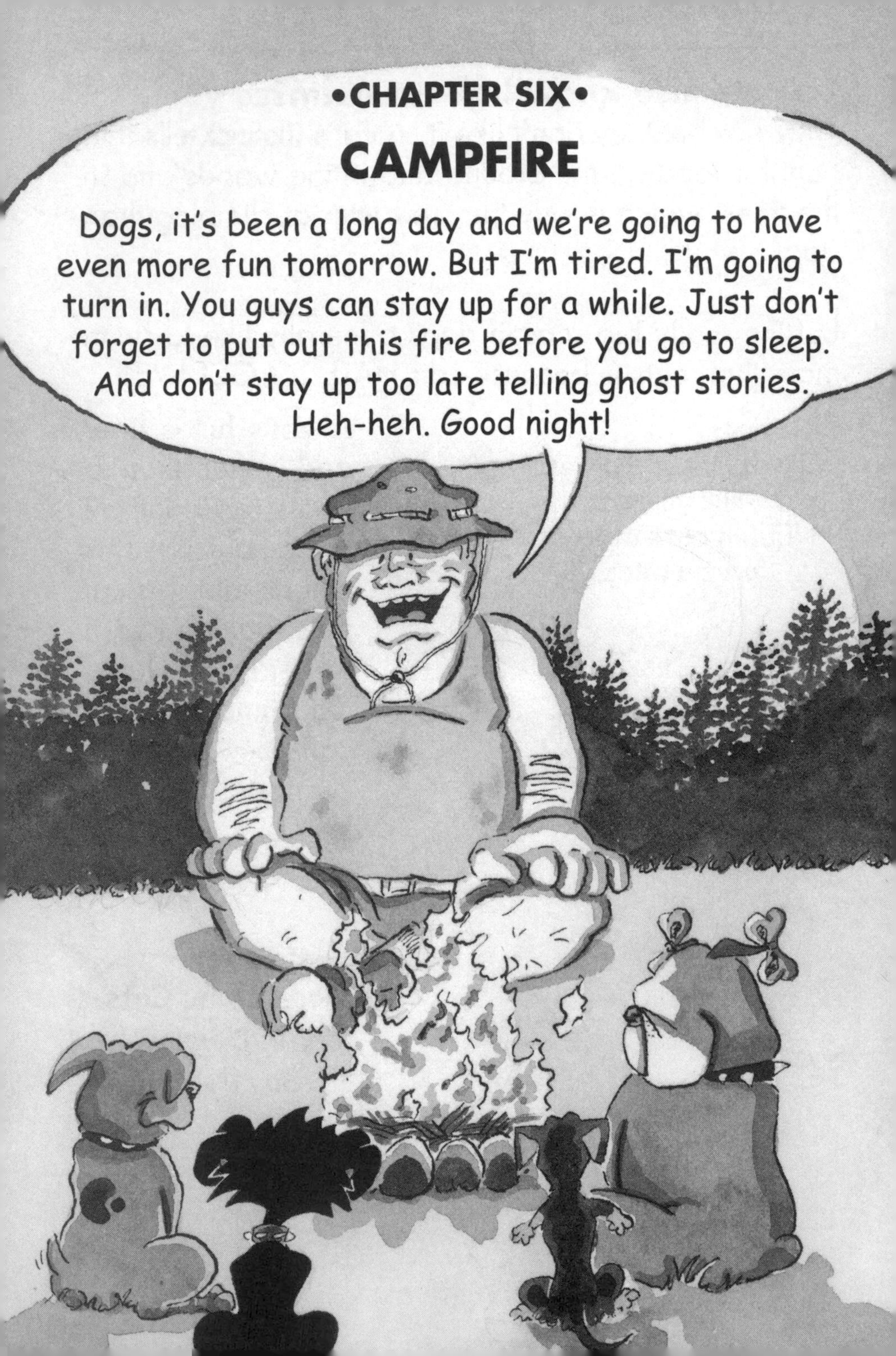
Dogs, it's been a long day and we're going to have even more fun tomorrow. But I'm tired. I'm going to turn in. You guys can stay up for a while. Just don't forget to put out this fire before you go to sleep. And don't stay up too late telling ghost stories. Heh-heh. Good night!

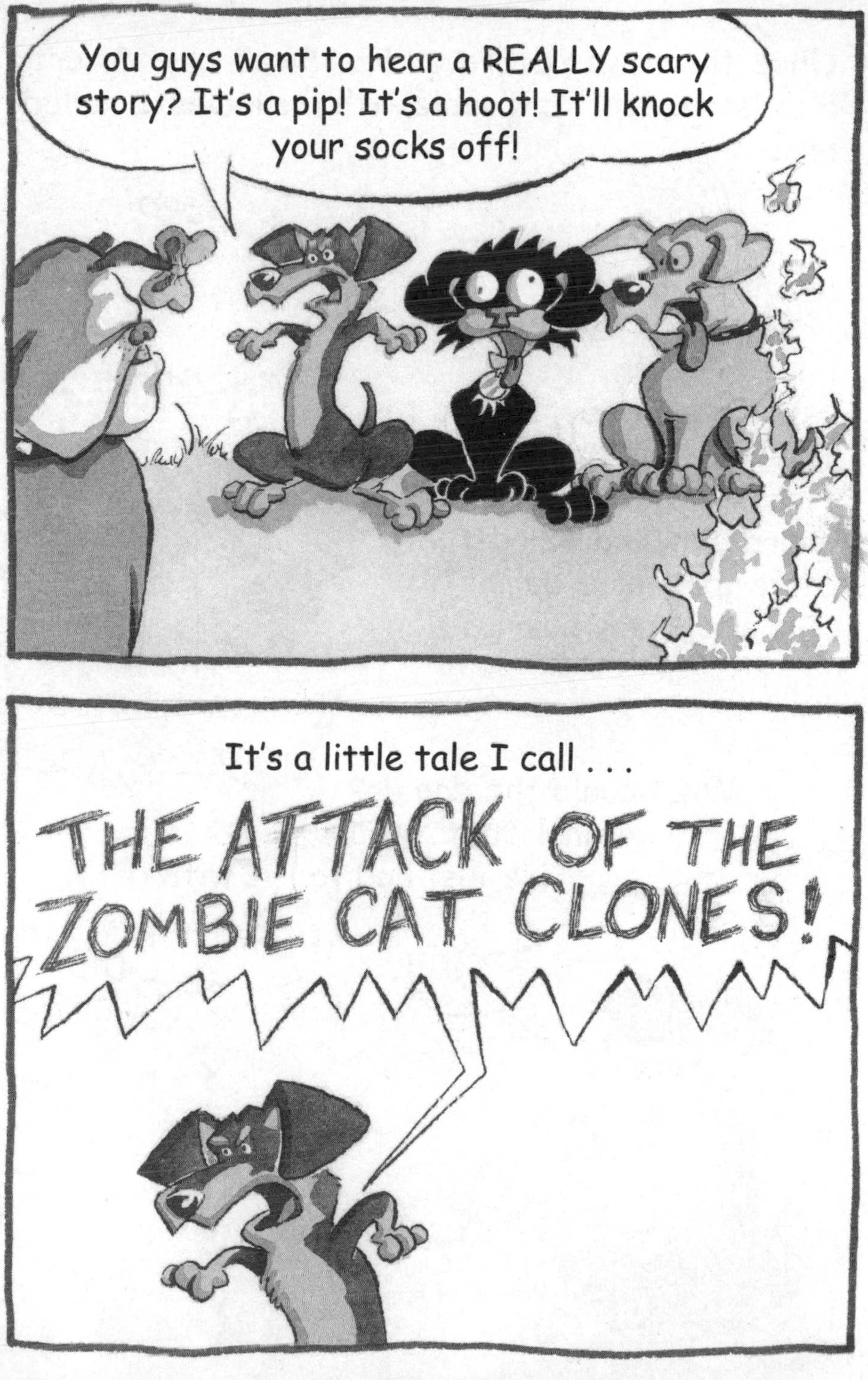
You guys want to hear a REALLY scary story? It's a pip! It's a hoot! It'll knock your socks off!
It's a little tale I call . . .
THE ATTACK OF THE ZOMBIE CAT CLONES!

Once there was a brave dog. Swell guy. Smart. Handsome, too. No trouble with the ladies. Smelled nice.

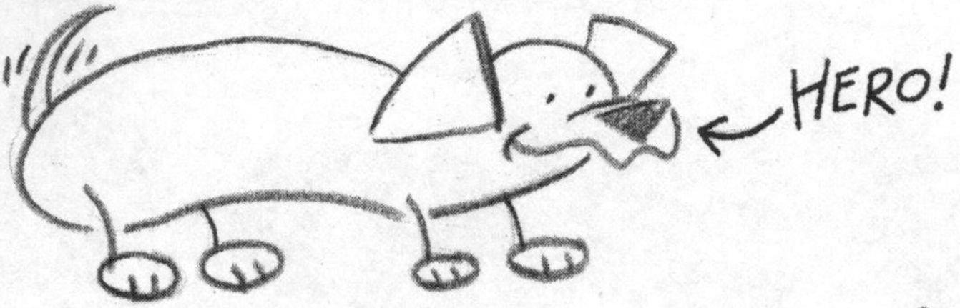
HERO!

But the poor guy, he had to live with this cat. Bad news, right? It was a cat. Looked weird. Smelled weirder. Litter box. Hair balls. The whole ugly business.

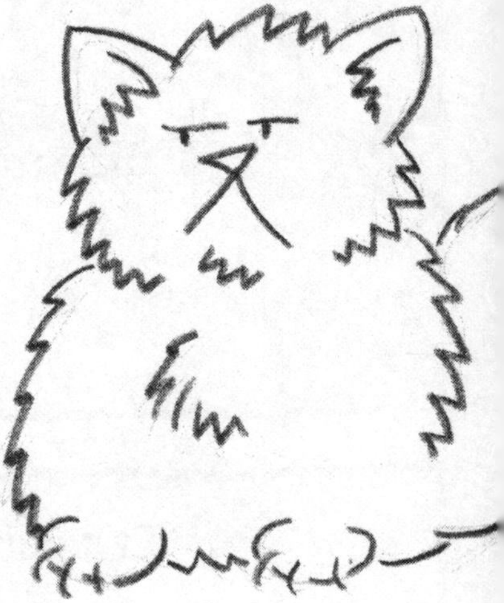

What could the dog do?
Nothing! That's what.
He just had to live with it.

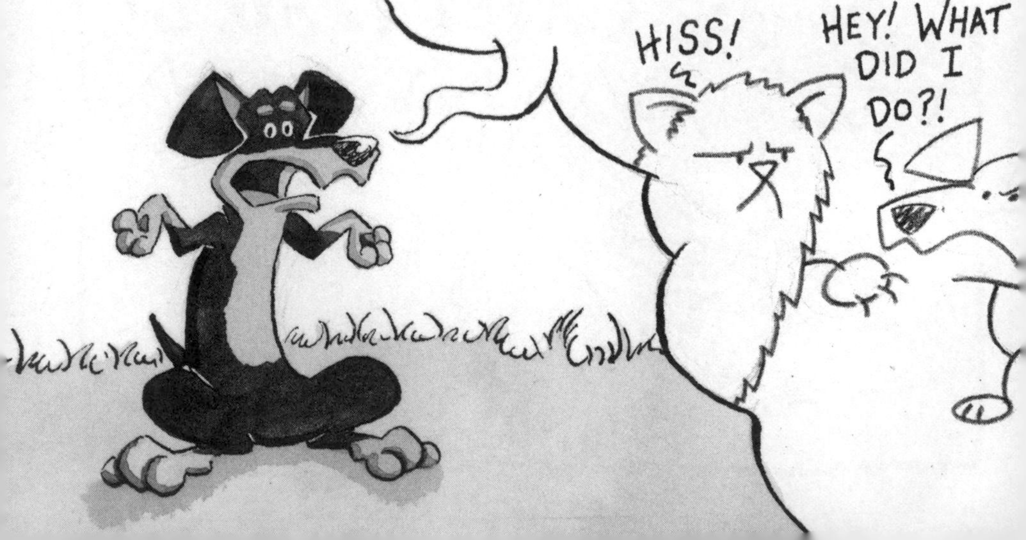
HISS!
HEY! WHAT DID I DO?!

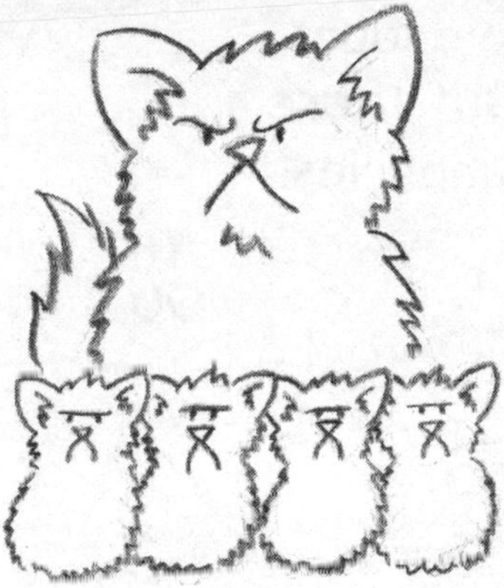

But then, one day—just when the dog thought things couldn't get worse, they got worse. WAY WORSE. One day, it was as if the cat EXPLODED! All of a sudden, there were these teeny, little cats all over the place. Plus, the original.

They were in the food. They were in the water.

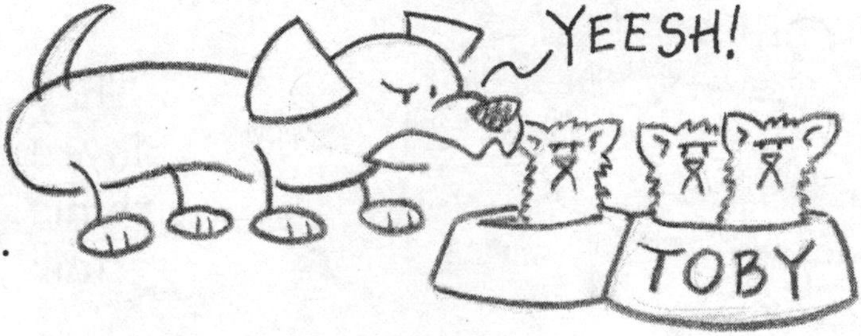
YEESH!
TOBY

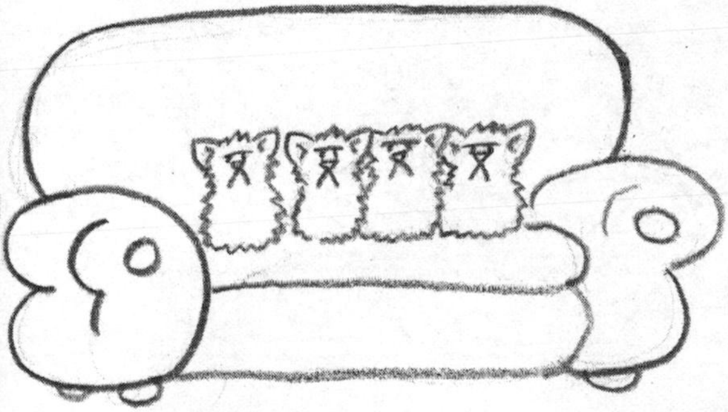

They were on the bed. They were on the couch.

Did I mention the food? They were in the FOOD, for crying out loud!

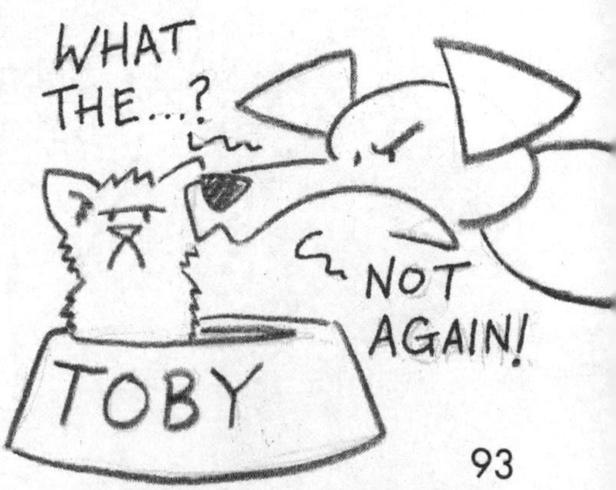
WHAT THE...?
NOT AGAIN!
TOBY

The dog did his absolute best to endure this whole gruesome situation. But these things, they had no sense of boundaries!

They played with his ears!

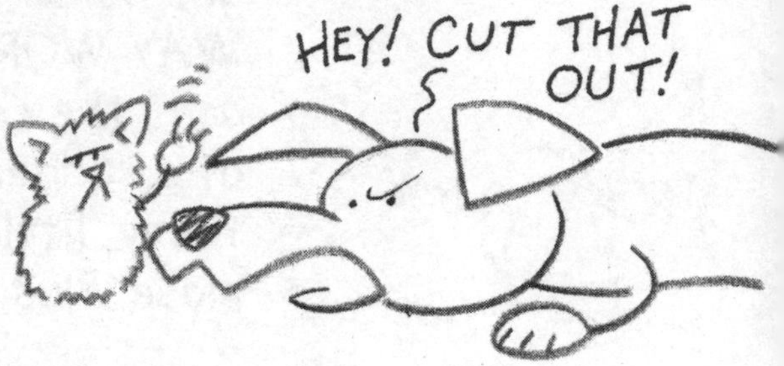
HEY! CUT THAT OUT!

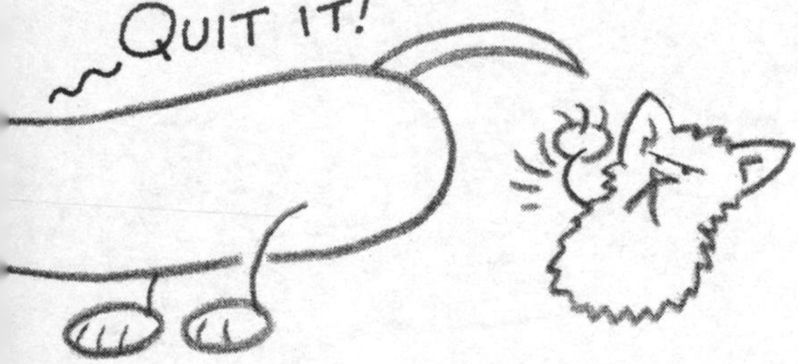
QUIT IT!

They played with his tail!

They tormented him day and night!

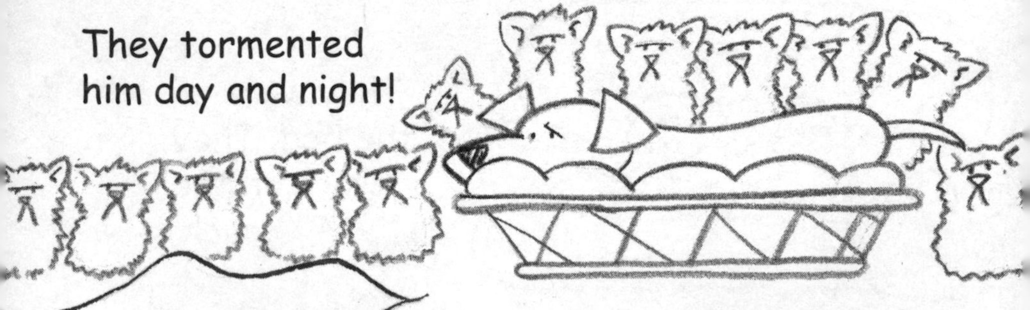

Soon the poor dog had no choice but to go completely . . .

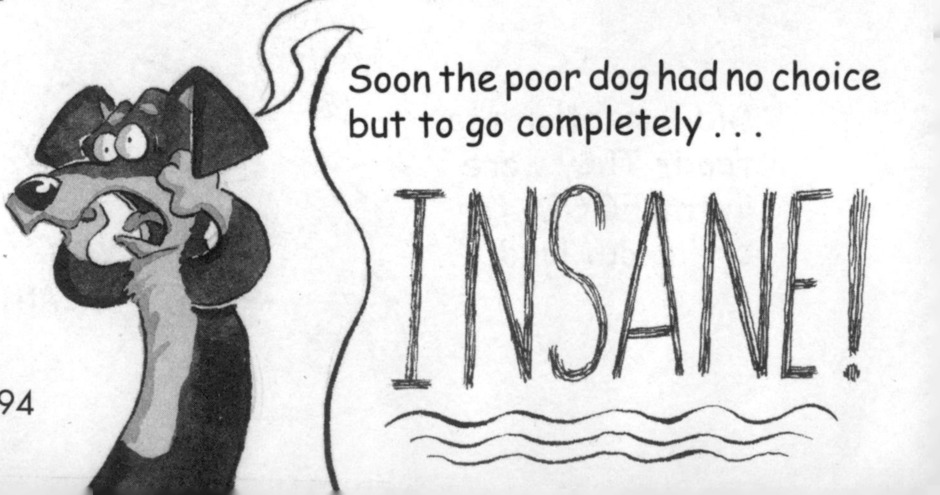
INSANE!

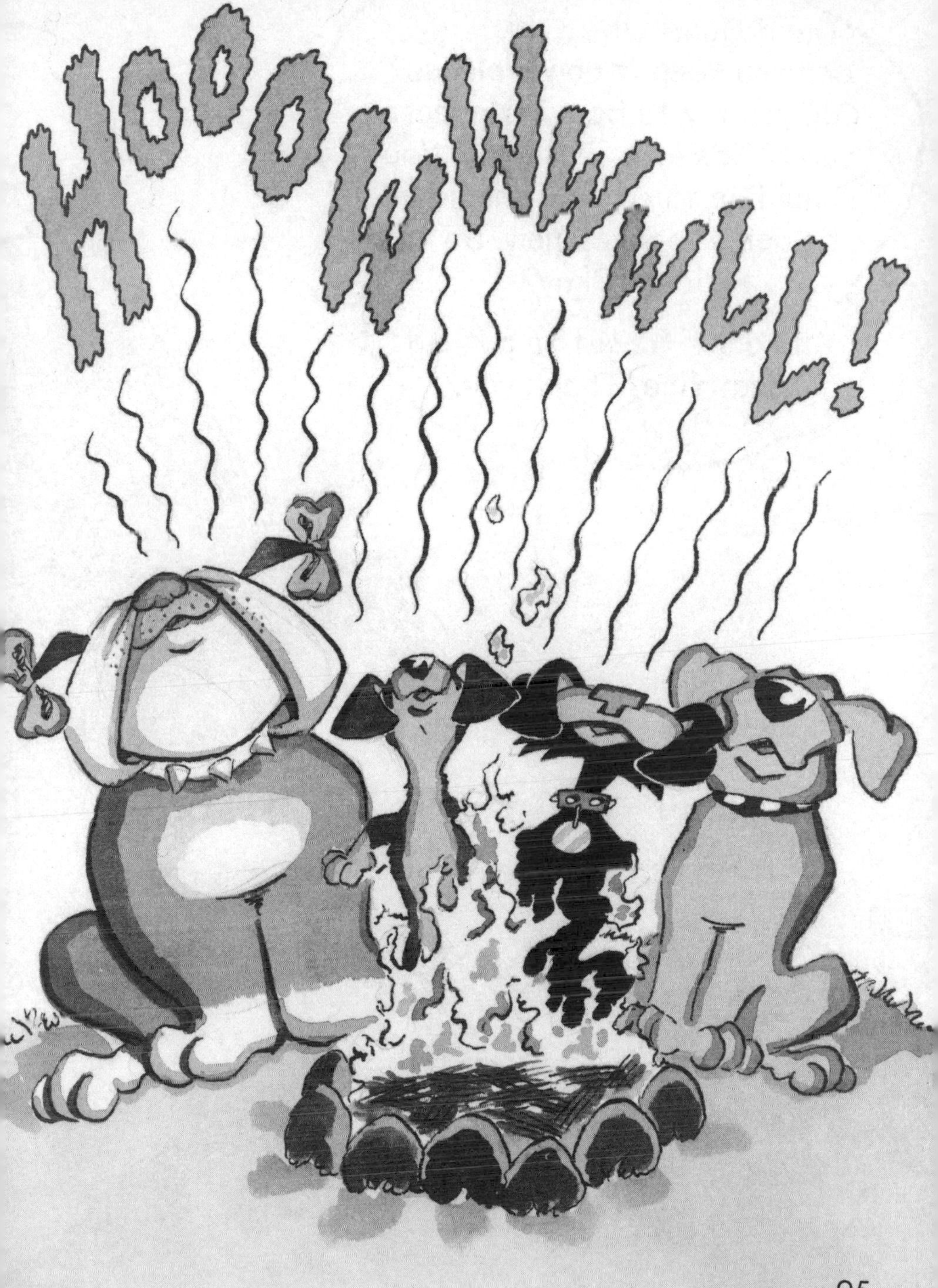
HOOOWWWWLL!

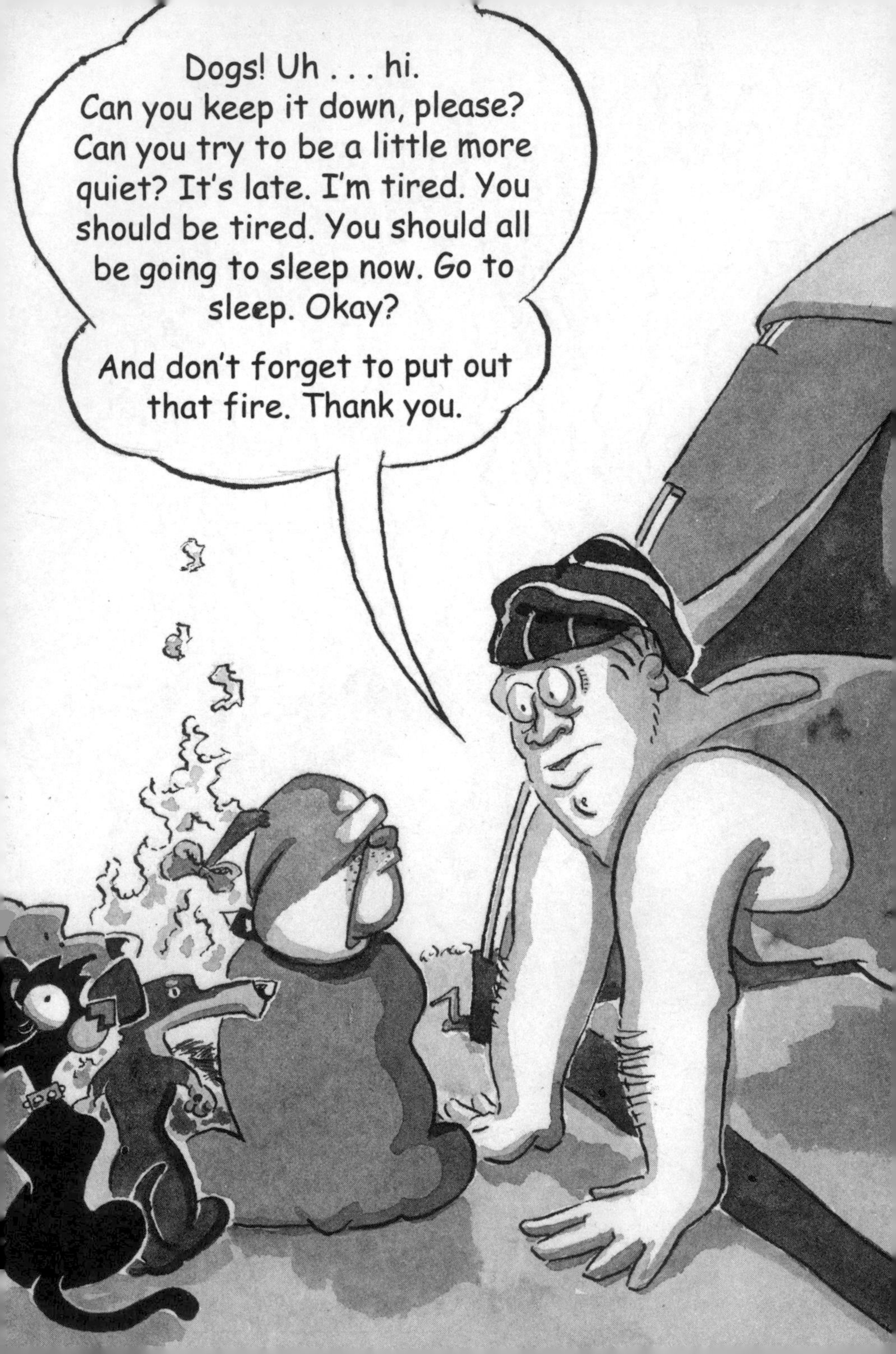
Dogs! Uh . . . hi. Can you keep it down, please? Can you try to be a little more quiet? It's late. I'm tired. You should be tired. You should all be going to sleep now. Go to sleep. Okay?
And don't forget to put out that fire. Thank you.

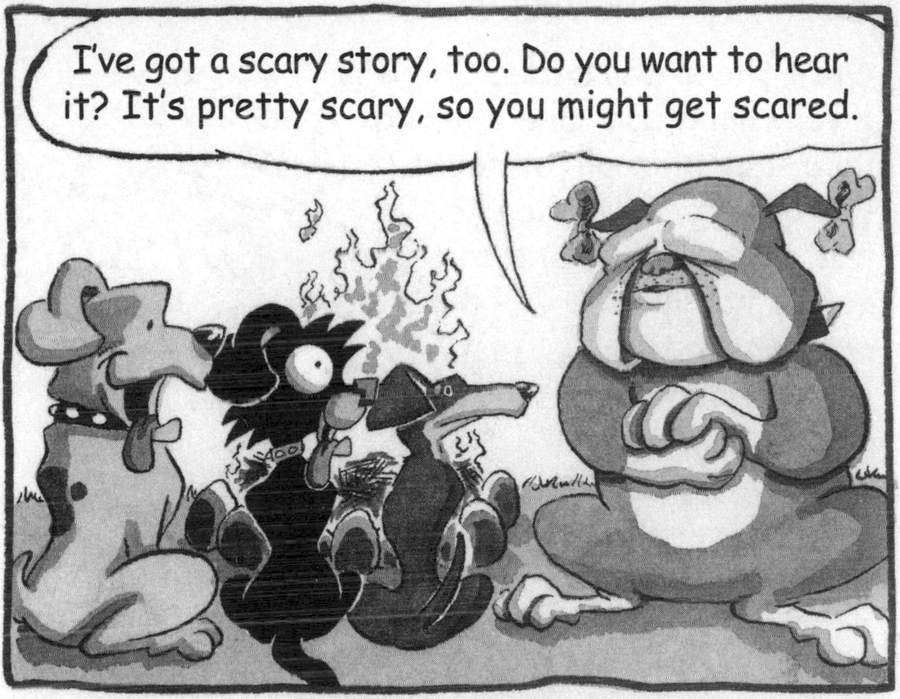
I've got a scary story, too. Do you want to hear it? It's pretty scary, so you might get scared.

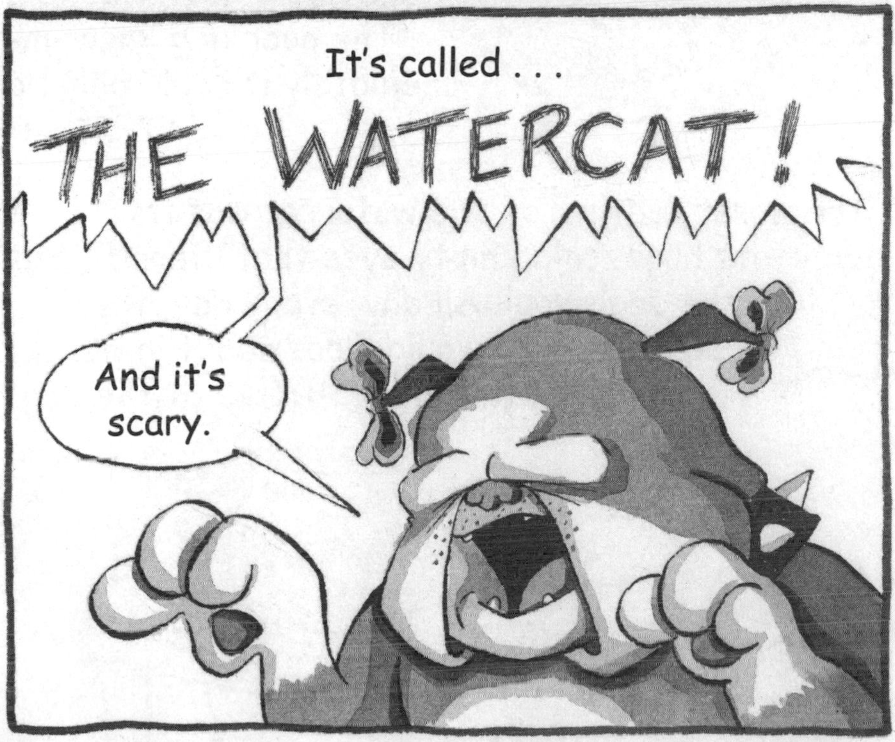
It's called . . .
THE WATERCAT!
And it's scary.

Once there was a dog. She was a very good dog. She chewed up a shoe a couple of times, but only because the shoe was asking for it. She rarely had an accident in the house. She was a good dog.

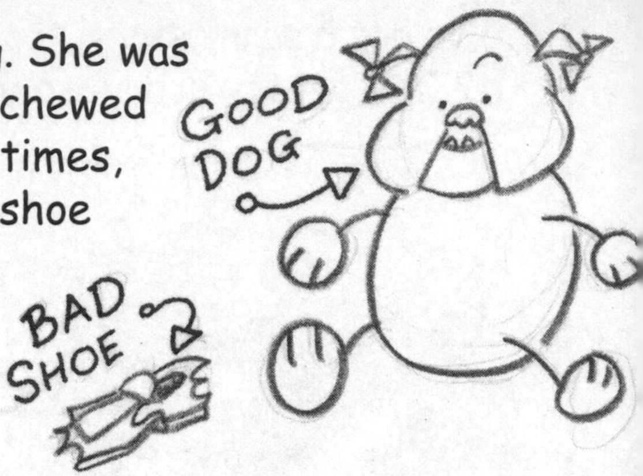
GOOD DOG
BAD SHOE

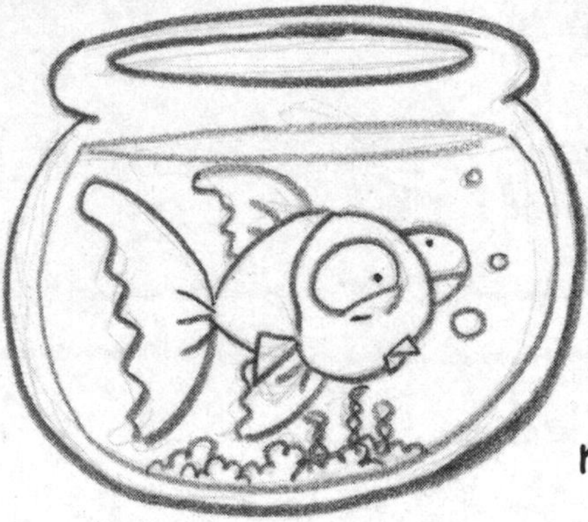

Then, one day, the dog's owner brought a horrible creature into the house. It was orange and scaly and had a huge flat tail. The poor dog knew immediately it could only be a WATERCAT!

The worst feature of the watercat was its eyes—its huge, cold empty eyes that stared deep into the dog's soul! All day, every day, the watercat would float about in its home staring, STARING at the dog.

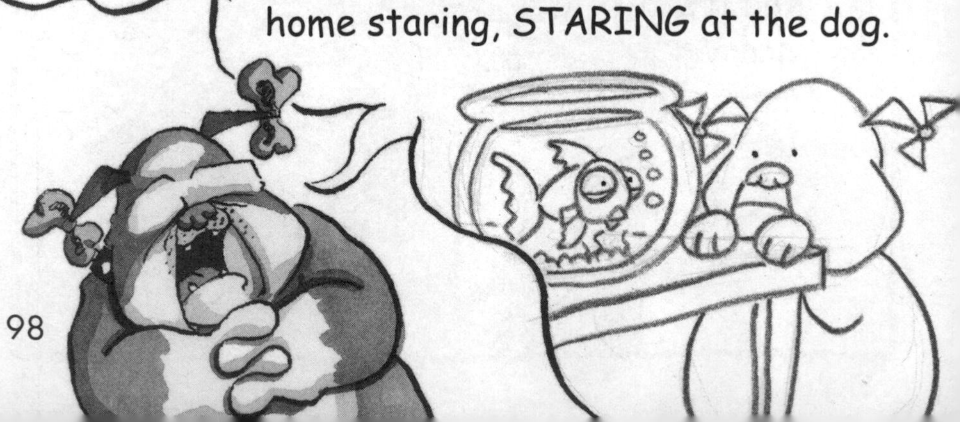

It stared at the dog when she was drinking out of the toilet, (which the dog knew she wasn't supposed to do). It stared at the dog when she sat on the sofa (which the dog knew she wasn't supposed to be on).

It stared at the dog when she was having an argument with the shoe (which the dog knew she wasn't supposed to do).

That's when the dog realized that the watercat was placed there by her owners to watch her every move and report her every crime! It was enough to make the poor dog go completely

INSANE!

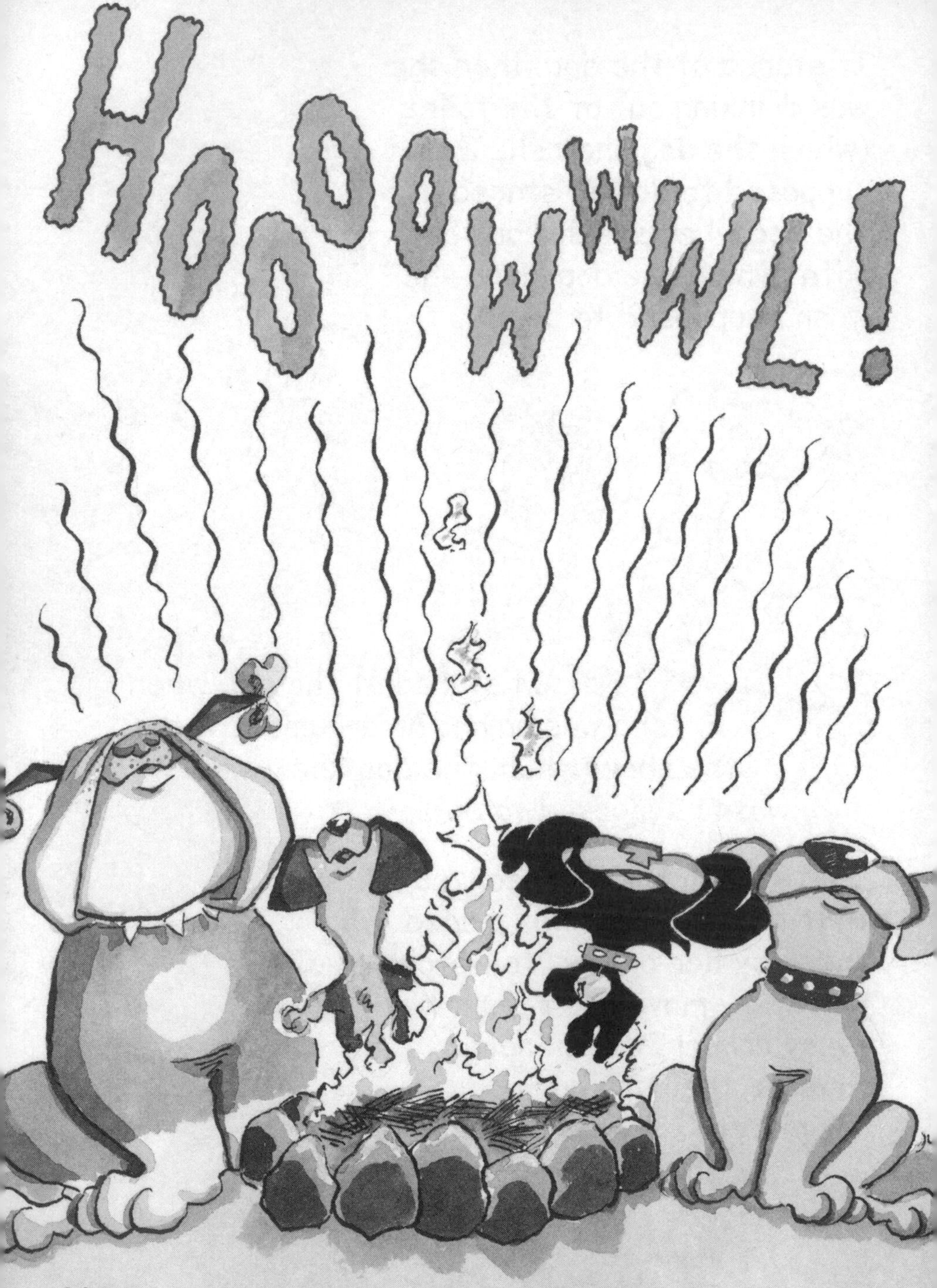
HOOOOWWWL!

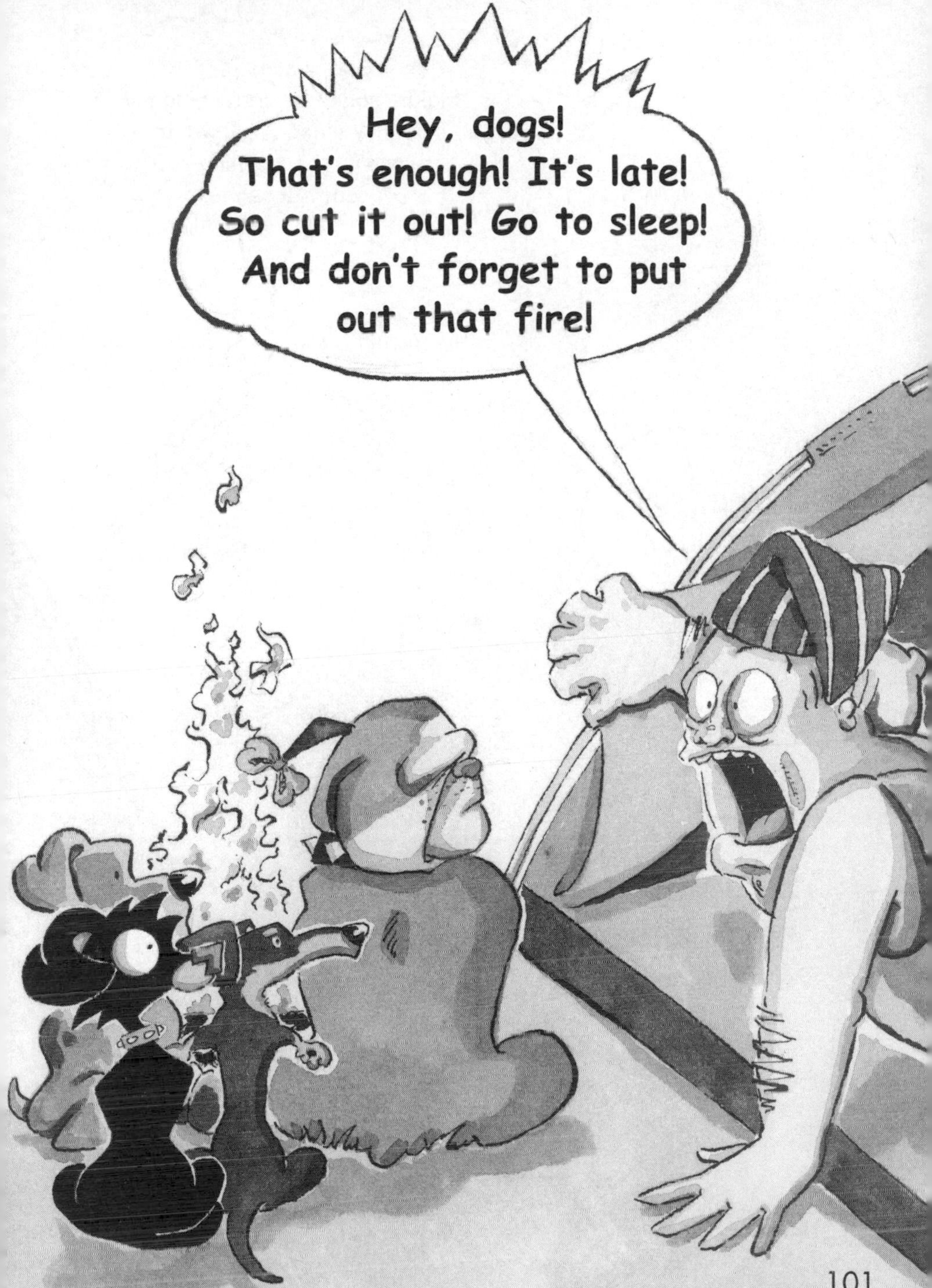
Hey, dogs! That's enough! It's late! So cut it out! Go to sleep! And don't forget to put out that fire!

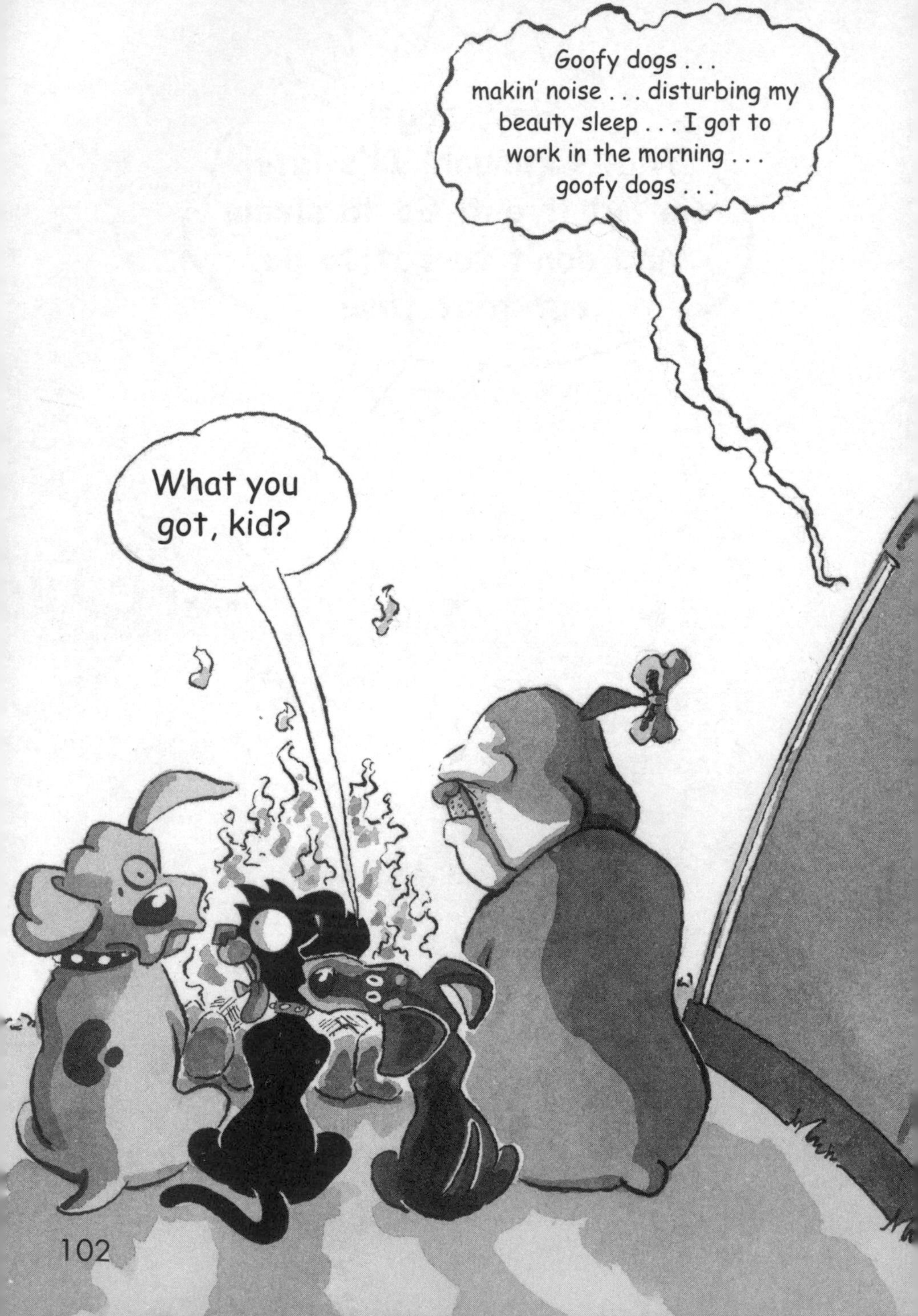
Goofy dogs . . .
makin' noise . . . disturbing my
beauty sleep . . . I got to
work in the morning . . .
goofy dogs . . .
What you
got, kid?

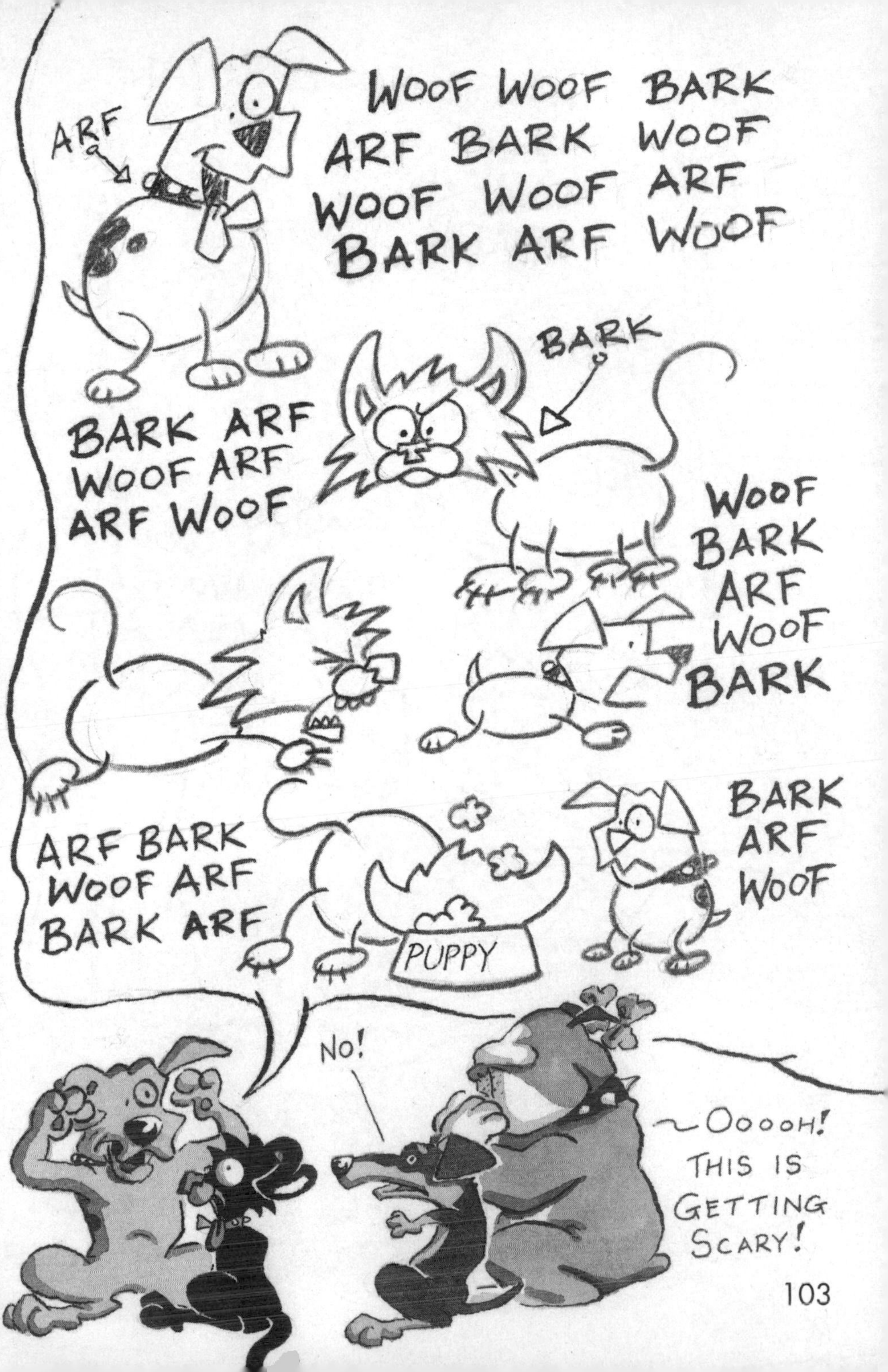
ARF
WOOF WOOF BARK
ARF BARK WOOF
WOOF WOOF ARF
BARK ARF WOOF
BARK
BARK ARF
WOOF ARF
ARF WOOF
WOOF
BARK
ARF
WOOF
BARK
ARF BARK
WOOF ARF
BARK ARF
PUPPY
BARK
ARF
WOOF
NO!
~OOOOH! THIS IS GETTING SCARY!

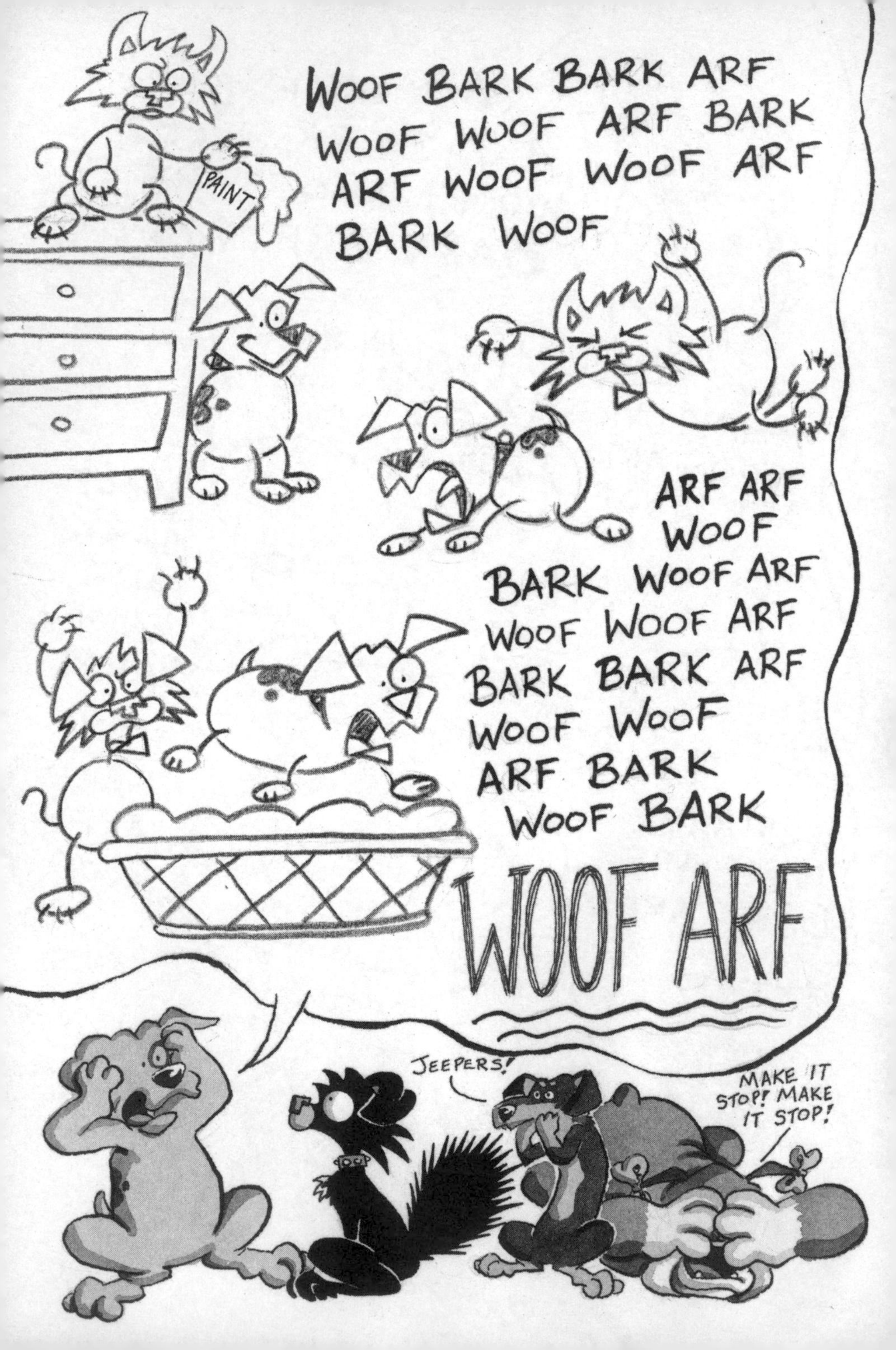
WOOF BARK BARK ARF
WOOF WOOF ARF BARK
ARF WOOF WOOF ARF
BARK WOOF
PAINT
ARF ARF
WOOF
BARK WOOF ARF
WOOF WOOF ARF
BARK BARK ARF
WOOF WOOF
ARF BARK
WOOF BARK
WOOF ARF
JEEPERS!
MAKE IT STOP! MAKE IT STOP!

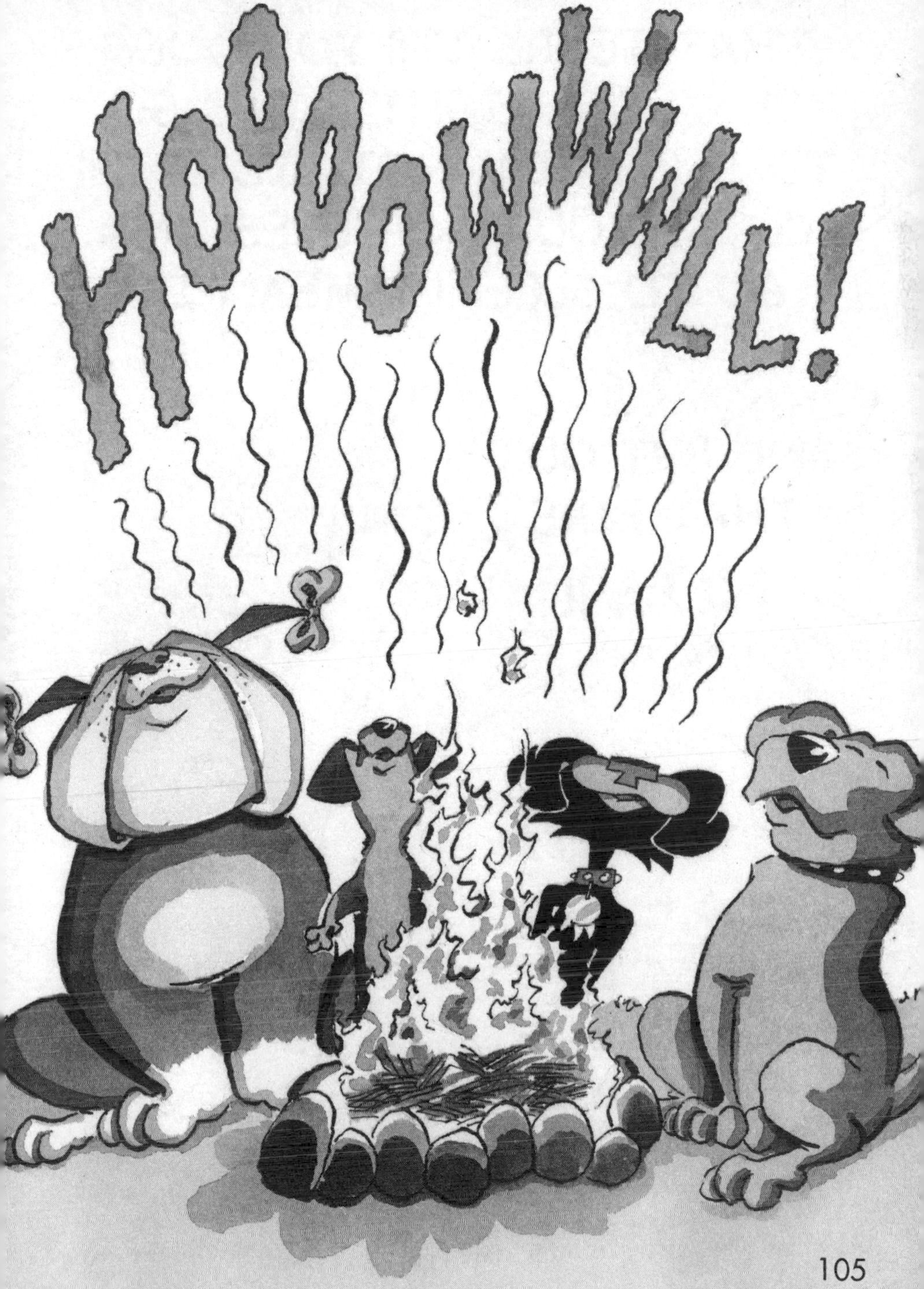
HOOOOWWWLL!

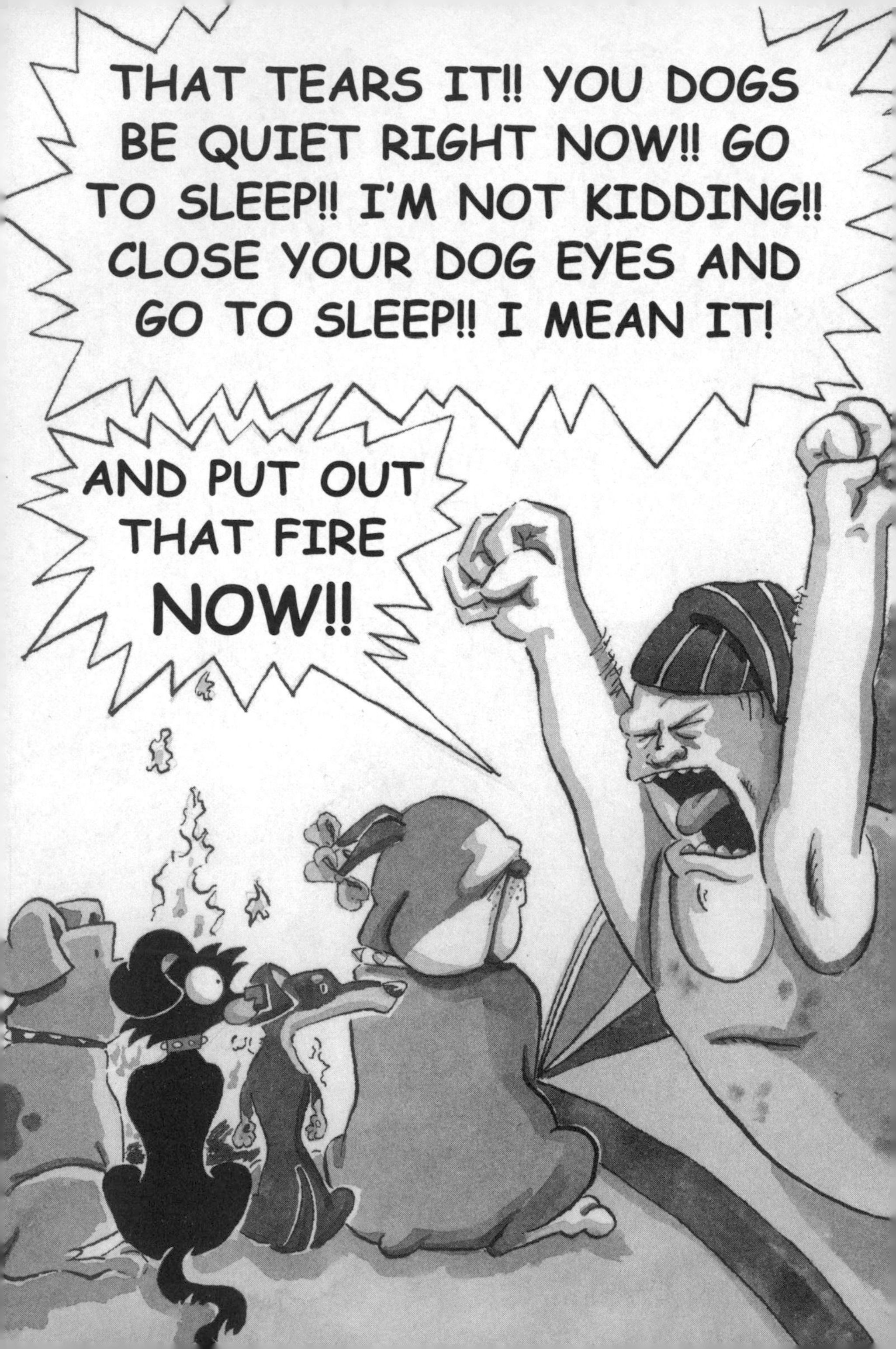
THAT TEARS IT!! YOU DOGS BE QUIET RIGHT NOW!! GO TO SLEEP!! I'M NOT KIDDING!! CLOSE YOUR DOG EYES AND GO TO SLEEP!! I MEAN IT!
AND PUT OUT THAT FIRE NOW!!

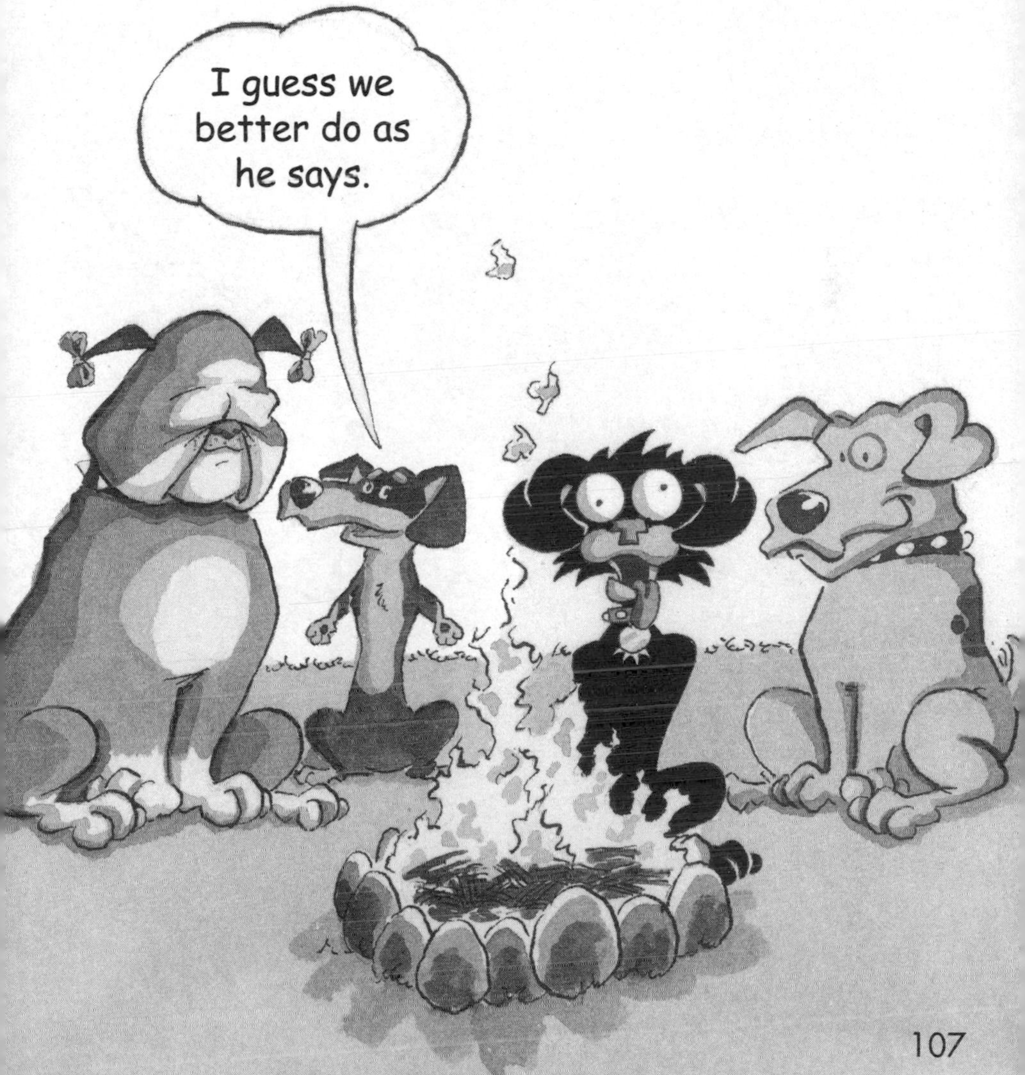
I guess we better do as he says.

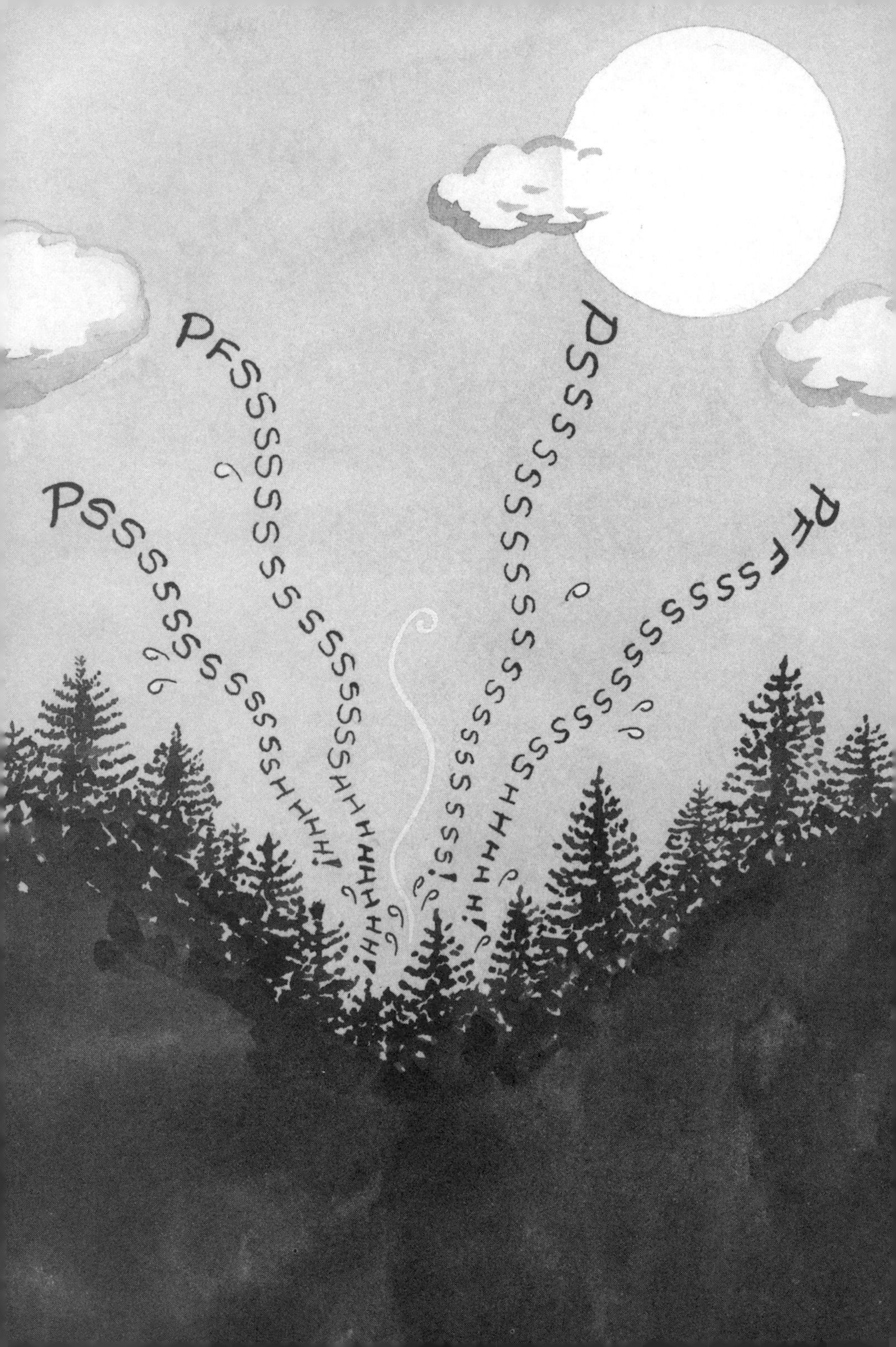
PSSSSSSSSSSSSSSHHHH!
PFSSSSSSSSSSSSSSSSSHHHHHHH!
PSSSSSSSSSSSSSSSS!
PFSSSSSSSSSSSSSSHHHH!

•CHAPTER SEVEN•

NATURE HIKE

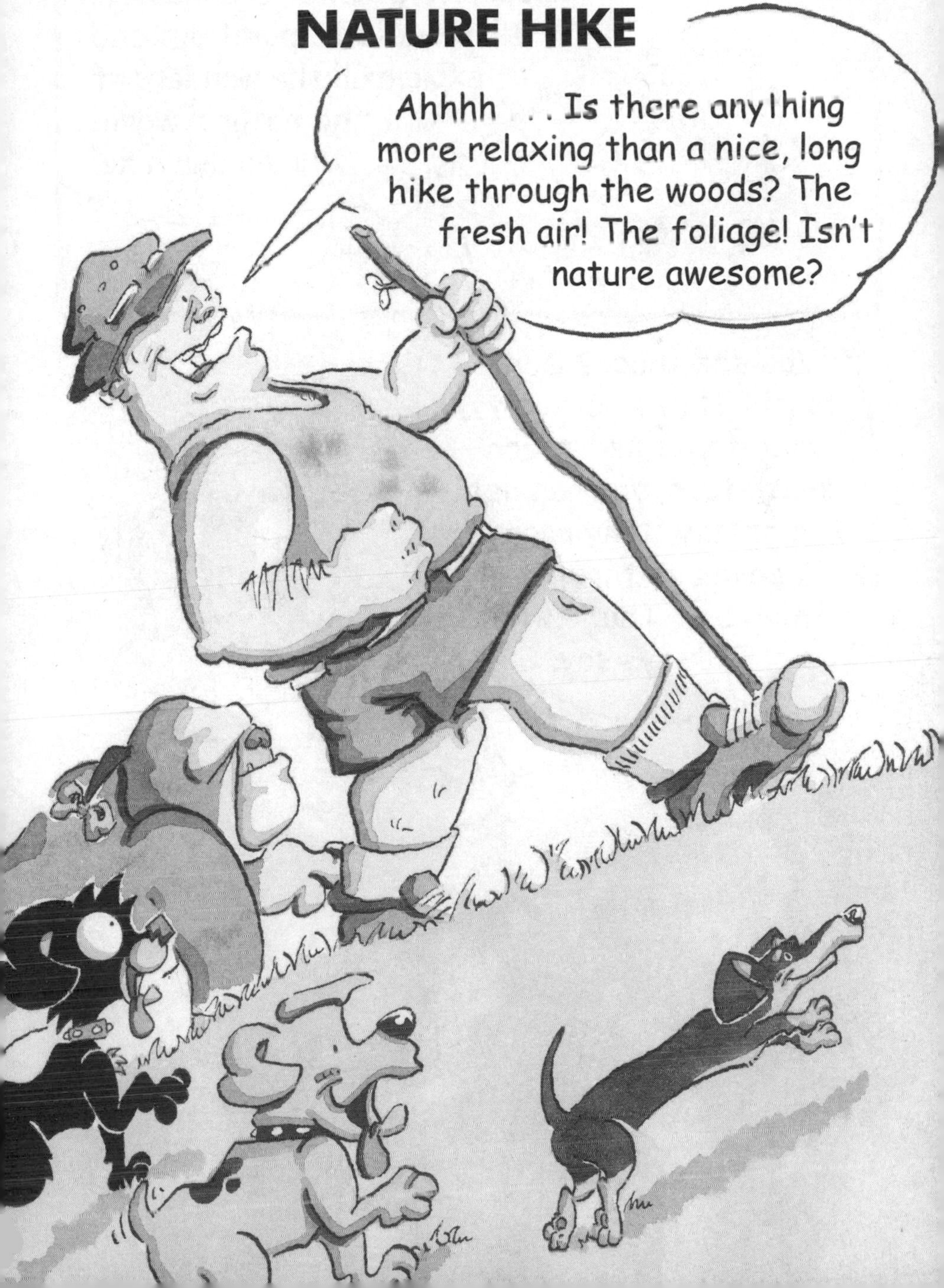
Ahhhh . . . Is there anything more relaxing than a nice, long hike through the woods? The fresh air! The foliage! Isn't nature awesome?

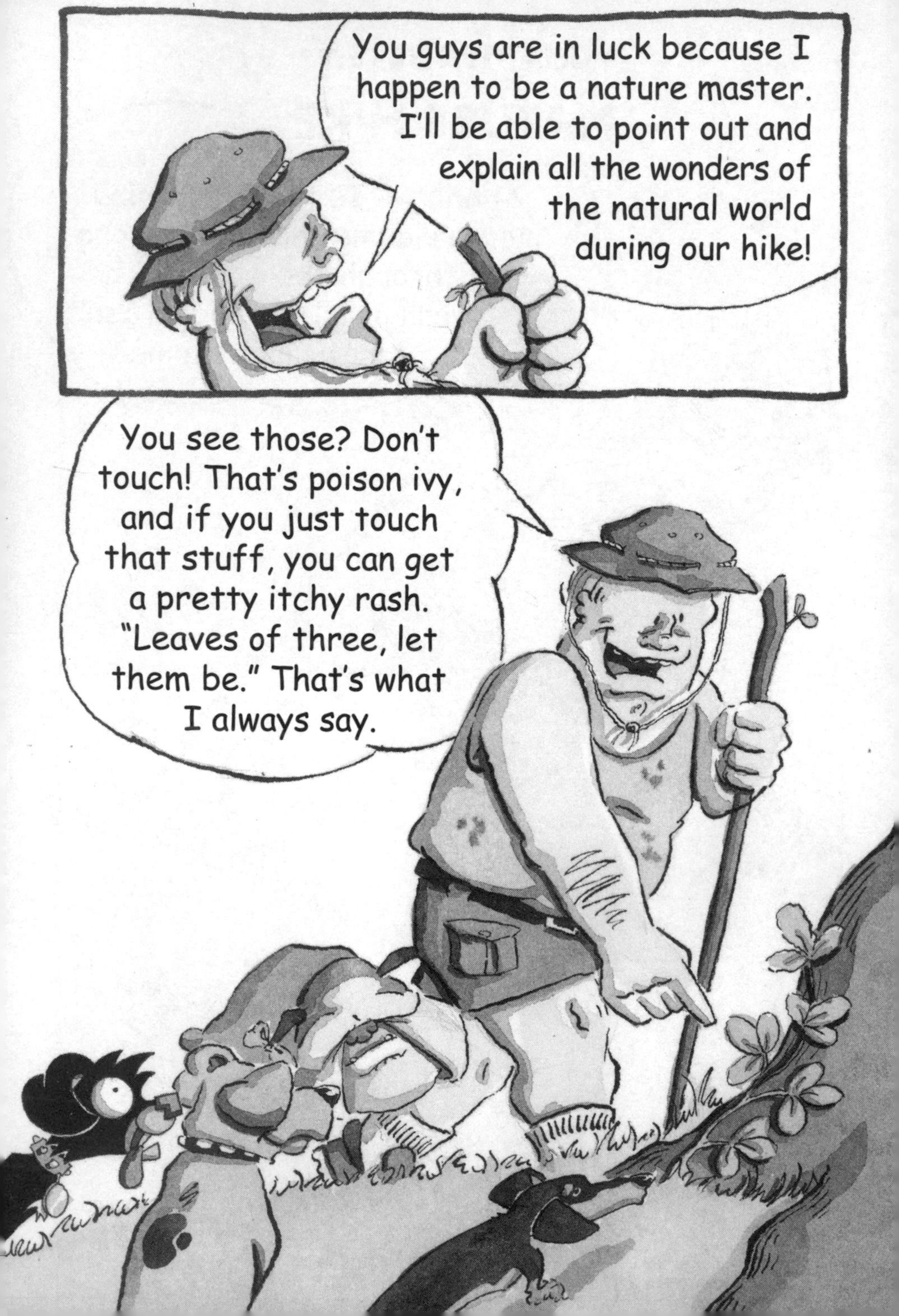

You guys are in luck because I happen to be a nature master. I'll be able to point out and explain all the wonders of the natural world during our hike!
You see those? Don't touch! That's poison ivy, and if you just touch that stuff, you can get a pretty itchy rash. "Leaves of three, let them be." That's what I always say.

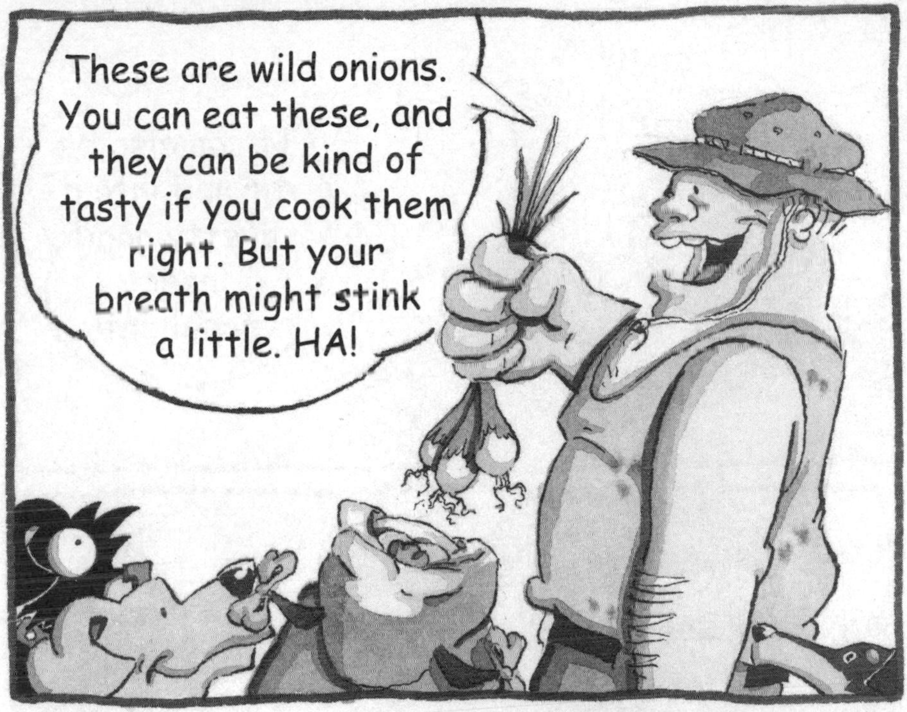
These are wild onions. You can eat these, and they can be kind of tasty if you cook them right. But your breath might stink a little. HA!

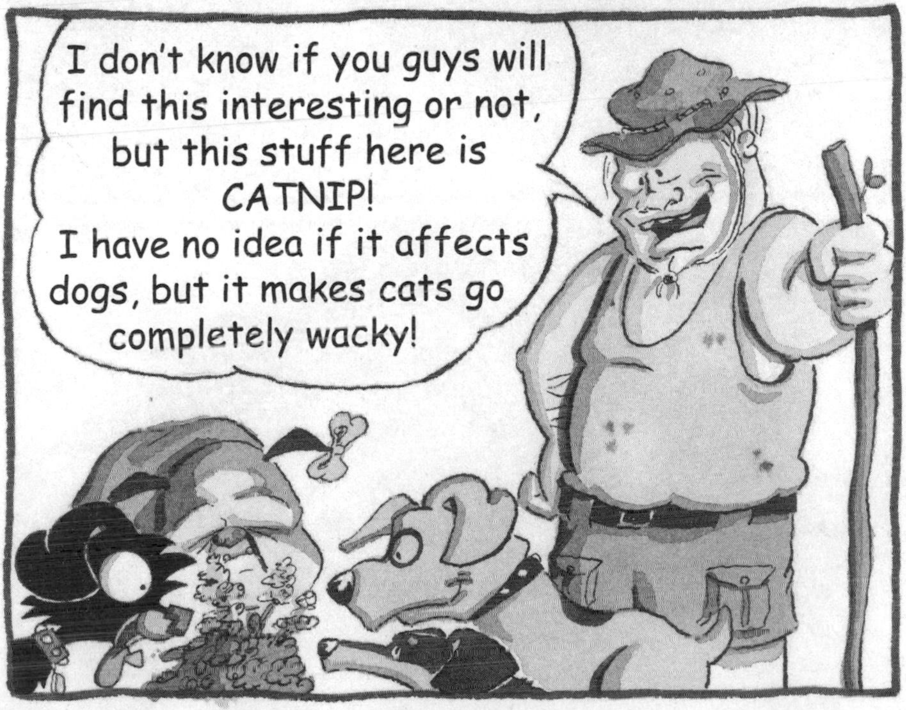
I don't know if you guys will find this interesting or not, but this stuff here is CATNIP!
I have no idea if it affects dogs, but it makes cats go completely wacky!

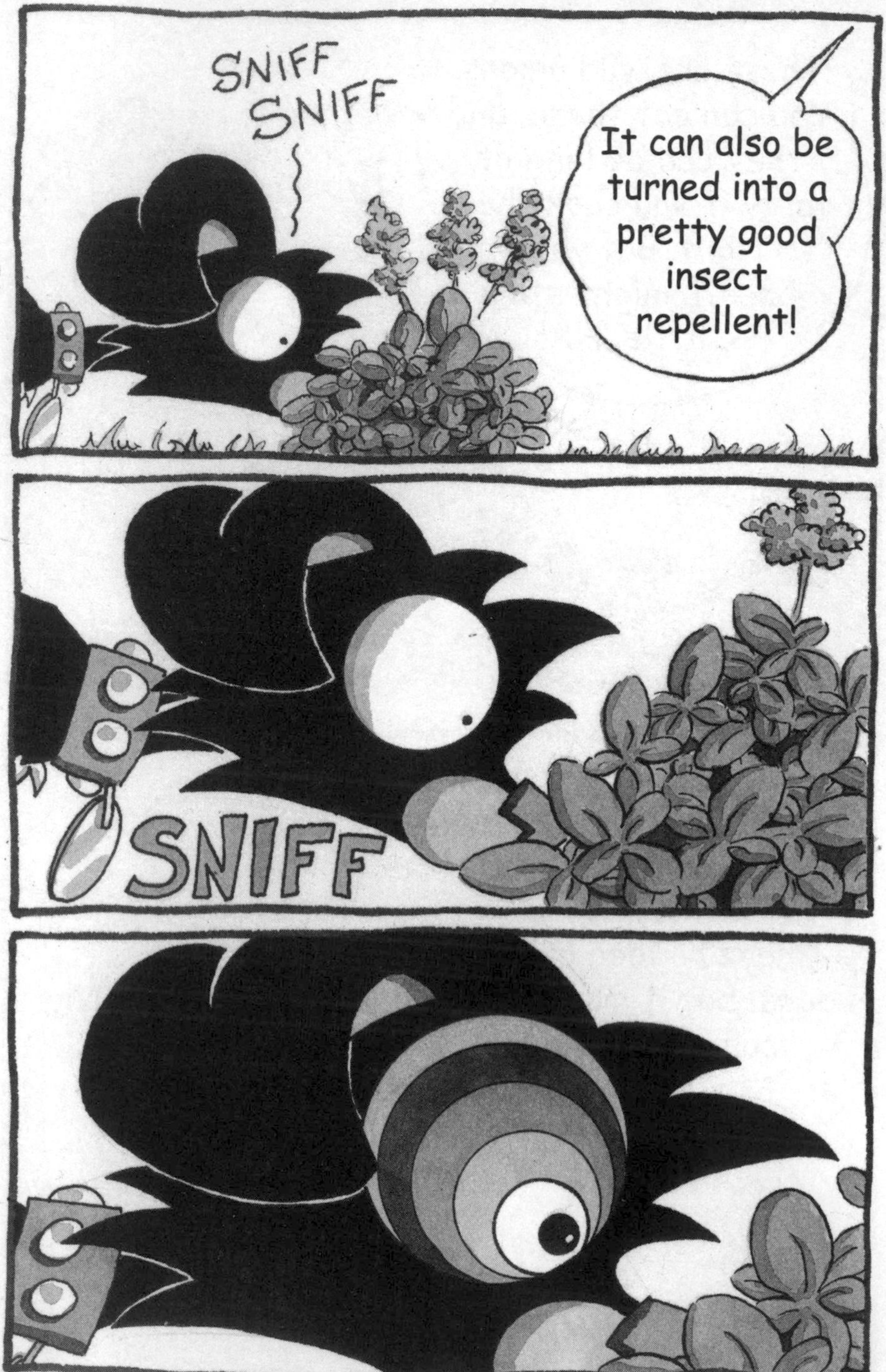
SNIFF
SNIFF
It can also be turned into a pretty good insect repellent!
SNIFF

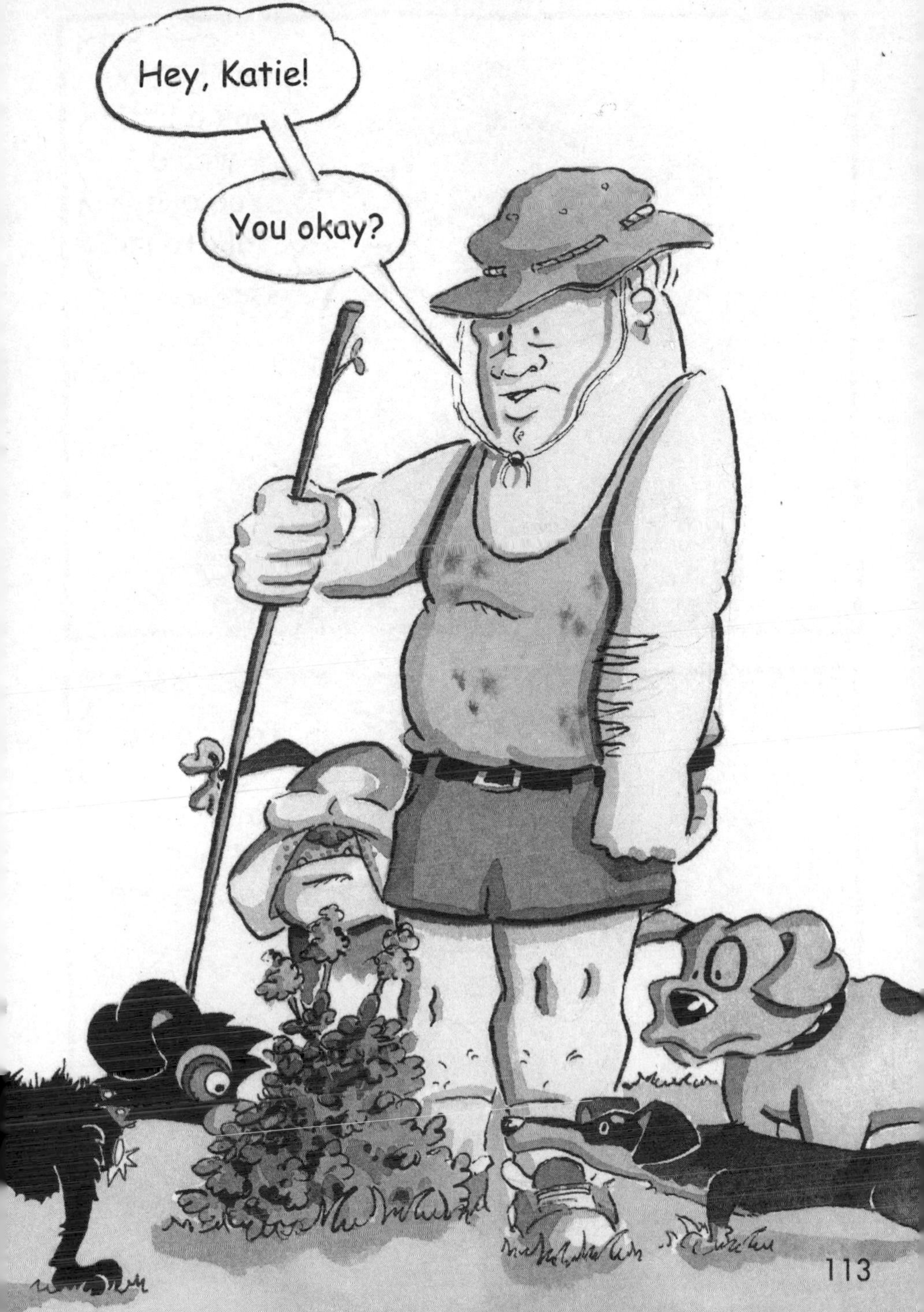
Hey, Katie!
You okay?

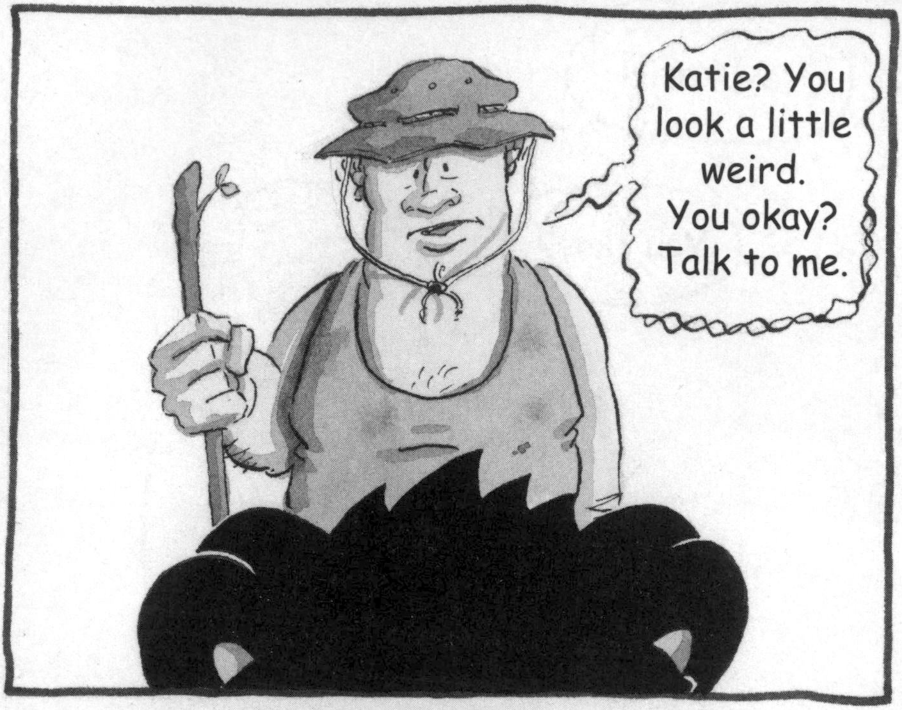
Katie? You look a little weird. You okay? Talk to me.

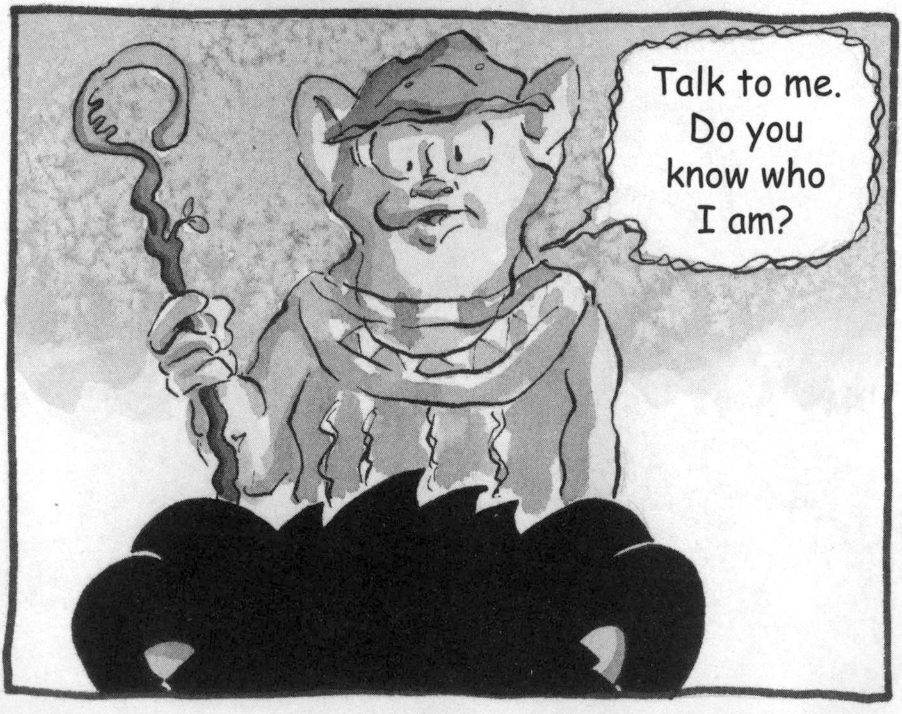
Talk to me. Do you know who I am?

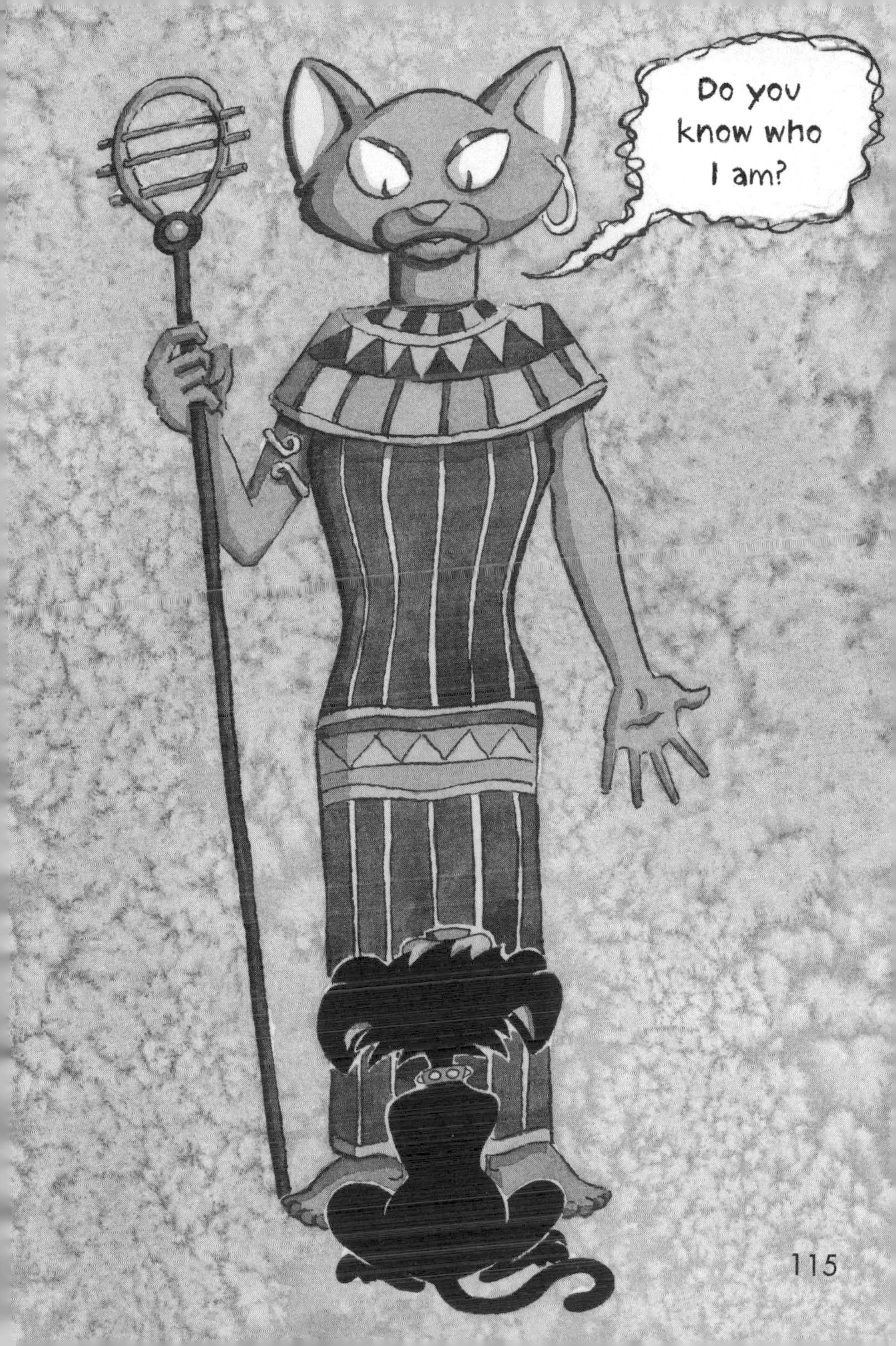
Do you know who I am?

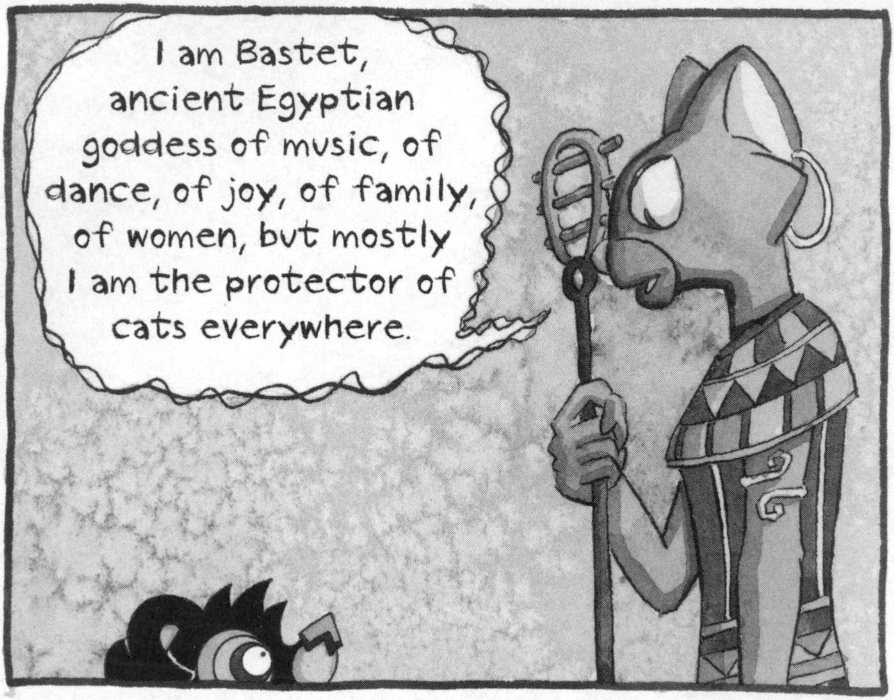
I am Bastet, ancient Egyptian goddess of music, of dance, of joy, of family, of women, but mostly I am the protector of cats everywhere.

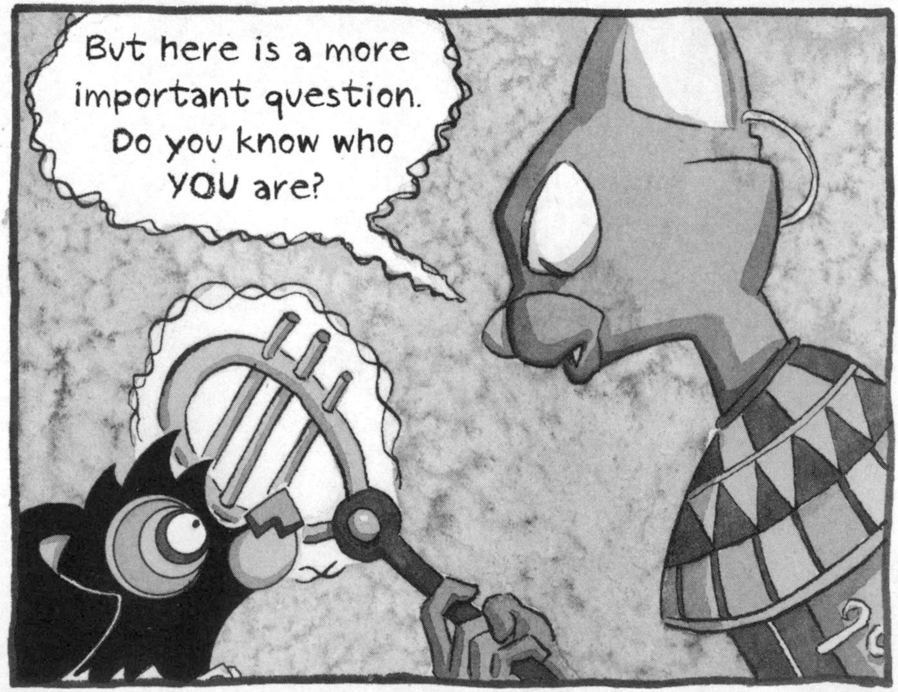
But here is a more important question. Do you know who YOU are?

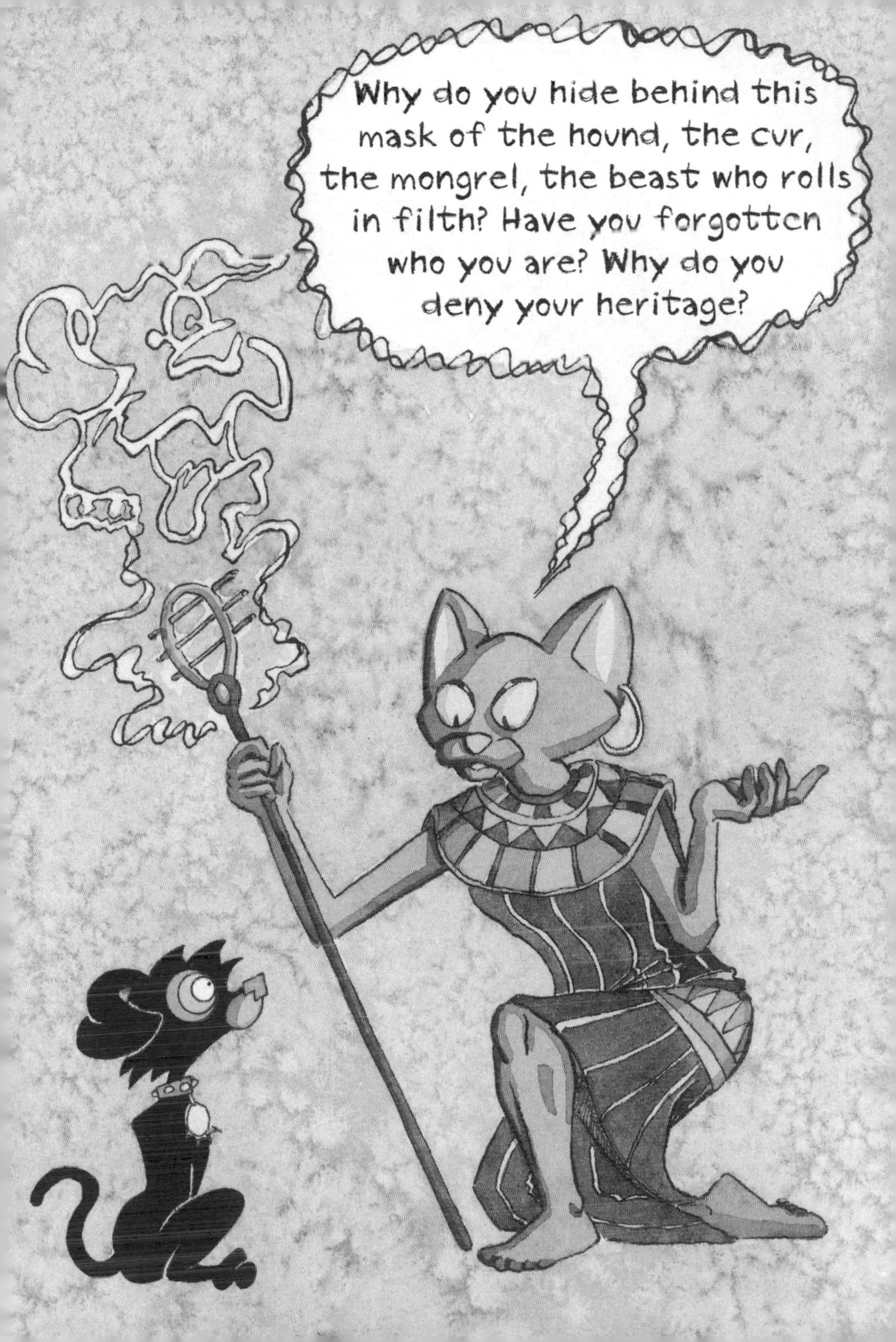
Why do you hide behind this mask of the hound, the cur, the mongrel, the beast who rolls in filth? Have you forgotten who you are? Why do you deny your heritage?

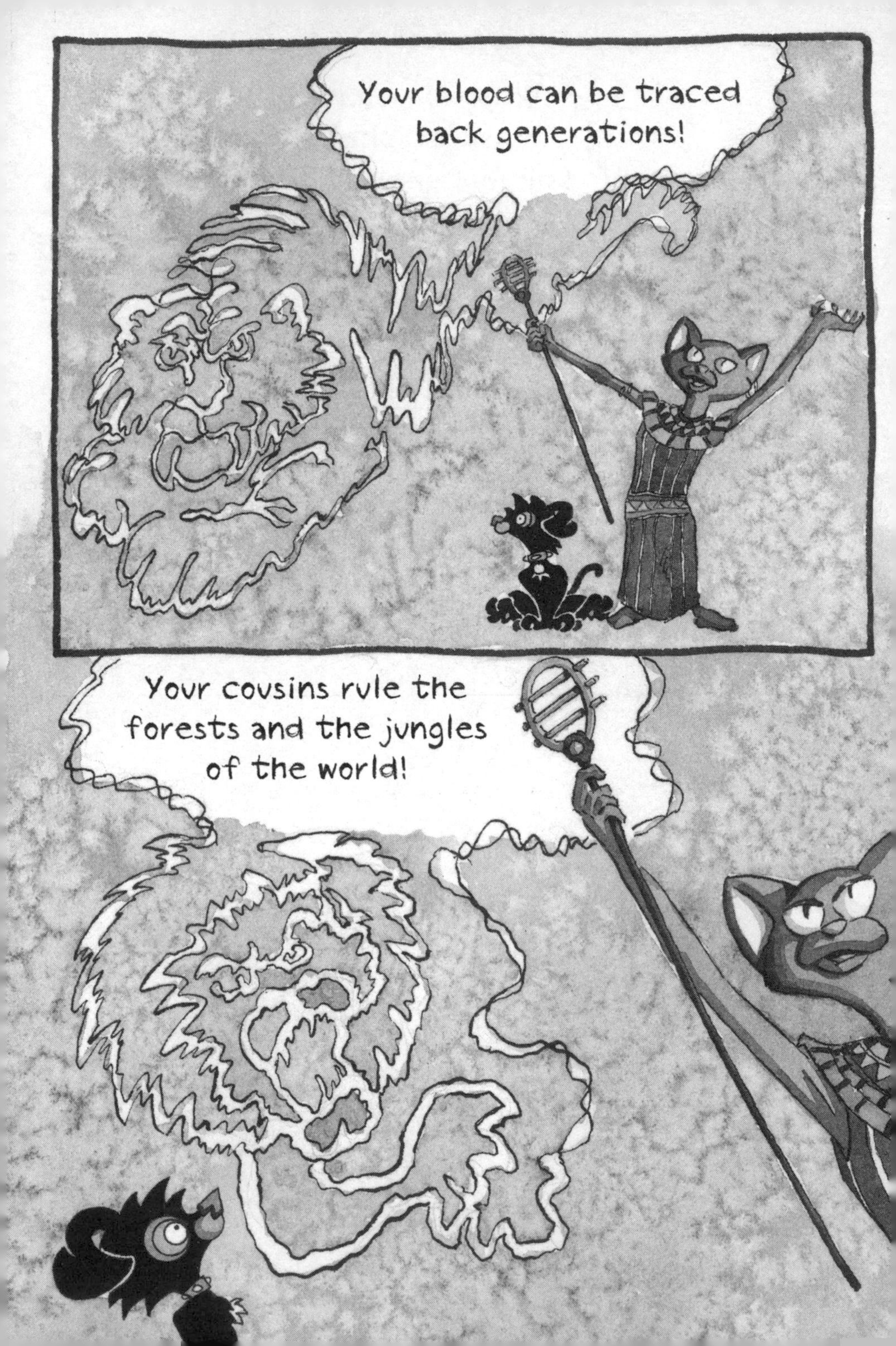
Your blood can be traced back generations!
Your cousins rule the forests and the jungles of the world!

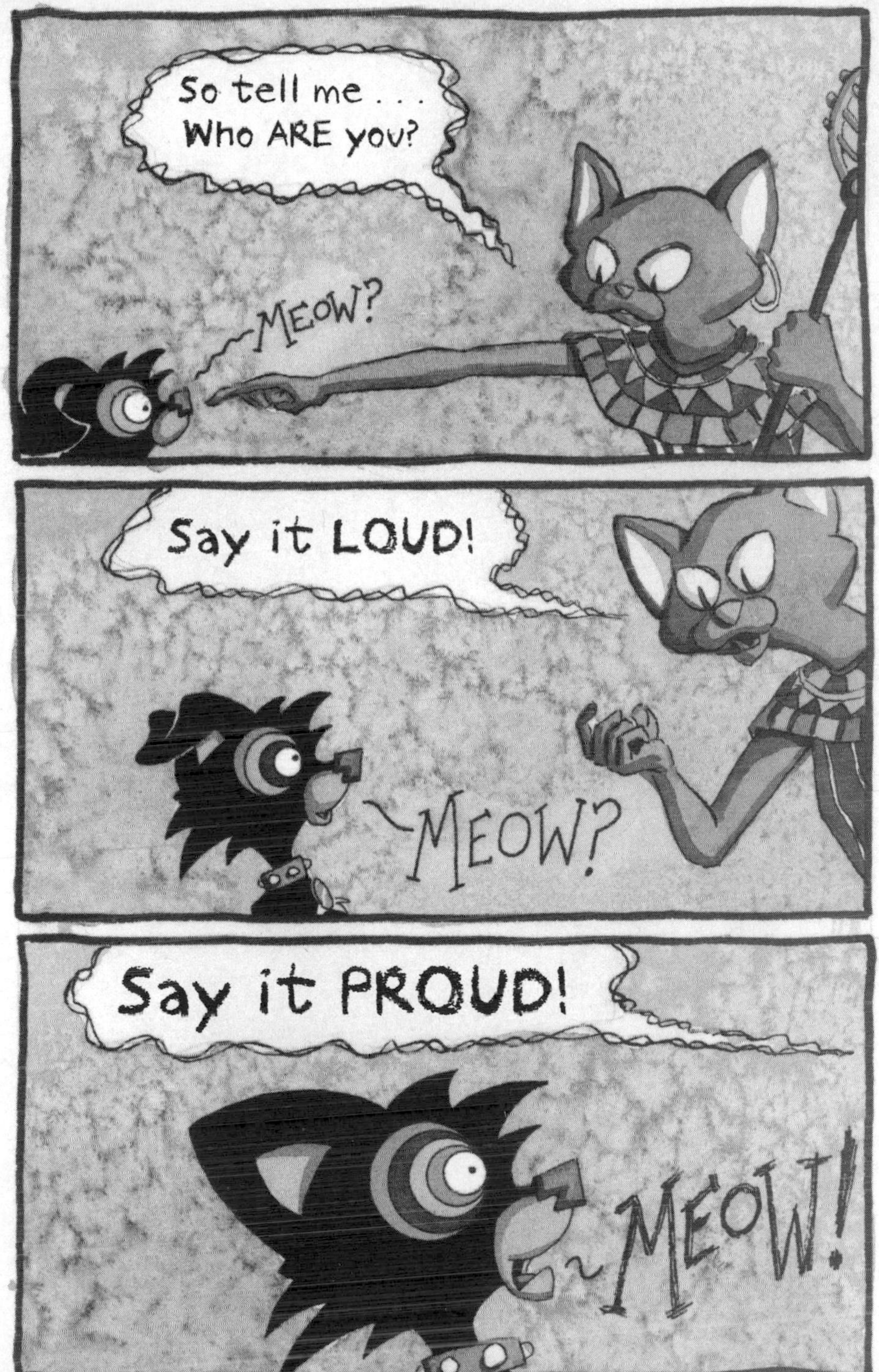
So tell me . . .
Who ARE you?
MEOW?
Say it LOUD!
MEOW?
Say it PROUD!
MEOW!

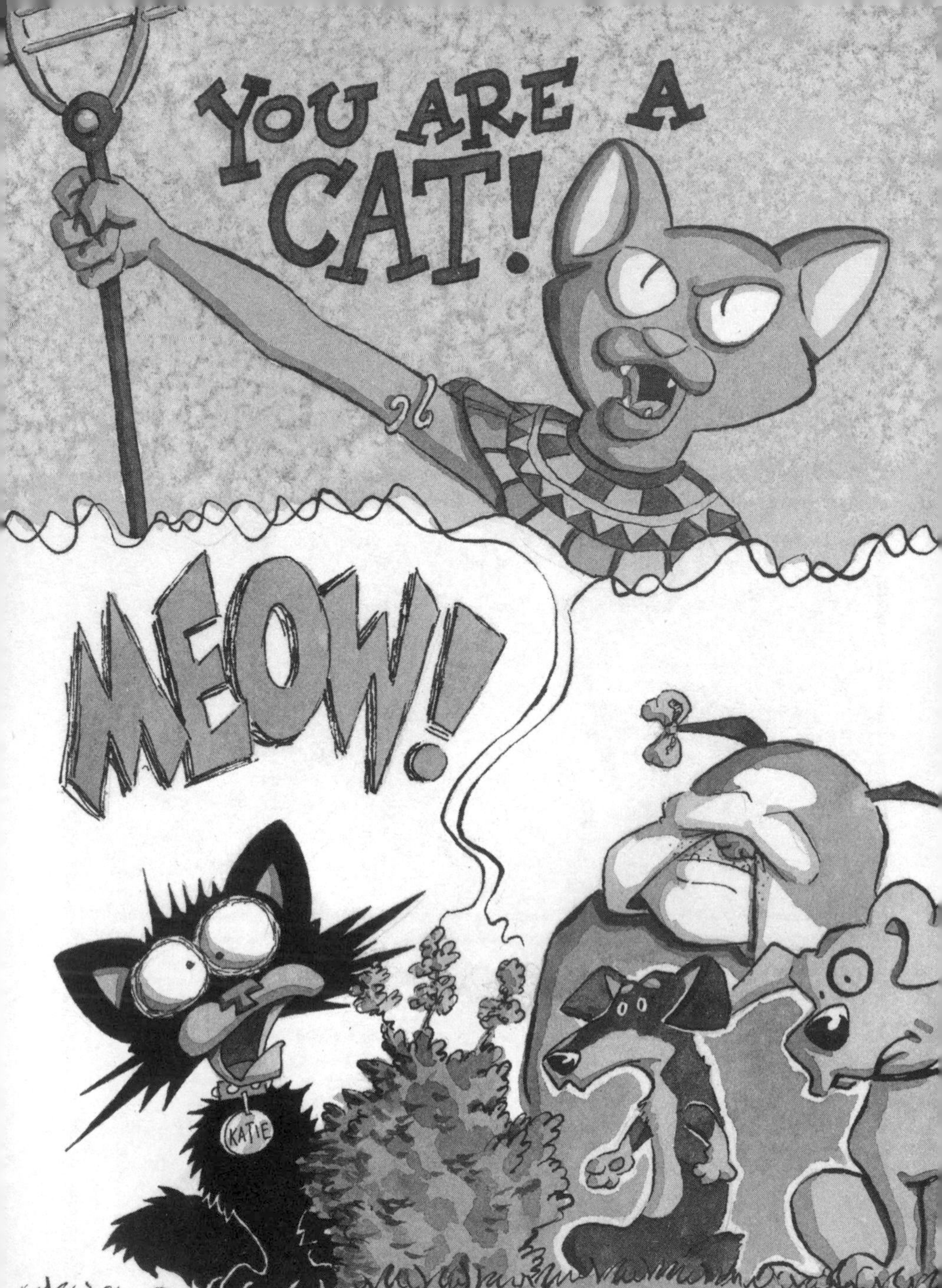
YOU ARE A CAT!
MEOW!
KATIE

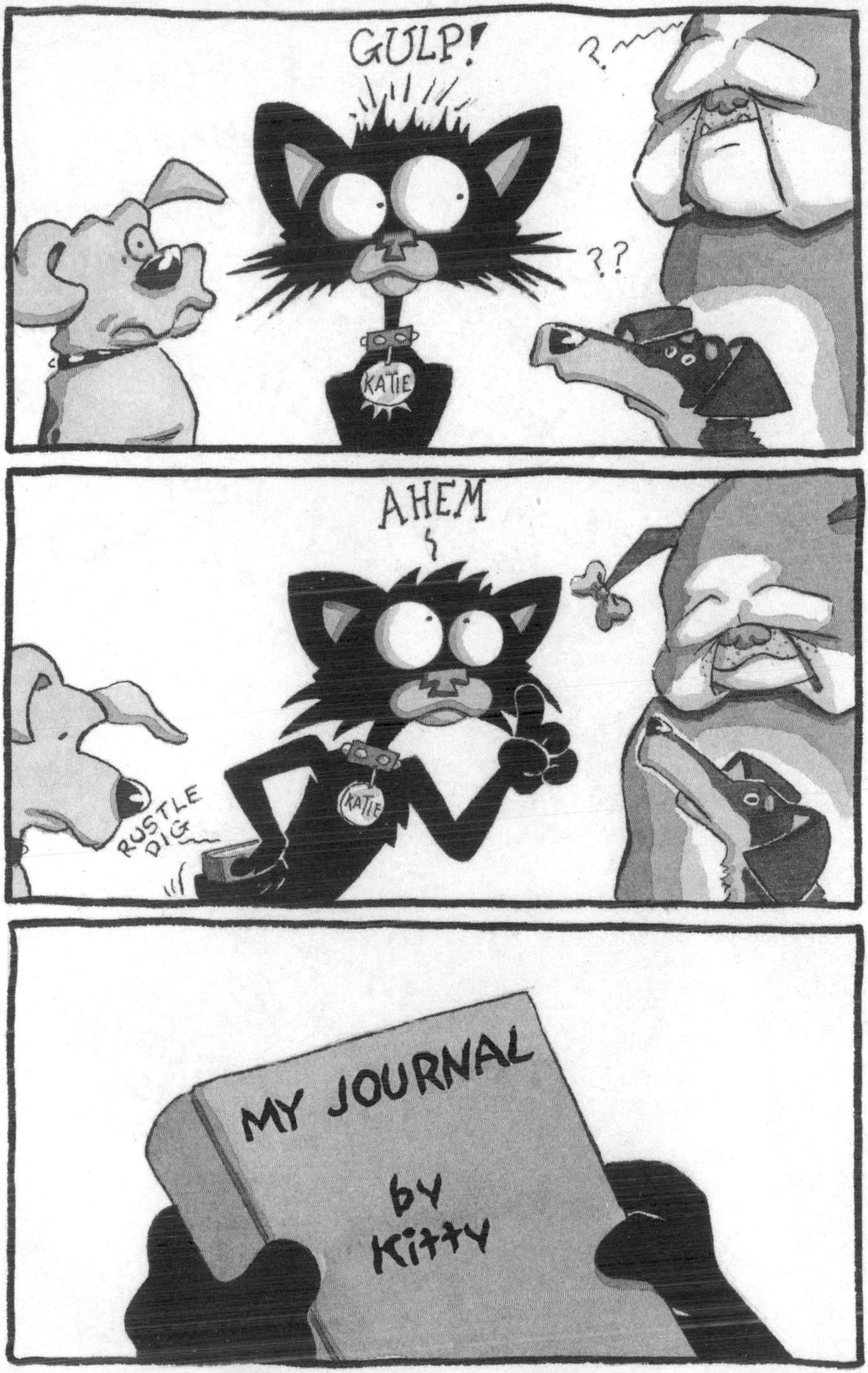
GULP!
?
??
KATIE
AHEM
RUSTLE
DIG
KATIE
MY JOURNAL
by
Kitty

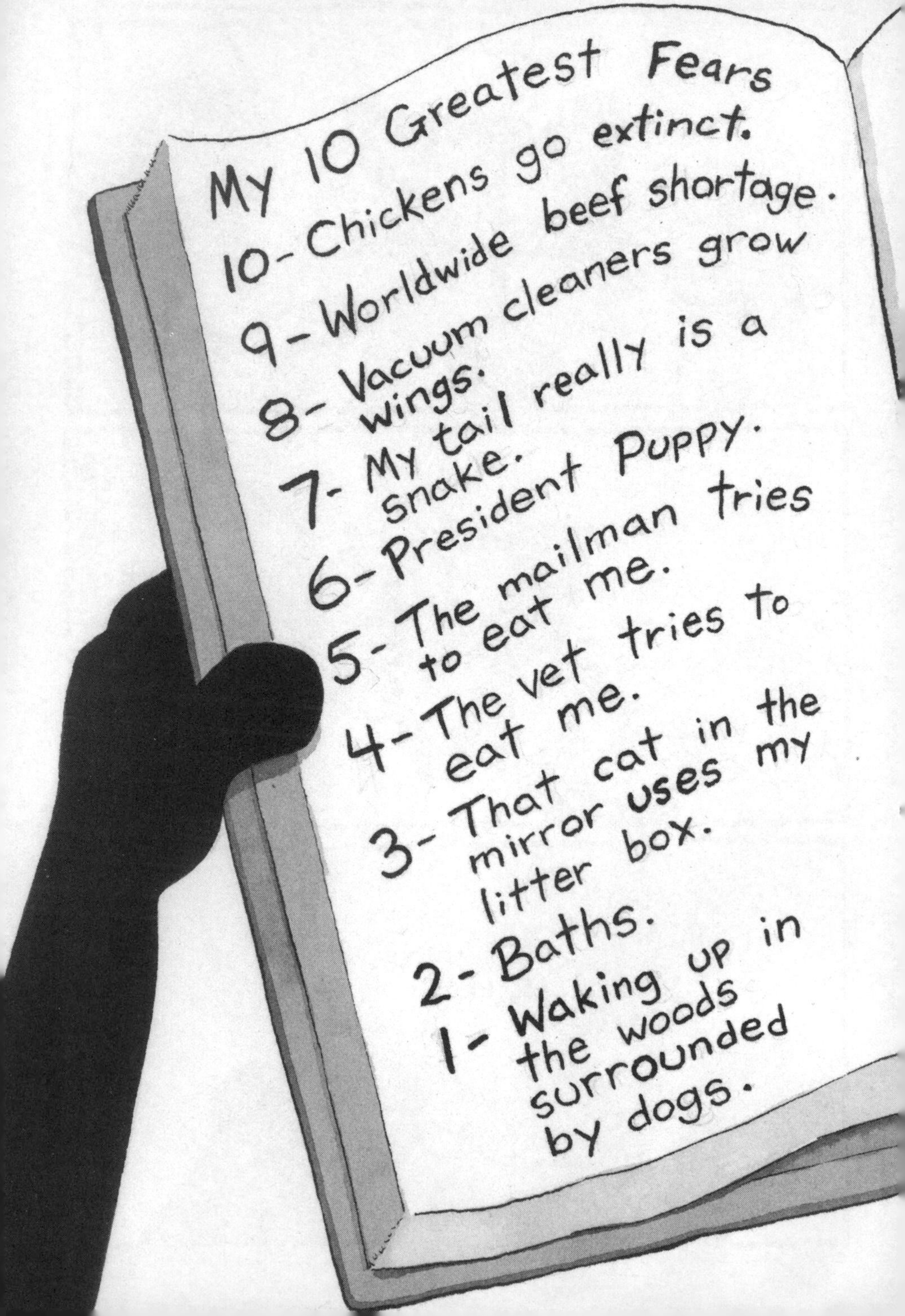
My 10 Greatest Fears
10- Chickens go extinct.
9- Worldwide beef shortage.
8- Vacuum cleaners grow wings.
7- My tail really is a snake.
6- President Puppy.
5- The mailman tries to eat me.
4- The vet tries to eat me.
3- That cat in the mirror uses my litter box.
2- Baths.
1- Waking up in the woods surrounded by dogs.

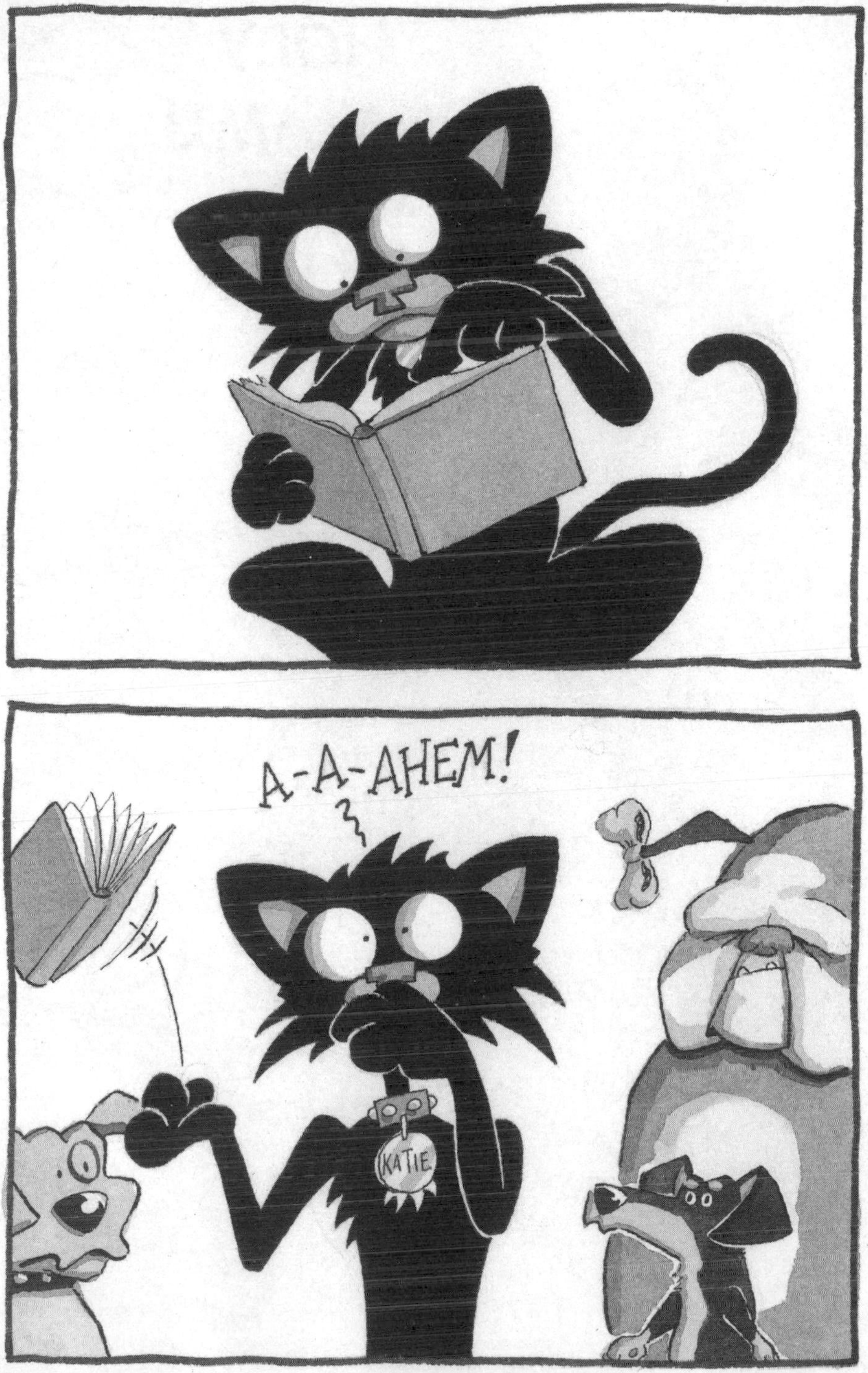
A-A-AHEM!
KATIE

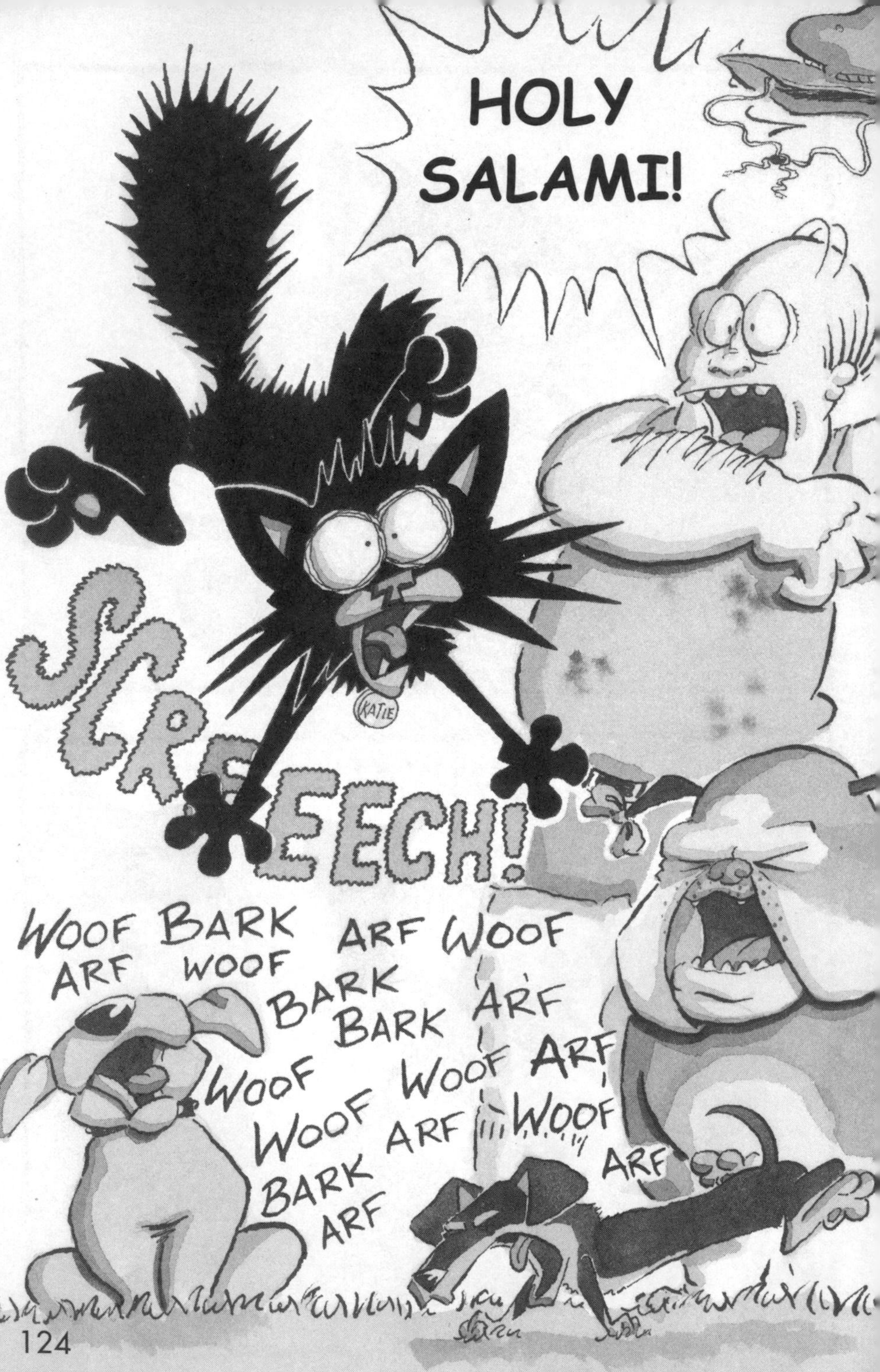
HOLY SALAMI!
SCREECH!
KATIE
WOOF BARK ARF WOOF
ARF WOOF
BARK
BARK ARF
WOOF
WOOF WOOF ARF
BARK ARF WOOF
BARK ARF
ARF

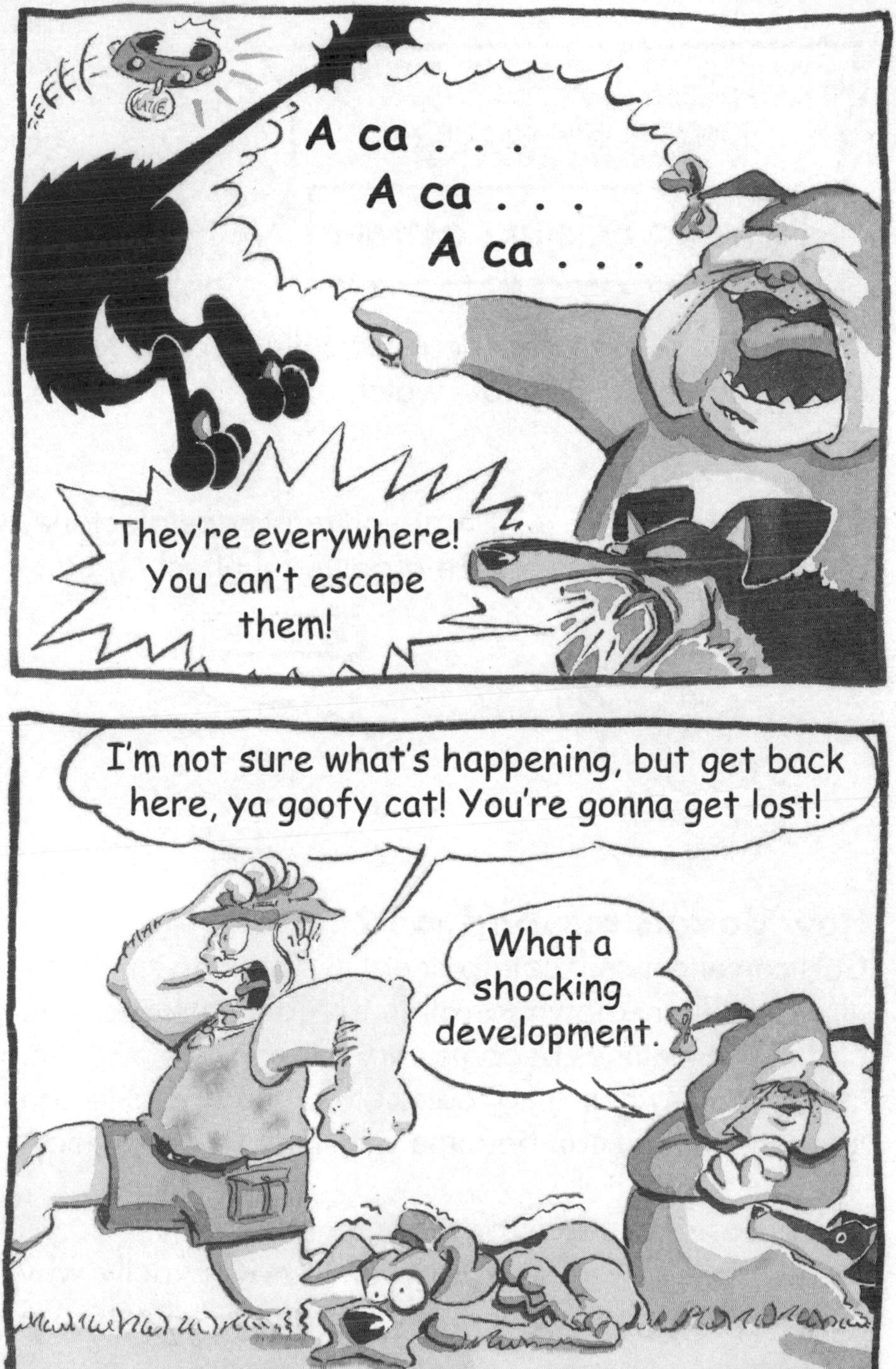
A ca . . .
A ca . . .
A ca . . .
They're everywhere! You can't escape them!
I'm not sure what's happening, but get back here, ya goofy cat! You're gonna get lost!
What a shocking development.

UNCLE MURRAY'S FUN FACTS

WHY DO CATS LIKE CATNIP?

This is really not a good time!

Only about 50 percent of cats actually respond to catnip, but for those that do—watch out!

What is catnip?

Catnip is a type of mint that contains nepetalactone, a chemical which can have a powerful effect on cats.

CRAZY SNIFF

MELLOW BURP

How do cats respond to it?

Cats can either sniff catnip or eat it. Cats who smell catnip have been known to roll in it, rub their faces in it, and can sometimes become very hyper and energetic. Interestingly, when a cat eats catnip, the opposite can happen: The cat can become very mellow and sleepy.

Why does this happen?

To be honest, even scientists don't know exactly why nepetalactone can have such a dramatic effect on a

PANIC
SLEEP
FOOD
COMPLETE MYSTERY

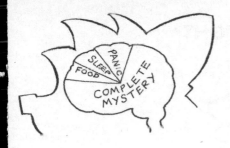

cat's behavior. All they know is that this chemical can make a cat go bonkers for as little as ten minutes to as much as two hours. This chemical has even been known to affect big cats like leopards and tigers.

I smell licorice!

Does catnip affect dogs?
Dogs don't go crazy over the scent of catnip like cats do, but they will get sleepy if they eat it. Some people will put a few catnip leaves in a dog's water bowl to help it calm down.

Is there such a thing as "dognip"?
The smell of anise seed, the same herb that flavors licorice, can make some dogs go completely nuts in the same way catnip can affect cats. But you have to be careful. The ASPCA warns that too much anise can really bother a dog's stomach.

Chemicals. Licorice. ASPCA. Got it! Just tell that cat to slow down!

•CHAPTER EIGHT•

LOST

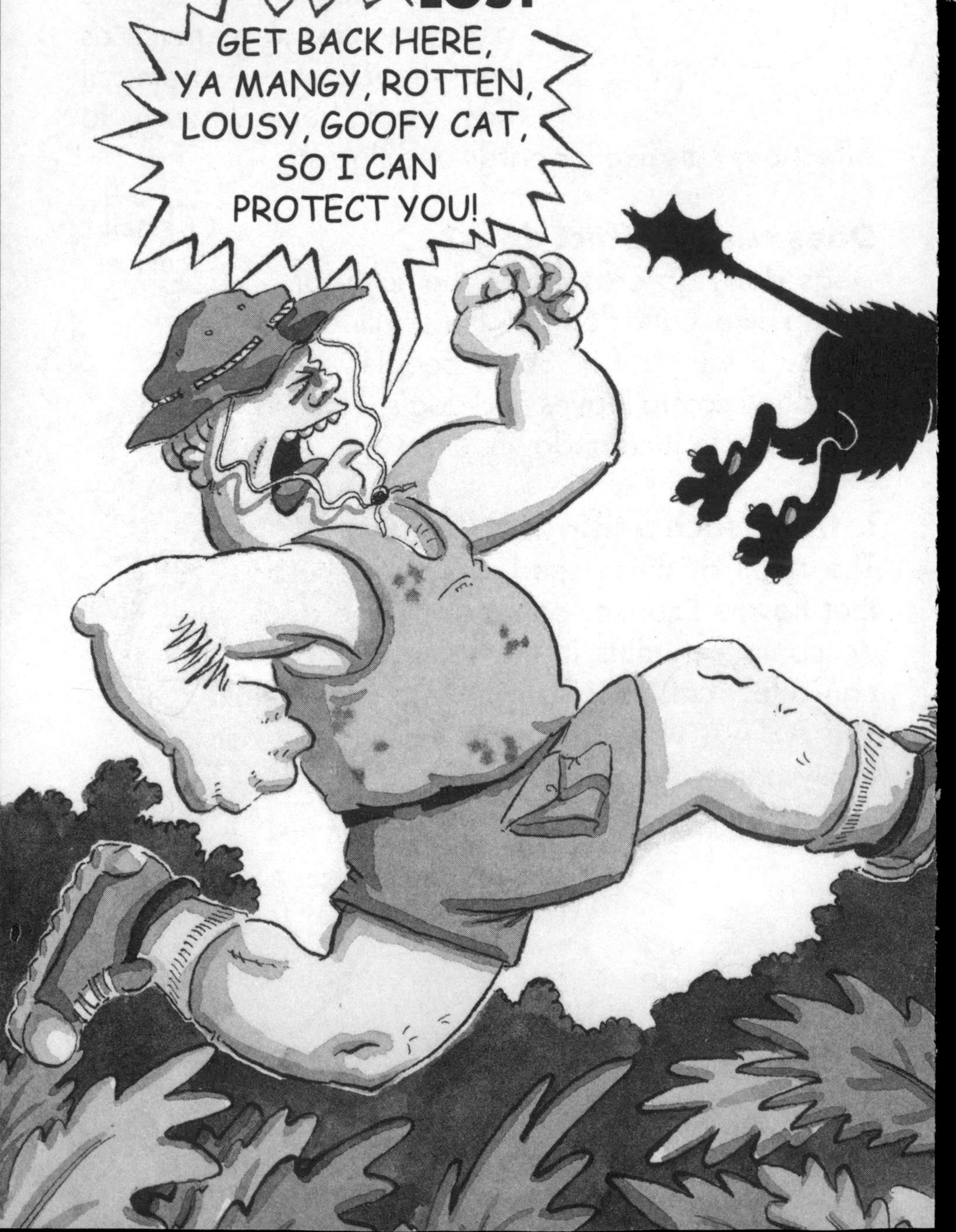
GET BACK HERE, YA MANGY, ROTTEN, LOUSY, GOOFY CAT, SO I CAN PROTECT YOU!

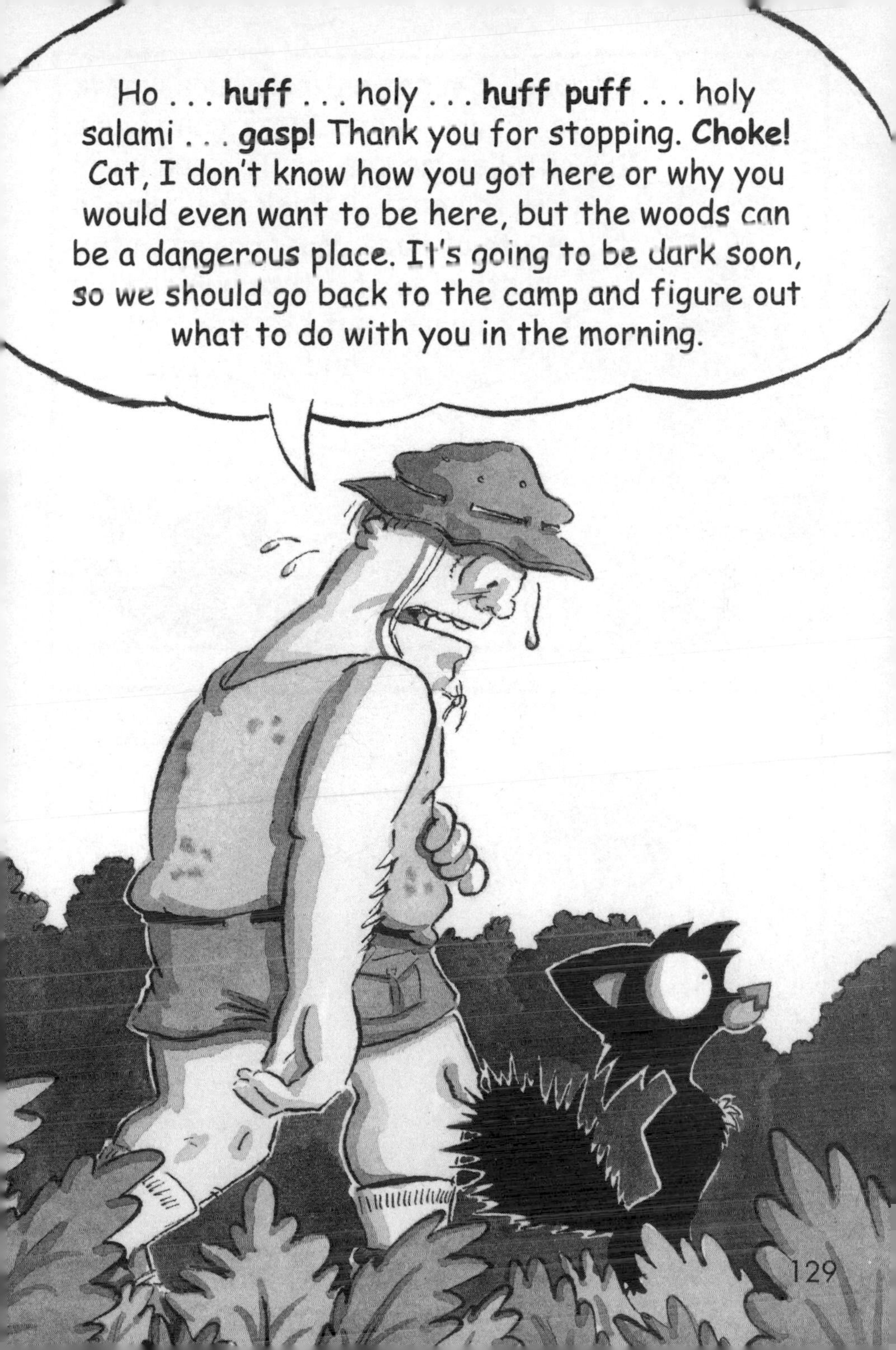
Ho . . . **huff** . . . holy . . . **huff puff** . . . holy salami . . . **gasp!** Thank you for stopping. **Choke!** Cat, I don't know how you got here or why you would even want to be here, but the woods can be a dangerous place. It's going to be dark soon, so we should go back to the camp and figure out what to do with you in the morning.

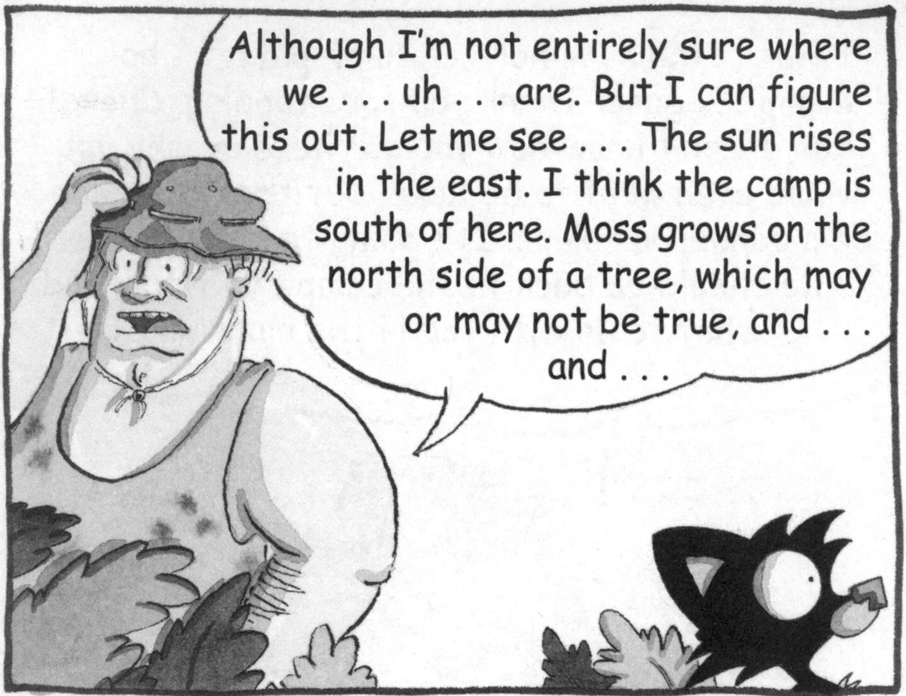
Although I'm not entirely sure where we . . . uh . . . are. But I can figure this out. Let me see . . . The sun rises in the east. I think the camp is south of here. Moss grows on the north side of a tree, which may or may not be true, and . . . and . . .

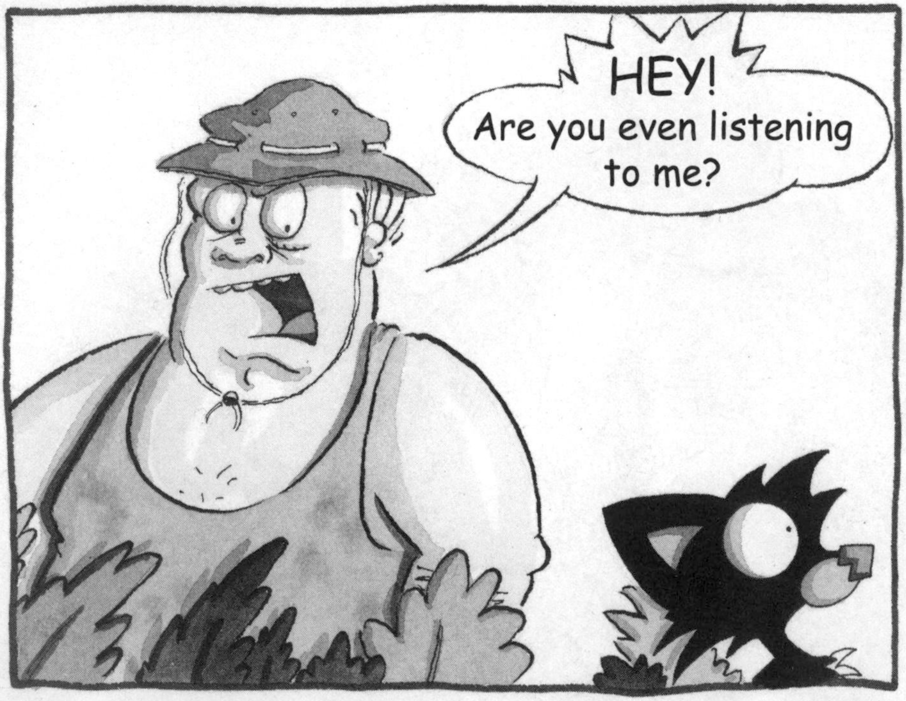
HEY!
Are you even listening to me?

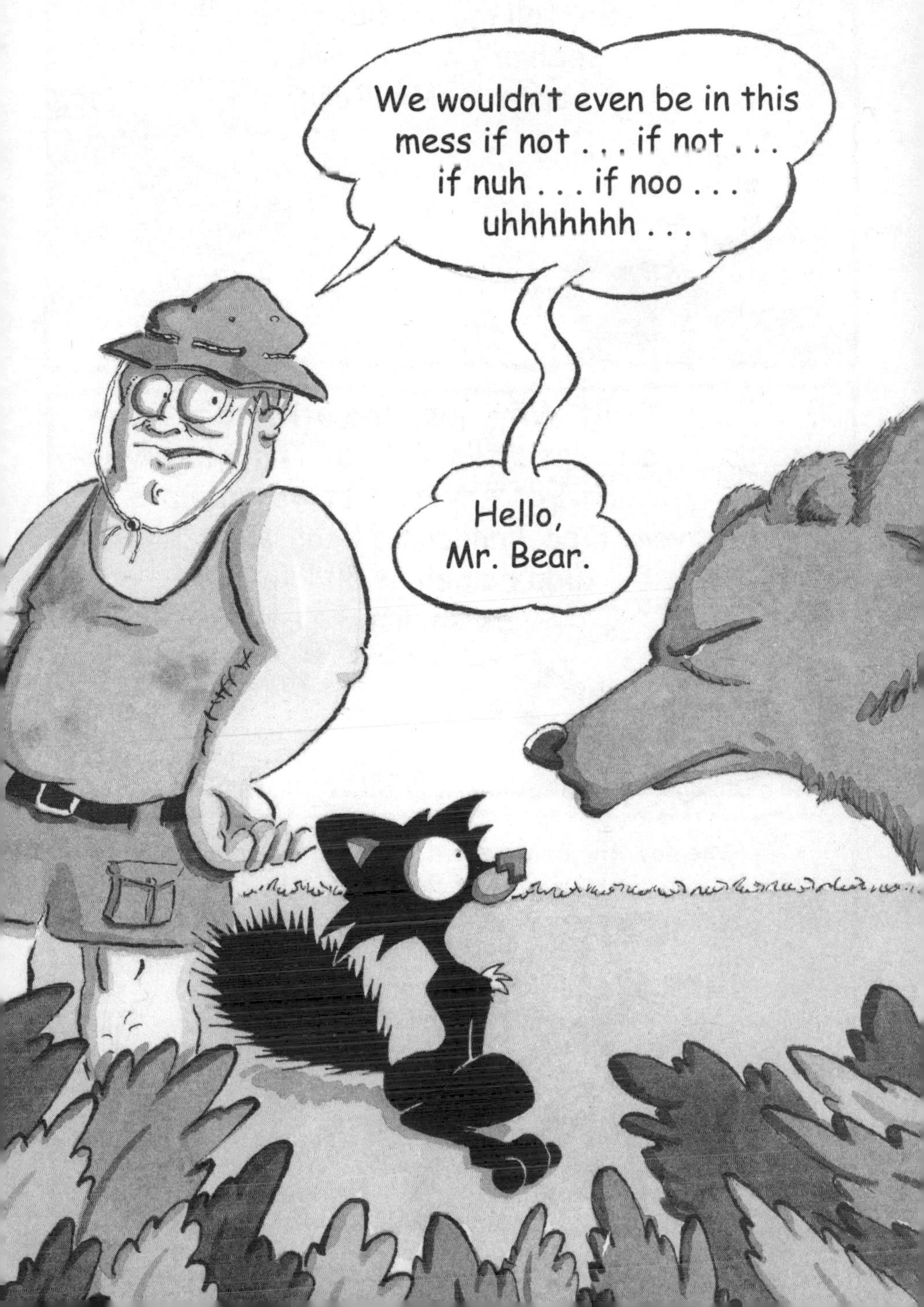
We wouldn't even be in this mess if not . . . if not . . . if nuh . . . if noo . . . uhhhhhhh . . .
Hello, Mr. Bear.

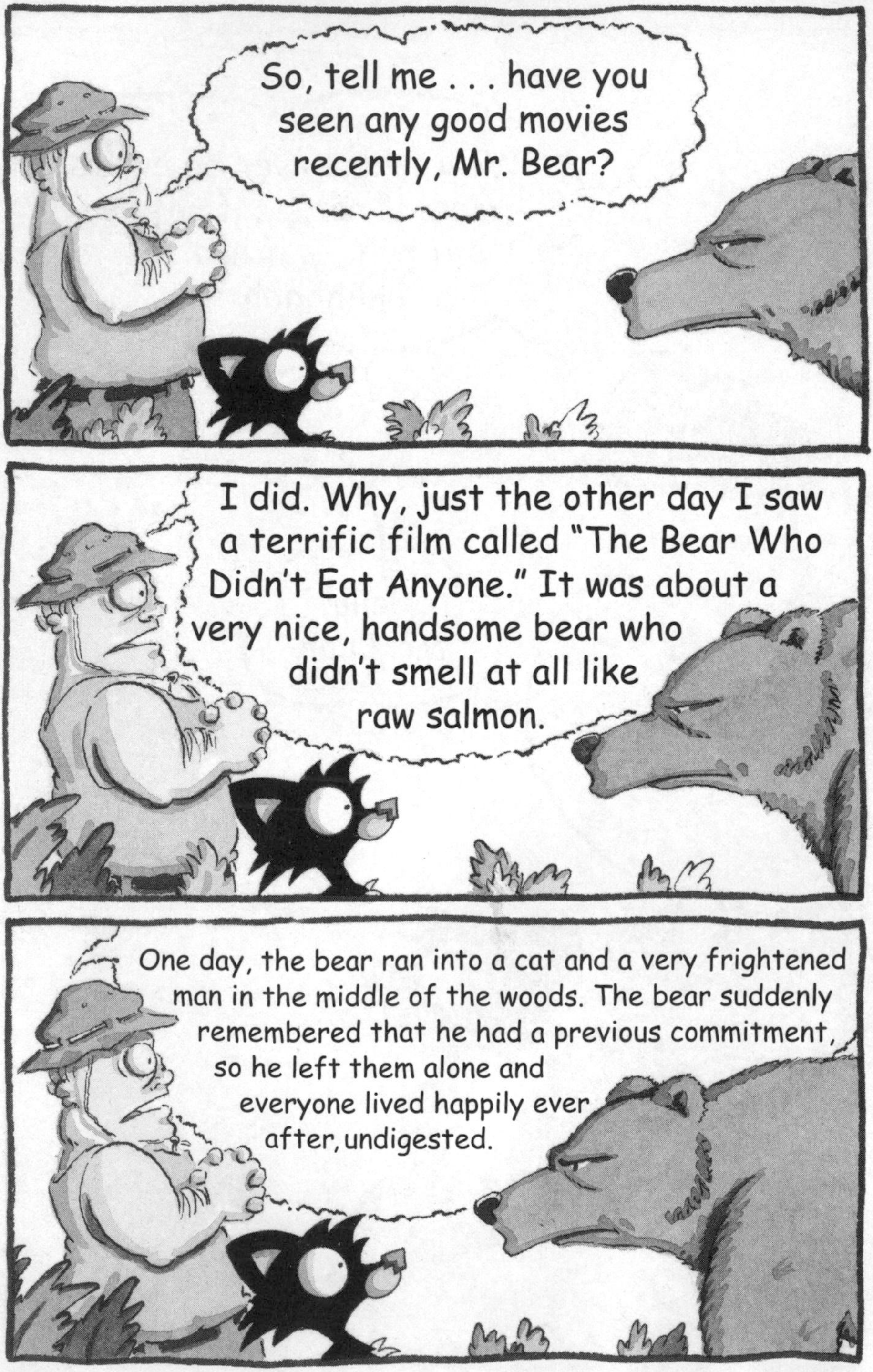
So, tell me . . . have you seen any good movies recently, Mr. Bear?
I did. Why, just the other day I saw a terrific film called "The Bear Who Didn't Eat Anyone." It was about a very nice, handsome bear who didn't smell at all like raw salmon.
One day, the bear ran into a cat and a very frightened man in the middle of the woods. The bear suddenly remembered that he had a previous commitment, so he left them alone and everyone lived happily ever after, undigested.

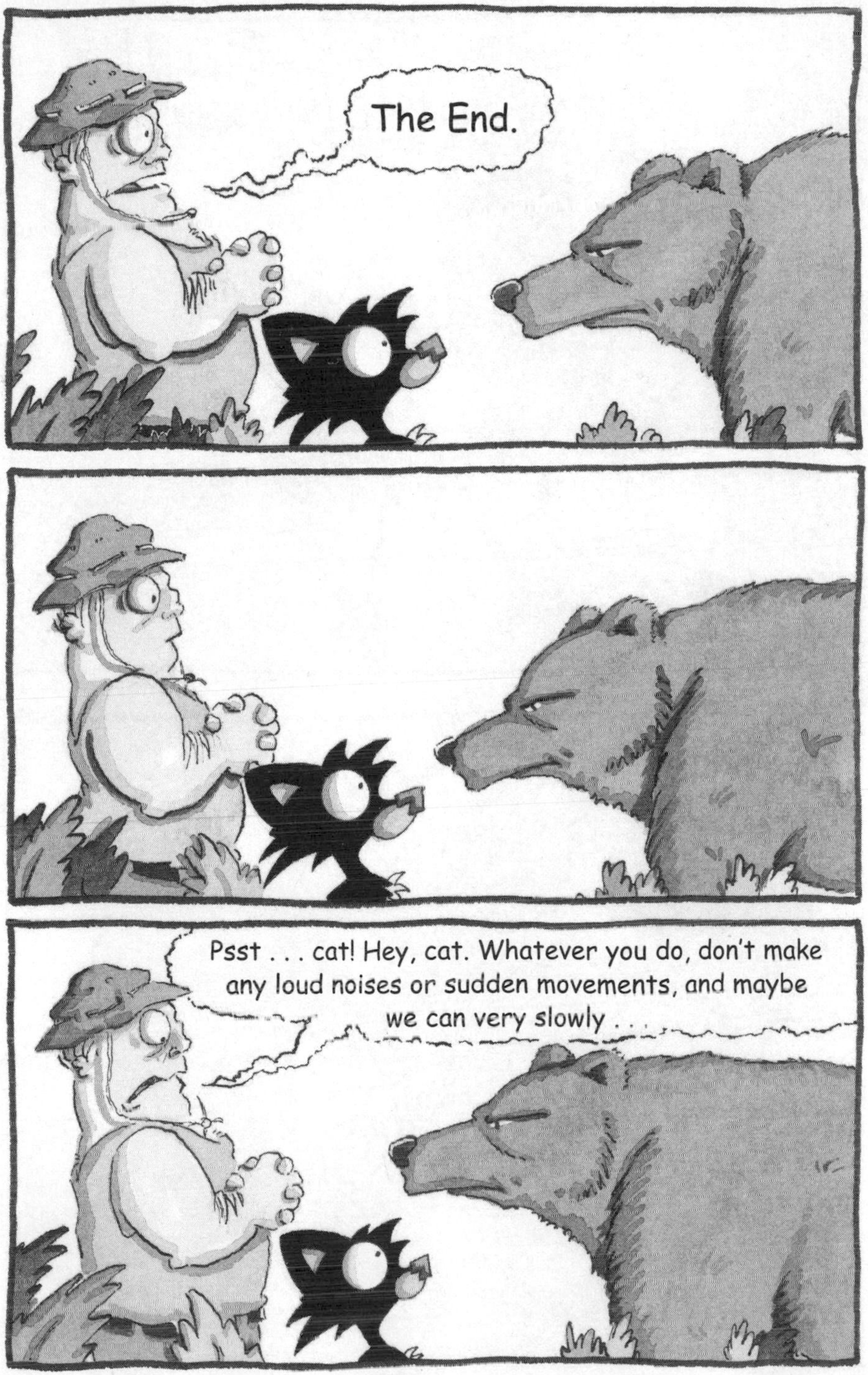
The End.
Psst . . . cat! Hey, cat. Whatever you do, don't make any loud noises or sudden movements, and maybe we can very slowly . . .

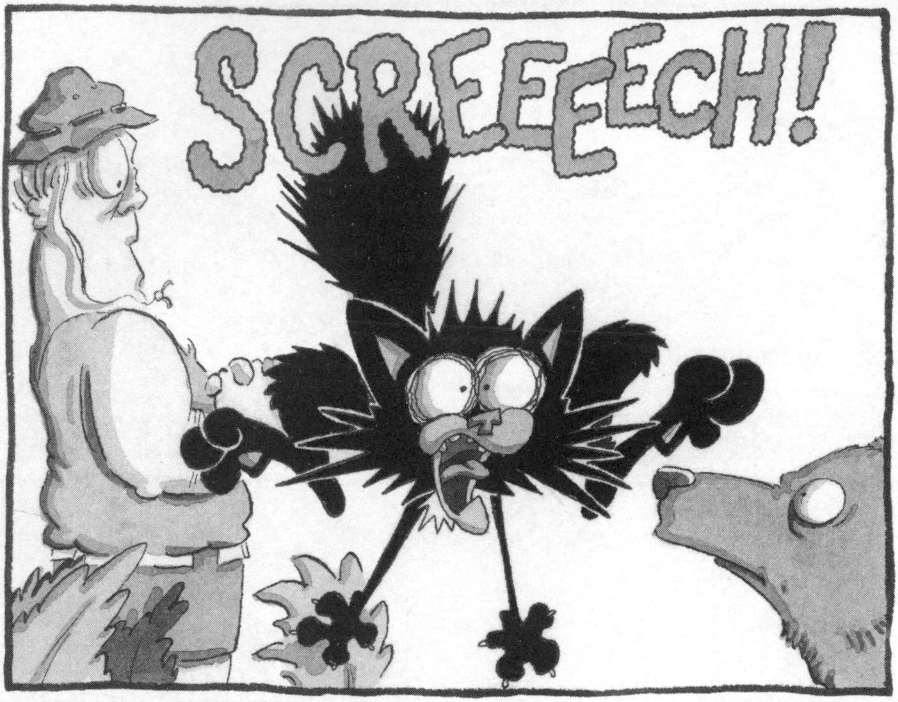
SCREEECH!

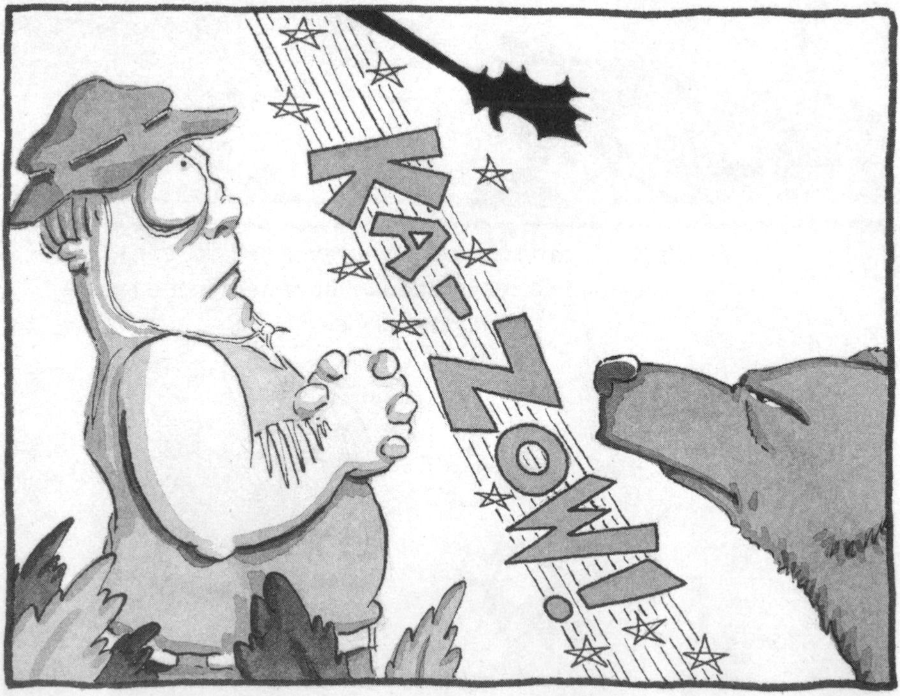
KA-ZOW!

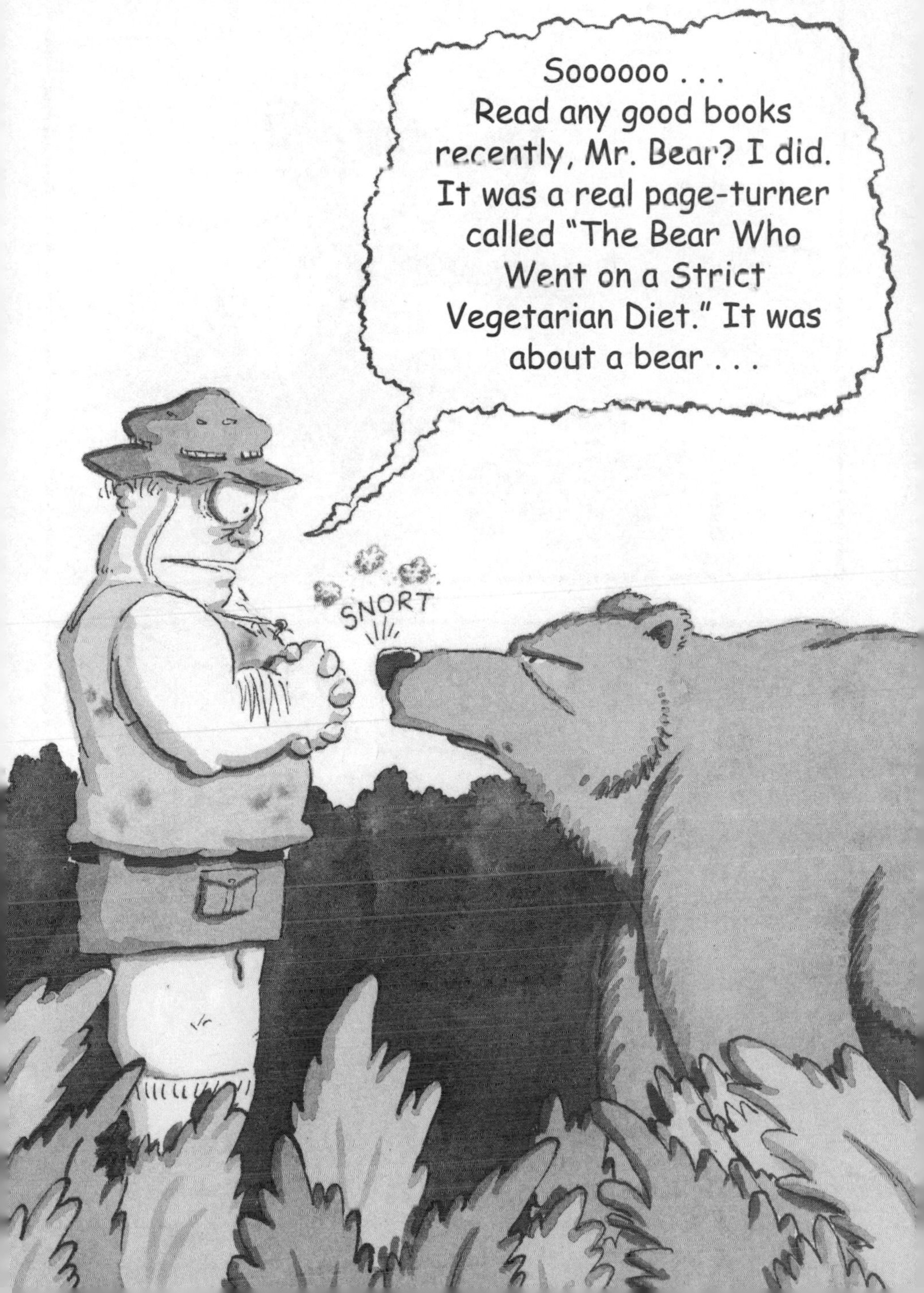
Soooooo . . .
Read any good books recently, Mr. Bear? I did. It was a real page-turner called "The Bear Who Went on a Strict Vegetarian Diet." It was about a bear . . .
SNORT

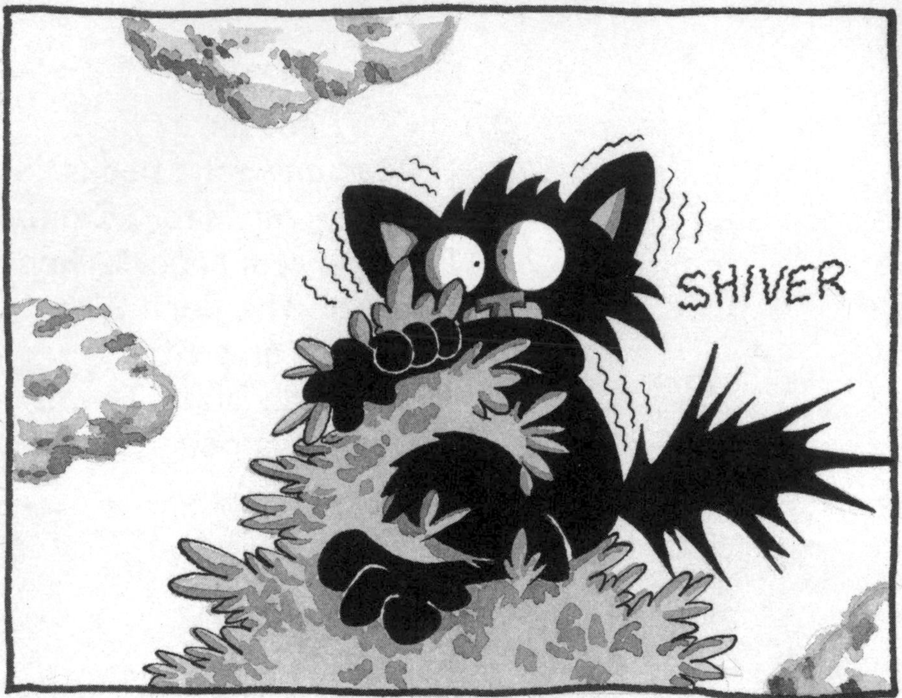
SHIVER

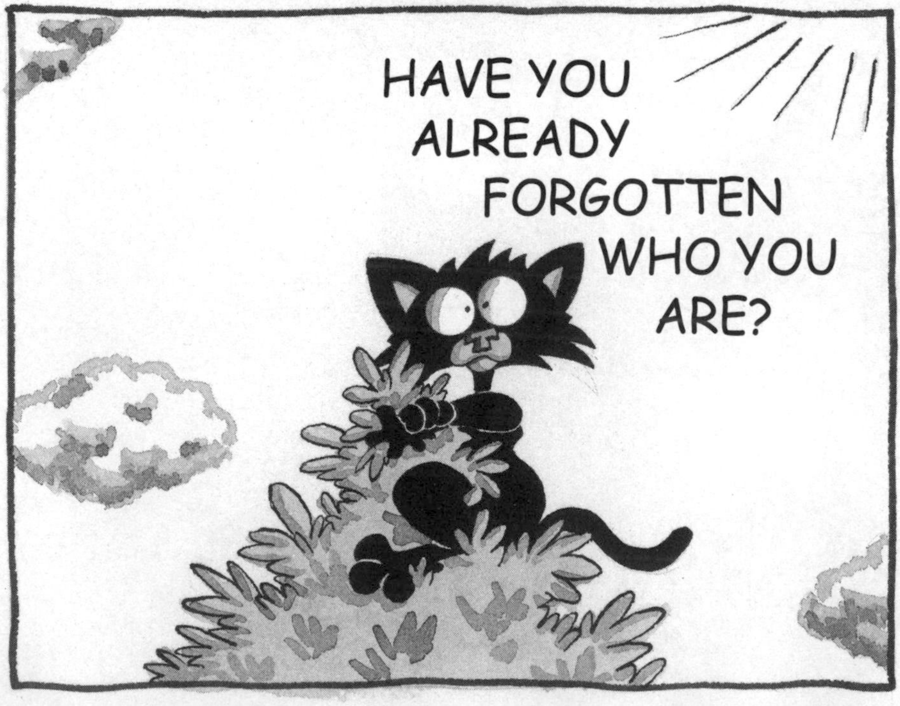
HAVE YOU ALREADY FORGOTTEN WHO YOU ARE?

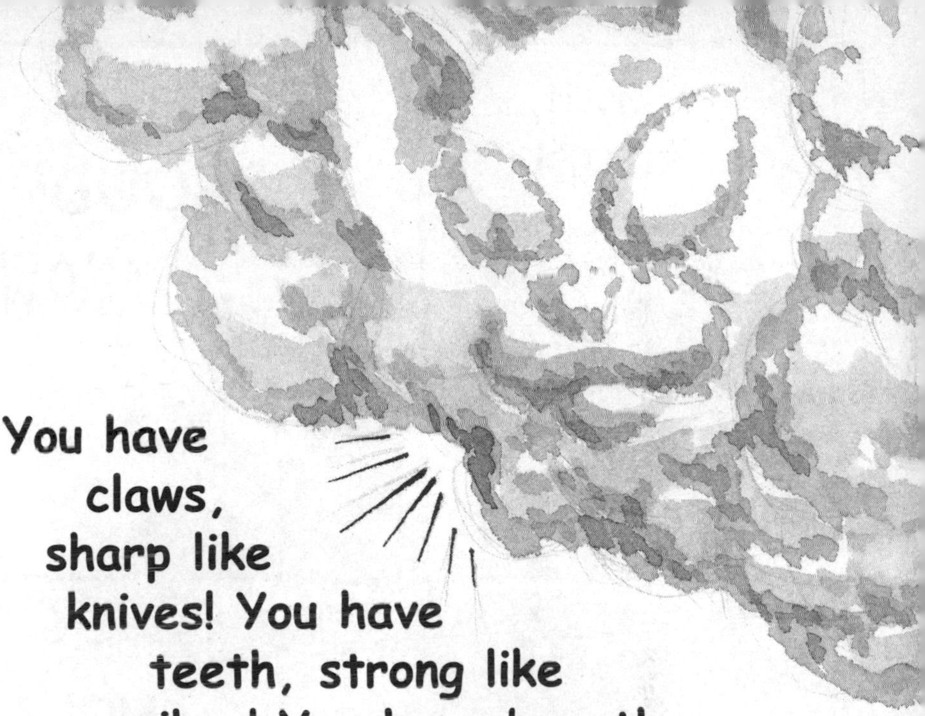

You have
claws,
sharp like
knives! You have
teeth, strong like
spikes! You have breath,
powerful like garlic left outside
on a hot day! No mere man can
frighten you! No mere
beast can defeat you!

Tell me who you are!

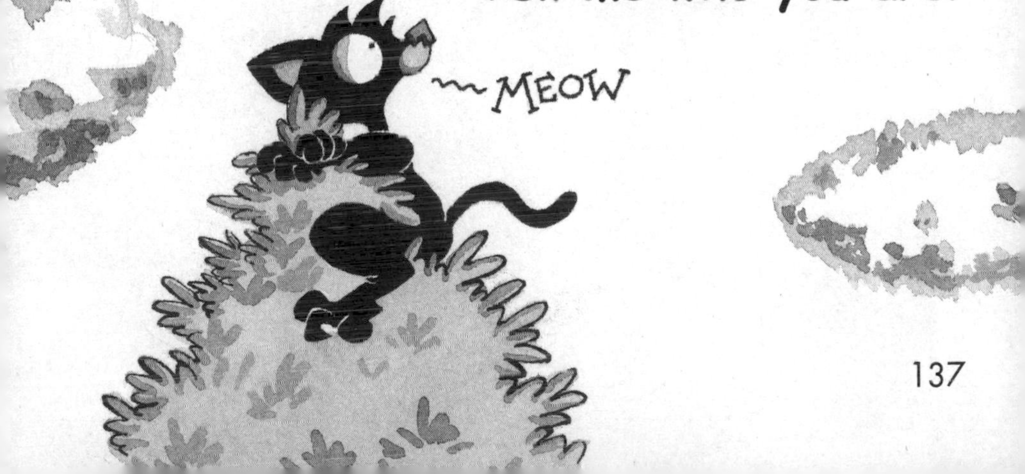
MEOW

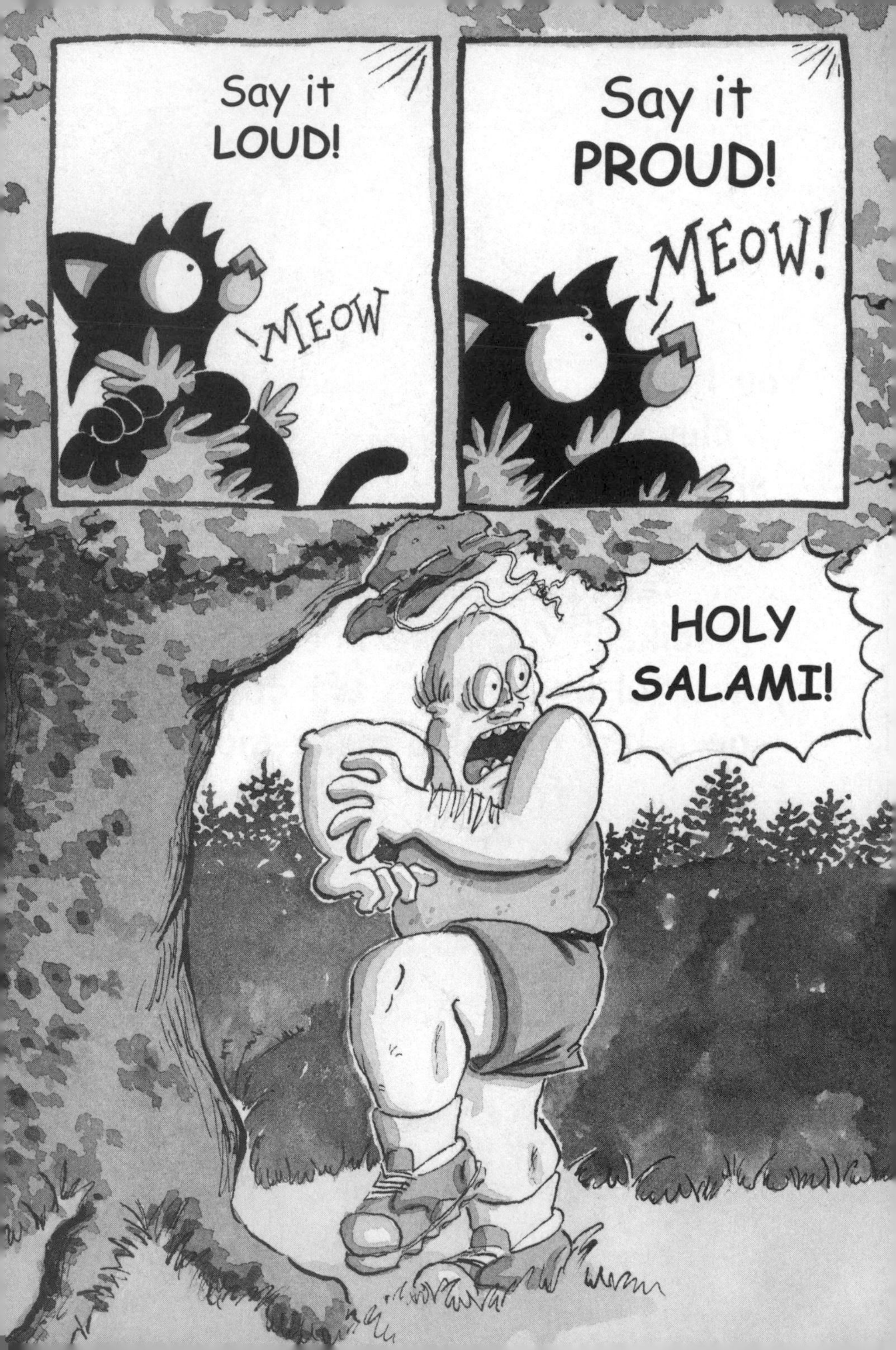
Say it LOUD!
MEOW
Say it PROUD!
MEOW!
HOLY SALAMI!

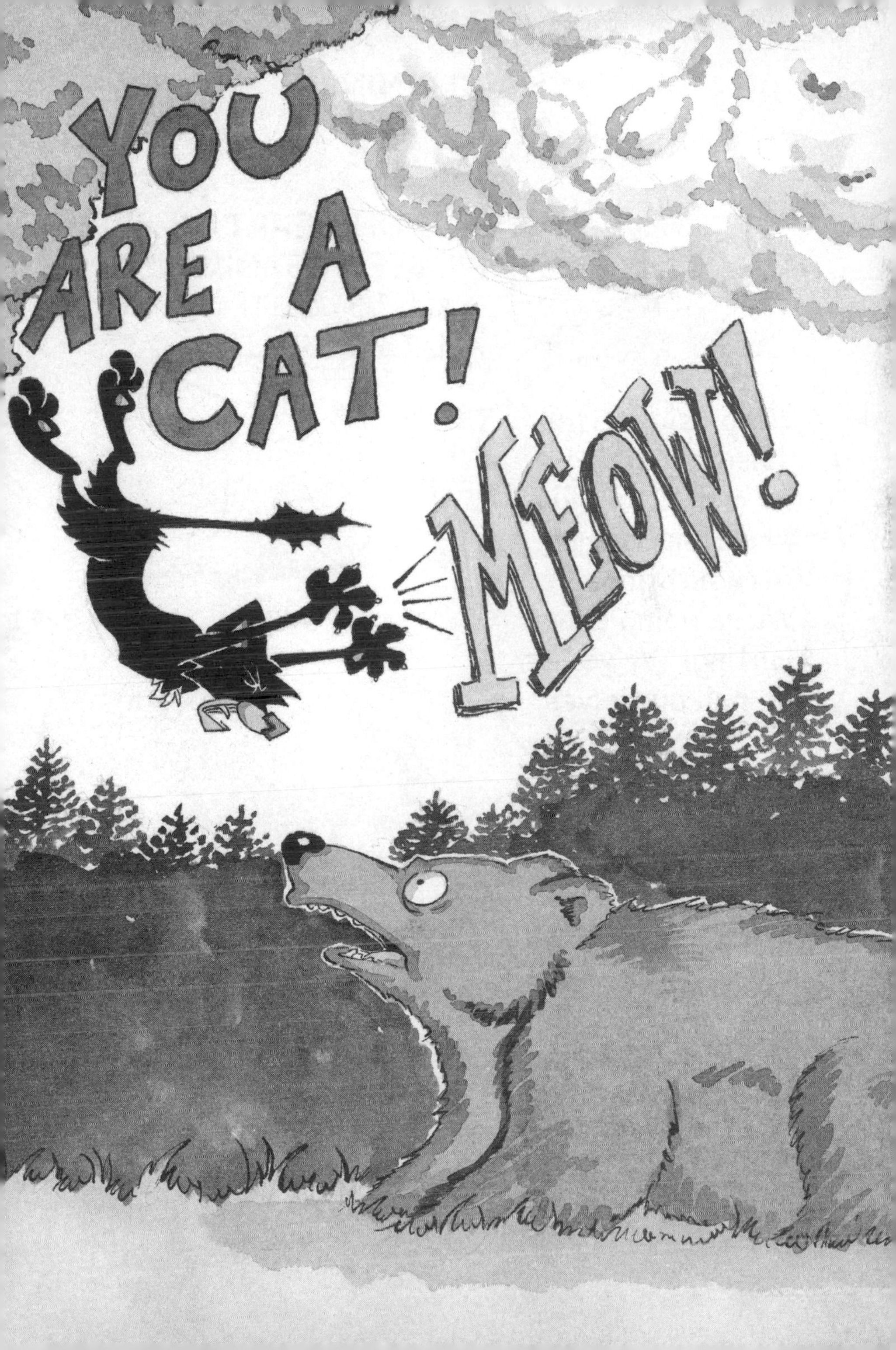
YOU ARE A CAT!
MEOW!

•CHAPTER NINE•

MEANWHILE . . .

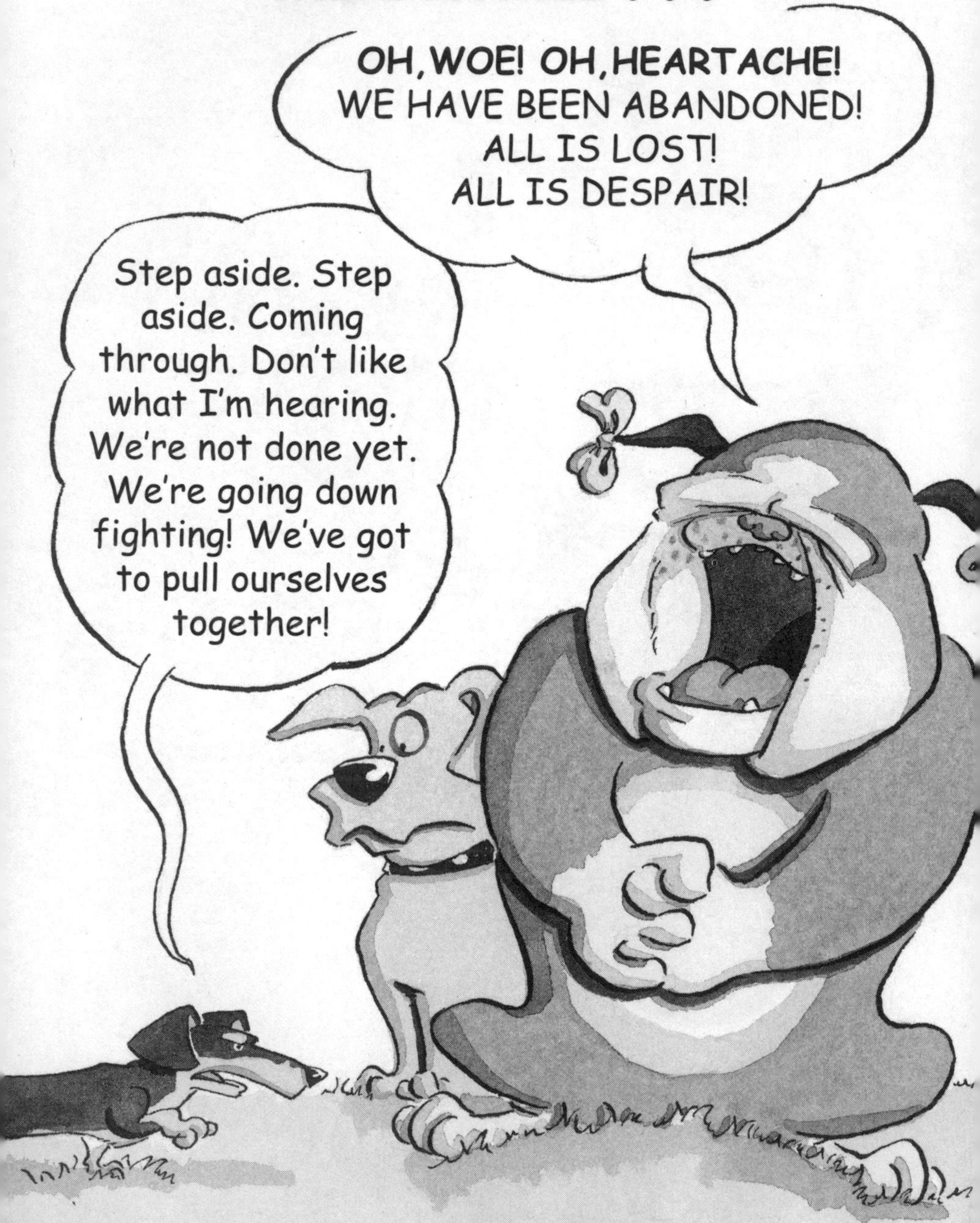
OH, WOE! OH, HEARTACHE! WE HAVE BEEN ABANDONED! ALL IS LOST! ALL IS DESPAIR!
Step aside. Step aside. Coming through. Don't like what I'm hearing. We're not done yet. We're going down fighting! We've got to pull ourselves together!

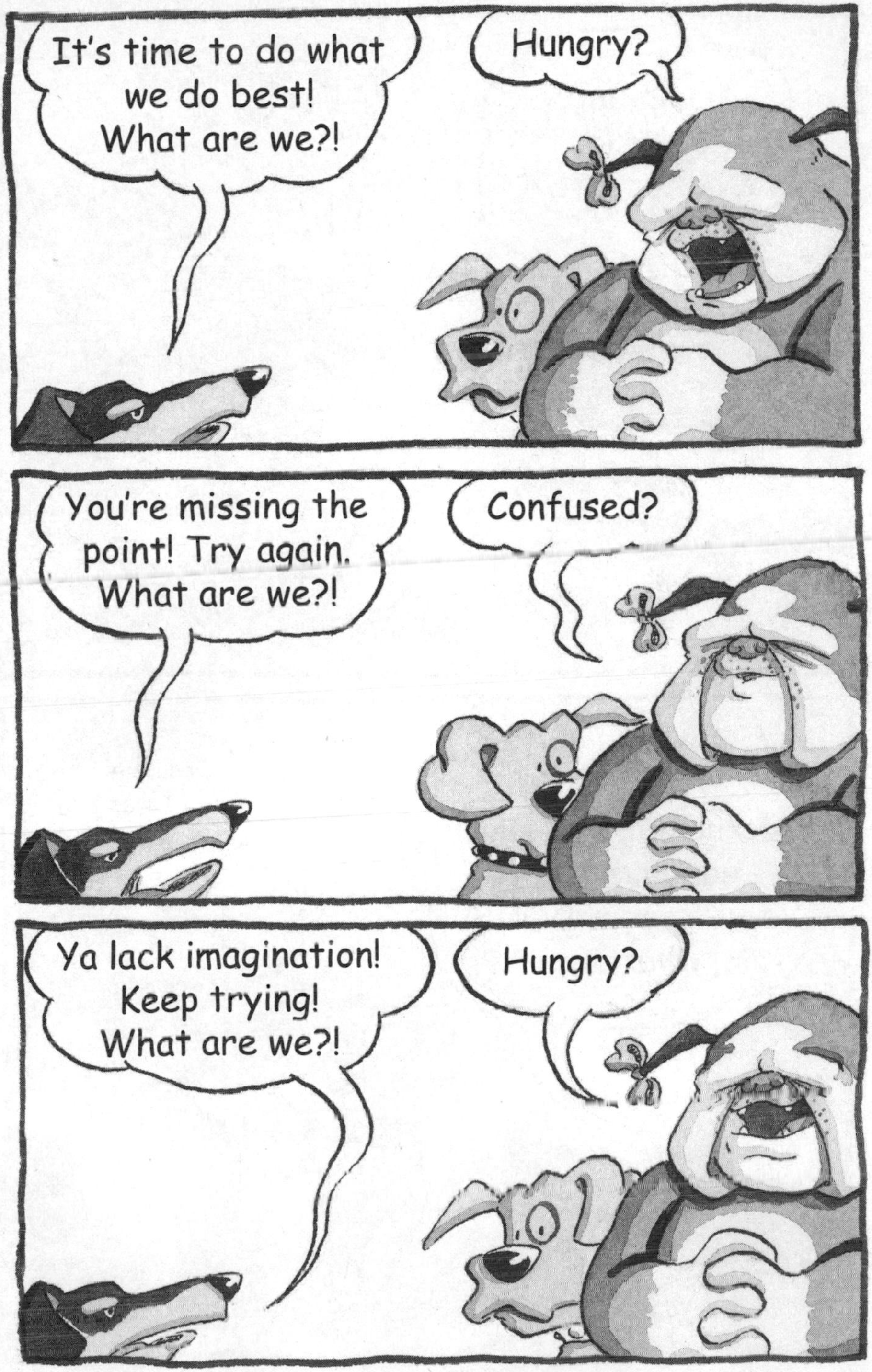
It's time to do what we do best! What are we?!
Hungry?
You're missing the point! Try again. What are we?!
Confused?
Ya lack imagination! Keep trying! What are we?!
Hungry?

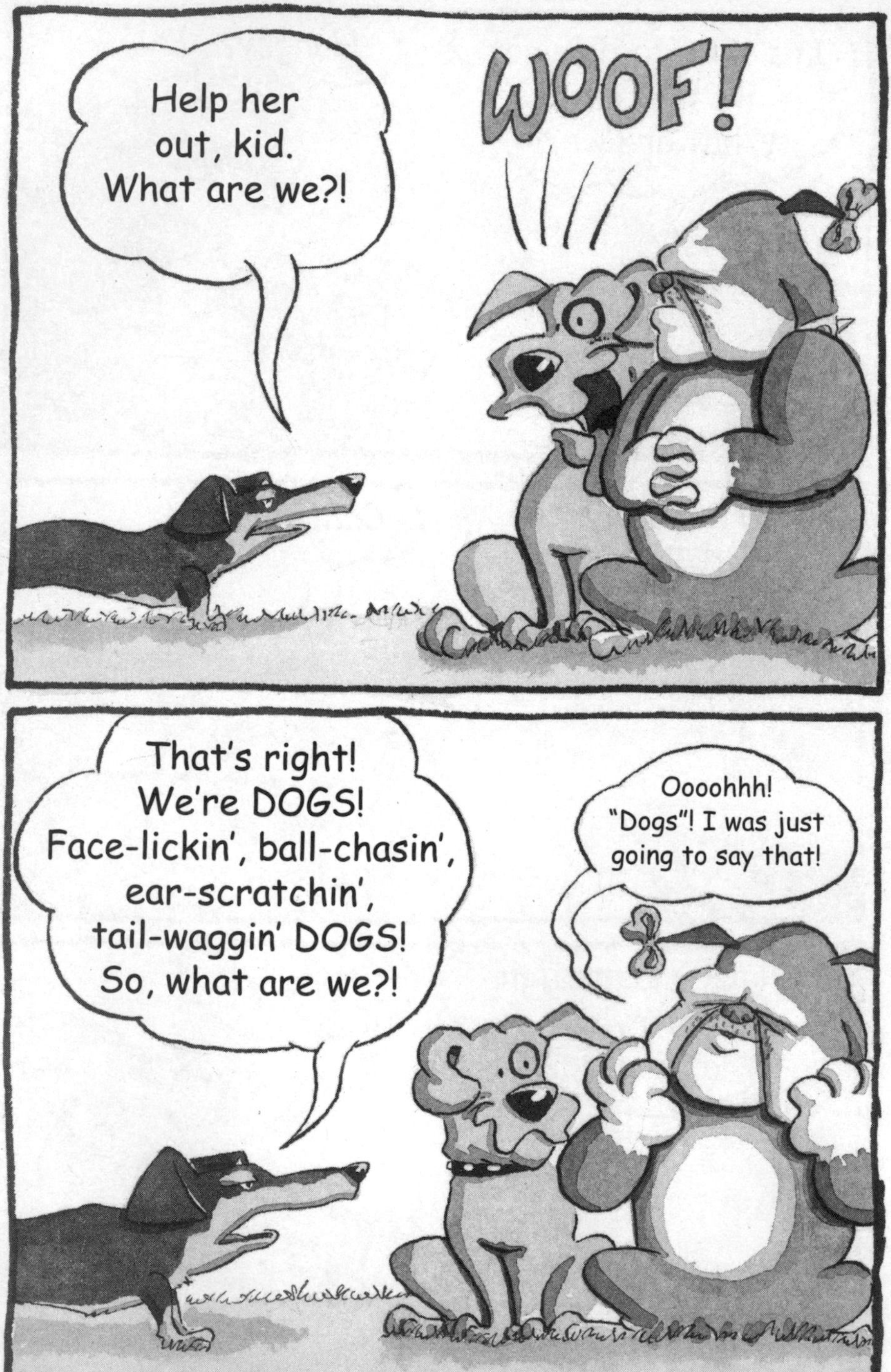
Help her out, kid. What are we?!
WOOF!
That's right! We're DOGS! Face-lickin', ball-chasin', ear-scratchin', tail-waggin' DOGS! So, what are we?!
Oooohhh! "Dogs"! I was just going to say that!

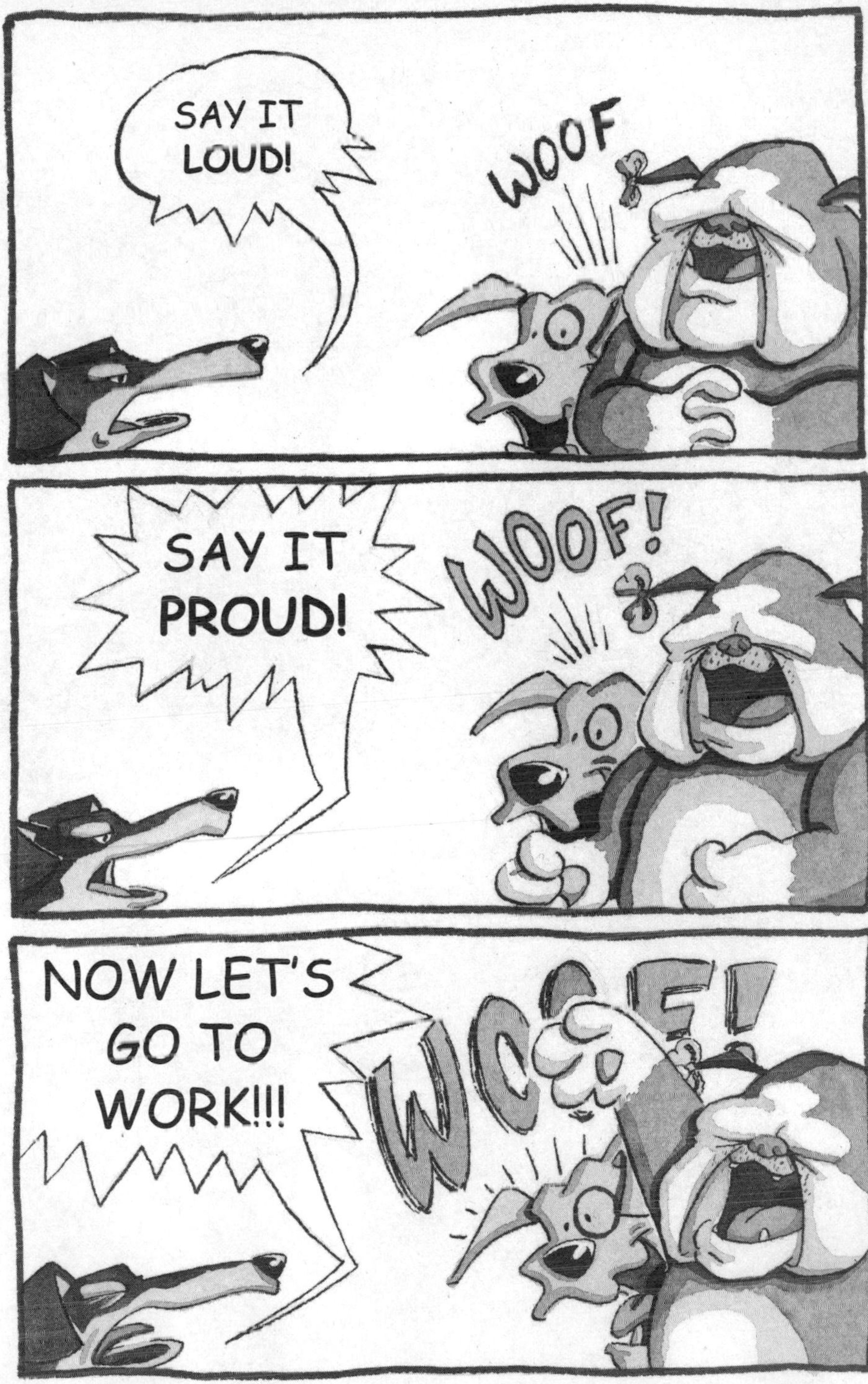
SAY IT LOUD!
WOOF
SAY IT PROUD!
WOOF!
NOW LET'S GO TO WORK!!!
WOOF!

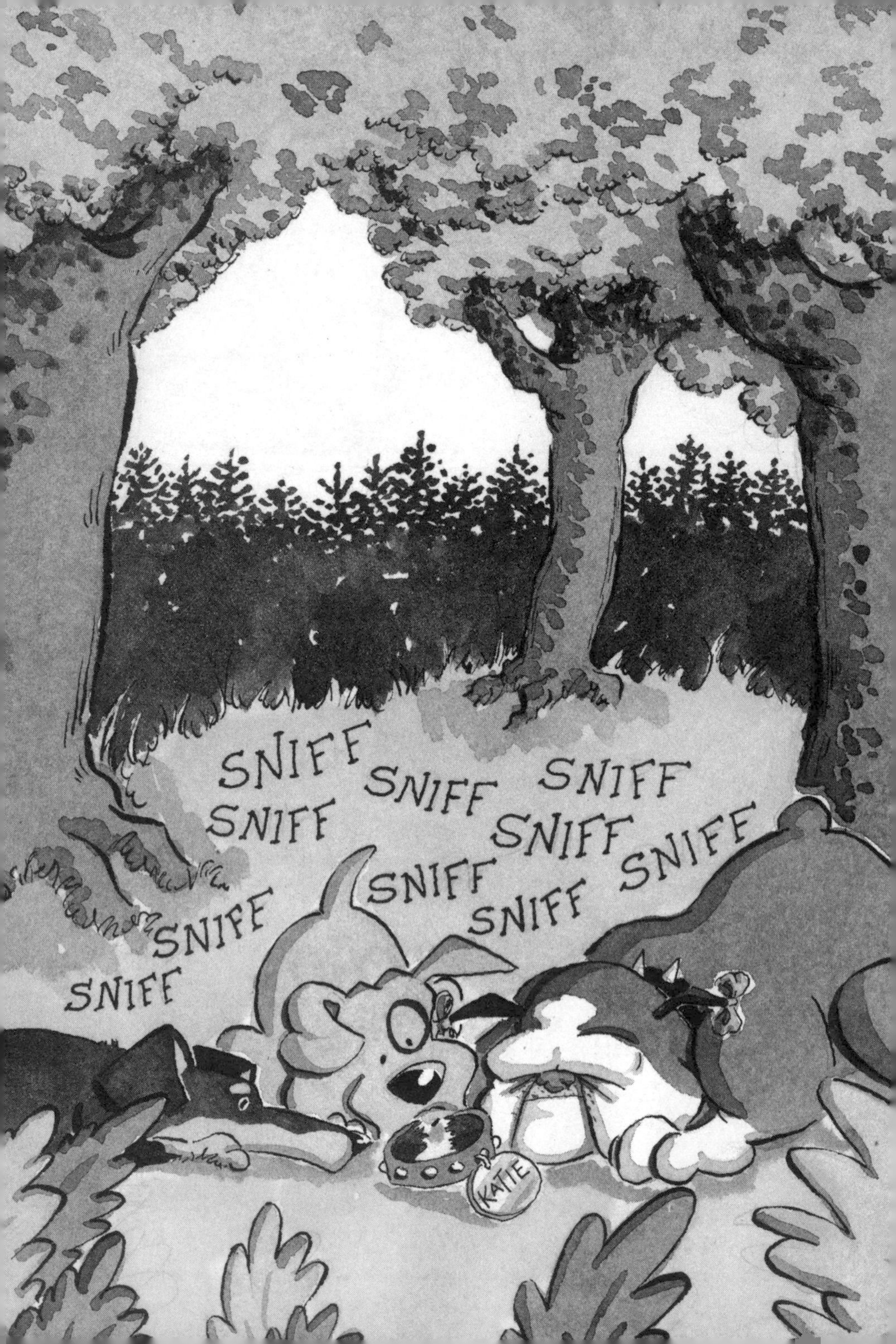
SNIFF
SNIFF
SNIFF
SNIFF
SNIFF
SNIFF
SNIFF
SNIFF
SNIFF
SNIFF
KATIE

•CHAPTER TEN•

REUNITED

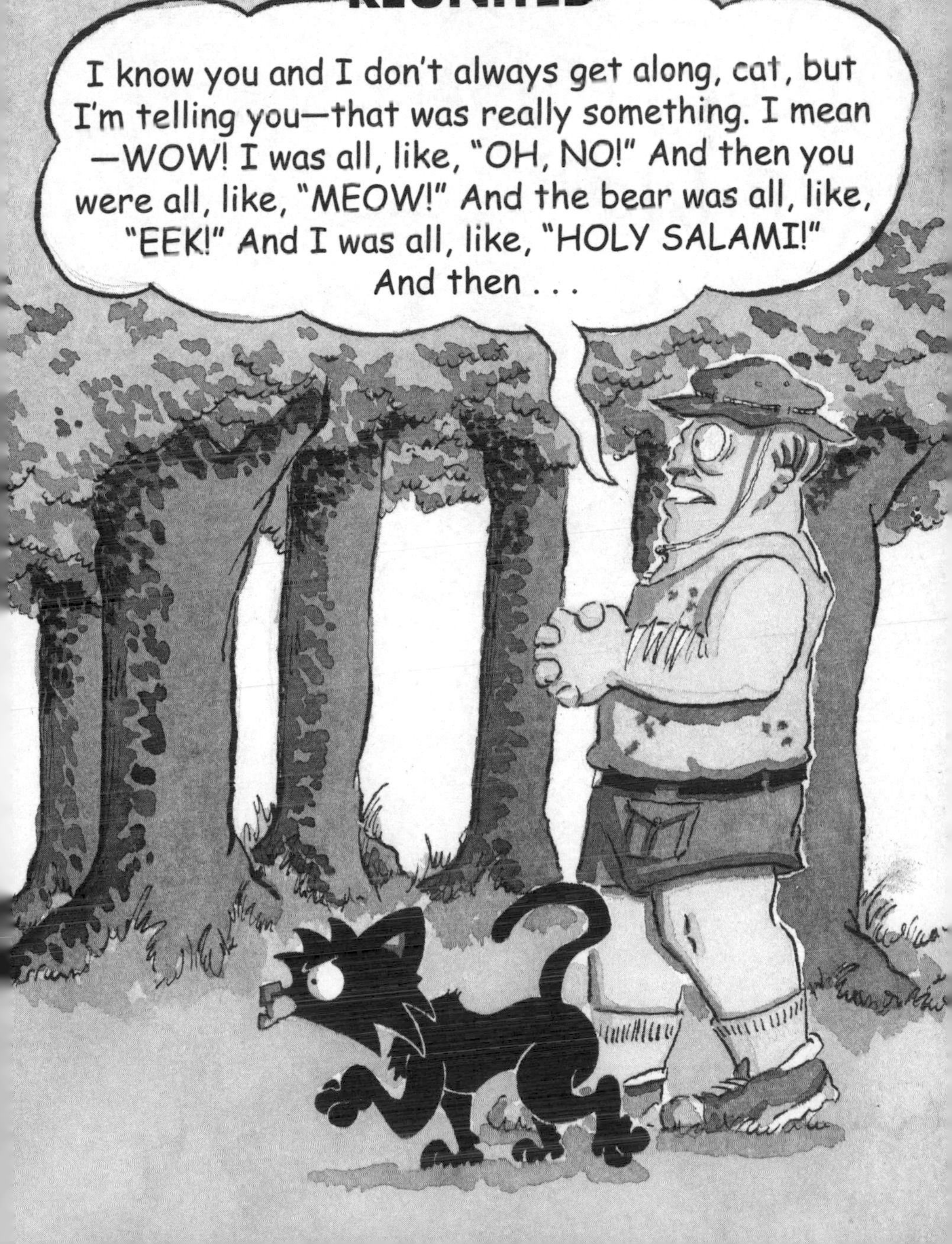
I know you and I don't always get along, cat, but I'm telling you—that was really something. I mean —WOW! I was all, like, "OH, NO!" And then you were all, like, "MEOW!" And the bear was all, like, "EEK!" And I was all, like, "HOLY SALAMI!" And then . . .

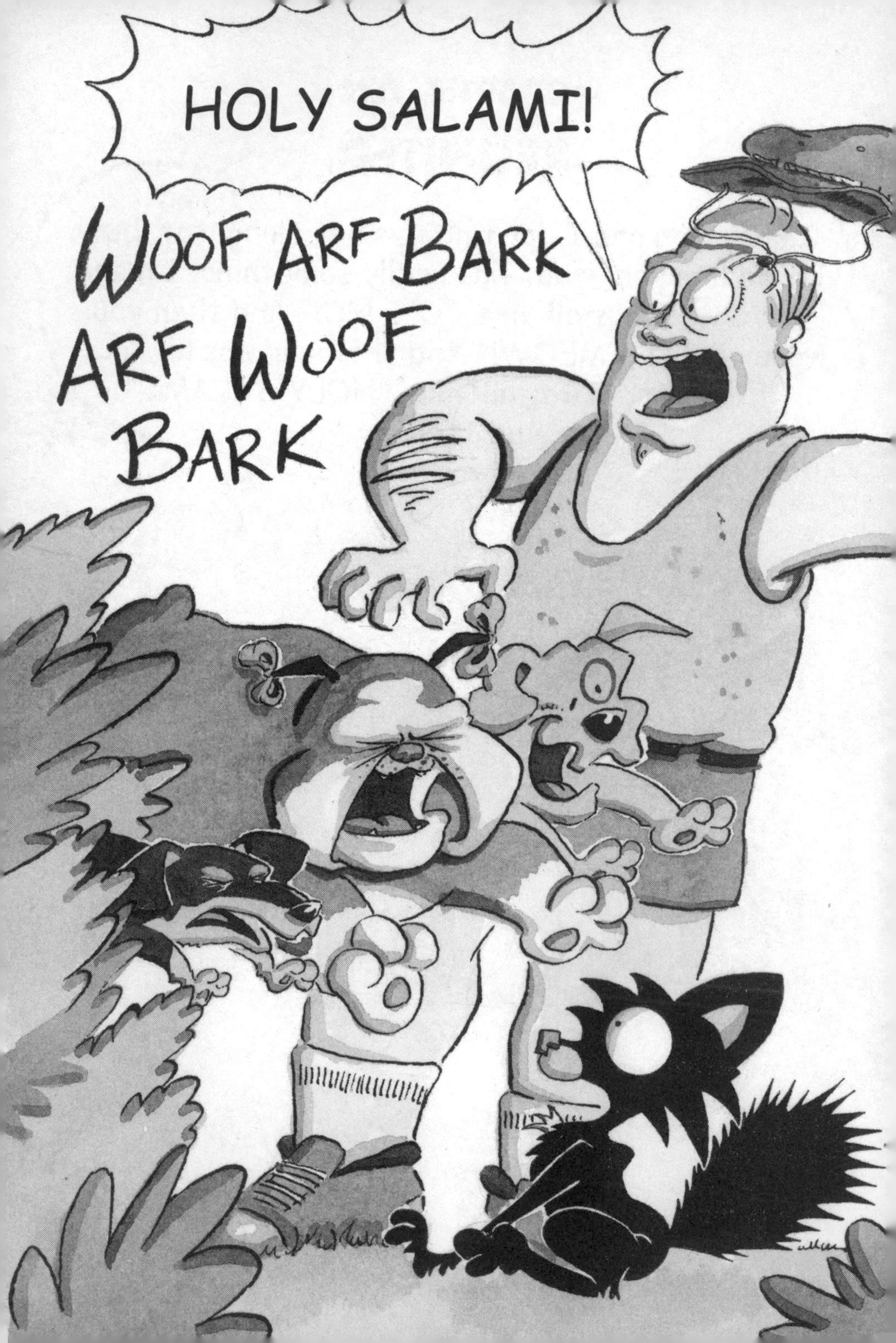
HOLY SALAMI!
WOOF ARF BARK
ARF WOOF
BARK

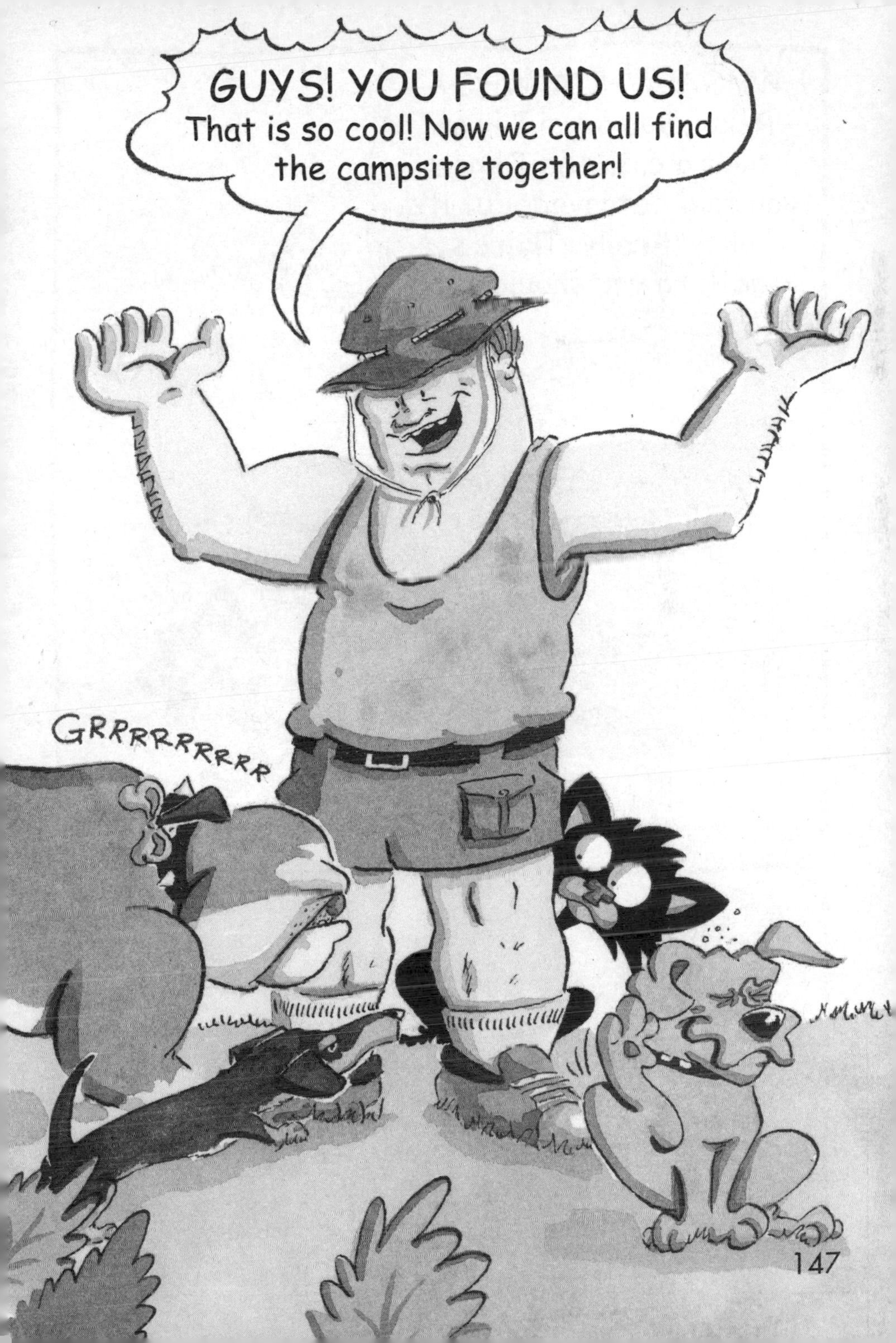
GUYS! YOU FOUND US!
That is so cool! Now we can all find the campsite together!
GRRRRRRRRRR

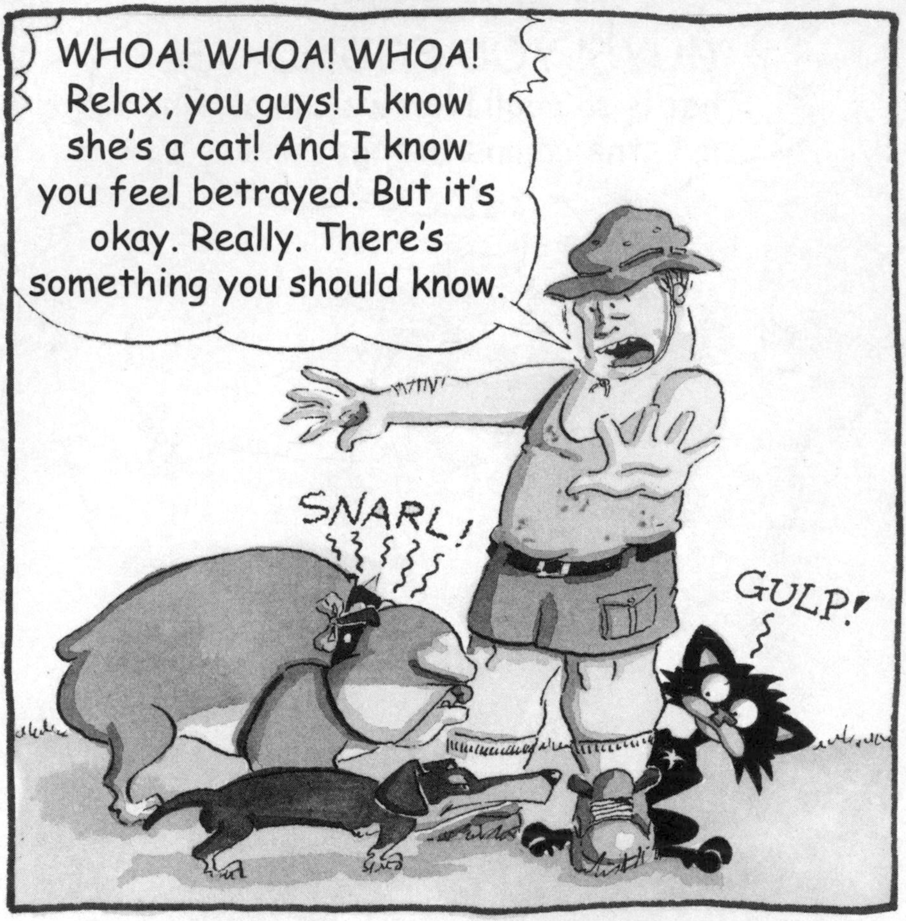
WHOA! WHOA! WHOA! Relax, you guys! I know she's a cat! And I know you feel betrayed. But it's okay. Really. There's something you should know.
SNARL!
GULP!

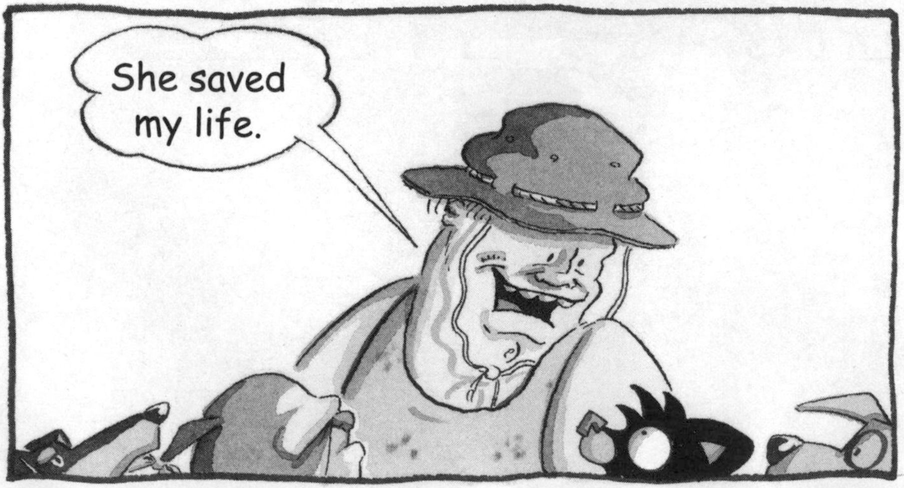
She saved my life.

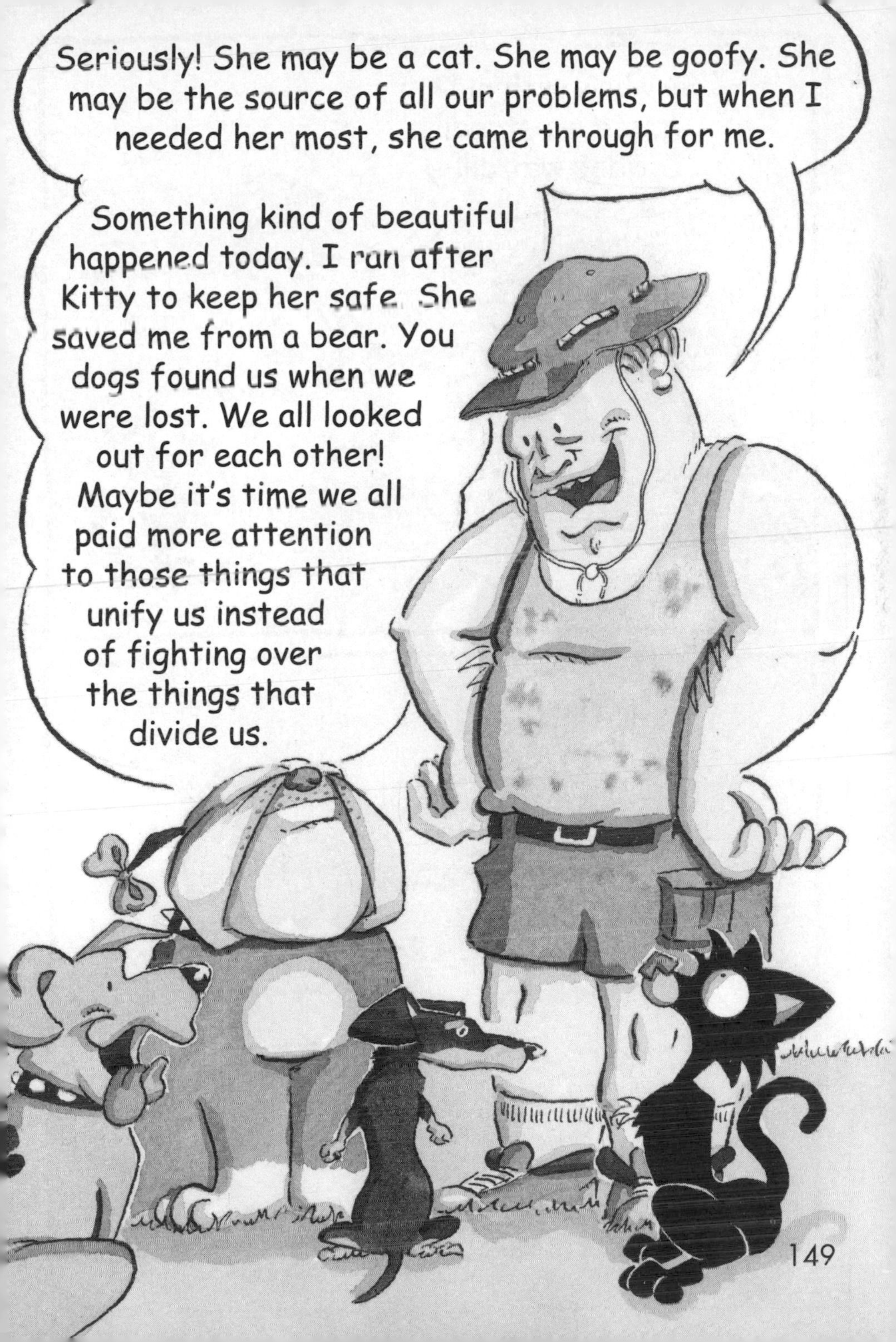
Seriously! She may be a cat. She may be goofy. She may be the source of all our problems, but when I needed her most, she came through for me.
Something kind of beautiful happened today. I ran after Kitty to keep her safe. She saved me from a bear. You dogs found us when we were lost. We all looked out for each other! Maybe it's time we all paid more attention to those things that unify us instead of fighting over the things that divide us.

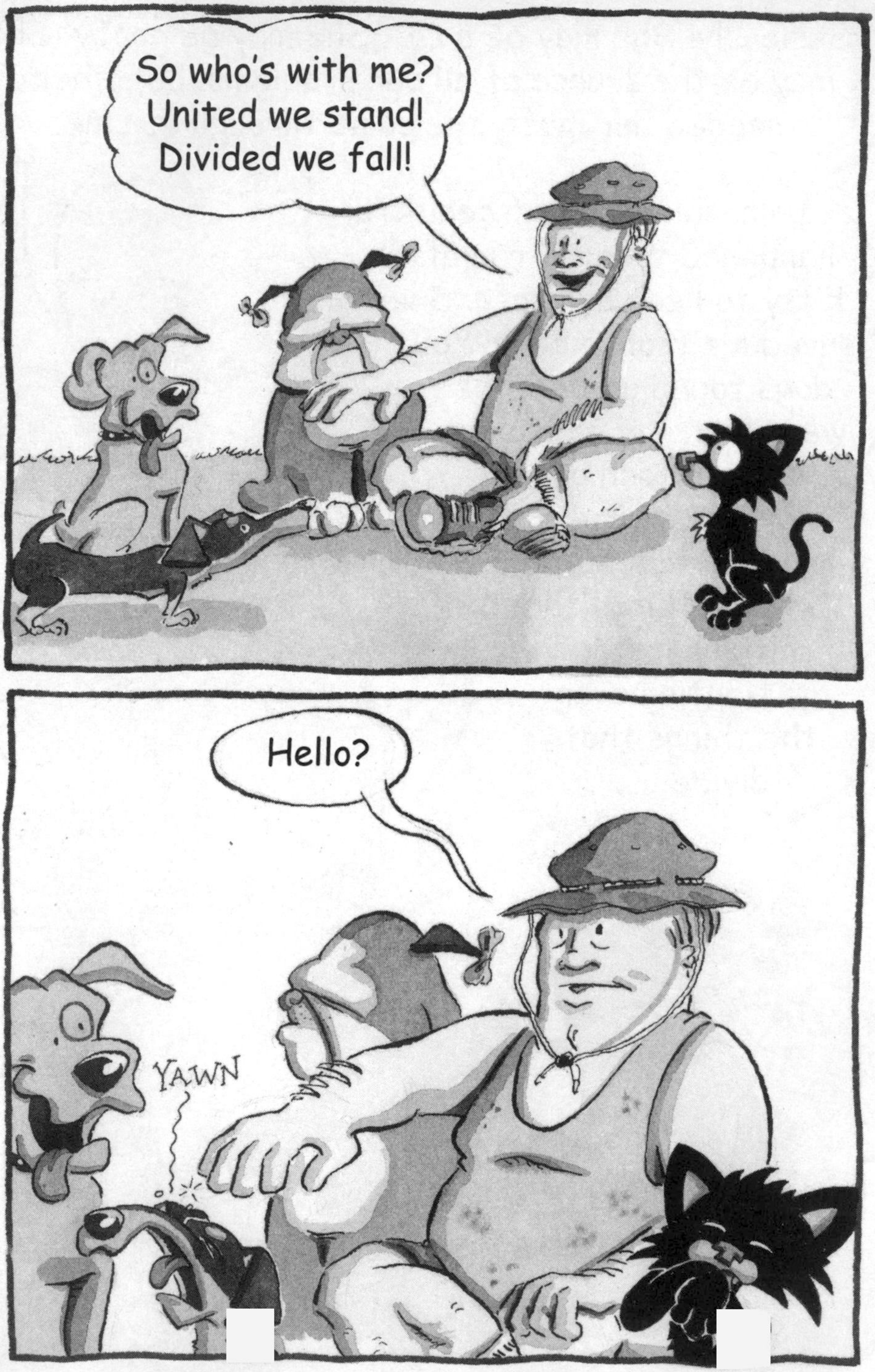
So who's with me? United we stand! Divided we fall!
Hello?
YAWN

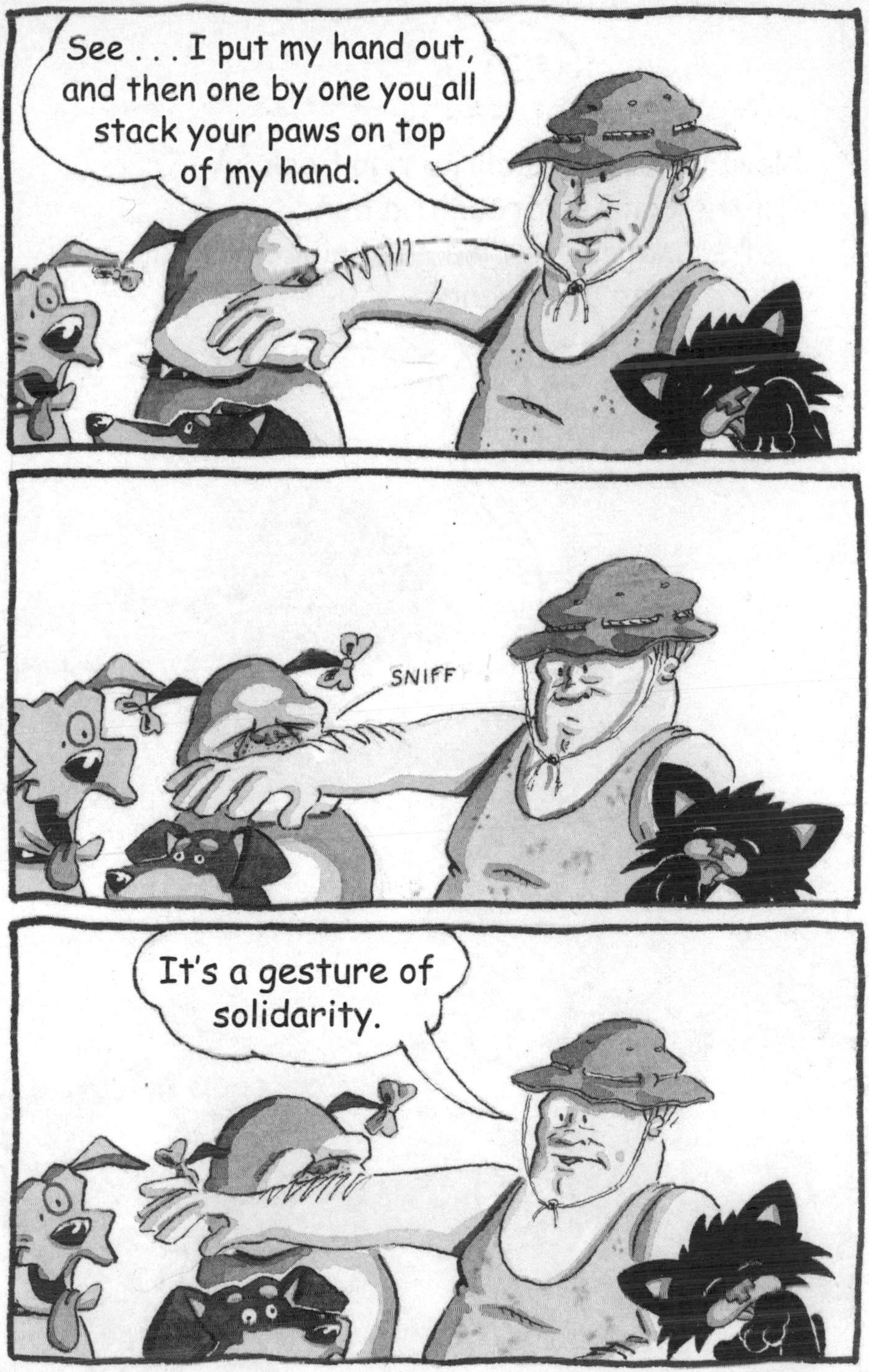
See . . . I put my hand out, and then one by one you all stack your paws on top of my hand.
SNIFF
It's a gesture of solidarity.

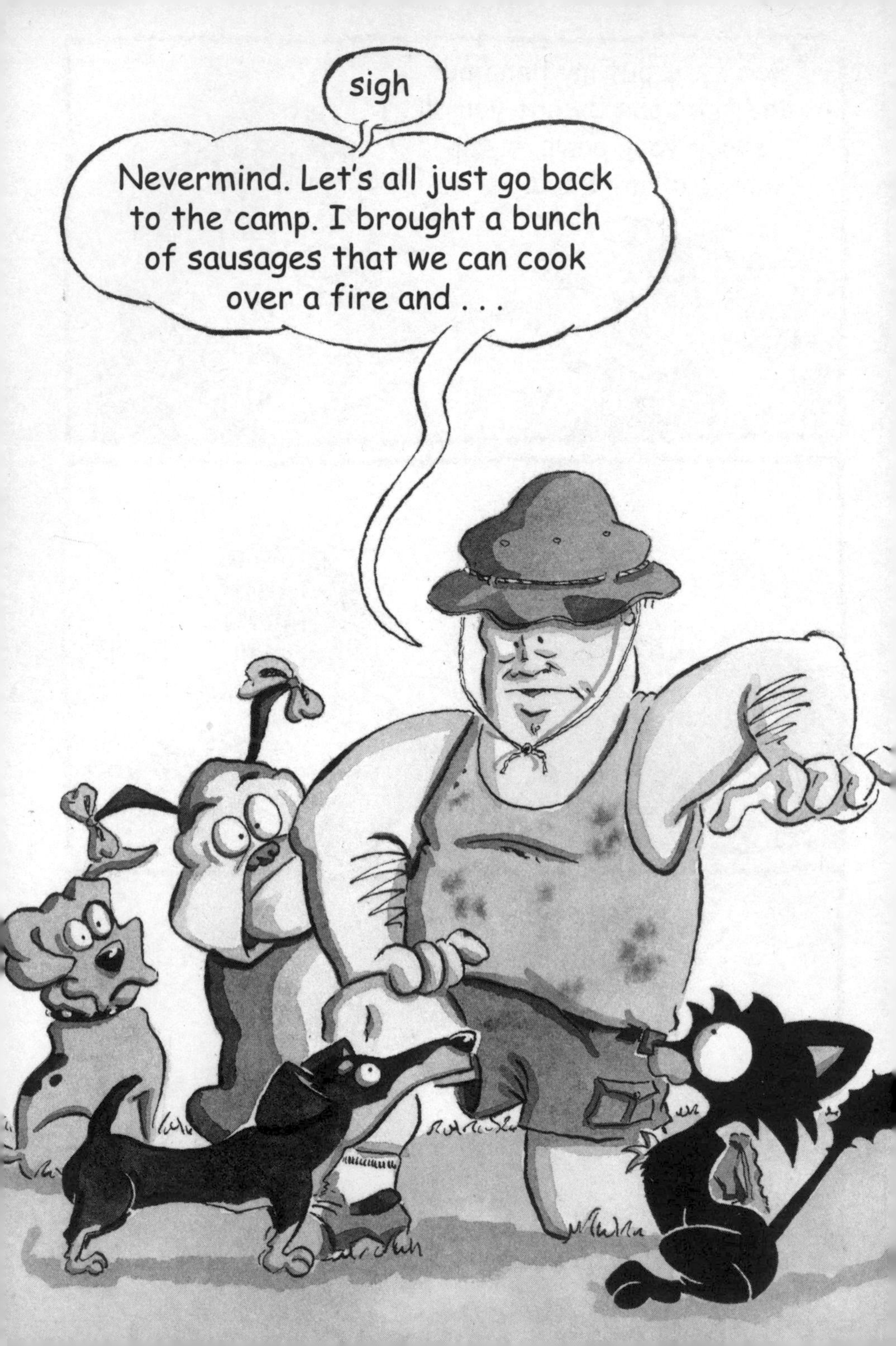
sigh
Nevermind. Let's all just go back to the camp. I brought a bunch of sausages that we can cook over a fire and . . .

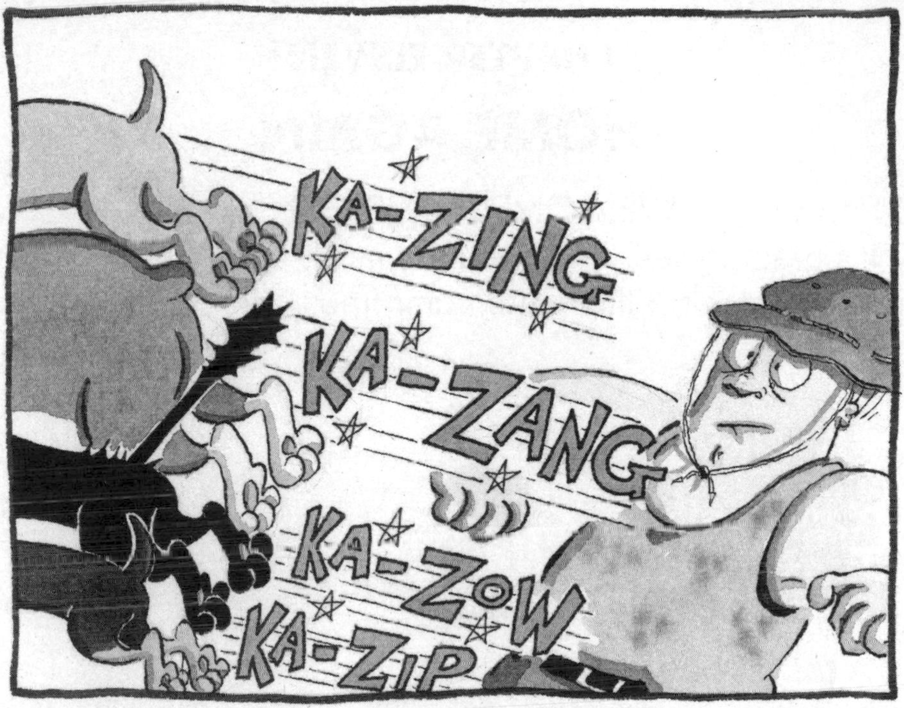
KA-ZING
KA-ZANG
KA-ZOW
KA-ZIP

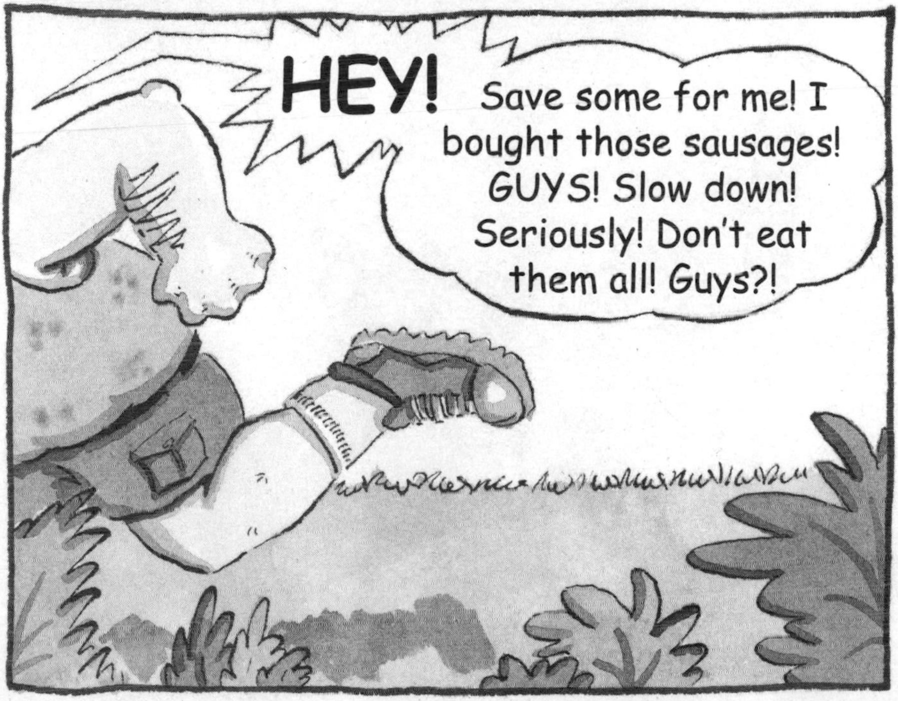
HEY!
Save some for me! I bought those sausages! GUYS! Slow down! Seriously! Don't eat them all! Guys?!

•CHAPTER ELEVEN•

HOME AGAIN

WELCOME HOME, PUPPY!

It's great to see you. You look much more like your old self. I think that camp really helped.

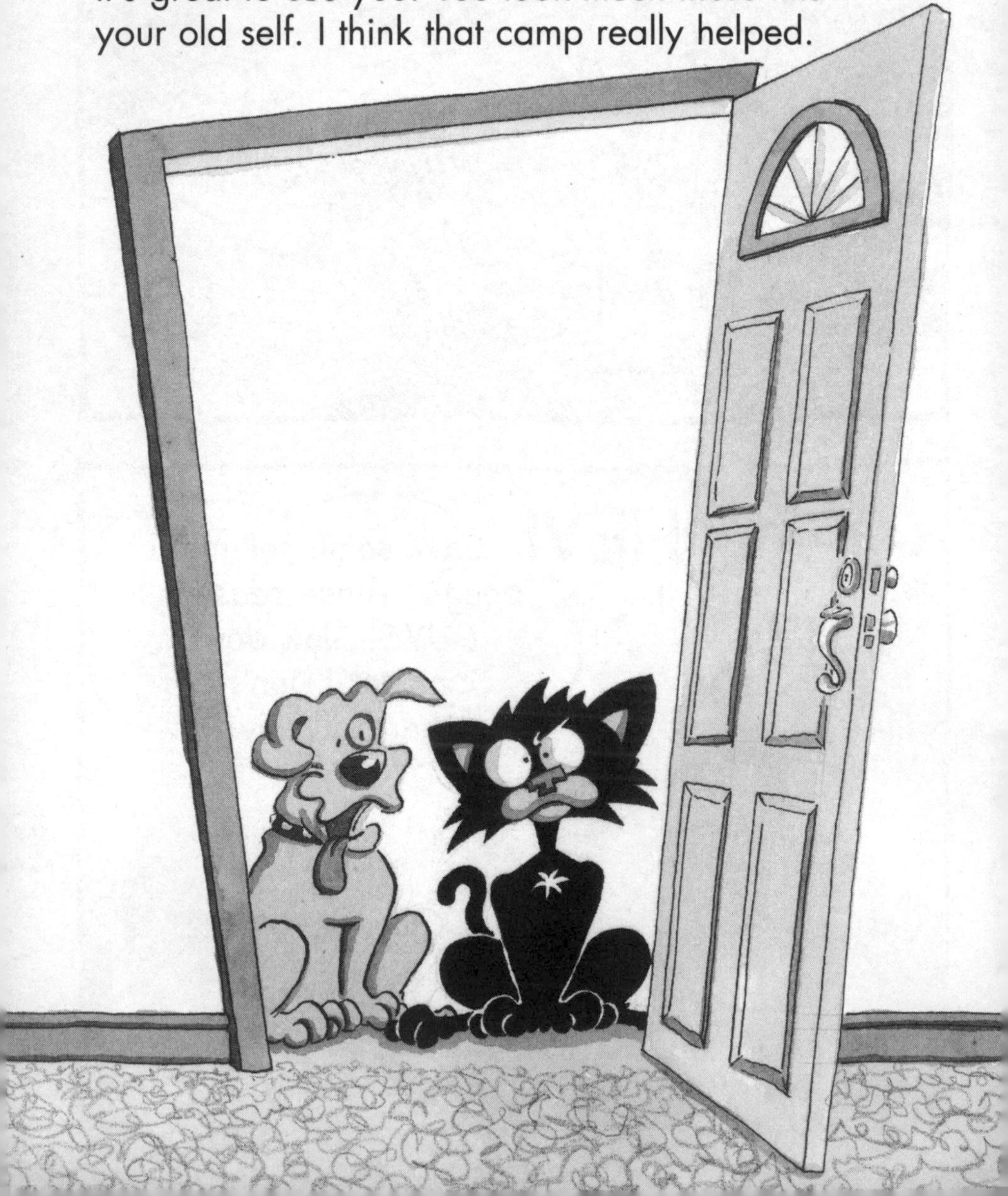

KITTY! Where have YOU been the past couple of days? Did you get lost? And what happened to your brand-new collar? Did you lose it already? Great. Oh well. I suppose it wasn't all that useful if you had it and STILL got lost.

The important thing is that you're both home safe and sound.

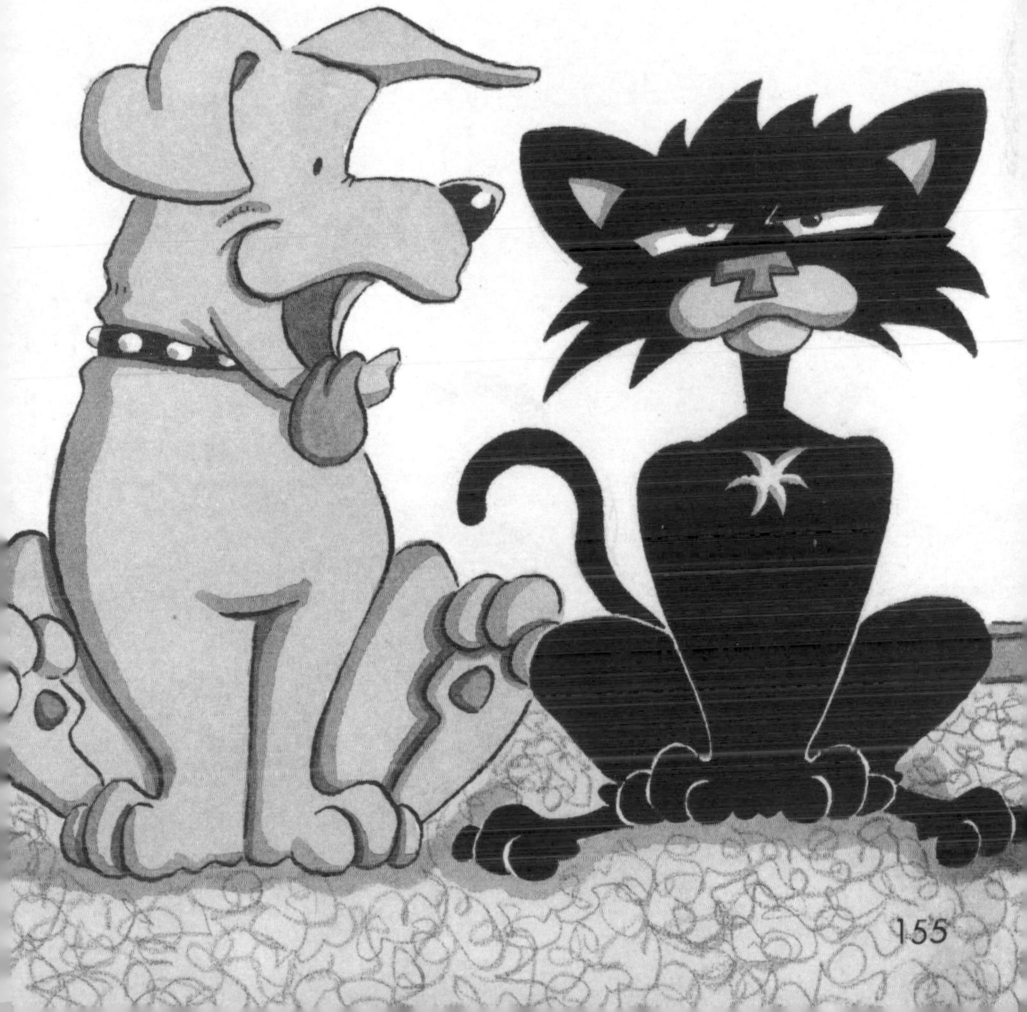

You guys look tired. Why don't you two go lie down and have a nice rest while I put together some food for you.

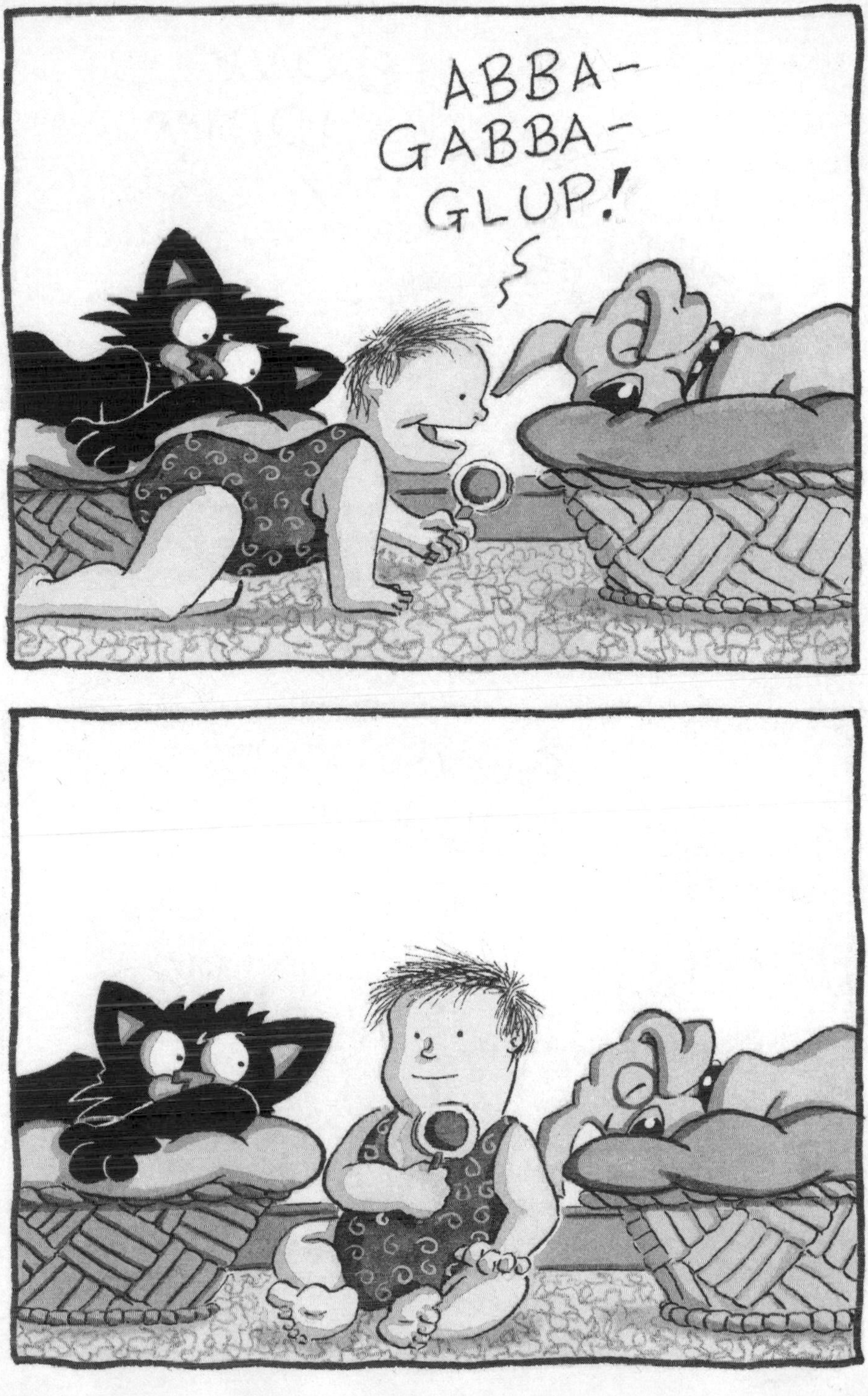
ABBA-
GABBA-
GLUP!

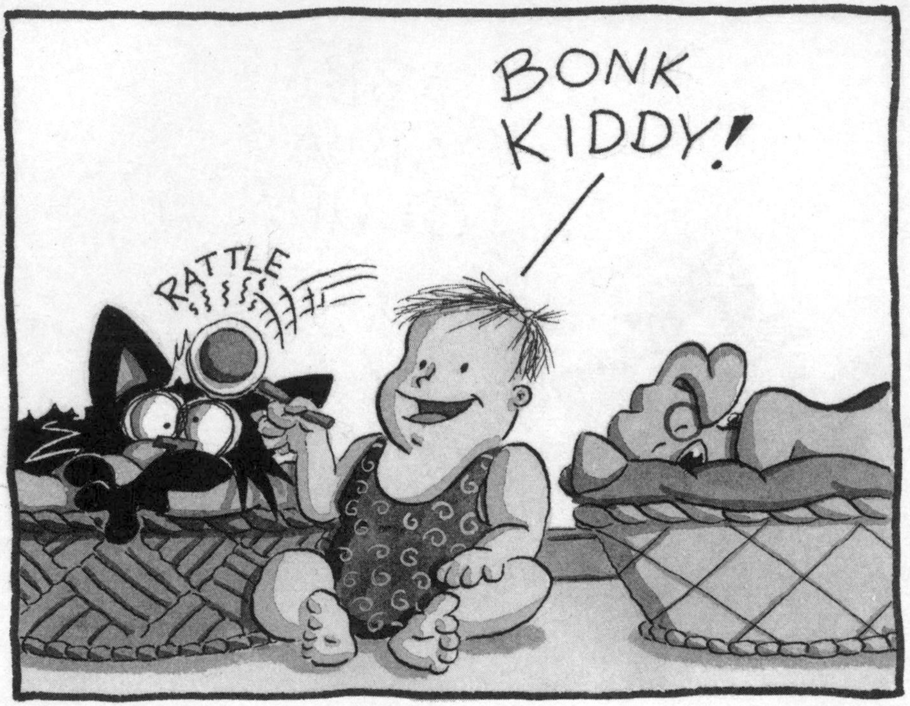
BONK KIDDY!
RATTLE

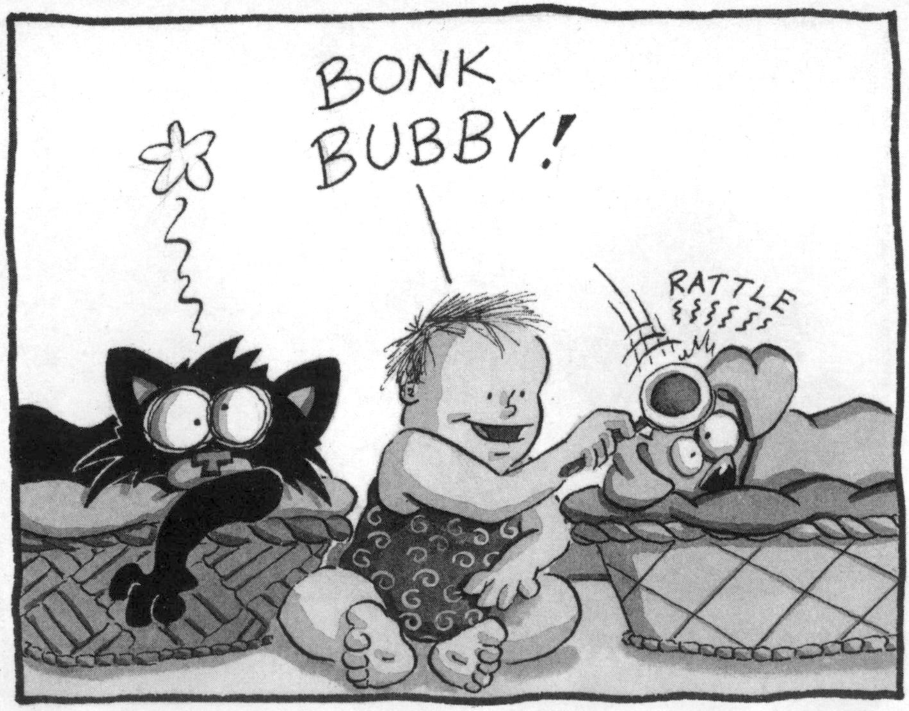
BONK BUBBY!
RATTLE

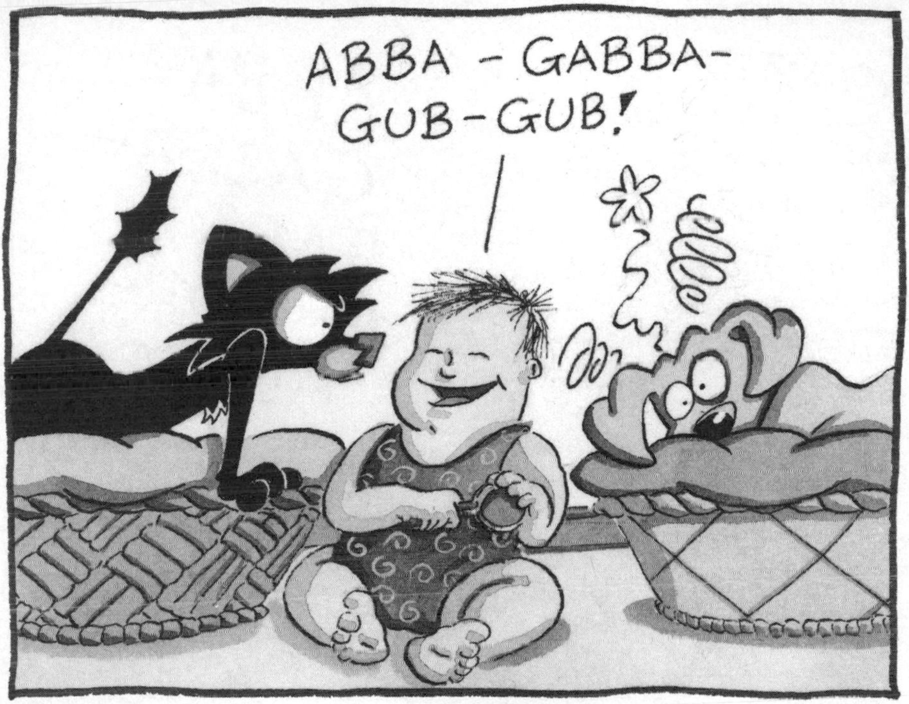
ABBA - GABBA-
GUB-GUB!

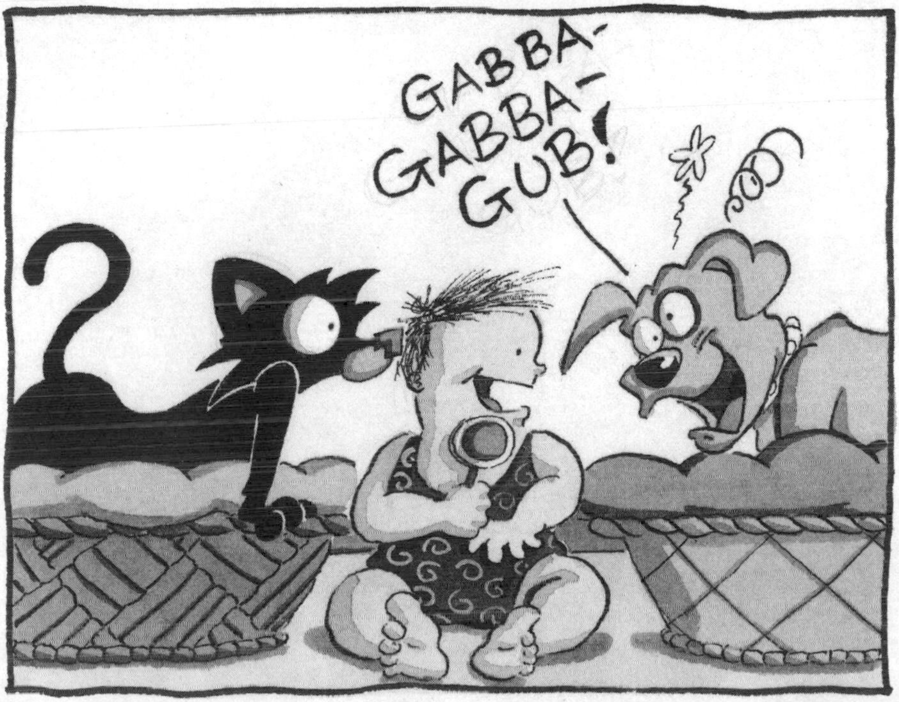
GABBA-
GABBA-
GUB!

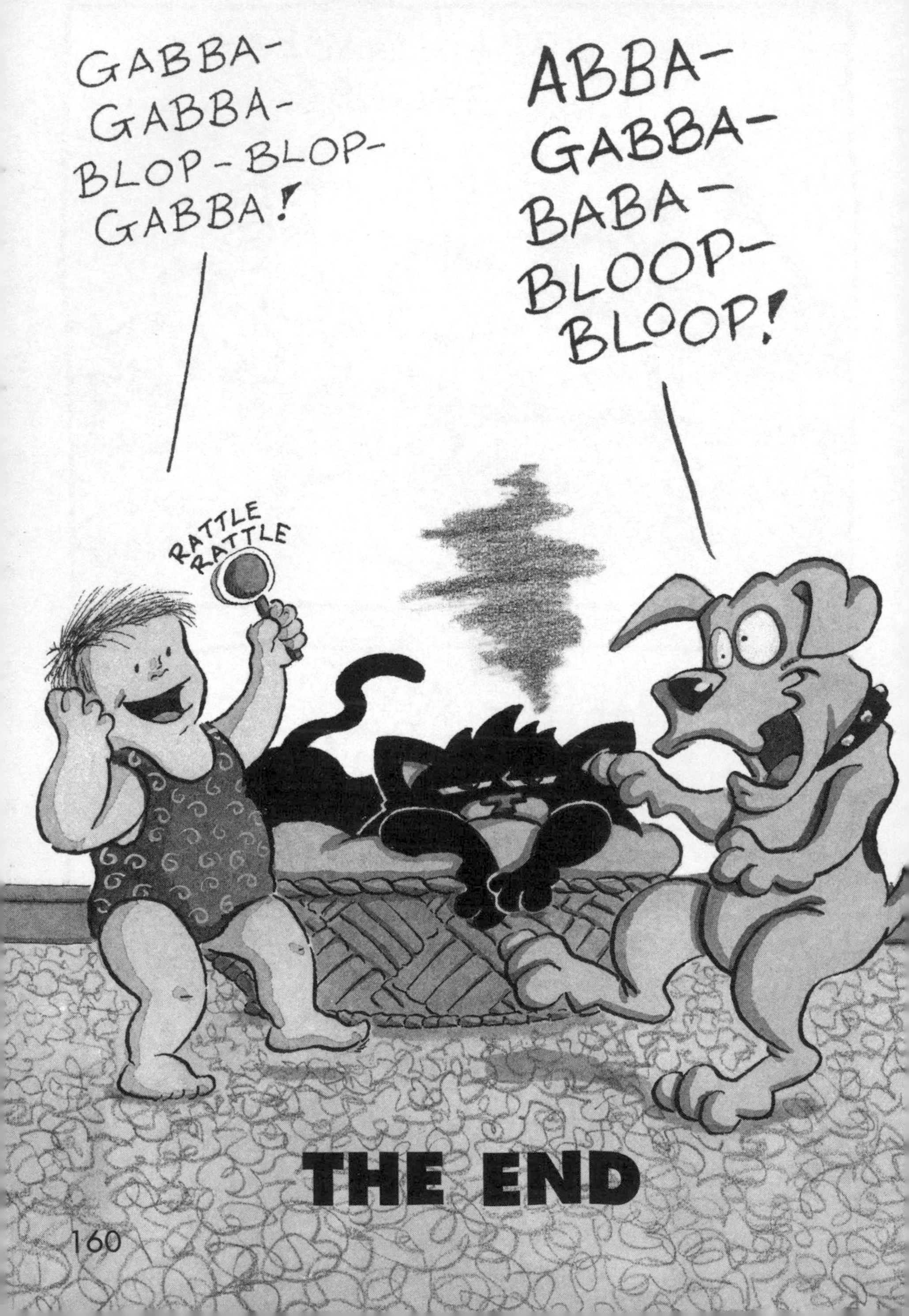
GABBA-
GABBA-
BLOP-BLOP-
GABBA!
ABBA-
GABBA-
BABA-
BLOOP-
BLOOP!
RATTLE
RATTLE
THE END

A CONVERSATION WITH NICK BRUEL

INTERVIEWED BY UNCLE MURRAY

Hi, Gang! It's me, good ol' Uncle Murray, here again to talk to Nick Bruel, author and illustrator of the book *Bad Kitty Camp Daze*. Nick, as you probably know, is a deeply private person. The only way he would agree to this interview was if I contacted him via shortwave radio at midnight during a full moon. I will now try to contact him in his secret, subterranean lair.

BWEEEOOO WEEOOO BWEEEEEEE

UNCLE MURRAY: Are you there, Nick? Come in, Nick! It's me, Uncle Murray! Come in! Come in!

NICK BRUEL: Uncle Murray, I'm sitting directly in front of you.

UNCLE MURRAY: We don't have a very strong signal! I am now going to attempt to modulate the frequency.

BWEEEEEEOOOOOOOO WEEEOOOOOOOOOOOO

NICK: What are you doing? I'm literally sitting three feet from you.

UNCLE MURRAY: Shhh! Your readers can't see us. I thought I would make things more interesting. Come in, Nick Bruel! Come in! Please speak to us from your hidden, underground fortress below Mount Kilimanjaro!

BWEEEEE . . .

NICK: Stop that.

UNCLE MURRAY: Sorry.

NICK: *Sigh.* So, what did you want to talk to me about?

UNCLE MURRAY: I don't know. What do you feel like talking about?

NICK: I guess we can talk about this book, *Bad Kitty Camp Daze.*

UNCLE MURRAY: That's a pretty good idea. Let's do that! So tell me, Nick, how did you come up with the idea for *Bad Kitty Camp Daze*?

NICK: Well, the idea for this book came to me one day as I was thinking about—

UNCLE MURRAY: Did you know that I'm in this book?

NICK: I did. As I was saying, the idea for this book came to me—

UNCLE MURRAY: I'm actually a pretty big part of this book.

NICK: You are. I know that. So as I was saying, the idea—

UNCLE MURRAY: One could argue that the title of the book should be *Uncle Murray Camp Daze*.

NICK: Well, this is really a book about Kitty, isn't it?

UNCLE MURRAY: I'm kind of a big part of a lot of these books, you know. *Uncle Murray Takes the Test. Uncle Murray School Daze. Uncle Murray Meets the Baby*. Those would all be pretty swell titles!

NICK: Are you done?

UNCLE MURRAY: *Uncle Murray vs. Uncle Murray*. That would be a little weird.

NICK: *Sigh.*

UNCLE MURRAY: Now I'm done.

NICK: The idea for this book came to me one day when I was thinking about how much my own daughter, Izzy, really likes summer camps. One summer she went to FOUR different summer camps, and she loved them all. She went to a canoe camp, an arts camp, a theater camp, and even a sports camp. It made sense for me to really think about making a book about camps, considering how much my daughter enjoyed them. The only problem is that I didn't really like camp when I was a kid.

UNCLE MURRAY: You didn't?

NICK: Nope. I only went to sleepaway camp one summer when I was a kid, and I really didn't like it there.

UNCLE MURRAY: Were you homesick?

NICK: A little. But mostly I didn't like it there because it was a terrible camp. In fact, I'll give you a real example of just how awful this camp was. But it's a little disgusting. Do you think you can handle it?

UNCLE MURRAY: [Straightening up in his chair] I can take it!

NICK: One day, at the camp I went to, I had to eat frogs.

UNCLE MURRAY: I'm sorry. I thought I heard you say you had to eat frogs.

NICK: That's right.

UNCLE MURRAY: Frogs. Like those slimy little green animals that jump around on lily pads. Frogs.

NICK: That's right.

UNCLE MURRAY: [Choking] That's . . . That's so gross. Is that even LEGAL?!

NICK: Actually, lots of people eat frogs. Some people even consider it a delicacy. They'll tell you they taste like chicken.

UNCLE MURRAY: Do they?

NICK: Nope. Frog tastes pretty much exactly like what you'd think frog *would* taste like.

UNCLE MURRAY: [Suppressing his gag reflex] I think I need to lie down.

NICK: I'm sorry.

UNCLE MURRAY: Can I ask you something before I go find an antacid?

NICK: Sure.

UNCLE MURRAY: Are you ever going to make any Uncle Murray books?

NICK: I don't know. I never really thought of it. You are *in* a lot of these books already.

UNCLE MURRAY: But I mean ones where I'm the star! You know—like *Uncle Murray vs. the Space Pirate Werewolves, Volumes I–VIII.*

NICK: Uhhh . . .

UNCLE MURRAY: Because if you ever do, I've already put together a brief outline that might help. [Reaches under his chair to pull out a massive stack of four thousand sheets of paper]

NICK: This is an outline?

UNCLE MURRAY: Or you could publish it just as it is! That's an even better idea! Those Caldecott/Newbery people won't know what hit 'em!

NICK: *Sigh.*

Big trouble comes in small packages.

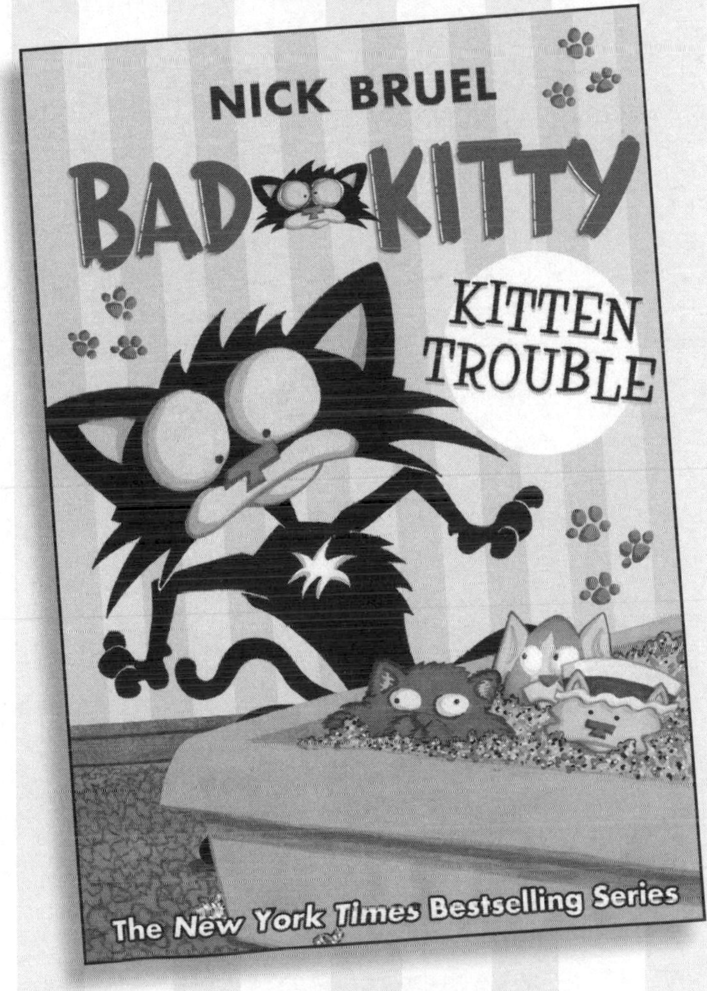
NICK BRUEL
BAD KITTY
KITTEN TROUBLE
The New York Times Bestselling Series

Keep reading for more Bad Kitty!

•CHAPTER ONE•

TODAY, MONDAY

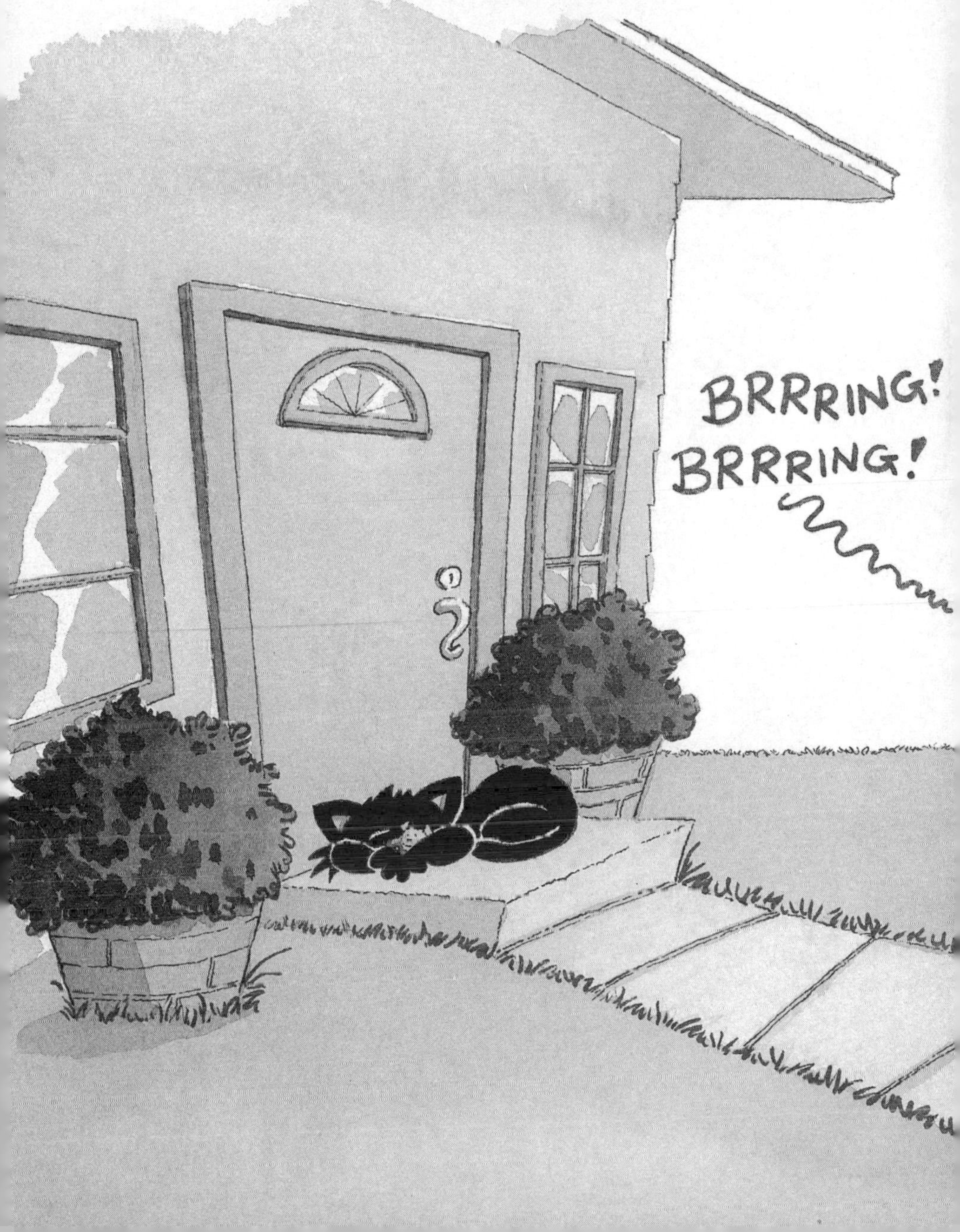
BRRRING!
BRRRING!

Kitty doesn't like that kid who delivers the newspapers.

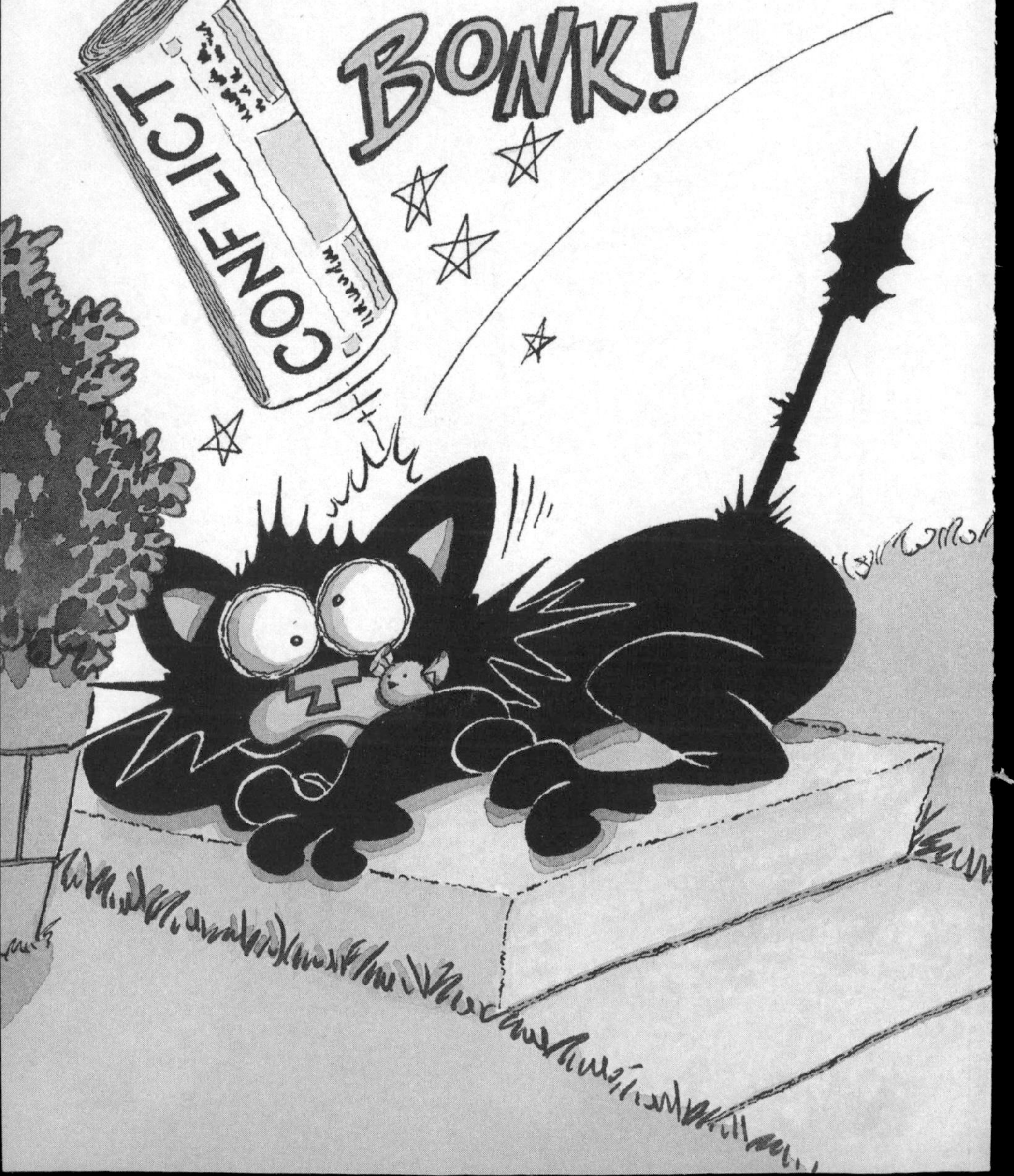
CONFLICT
BONK!

Every day, the same thing—he bonks her on the head with the newspaper, and then he rides off on his bike saying . . .

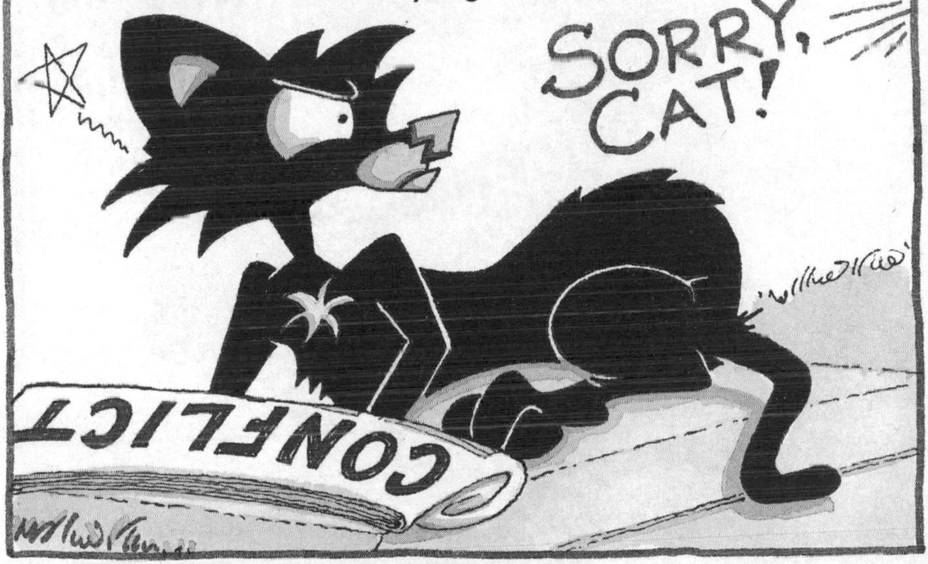
SORRY, CAT!
CONFLICT

Kitty doesn't like that kid's bike. Kitty doesn't like that kid's bell. Kitty really doesn't like that kid at all. So Kitty's decided to do something about it.

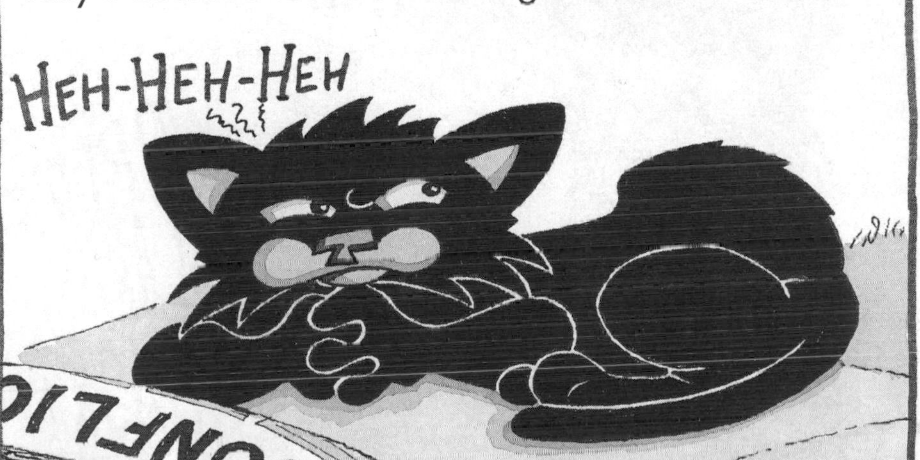
HEH-HEH-HEH

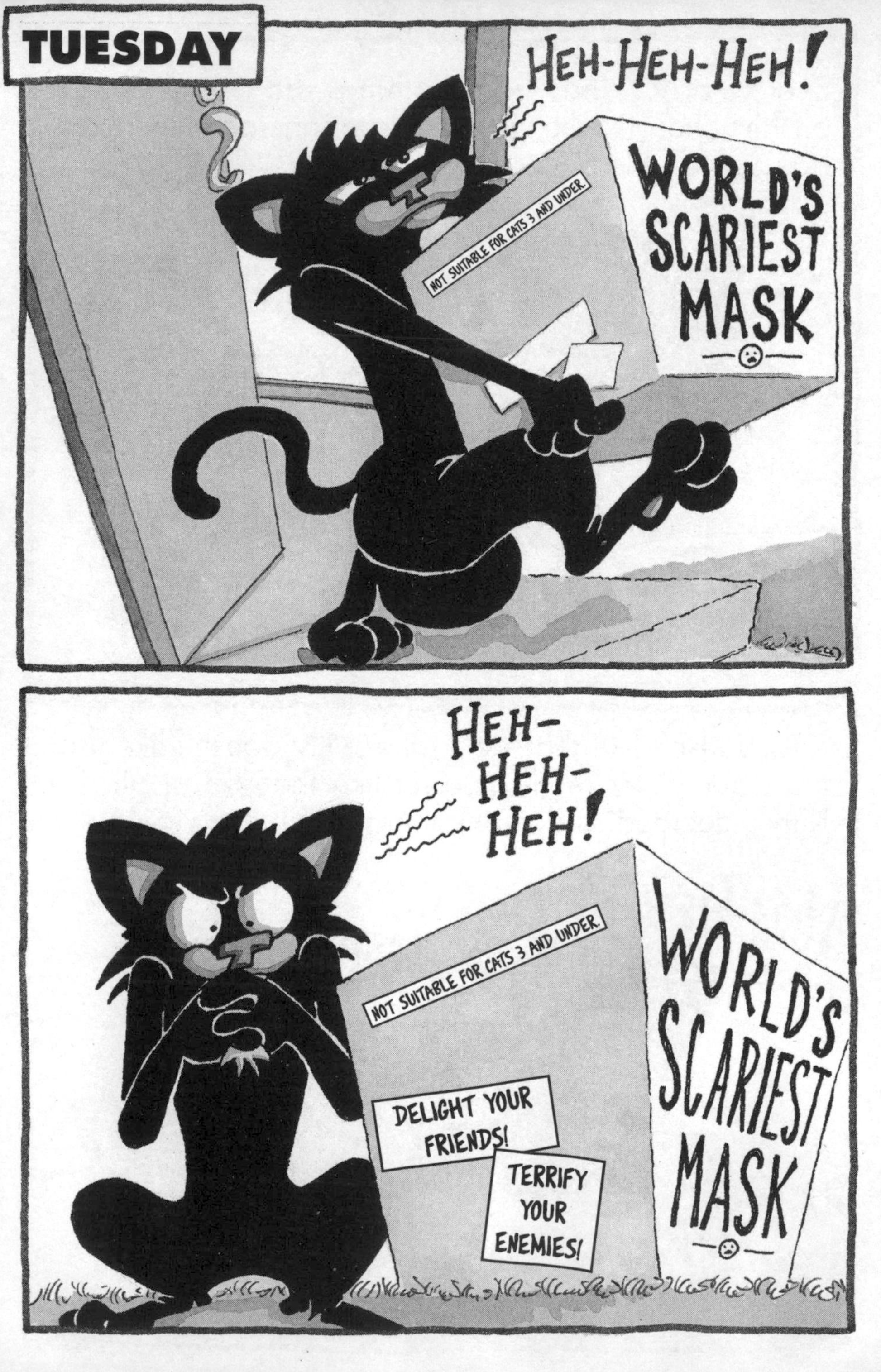
TUESDAY
HEH-HEH-HEH!
NOT SUITABLE FOR CATS 3 AND UNDER.
WORLD'S SCARIEST MASK
HEH-HEH-HEH!
NOT SUITABLE FOR CATS 3 AND UNDER.
WORLD'S SCARIEST MASK
DELIGHT YOUR FRIENDS!
TERRIFY YOUR ENEMIES!

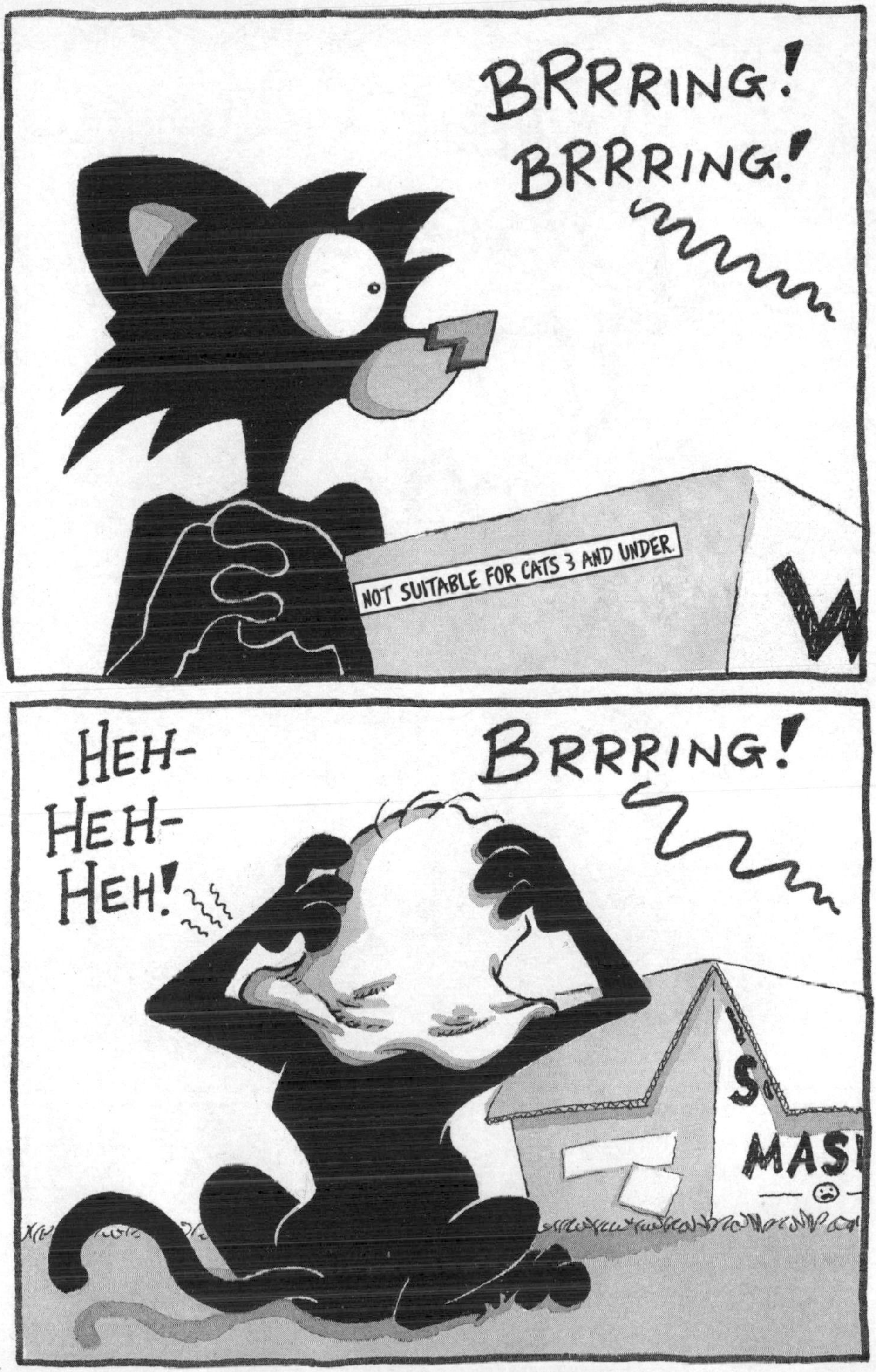
BRRRING!
BRRRING!
NOT SUITABLE FOR CATS 3 AND UNDER
HEH-
HEH-
HEH!
BRRRING!

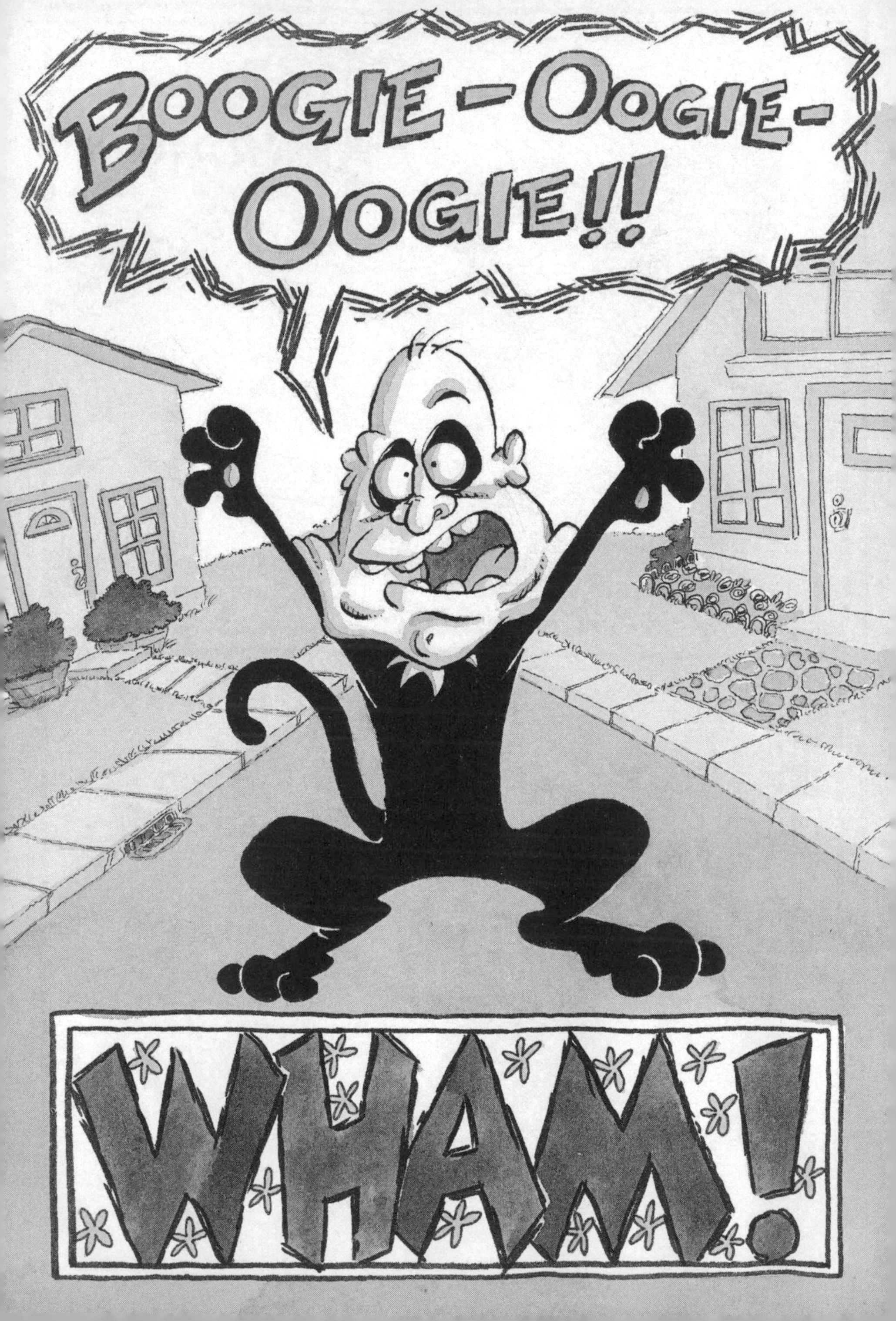
BOOGIE-OOGIE-OOGIE!!
WHAM!

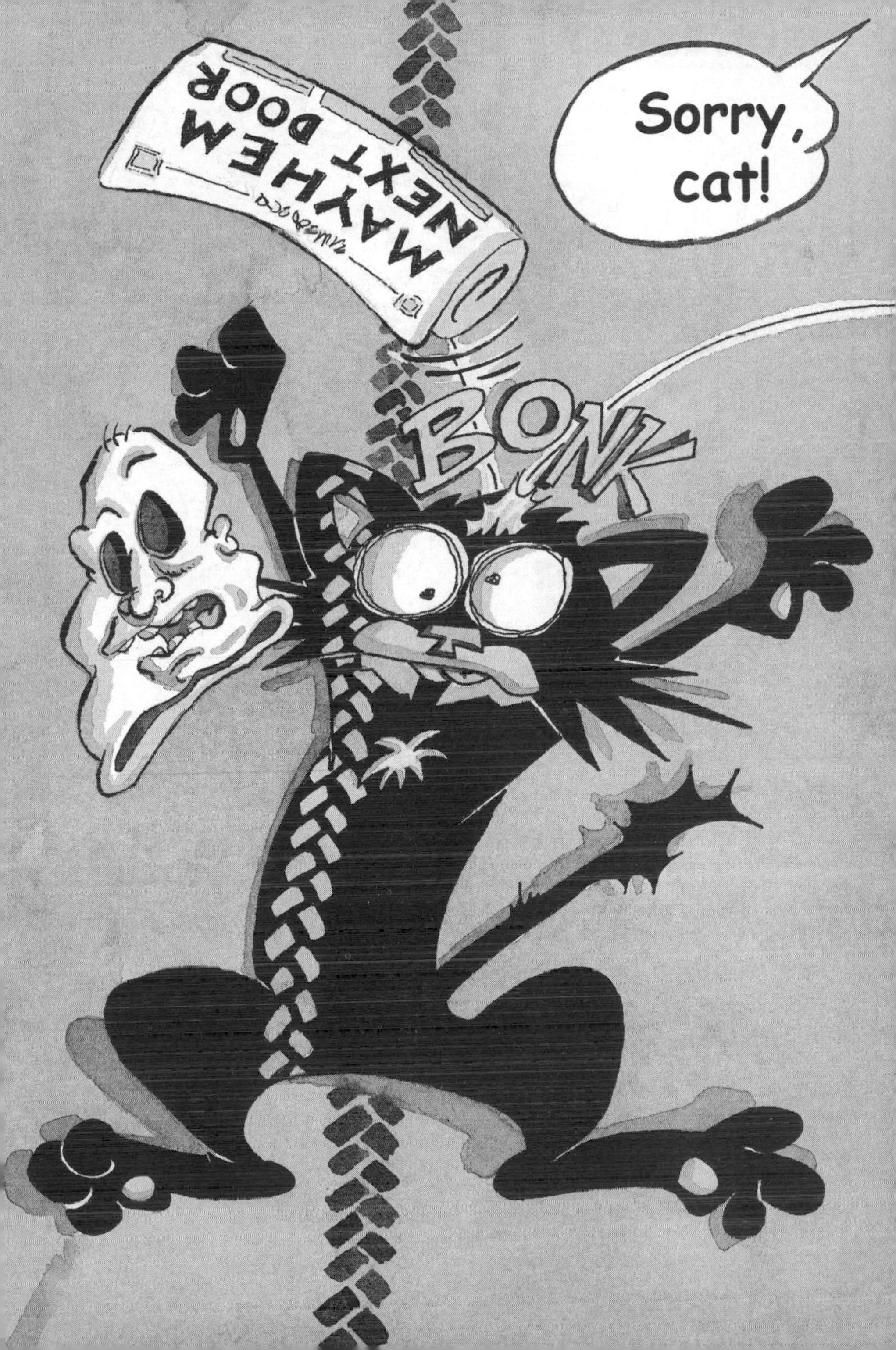
MAYHEM NEXT DOOR
Sorry, cat!
BONK

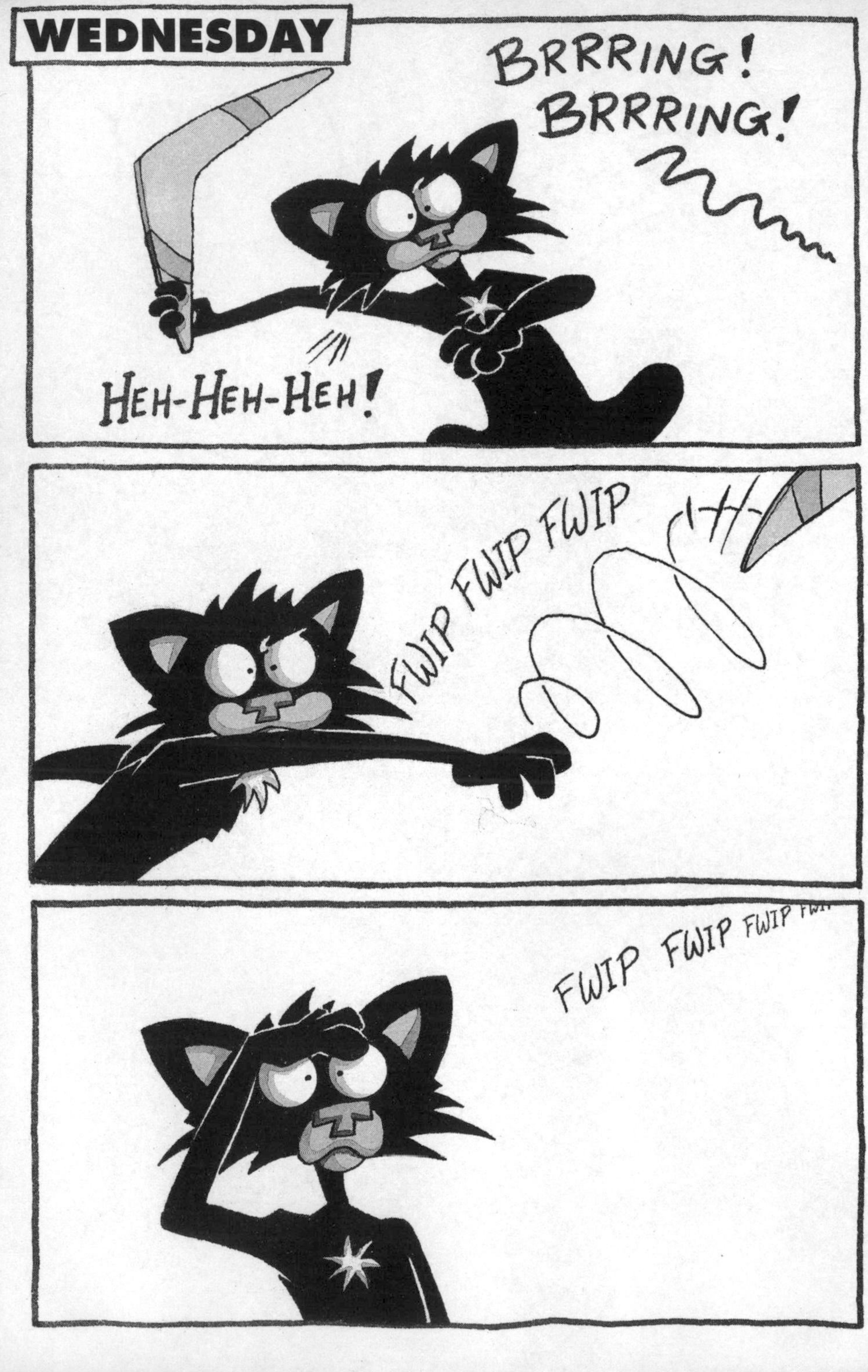
WEDNESDAY
BRRRING! BRRRING!
HEH-HEH-HEH!
FWIP FWIP FWIP FWIP
FWIP FWIP FWIP